even more
Pongwiffy
stories

This omnibus edition published in Great Britain in 2019 by Simon & Schuster UK Ltd
A CBS COMPANY

Pongwiffy and the Pantomime first published by Puffin Books in 1997
Pongwiffy and the Spellovision Song Contest first published by Puffin Books in 2003
Pongwiffy: Back on Track first published by Bloomsbury in 2009

Text copyright © Kaye Umansky 1997, 2003 and 2009
Revised text copyright © Kaye Umansky 2009
Illustrations copyright © Katy Riddell 2019

This book is copyright under the Berne Convention.
No reproduction without permission.
All rights reserved.

The right of Kaye Umansky and Katy Riddell to be identified as the author and
illustrator of this work has been asserted by them in accordance with sections 77
and 78 of the Copyright, Design and Patents Act, 1988.

1 3 5 7 9 10 8 6 4 2

Simon & Schuster UK Ltd
1st Floor, 222 Gray's Inn Road
London
WC1X 8HB

www.simonandschuster.co.uk

Simon & Schuster Australia, Sydney
Simon & Schuster India, New Delhi

A CIP catalogue record for this book is available from the British Library.

PB ISBN 978-1-4711-6742-3
eBook ISBN 978-1-4711-6743-0

This book is a work of fiction. Names, characters, places and incidents are either the product
of the author's imagination or are used fictitiously. Any resemblance to actual people
living or dead, events or locales is entirely coincidental.

Printed and bound by CPI Group (UK) Ltd, Croydon, CR0 4YY

Simon & Schuster UK Ltd are committed to sourcing paper
that is made from wood grown in sustainable forests and support the Forest
Stewardship Council, the leading international forest certification organisation.
Our books displaying the FSC logo are printed on FSC certified paper.

CONTENTS

WITCHES AND FAMILIARS

SOURMUDDLE & SNOOP

PONGWIFFY & HUGO

SHARKADDER & DEADEYE DUDLEY

AGGLE BAG & IDENTIKIT
BAG AGGLE & COPICAT

SLUDGEGOOEY & FILTH

MACABRE & RORY

BENDYSHANKS & SLITHERING STEVE

GAGA & BATS

BONIDLE & SLOTH

SCROFULA & BARRY

GREYMATTER & SPEKS

RATSNAPPY & VERNON

even more

Pongwiffy

stories

Pongwiffy and the Pantomime

CHAPTER ONE
A Brilliant Idea

'No!' shouted Grandwitch Sourmuddle, thumping the table with her clenched fist. 'No-no-no-no-NO! We are *not*, positively, absolutely, definitely *not* holding a coffee morning, d'you hear? I hate coffee and I detest mornings. All that sitting around with your little finger stuck out, it's not natural. Never, I say! Never, never, never!'

She gave a final thump, folded her arms and sat back, glaring. There was a short pause.

'I take it that's a no, then, Grandwitch?' asked Witch Greymatter, who was secretary that night.

'Yes,' said Sourmuddle emphatically. 'No. Yes, no, that is.'

Greymatter took up her pencil and scribbled through the last item on the list that lay before her.

'Well, that's that, then,' she said with a little sigh. 'We've been through all the suggestions. Jumblesale – barndance – quiznight – craftfair – sponsoredknit – paintyourbroomstickinafunnywayday – swiminggala – flowershow – coffeemorning.'

There fell another silence.

'It's no good,' said Witch Sludgegooey finally. 'I just can't seem to get excited about any of them.'

It was the usual monthly Coven Meeting in Witchway Hall. Twelve Witches and their assorted Familiars sat around the long table set centre stage. Outside, the chilly winds of autumn prowled around the place, rattling at the windows and whistling through every knothole.

So far, the Meeting hadn't gone well. The main item on the agenda was to think of a way in which they could boost the kitty. Christmas was fast approaching and Coven funds were horribly low. Besides, there's something about that in-between time after Hallowe'en and before the end of December that makes you want to fill it with – well, something.

8

'Tea-break time, I think,' announced Sourmuddle to general relief. 'I've got brain-ache. How are you doing with those sandwiches, Pongwiffy? We're all starving out here!'

'On my way-hee!' sang a cheerful voice from the backstage kitchen. 'Wow, have I got a feast for you!'

There followed a loud yell, a resounding crash and a lot of tinkling.

There was a short pause, then the thirteenth Witch advanced from stage left. A piece of ham stuck to the sleeve of her disreputable cardigan. Her shoes were wet and steaming. She was holding a china handle – all that remained of the Coven teapot. Perched on her hat was a small, grim-faced hamster. He was attempting to wipe what appeared to be a large dollop of mustard from his front.

'Oops!' said Pongwiffy sheepishly.

There were a lot of tuttings, black looks and mutterings of 'typical'.

'I dropped the tray tripping over Hugo,' explained Pongwiffy. 'Blame him. It's all his fault.'

'It *not*,' snapped the Hamster on the hat.

'Of course it is. How was I supposed to know you were right under my feet? If you weren't such a little squirt, I'd have noticed you, wouldn't I?'

'So I take it there's no sandwiches, then?' interrupted Sourmuddle.

''Fraid not,' confessed Pongwiffy. 'There's a nice piece of ham here, fresh off my cardigan, if anybody would like to . . . No? I'll eat it myself, then.' Which she proceeded to do, with relish.

'Sit down, Pongwiffy, and don't say another word,' ordered Sourmuddle.

The failed sandwich-maker pulled out a chair and sat on it, still chewing.

'Now what?' demanded Witch Macabre. 'How are we supposed tay have a tea break if there's noo tea?'

'We think we should call it a night and go home, don't we, Bag?' said Witch Agglebag, stifling a yawn.

'We certainly do, Ag,' replied her twin, Witch Bagaggle. 'We've got two cauldrons full of hot soup at home, just waiting for us to soak our feet in.'

'Can't go home,' ruled Sourmuddle. 'Not until we've made a decision. Besides, I'm all right. I knew it was Pongwiffy's turn to do the catering, so I've brought my emergency flask. Where is it, Snoop?'

'Right here, Grandwitch,' said the small red Demon at her elbow, producing a bright yellow flask with an air of triumph. Everyone watched enviously as he unscrewed the plastic cup and proceeded to pour. Nobody else had thought to bring one.

'Well, I think it's stupid,' grumbled Macabre. 'Having a tea break when there's noo tea.'

'In that case,' said Sourmuddle, taking a sip, 'we'll just have to make small talk.'

'What's that, then?' enquired Macabre suspiciously.

'It's where we chat pleasantly amongst ourselves. Asking about each other's relations and so on,' explained Sourmuddle. 'For example, I say –' she put on a high-pitched, unconvincing voice, 'I say, "*Dooo* tell me, Witch Sharkadder, how is your delightful cousin, the famous Dwarf chef Pierre de Gingerbeard, of whom we hear you name-drop so much?" And Sharkadder says, "Very well, thank you, Grandwitch, how kind of you to ask."'

'No, I don't,' said Sharkadder tragically, looking up from applying a fresh coat of bright green lipstick. 'Poor Cousin Pierre. He fell into the pancake mix last week. Got badly battered.'

A heavy silence fell as everybody thought sad thoughts about Sharkadder's unfortunate cousin. Outside, the wind moaned. It was all rather depressing.

'Anybody fancy a game of charades?' suggested Pongwiffy in an attempt to brighten things up a bit.

11

'No,' said Sourmuddle. 'And I thought I told you to keep quiet.'

'How about a sing-song, then? That'd cheer us all up, wouldn't it?'

'We're not here to be cheerful,' Sourmuddle told her severely. 'We're here to think of a moneymaking idea.'

'What have you come up with so far?' asked Pongwiffy, who had been stuck out in the kitchen all night.

'The usual stuff,' sighed Greymatter. 'Nothing we haven't done a hundred times before. Nobody can face another jumble sale, and a quiz night's no good because the Skeletons held one only last week, and the Zombies are having a barn dance, and Sourmuddle's got this thing about coffee mornings . . .'

'Quite right too,' agreed Pongwiffy. 'We don't want to get bogged down in boring old stuff like that. What we need is something challenging. A new, exciting project that makes use of all our amazing talents. Some sort of Christmas show, perhaps. That'd be fun, wouldn't it?'

At this, Witches and Familiars alike sat up and began to look interested.

'You mean, an opera or something?' asked Greymatter, whose tastes ran towards the highbrow.

'Not an opera,' said Pongwiffy definitely. 'Too posh.'

'Us could do a musical, though!' That was Dead Eye Dudley, Sharkadder's battered tomcat. One of his nine lives had been spent as ship's cat on a pirate brig and as a result he was seriously Into Shanties. 'Us could do a musical an' call it *Cats*!'

IdentiKit and CopiCat, the twins' Siamese Cat Familiars, nodded eagerly. Everybody else laughed like drains.

'Ha!' scoffed Pongwiffy. 'Whoever'd want to go and see a show called *Cats*? Craziest idea I've ever heard.'

'Take no notice, Duddles darling,' said Sharkadder coldly. 'Mummy thinks it's a perfectly sweet idea. You can be the star and sing one of your lovely shanties.'

'No, he can't,' argued Pongwiffy. 'What would he sing about? Fish heads? His flea problem? Scrabbling around in cat litter? You might as well have a musical called – called *Hamsters*!'

Hugo froze in mid-guffaw.

'And vot wrong viz zat?' he enquired stiffly.

'If it comes to it, what's wrong with *Snakes*?' chipped in Slithering Steve, Bendyshanks's Snake.

'Or *Rats*?' piped up Vernon, Ratsnappy's Rat.

'*Vultures* is a catchy title, don't you think?' suggested Barry, Scrofula's Vulture, not very hopefully.

'Or *Haggis*,' poked in Rory, Macabre's Familiar, who was one.

'*Demons!*' (Sourmuddle's Snoop)

'*Fiends!*' (Sludgegooey's Filth)

'*Owls!*' (Greymatter's Speks)

Gaga's Bats flapped about excitedly, obviously making a bid for attention. The only Familiar who didn't have an opinion was Bonidle's Sloth, who, like his mistress, was fast asleep.

'Order!' commanded Sourmuddle, banging her gavel. 'Order, I say! We're not doing a musical about any of you Familiars and that's final. Your job is to help us Witches, not to go swanning off taking starring roles in musicals.'

'Oh no it isn't!' mumbled the Familiars.

'Oh yes it is!' chorused the Witches.

'I've just had a brilliant idea,' said Pongwiffy.

Nobody heard.

'Oh no it isn't!' argued the Familiars, warming to their theme.

'Oh yes it is!' insisted the Witches.

'*I said I've just had a brilliant idea!*' repeated Pongwiffy, more loudly.

Still nobody heard.

'Oh no it isn't!'

'Oh yes it is!'

'I SAID I'VE HAD A BRILLIANT IDEA!'

This time everybody heard. Excitedly, she leapt on to her chair. She had one of those Looks. One of those flushed, bulgy-eyed Looks that everyone knew so well.

'Oh no it isn't!' she squawked. 'Oh yes it is!' She waved dramatically at a point just left of Agglebag's shoulder. 'It's behind you!'

'What is?' said Agglebag anxiously, turning to look.

'No, no, not *really*. I'm just saying that. What does it remind you of?'

'It reminds me that I must ring for the men in white coats to take you away, Pongwiffy,' said Sourmuddle briskly. 'Get down before I lose my temper.'

'Not until you've heard my brilliant idea for the Christmas show,' insisted Pongwiffy.

'Which is?'

'Hold on to your hats, girls,' crowed Pongwiffy, and struck a pose. 'We . . .' She paused for dramatic effect. '*We are going to put on a pantomime!*'

CHAPTER TWO
Which One?

'A pantomime, eh?' mused Sourmuddle. 'I went to one of those once, when I was a slip of a girl. It was all about a poor young woman who did a lot of housework, and a posh fairy in a blue net frock turned up and gave her some grass boots and sent her off to play ball in some sort of converted vegetable. I was sick on ice cream at the interval, I recall. Ah me! Happy days.'

'That was *Cinderella*,' nodded Pongwiffy. 'Although I don't think you've got the plot quite right, Sourmuddle. It was glass slippers, not grass boots.'

'Could be,' agreed Sourmuddle. 'My memory's not what it was. I was definitely sick, though.'

'I don't think it should be *Cinderella*,' said Sharkadder excitedly. 'I vote we do *Dick Whittington*. And I can play the title role, because I've got the right sort of legs for Principal Boy. And Dudley can be my faithful cat.'

'Nonsense,' argued Ratsnappy. 'It's obvious we should do *The Pied Piper*, because I can play the recorder. You said we should make use of our amazing talents, Pongwiffy. And Vernon can be chief rat, can't you, Vernon? And we can use some of your relations as extras.'

Vernon looked excited.

'I think you'll find all the rats get drowned in that story,' remarked Greymatter.

Vernon stopped looking excited and became anxious instead.

'Who'll write it, though?' enquired Bendyshanks. 'I mean, we can't just make it up as we go along. There has to be a proper script and everything.'

'Oh, no problem,' said Pongwiffy rashly. She was much too carried away with her idea to let anything stand in her path. 'I'll write it. It'll probably only take me an evening. I've always fancied myself as a playwright. I'll direct it too. I'll do everything. All we need to do is decide which one. We'll use the little-pieces- of-paper method. Everyone must write down the character she wants to play and we'll see which pantomime crops up most often. Agreed?'

Everyone agreed.

'I'll do the honours, then,' said Sourmuddle, and twiddled her fingers. Instantly, twelve stubby pencils and little scraps of paper materialised on the table before the Witches. Sourmuddle herself had a quill pen and a smart silver inkpot and a large piece of parchment with her name and address prominently displayed at the top, but nobody said anything. She was Grandwitch. She could do what she liked.

'Wazapnin'?' muttered Bonidle, awaking from a deep sleep and finding herself required to do something. 'Is it mornin'?'

'We're putting on a pantomime,' explained Pongwiffy. 'Everyone has to write down who they want to be. If I was you, I'd go for something undemanding, Bonidle. Like a fallen log. Right, off you go.'

There was a bit of excited whispering and the sound of busily scratching pencils.

When everyone had finished, Pongwiffy passed her

hat along and they all solemnly dropped their papers in. Sourmuddle made a big thing about rolling up her parchment and tying it with red ribbon before placing it with the others.

'Right,' said Pongwiffy. 'Let's see what we've got.'

Everyone waited with bated breath while she began to unfold the scraps of paper.

'The twins want to be the Babes in the Wood,' she announced. Agglebag and Bagaggle nudged each other and giggled. 'Well, that's all right, I suppose. Sharky's sticking with Dick Whittington. Sludgegooey's written . . . *Snow White?*'

'That's me,' said Sludgegooey eagerly. 'I've always thought of myself as a Snow White sort of person.'

Everyone's jaws dropped in disbelief.

'I'd wash,' she added defensively.

'Hmm,' said Pongwiffy, unpersuaded. She turned to the next piece. 'Bonidle's put Sleeping Beauty. No problem there, she can do it with her eyes closed. Bendyshanks wants to be . . . *Cleopatra?*'

'Oh, I do, I do!' cried Bendyshanks, all aglow with enthusiasm. 'I've always wanted to play her. I did a course on belly dancing once. And Steve can be my poisonous asp. Oh, say I can, Pongwiffy! It's the answer to a dream!'

19

'Oh dear,' groaned Pongwiffy. 'This is going to be harder than I thought. Ratsnappy's sticking with the Pied Piper, and Scrofula's gone for – wait for it – Rapunzel.'

The assembled company rocked with mirth and tapped their foreheads pityingly.

'So?' said Scrofula, who had what can only be described as Problem Hair. 'What's so funny? You said we can be whoever we like.'

But Pongwiffy had moved on to the next one and was holding her head in despair.

'What's this say, Macabre? *Lady Macbeth*?'

'Aye,' said Macabre definitely.

'That's not a pantomime character,' objected Bendyshanks.

'Neither's Cleopatra,' snapped Macabre.

'She can dance, though,' shot back the would-be Queen of the Nile. 'I bet Lady Macbeth never went on a belly-dancing course.'

'She wouldnae want to,' scoffed Macabre. 'None o' that sissy stuff up in Scotland.'

Pongwiffy sighed, and turned to the three remaining suggestions. Greymatter had, for some reason, plumped for Sherlock Holmes. Sourmuddle's childhood experience had apparently left her with a deep-seated desire to be a posh fairy in a blue frock. Last of all was Gaga's piece of paper, on which was written, in wildly enthusiastic writing,

PANTOMIME HORSE –
BACK END PREFERRED!!!!

'Well,' said Pongwiffy despairingly. 'This is ridiculous. There's not even two characters from the same story. Some of you have got to change.'

'Not me,' said Sourmuddle stoutly. 'I'm leader of this Coven. If I can't be a fairy, I don't want to be in it.'

'But it's impossible,' argued Pongwiffy. 'How do you come up with a storyline that has to include three princesses, an Egyptian dancing queen, a posh fairy, Lady Macbeth, a couple of lost babies, a rat exterminator, Dick Whittington, a fictional detective and a pantomime horse's bum?'

'Well, that's your problem, Pongwiffy,' said Sourmuddle tartly. 'You said you could write the script in an evening, I seem to remember.'

'Well, yes, but –'

'There you are, then. It'll be a nice challenge for you. I suggest you take it home and work on it.'

And that is exactly what Pongwiffy did.

CHAPTER THREE
The Goblins' Invitation

W est of Witchway Wood, on the foothills of the Lower Misty Mountains, lies an area of outstanding natural unsightliness, known as Goblin Territory. It is a bleak, windblown place, full of craggy rocks and drippy caves. Nothing grows there, apart from scrubby gorse bushes, the odd twisted tree and unpleasant plants of the stinging variety. You would have to be really stupid to live in Goblin Territory.

Being stupid was something that came easily to the Gaggle of Goblins who lived there in the biggest, dampest, drippiest cave of them all: Plugugly,

Stinkwart, Hog, Slopbucket, Lardo, Eyesore and Sproggit. Seven daft Goblins with six brain cells between them.

Right now, they had just woken up and were thinking about breakfast. Not doing anything about it, you understand, because there wasn't any. Just thinking about it.

'I wish we 'ad sausages,' sighed Stinkwart as they sat in a gloomy circle, staring at the empty frying pan. 'Six fat bangers sizzlin' in a pan. Lovely.'

'There's seven of us,' Slopbucket reminded him. 'I fink,' he added doubtfully. (Goblins are not good at counting. They get confused after two.)

'I know *that*,' said Stinkwart pityingly. 'Fink I'm stupid? I said six 'cos then I can 'ave two, see?'

The Goblins thought about this for a while. There seemed something a bit wrong with Stinkwart's maths, but nobody was sure enough to say so.

'How come Stinkwart gets two?' remarked Eyesore after a bit. 'Two's more than one, innit? How come he gets two sausages and the rest of us only gets one? Huh? Huh?'

'Because I thought of 'em!' cried Stinkwart triumphantly. 'I thought of 'em, so I gets the most. Right?'

23

'I'll fight you for the extra one,' challenged Slopbucket, flexing his muscles. Everyone cheered up. An early morning punch-up over non-existent sausages wasn't quite as good as eating breakfast, but it was a way of filling in the time.

The fight, however, never got off the ground, because just at that moment, there came a knock on the front boulder. Everyone looked startled. Visitors were rare, particularly at this hour of the morning.

'Go on, Plug,' chorused six voices. 'See who it is.'

Plugugly reached for the saucepan he habitually wore on his round, bald head. He was the official doorkeeper and he liked to look properly dressed. He stumped to the boulder, rolled it a tiny way to one side and spoke through the crack.

'Yes?' he said. 'Whatcha want?'

'It is the post,' a gravelly voice informed him. 'I is your Post Troll. I has brung you A Letter.'

'Derrr – a what?' said Plugugly.

'A Letter,' repeated the voice, adding helpfully, 'It is a paper fing wiv a stamp on.'

'Cor,' said Plugugly, quite overwhelmed. The Goblins had never had A Letter before.

There was a crackling noise and a square white envelope slid through the gap and fell with a plop at

24

his feet. Nervously, Plugugly stooped and picked it up. The rest of the Goblins shuffled up and peered over his shoulder. It was addressed to:

The Goblins, The Cave
Goblin Territory, Lower Misty Mountains

To the Goblins, who couldn't read, it just looked like squiggly black marks.

'Better open it, I suppose,' remarked Eyesore doubtfully. 'Go on, Plug.'

Fingers trembling, Plugugly tore it open. It contained a single card covered with yet more incomprehensible squiggles. The Goblins examined it wonderingly.

'Wot's it say?' asked Sproggit.

'Dunno,' confessed Plugugly. 'Anyone got any idears?'

The card was passed around for inspection.

'Thass an H, innit?' said Hog doubtfully, pointing at a G. But that wasn't much help.

'Wot we gonna do?' wailed Lardo. 'We got A Letter an' we can't read it. Wot we gonna do?'

They stared wildly at each other, biting their knuckles and wringing their hands with frustration.

'I know!' cried Plugugly suddenly. 'We'll get de postie to read it to us!'

Everyone cheered and clapped him on the back. Plugugly glowed. He hadn't had many good ideas lately. Perhaps this was the start of a whole new Good Idears era.

The Post Troll was stomping down the slope, merrily whistling a little ditty entitled 'Post Troll Pete and His Oversized Feet'. He was surprised to hear wild shouts, then find himself suddenly surrounded.

'Read dat,' instructed the Goblin with the saucepan on his head, thrusting out the card.

'What about that magic lickle word?' said the Post Troll, wagging a reproving finger.

The Goblins looked blank.

'You know,' prompted the Post Troll. 'What has you got to say? When you is wanting a favour?'

'Or else?' suggested Slopbucket doubtfully.

'I is referrin' to "please",' the Post Troll told him severely. 'Read that *please*.'

'We can't,' explained Eyesore sadly.

'So you read it,' ordered Plugugly.

The Post Troll gave up. He snatched the card and read: '"The Great Gobbo invites you to a Grand Christmas Eve Fancy Dress Ball at Gobbo Towers.

A prize will be awarded for the best costume." There. *Now* what do you say?'

More blank faces.

'T'ank you!' shouted the Post Troll. 'T'ank you!'

'Dat's all right,' said Plugugly. 'Any time.'

Shaking his head in despair, the Post Troll thrust the card back at Plugugly, shouldered his bag and stomped off down the hill.

'Cor,' said Plugugly, sounding quite choked. 'We got an invitation. To a ball.'

They could hardly take it in. The Great Gobbo, chief of all the Goblin tribes, wanted them – *them* – at his ball! What an honour.

'I've always wanted to visit that there Gobbo Towers,' said Lardo wonderingly. 'It's dead swanky. My old mum knew someone what worked up there. There's somethin' called A Hinside Toilet.'

'Nah!' breathed Hog, clutching at his heart. 'That's what you call sophicist … sophitis … sosiph … posh.'

'An' there's a proper table with legs wot you eat off.'

'Imagine eatin' off table legs,' gasped Slopbucket, terribly impressed, as anyone would be who was used to eating off the floor.

'An' the Great Gobbo sits on a whackin' great

27

throne,' continued Lardo. 'An' all these beautiful She-Goblins in pink bikinis feeds him grapes.'

'Oo-er,' gulped his audience, their eyes coming over all glazed at the thought of the She-Goblins in their pink bikinis. Young Sproggit was so overcome he had to go and sit down under a tree.

'What's fancy dress when it's at 'ome?' Eyesore wanted to know.

'I know!' squeaked Hog, jumping around with his arm in the air. 'It's where you dresses up fancy. You has to go lookin' like someone else, see.'

'Well, dat's easy,' said Plugugly, relieved. 'We'll swap clothes an' go as each udder.'

'Erm – no, I don't fink that'll do,' said Hog. 'Iss gotta be someone special. Like a Spanish lady. Or a goriller. Iss gotta be a proper costume, see?'

'Sounds tricky,' commented Lardo, shaking his head. 'Proper costumes don't grow on trees.'

Seven anxious pairs of eyes roamed over the few scrubby trees growing on the slope. Nope. No costumes there.

'We'll fink about de costumes,' decided Plugugly. 'We'll 'ave a long, hard fink. We ain't lettin' costumes stop us from goin' to de ball. We just 'ave to use our 'eads. Right?'

The Goblins looked at each other doubtfully.

'I 'ad my 'ead examined once,' remarked Lardo. 'They couldn't find nuffin'.'

And, brows furrowed in deep concentration, they made their way back up to the cave in order to begin the unaccustomed process of thinking.

CHAPTER FOUR
The script

I think I've got writer's block,' announced Pongwiffy. She was wading to and fro in a sea of inky puddles and screwed-up pieces of paper in Number One, Dump Edge, which is the hovel where she lives. Obviously, things were not going well on the creative front.

'Vot ze problem?' asked Hugo, who was sitting in a teacup, filling in *The Daily Miracle* crossword puzzle.

'What's the *problem*?' cried the demented playwright, clutching her head with ink-stained fingers. 'I'll tell you the problem. I've got a cast of thousands which

I've somehow got to fit into a storyline. I've got to think of jolly songs and some dances and a happy ending. And there's got to be a funny bit with a horse and a bit where everyone goes, "He's behind you!" And everything has to be in rhyming couplets – and that's hard, I might tell you.'

Hugo put down the paper with a little sigh.

'Vot you done so far?'

'Not much,' admitted Pongwiffy. 'Right now I'm trying to come up with a plot and a snappy title. The one I've thought of sounds a bit long.'

'Try me.'

Pongwiffy snatched up a piece of paper and read: '*Sherlock Holmes Solves the Mysterious Case of the Missing Babes in the Wood Who are Spotted by Three Princesses After They Have Been Cruelly Left There by Lady Macbeth Riding Half a Pantomime Horse and They Have a Dream About Cleopatra But are Rescued by the Pied Piper and Dick Whittington and They Get Three Wishes from a Fairy and Live Happily Ever After.*'

'Is good plot,' nodded Hugo encouragingly. 'Plenty of action.'

'That's not the plot. That's the title. Oh dear! I knew it was too long.'

31

'Don't vorry about ze title,' advised Hugo. 'Script first. Title later.'

'I know, I know. But that's easier said than done. These rhyming couplets are very tricky, you know. I've had a go at Sherlock Holmes's opening speech, but I'm stuck.'

'Read me vot you done.'

Pongwiffy fished about and came up with another piece of paper.

'Ahem. "*Enter Sherlock Holmes.*"'

There was a pause.

'Go on,' said Hugo.

'That's it.'

'Zat's *it*? But 'e not say nussink!'

'I know. I told you I was having trouble with his opening speech.'

'Vell,' said Hugo, shaking his head. 'Zat no good. Zis Sherlock, 'e important character. 'E got to 'ave lines to say. 'E got to say sumsink like –' he scratched his head, 'sumsink like, "*I Sherlock 'Olmes. 'Ow do you do? I searchink for a vital clue.*"'

'What?' hissed Pongwiffy, electrified. 'What did you just say, Hugo?'

Hugo looked surprised, gave a little shrug, then repeated it.

32

'I Sherlock 'Olmes. 'Ow do you do?
I searchink for a vital clue.'

'But it's brilliant!' cried Pongwiffy, casting about for another sheet of paper. 'Hang on, let me write it down!'

Ink sprayed everywhere as she scribbled madly.

'Right. Got it. What might he say next, do you think?'

Hugo pondered briefly, then said:

'Ze Babes are missink in ze vood.
No news of zem. Zis is not good.
I' ave to solve zis mystery
Or zose poor Babes is 'istory.'

'Hugo! But this is sheer poetry! I never knew you had it in you!'

Pongwiffy's pen fairly flew as she committed the immortal lines to paper.

'Go on!' she begged. 'What happens next?'

'Vell . . .' said Hugo slowly, 'vell, zen zis Sherlock, 'e go off to ze vood to look for ze Babes. And 'oo should 'e meet but Snow Vhite and 'er friends Rapunzel and Sleepink Beauty, dancink gracefully round a tree.'

'Of course! That gets a dance in! Hang on, I must

make a note to book the Witchway Rhythm Boys. Right, go on! What do they say?'

Hugo vaulted from the cup, twirled an imaginary skirt, batted his eyelashes and declaimed:

> *'I am Snow Vhite, as you can see.*
> *Zose are my good friends 'ere viz me.*
> *Ve laugh an' play an' 'ave such fun,*
> *And zen ve lie down in ze sun.'*

'Fun! Sun! Incredible!' marvelled Pongwiffy. 'Go on. What does Scrofula say?'

With absolutely no hesitation, Hugo replied:

> *'I am Rapunzel viz long hair*
> *And Sleepink Beauty's over zere.'*

'Amazing! Fantastic! How do you think of it?'

'I dunno,' said Hugo with a modest little shrug. 'It just come, you know?'

'Well, I never!' crowed Pongwiffy, rocking to and fro. 'What talent! And I never even knew. Oh, this is too good to be true!'

Just then there was a knock on the door.

'Coooooeeee! Pong! It's me!' came a voice.

'Botheration! It's Sharky. And just as the panto was beginning to take shape. Go and put your feet up, Hugo, you little genius. Rest your brains for a bit. We'll carry on the minute I get rid of her.'

She scuttled to the door and flung it open.

'Yes? What is it, Sharky? I'm rather busy at the moment. Writing the panto, you know.'

'Oh? Really?' said Sharkadder, peering curiously at the heaps of crumpled paper. 'Well, I won't stop long. It's very cold out here. I don't suppose ... ?'

She looked hopefully past Pongwiffy in the direction of the kettle.

'No,' said Pongwiffy. 'Not a chance.'

'Oh, well. I'll be off, then. Don't want to interrupt the creative flow. Is it – er – coming along all right?'

'Oh, fine, fine,' declared Pongwiffy. 'I'm getting on like a hovel on fire. It's fairly flowing out of me. Should have it all wrapped up in no time.'

'Well, I never,' breathed Sharkadder, terribly impressed. 'I never knew you were a writer, Pong. It just goes to show. You can be friends with someone for years and not discover all their hidden talents.'

'Amazing, isn't it?' said Pongwiffy with a light little laugh.

'Ahem!'

From behind there came the distinct sound of a Hamster's warning cough.

'Have you – er – got to Dick Whittington's bit yet, by any chance?' enquired Sharkadder, trying to sound casual. 'Not that I'm *that* interested, ha ha, it's just that I was wondering if I've got a lot of lines to say. By any chance.'

'You haven't entered yet. You have to be patient. I've got loads of other stuff to fit in first. This is a team effort, Sharkadder. We don't want any prima donnas.'

'Oh. Yes, of course. I quite understand that,' said Sharkadder humbly. 'I'll let you get on, then, shall I?'

She turned and respectfully began to tiptoe away. Then she paused.

'Er – just one thing. I don't have to *kiss* anybody, do I?'

Pongwiffy glanced back at Hugo, who shrugged.

'I don't know yet,' said Pongwiffy furtively. 'Haven't quite decided. If it's in the script, you'll have to. That's show business.'

'Well, I'm not kissing Sludgegooey or any of that lot,' declared Sharkadder firmly. 'Even if I am Principal Boy. I do have some pride. If there's any

37

princess-kissing to be done, you'll need a Prince Charming.'

'Excuse me,' interrupted Pongwiffy sternly. 'Who's writing this panto?'

'Why – you, of course, Pong.'

'Correct,' said Pongwiffy. 'Me. With, perhaps, a bit of help from Hugo. And I don't need to be told how it should be done. Anyway, we don't have a Prince Charming. Nobody wanted to be him.'

'Well, you could always import one. And I've got just the person.'

'Who?' asked Pongwiffy.

Sharkadder told her.

'Don't make me laugh,' said Pongwiffy.

'I'm not. I can't think of anyone else, can you?'

Pongwiffy couldn't. There was a distinct lack of princely material in Witchway Wood.

'That's settled, then,' said Sharkadder gaily. 'We'll go and tell him the good news this afternoon.'

'Well – all right,' sighed Pongwiffy reluctantly, adding, 'Now, if you don't mind, Sharky, I'd like to get back to my script. I feel a couplet coming on.'

And she shut the door.

'There's got to be a Prince Charming, mind,' Sharkadder's voice called faintly. 'It's traditional.'

'She right, Mistress,' said Hugo. 'Zere has. It is.'

'Hmm. All right, we'll stick him in at the end, just before the happy ending. Right, come on then, polish your brains up, Hugo. Let's get this script on the road!'

CHAPTER FIVE
prince Ronald

Sharkadder's nephew, who was rather grandly known as Ronald the Magnificent (but only to himself), was in his attic room at the Wizards' Clubhouse. Well, actually, it wasn't so much a room. More a cupboard, really.

The allocation of rooms at the Clubhouse was based on the time-honoured Beard System. The Wizard with the longest beard got the big, posh room with the decent rug and the potted plant. The second longest beard was awarded the second poshest (slightly smaller rug, slightly deader plant) – right down to

Ronald, who had no beard at all and therefore got the attic with no rug, no plant and everyone else's discarded furniture. Sadly, this didn't include a chair. Ronald spent all his time standing up or lying down, with very little in between.

Right now, he was bent over his desk, which was awash with ancient books, scraps of paper covered in scribbly notes and a host of little jars and bottles filled with mysterious substances. Rising from the clutter was a Bunsen burner, currently set at a low flame under a copper pot. The official name for this pot, as any Wizard will tell you, is a crucible. Ronald's crucible contained a simmering, milky-white substance which was giving off thin wreaths of ghostly white smoke.

It was very clear that some sort of Wizardly experiment was taking place!

In fact, for the last few weeks, Ronald had been secretly working on an exciting, new, mould-breaking formula for an Extra Strong Invisibility Serum. If his calculations were right, a small sprinkle of this wonderful new serum would bring on a state of instant and complete vanishment. There was nothing like it on the market, unless you counted Invisibility Pills (unreliable with a terrible taste) or old-fashioned Cloaks of Invisibility (a shocking nuisance because

41

they were never to be found and always needed dry-cleaning).

The idea had come to him in an inspired flash one day, when he was eating a packet of Polos. If he could just isolate the holes and, using his amazing Wizardly skills, combine them scientifically with a bit of this and a bit of that, and maybe just a touch of the other . . .

Weeks of highly secret research had followed. Long, lonely hours spent huddled over his candle, working out difficult times tables and doing complicated things with a compass. Much poring over the pages of ancient tomes. Much tramping about at dawn in soggy countryside, tracking down various rare plants and herbs. Much eating of Polos.

Still. It was worth it. If the serum worked, he would be the toast of the town in Wizardly circles. He might be asked to write an article about it for *The Wizard's Weekly*. Why, he'd be famous! People might even stop teasing him. People might say things like, 'Say, you've got to hand it to young Ronald, he's really come up with the goods this time. Someone should get him a chair, don't you think?'

And if they didn't, well, see if he cared. He would just bottle the serum up, sell it for a vast profit – and use the money to buy *himself* a chair. A big, flash one. With a cushion. Ha!

Carefully, he measured out half a teaspoon of powder from a little jar labelled 'Dried Scotch Mist' and added it to the bubbling mixture in the crucible. He followed this with a pinch of Essence of Fog and three drops from a small phial containing a black, slippery substance which was, apparently, Extract of Shadow. There was a series of small explosions as the new substances got to know each other. Then the mixture settled down and simmered away happily. Ronald let out a relieved breath. So far, so good. Now all that remained was to add the final vital ingredient – a handful of Fresh Snow.

Gleefully, he reached for the stoppered flask. Then: 'Blast!' shouted Ronald. 'Blast, bother and blow!'

The flask was empty, apart from a small amount of brackish-looking water. That was the trouble with snow. It had a very short sell-by date. Now he'd have to wait until the next snowfall – whenever that might be – then go out and collect some more. What a disaster!

To add to his troubles, there came the sound of footsteps climbing the stairs. Ronald gave a guilty start, turned off the Bunsen burner, grabbed up the crucible (burning his fingers in the process) and hastily tipped the milky-white stuff down the cracked sink in the corner. He then scooped everything – Bunsen burner, crucible, books, papers, jars, the lot – into a cardboard box, which he kicked under the bed. Finally, he ran around the room, flapping at the air to dispel the white mist and the telltale smell.

The reason for his panic was the small notice that was displayed on his wall. It read:

STRICTLY NO MAGICAL EXPERIMENTS
IN THE BEDROOMS!

It was a sensible rule. In the past, Wizardly research carried out in bedrooms had proved a major fire risk. Alone and unaided, Fred the Flameraiser had burned down the entire Clubhouse at least three times. Of course, with oodles of Magic at their disposal, it didn't take the Wizards long to rebuild it. Nevertheless, it was a terrible nuisance, and nobody could ever agree on the exact shade of wallpaper. In the end, it had been decided that all Magical experiments must be conducted in the special fireproof laboratory which was located in the basement.

The trouble was, the lab was a very public place.

44

Your fellow Wizards tended to wander in, peer over your shoulder, enquire what you were working on, sneer a bit, then sneak off and pinch your idea.

Ronald didn't want anyone to know what he was working on. Not yet. Not until he'd cracked it.

There came a thunderous knocking at the door.

'Just a minute,' called Ronald, snatching up a can of *Reeka Reeka Roses* air-freshener and spraying it around.

Hastily, he threw himself down on his bed and looked casual. Only just in time. The door opened and a head, topped with a tangled green beehive hairdo, peered around it. It was Brenda, the Zombie receptionist.

'You got visitors,' announced Brenda, through a mouthful of bubblegum. 'I told 'em they ain't supposed to come outside of visitin' hours, but –'

'Out of the way, young woman!' interrupted a crisp voice that Ronald recognised with a sinking heart. 'We're here on Witch business!'

The door was flung open and Ronald's visitors stamped in.

'Oh,' said Ronald, rising from his bed with little enthusiasm. 'It's you, Aunt Sharkadder.'

'Good afternoon, Ronald, dear. Pong and I thought

we'd pay you a surprise visit. Say hello to Ronald, Pongwiffy.'

Pongwiffy and Ronald curled their lips at each other in mutual dislike.

'So! This is your room, is it?' cried Sharkadder gaily. 'Well, well, well. It's got a funny smell, hasn't it? Like cheap air-freshener with an underlying whiff of cooked marsh gas.'

'That's his aftershave,' said Pongwiffy.

'I hardly think you're in a position to comment on horrible smells, Pongwiffy,' said Ronald with a sniff.

'Actually, I consider myself a bit of an expert,' said Pongwiffy, who did. 'And if you really want to know what I think,' she added, 'I think Ronald's been cooking up a bit of Magic on the sly. Right here, in the shoebox he calls his bedroom.'

'No, I haven't,' lied Ronald, going red.

'Yes, well, I must say I expected something a bit grander,' remarked Sharkadder. 'After everything you've told me, Ronald, I rather had the impression that you Wizards lived in style. Well, come on, then. Haven't you got a kiss for your aunty?'

There came a snigger from the doorway. Ronald went pink. It wasn't done to admit you had a Witch aunty. Particularly one who kissed you.

46

'All right, Brenda, I won't keep you,' he said uncomfortably. 'Thanks awfully for bringing them up and everything. Er – you won't forget about that chair I asked for, will you? Super earrings, by the way.'

Brenda popped a rude bubble and withdrew. Sharkadder clutched Ronald in a tight embrace and planted a bright green lipsticky kiss on his forehead.

'There!' she said. 'That's because I haven't seen you for ages. How come you never visit me for tea any more, you bad boy?'

'Actually, you haven't invited me,' Ronald pointed out, struggling from her grasp.

'Oh, poo! You're more than welcome any time you like. Day or night, the kettle's always on for my favourite nephew. Haven't I always said that, Pong?'

Pongwiffy was wandering around Ronald's room, fiddling with things. She pulled the handle off his wardrobe. She tried out his bed and broke a spring. She opened his diary, ran her eyes down a page and sneered.

'You put that down, Pongwiffy,' said Ronald. 'Tell her, Aunty. She's touching my things.'

'Just having a look,' said Pongwiffy. 'Professional interest, you understand. What's this?' She turned a page and read aloud: *"1 September: Got up ... Hung*

47

about ... Had a nurly nite ... Luked for a char ... Didunt find one. 2 September: Got up ... Sossijuss for super ... Had another nurly nite ... Still no char.' Badness me, Ronald, what an exciting life you do lead. What are all these Nurly Nites of which you speak? And what's all this about a char?'

'Stop it! You can't read that – it's private!' Ronald protested and made a leap.

Pongwiffy evaded him and gleefully continued turning pages. 'Aha! Here's something interesting. *"Werked in bedroom on new seecret formuler."* I knew it! So where's all the stuff? Is that what's in that big cardboard box I see poking out from under your bed?'

'Put it down!' howled Ronald. 'You've got no right to read people's diaries.'

'Oh, all right, keep your hair on. Just thought you might like a few writing tips.'

Pongwiffy threw the diary over her shoulder. Ronald caught it and thrust it deep into his robe.

'Ha!' he scoffed. 'Since when do you know anything about writing, Pongwiffy?'

'Since I became a playwright, *actually*,' said Pongwiffy with a smug air.

'A playwright? You? Don't make me laugh.'

'I am so. Aren't I, Sharky?'

'Well, yes. As a matter of fact, Ronald, that's why we're here. We've come to offer you a wonderful opportunity. It's a tremendous honour and you're a very lucky young man.'

'Oh, really?' groaned Ronald. He was getting a bad feeling. 'What's that, then, Aunty?'

'You,' announced Sharkadder, 'are going to be Prince Charming in the lovely pantomime that Pongwiffy's writing. Won't that be fun?'

Ronald suddenly came over all weak. His legs gave way and he collapsed on to his bed with a little moan.

'Why?' he managed to choke out. 'Why me?'

'Because there's nobody else,' said Pongwiffy bluntly. 'I didn't really want you, but Hugo says we have to have a prince. To kiss all the princesses.'

'*All* the princesses?' repeated Ronald faintly. 'How many would that be?'

'Three,' said Pongwiffy gleefully. 'Snow White, Rapunzel and Sleeping Beauty. Played by Sludgegooey, Scrofula and Bonidle.'

It was all too much. Ronald rallied.

'No!' he cried. 'I won't do it! I won't!'

'I beg your pardon, Ronald?' purred Sharkadder in a voice like razor blades cutting through silk. 'Did I hear you say you won't?'

'That's right. I'm sorry, Aunty, but I'm a serious Wizard. I'm working on a new project. I can't spare the time.'

'Oh dear. That *is* a pity, isn't it, Pong?'

'It certainly is,' agreed Pongwiffy sadly. 'I guess there's nothing else for it. We'll just have to report him. We'll just have to go down right now and announce that he's been breaking the rules and working on a silly old secret formula in his room. Come on, Sharky. We'll take the evidence with us.'

Purposefully, they moved towards the bed.

'Wait!' cried Ronald.

They paused.

'Yes?' said Sharkadder. 'Is there something you wanted, Ronald?'

'When's the first rehearsal?' said Ronald brokenly.

CHAPTER SIX
The Read-Through

The first rehearsal took place in Witchway Hall. A large circle of chairs had been placed on the stage. Everyone was present, with the exception of the eagerly awaited playwright and her assistant. Ronald was there too, maintaining a stiff air of aloofness and standing apart from the rest of them. This was for the following reasons:

1. It showed he didn't want to be there.
2. No chair. Again.

There was an air of expectancy and great excitement. It was common knowledge that Pongwiffy had finished writing the script. She and Hugo had been shut up in Number One, Dump Edge for days, refusing to answer the door except for important deliveries of ink, paper and takeaway pizzas with extra skunk topping. Various would-be thespians had come knocking to see how their parts were coming along, but to no avail. Gaga's Bats had been sent to spy through the window and had reported scenes of great industry, with candles burning at both ends and a steadily growing pile of manuscript.

Then, that very morning, the hovel door had burst open and the pair of them had staggered out into the fresh air, spraying each other with fizzy demonade and thumping each other's backs in celebratory fashion. When questioned, however, they had refused to give away a thing.

'Wait until this evening,' Pongwiffy had said mysteriously. 'All will be revealed then.'

And now it *was* this evening and the tension was wound up to breaking point. There were a lot of flushed faces, damp palms and peals of high, nervous laughter. People kept saying that, of course, they didn't *mind* if they only got a small part, oh dear me no. But they didn't mean it. Barry the Vulture was so flustered by it all that he had gone off somewhere to be quietly sick. Gaga was in the last stages of complete hysteria and kept rushing off to hang from the curtains. Only Sourmuddle looked confident. As Grandwitch, she could be sure of a decent part – or, as she told Snoop, she'd want to know the reason why.

Just as the excitement reached fever pitch, the long-awaited writing team arrived. Pongwiffy was clutching a fat sheaf of papers under her arm and wearing a look of great triumph. Hugo sat perched on her hat, looking pale but proud.

'Aaaah!' breathed the expectant company. 'Here they are.'

'Yep!' cried Pongwiffy, almost bursting with importance. 'Here we are – and the panto's finished, like I said it would be. And, what's more, it's all in poetry.'

'What's it called?' shouted Ratsnappy.

'It's called *Terror in the Wood*.'

Everybody tried it out. *Terror in the Wood*. It wasn't exactly traditionally pantomime-ish, but it had a certain something.

'I've got copies of everybody's part and I suggest that the first thing we do is have a read-through. I'll talk you through the story and when it comes to your bit, read it out. I shall be looking for volume, clarity and a deep sense of commitment.'

Pongwiffy bustled around the circle, handing out sheets of paper covered with spidery writing. Eager hands received them and heads bowed as everybody studied their part. She took her seat and held up her hand dramatically.

'Right,' she said. 'Imagine it. The orchestra has played the overture. The stage is in darkness. The curtains part. Slowly, the lights come up on Sherlock Holmes's study. Enter Sherlock with his magnifying glass. Go on, Greymatter. That's you.'

'What about Speks?' said Greymatter. 'He wants to be in the panto too. Don't you, Speks?'

The small owl seated on the back of her chair agreed that yes, indeed, he would very much like to be in the panto.

'Not possible,' said Pongwiffy. 'There isn't a part for him.'

'He can play Watson,' insisted Greymatter. 'Watson, my faithful owl, who helps me with all my cases.'

'Watson wasn't an owl,' argued Pongwiffy.

'Sherlock Holmes wasn't an elderly Witch with a rather nasty perm, but that hasn't stopped

Greymatter,' Sharkadder chipped in. 'Don't be mean, Pong. Let Speks be Watson.'

'Yes!' came several voices raised in agreement. 'Speks for Watson!'

Pongwiffy sighed. They hadn't even started and already people were arguing.

'All right,' she said. 'All *right*. Enter Sherlock Holmes with his magnifying glass and his ridiculous owl called Watson. Go on, Greymatter. Say your opening lines.'

'Ahem,' said Greymatter. 'Right. Er –

> *And now at last our panto's done.*
> *We hope you had a lot of fun.'*

'I think you've got the pages mixed up,' said Pongwiffy stiffly. 'That's the end.'

'Oh – right. Sorry. Um –

> *I'm Sherlock Holmes. How do you do?*
> *I'm searching for a vital clue.*
> *The Babes are missing in the wood –'*

She broke off as Agglebag and Bagaggle clutched at each other with excited little screams.

'That's us!' squeaked Agglebag. 'We're the Babes, Bag!'

'I know, Ag, I know! Oh my!'

'Shush!' Pongwiffy warned them sternly. 'No interruptions, if you please. Carry on, Greymatter. And try to sound less like a brick.'

Greymatter adjusted her glasses and carried on reading.

> *'The Babes are missing in the wood.*
> *No news of them. This is not good.*
> *I have to solve this mystery*
> *Or those poor Babes is history . . .*

'Actually, Pongwiffy, that should read *are* history. Hope you don't mind my mentioning it.'

Pongwiffy gave a little frown.

'Well, all right, change it if you must. But I don't want you to think you can go round changing lines just because they don't suit you. We creative types can get very upset when people mess about with our work. It took me a long time to write this pantomime. Long, lonely hours, just me, my pen and my incredible imagination . . .'

'*Ahem!*' came a warning cough from her hat.

'Well, all right, Hugo helped a bit.'

'*AHEM!!*'

'A lot,' amended Pongwiffy hastily. 'Hugo helped a lot. Anyway, at this point you sing a jolly song, Greymatter, but we won't bother about that now. We'll move on to the next scene, which is set in a lovely woodland glade, with Snow White, Rapunzel and Sleeping Beauty dancing gracefully around a tree.'

'What?' chorused Sludgegooey, Scrofula and Bonidle, sounding startled.

'You heard. You've got to do a graceful dance.'

'What – now?' asked Sludgegooey. 'In front of everyone?'

'No, not now. We'll work on the dance another time. Just say your lines.'

Sludgegooey pulled her nose with filthy fingers and intoned:

> *I am Snow White, as you can see,*
> *These are my good friends here with me,*
> *We laugh and play and have such fun*
> *And then we lie down in the splodge.'*

'What?' said Pongwiffy.

'There's an inkblot over the last word. I can't read

57

it. What do we lie down in, Pongwiffy? After we've had all this fun?'

'Sun,' said Pongwiffy coldly. 'You lie down in the sun. It's obvious. It's got to rhyme with fun. Anyway, you'd hardly lie down in a cowpat, would you?'

'I might,' said Sludgegooey defensively.

'*You* might. But Snow White wouldn't, would she? You've got to stay in role. Right, your turn, Scrofula.'

Scrofula held up her sheet of paper and read:

> *'I am Rapunzel with long hair*
> *And Sleeping Beauty's over there.*

'How come my bit's shorter than Sludgegooey's?'

'And how come I don't get anything to say at all?' Bonidle wanted to know.

'Because you're asleep, of course,' snapped Pongwiffy, beginning to sound exasperated. 'Anyway, you've got a line.'

'Have I? What is it?' asked Bonidle.

'"*ZZZZZZZZ*," ' said Pongwiffy. 'Now do it.'

Obediently, Bonidle did it. And that was the last they heard from her that evening.

'Right,' said Pongwiffy. 'On to the next bit. Sherlock Holmes questions the witnesses.'

58

'When does the fairy come in?' Sourmuddle wanted to know.

'Not yet,' said Pongwiffy through gritted teeth. 'Be patient, Sourmuddle, everyone can't enter at the same time.'

'I'm Grandwitch,' said Sourmuddle tartly. 'I can enter any time I like.'

'Not in a pantomime. You've got to wait your turn. Carry on, Greymatter.'

The great detective cleared her throat.

> *'Ah ha! Now, who is this I see?*
> *Three beauties dancing round a tree.*
> *Good morrow to Your Royal Highnesses.*
> *Excuse me while I –* clear my sinuses?'

Greymatter stopped, looking puzzled.

'Ah. That's where we have a bit of stage business,' explained Pongwiffy. 'You've got hay fever. You have to stop and blow your nose. It's the only word that rhymes with Highnesses, see. We were rather pleased with that bit, weren't we, Hugo? Carry on.'

> *'The Babes are gone! There is no trace!*
> *It is a most mysterious case.*

> *I wonder where those Babes can be.*
> *Oh, can you help, Princesses three?'*

There was a long pause. Macabre gave Sludgegooey an almighty nudge.

'Oh – is it me? Right. Um –

> *'We saw them pass a short while back.*
> *They went along that little track.*
> *They have been taken off by force*
> *By a Scottish woman on a horse.'*

'That's me,' Macabre informed everybody proudly. 'Hear that, everyone? Ma bit's comin' up soon.'

'What about the fairy?' demanded Sourmuddle again. 'I'm warning you, Pongwiffy, I'm not waiting much longer. It's the fairy that everyone's anxious to see, after all.'

'Dick Whittington is still conspicuous by his absence, I note,' remarked Sharkadder with more than a touch of pique.

'I think it's time the Pied Piper got a look-in, don't you, Vernon?' complained Ratsnappy.

'What about Cleopatra?' clamoured Bendyshanks. 'Where's she, I'd like to know?'

'And another thing,' piped up Scrofula. 'What about Barry? If Sherlock Holmes can have a faithful owl, why can't Rapunzel have a faithful vulture?'

'It isn't possible,' explained Pongwiffy wearily. 'There just isn't room in this panto for all the Familiars. Those who haven't got a part get to do other things.'

'Like what?'

'Like scenery-shifting. And Noises Off.'

This statement was greeted by quite a lot of noises off, most of them raised in shrill complaint.

Pongwiffy and Hugo exchanged meaningful glances. It seemed that rehearsals were going to be a bit of a trial.

CHAPTER SEVEN

Preparations

Putting on a pantomime is not something that can be taken lightly – as Pongwiffy soon learnt.

To begin with, there was the question of music. The Witchway Rhythm Boys were the obvious choice, being local, so Pongwiffy went along to the specially soundproofed hut where they rehearsed.

'How much do we get paid?' enquired Arthur, the small Dragon who played the piano. (Dragons rarely become pianists, but Arthur was unusual. In fact, he was quite good, apart from an unfortunate tendency to set his instrument on fire during the faster passages.)

'What d'you mean, *paid*?' snapped Pongwiffy. 'This is a great honour, you know, being asked to perform in my panto.'

'We always get paid for gigs,' Arthur told her. 'Union rules.'

'Yeah, man,' agreed Filth the Fiend, Sludgegooey's Familiar, who played drums in his spare time. 'Gotta come up with the bread.'

'Toim's money,' nodded O'Brian, the Leprechaun, who played penny whistle.

'Well, I'm flabbergasted,' said Pongwiffy. 'Your selfishness defies belief. After all the employment we Witches have given you in the past.'

'Yes, but we never got paid for it, did we?' Arthur reminded her. 'We're getting popular now. We can pick and choose. We've got the Skeleton disco next week and the Zombie barn dance and a Vampire ruby wedding Sunday fortnight. We're an up-and-coming band, we are. No pay, no play. That's the deal, right, boys?'

'To be sure,' said O'Brian firmly.

'You said it, man,' agreed Filth.

So Pongwiffy had to cough up.

Then there was the question of costumes. After a bit of thought, Pongwiffy decided to hire them. It virtually emptied the kitty, but costumes are one of the most important aspects of any production and Witches aren't known for their nifty work with a needle. She got Hugo to take everybody's measurements and sent off a list of requirements to Gentleman Joe's Theatrical Costume Hire Company, which advertised in *The Daily Miracle* and promised to deliver.

Then there was the scenery to consider. Pongwiffy engaged the services of a local artist, a Vampire by the name of Vincent Van Ghoul, who wore a red beret and matching smock and lived in paint-splattered squalor in the small shed he grandly called his studio. Vincent eked out a living as a portrait artist and welcomed the chance to do something a bit

64

different.

'There are three scenes,' Pongwiffy told him. 'The first is Sherlock Holmes's study.'

'Great,' said Vincent eagerly. 'I'll paint it red. Nice vase of red poppies on the table. Bowl of tomatoes. That sort of thing.'

'The next is a woodland glade,' explained Pongwiffy.

'No problem,' said Vincent. 'I'll set it in autumn. At sunset. Nice red trees and a carpet of red leaves, I feel.'

'Hmm. And then there's the ballroom scene.'

'I see it all!' cried Vincent. 'Red velvet curtains with pots of red geraniums!'

That's the trouble with artistic Vampires, of course. They are red-fixated.

Then there was publicity to think about. There were posters to be designed. After a bit of thought, Pongwiffy came up with the following:

Grand Pantomime
The Witchway Players
proudly present
TERROR IN THE WOOD
December 20 7.00 sharp
Witchway Hall –
Bring Your Fiends

(*STRICTLY NO GOBLINS!!*)

There were programmes to be printed and special invitations to be sent out to important people. Pongwiffy wrote a list of these, starting with royalty. The local Royal Family consisted of King Futtout, Queen Beryl and their daughter, Princess Honeydimple. They weren't particularly popular, but as their palace bordered Witchway Wood, it would have been unneighbourly not to send them an invitation.

Scott Sinister, the famous film star, was also down for an invite.

'I thought you'd gone off him,' Hugo reminded Pongwiffy, peering over her shoulder at the VIP list.

'So did I,' sighed Pongwiffy, 'but when it comes down to it, there is a corner of my heart that will be for ever Scott's. We've had our ups and downs, Scott and me, but that's what makes our relationship so excitingly special. I'm going to send him a handmade invite with "Don't Bring Lulu" at the bottom.'

(This will make sense to readers who have followed the previous exploits of Pongwiffy. If this doesn't include you – no matter. It is enough to know that Pongwiffy and Luscious Lulu Lamarre, the great actor's girlfriend, Do Not Get On.)

Other VIPs included Pierre de Gingerbeard (provided he was well enough) and the Yeti Brothers, Conf and Spag, who ran all the fast food establishments in the area. The only reason they appeared on the list was because Pongwiffy was rather hoping they might slip her a free pizza.

'Vot about ze Vizards?' Hugo reminded her.

'Oh, poo!' said Pongwiffy. 'What do we want silly old Wizards in the audience for?'

'Ronald vill be 'appy,' Hugo remarked. ''E don't vant it known zat 'e in Vitch panto. 'E don't vant to kiss Vitches. 'E sink all 'is friends vill laugh at 'im.'

'Good point,' said Pongwiffy, and promptly added the Wizards to the VIP list. 'They'll all have to pay though,' she added. 'The whole point is to raise money.'

Then, armed with a hammer and a mouthful of nails, she went scuttling off to pin posters to trees.

It wasn't really necessary. By now, word had got around. The Familiars had their hands full chasing away curious onlookers who crowded around Witchway Hall every evening, peering through the windows in the hope of getting a glimpse of rehearsals in progress.

And so the weeks went by in a dizzy whirl of

67

activity – and almost before anyone realised it, autumn had given way to winter and the grand opening night was almost upon them.

CHAPTER EIGHT
Fancy Dress

Plugugly was skulking behind a bush down in Witchway Wood, straining to hear the conversation of two Skeletons who stood a short distance away, examining a poster displayed on a tree.

'Looks like the Witches are putting on some sort of show, darling,' remarked the first Skeleton. You could tell he was a male Skeleton, because he was wearing a bow tie.

'Hmm,' said his female companion, who was all decked out in a blonde wig. 'A pantomime, no less. Are we doing anything Saturday night, darling?'

'I doubt it,' said the other. 'Might as well go. Everyone else'll be there.'

'Except the Goblins, of course,' nodded the bewigged one. 'They're barred. The Witches won't let them attend anything these days. See?' She pointed a finger bone. '*Strictly No Goblins*. And quite right too.'

They laughed, linked arms and strolled on.

Ears burning, Plugugly hurried back to the cave to tell the others.

Eagerly, he burst in, blurting out, 'Guess wot? Dere's a pantymine, an' . . .'

'Ssssh!' said everyone.

All eyes were on Stinkwart, who was standing on a handy rock. He was wearing two large, branching twigs on his head and appeared to have reddened his nose with crushed holly berries.

'We're inspectin' each uvver's costumes fer the fancy dress ball,' explained Hog. 'We're tryin' ter guess 'oo we are.'

'Sorry,' whispered Plugugly and sat down. This was important. The bad news about the pantomime could wait.

'Right,' said Stinkwart. ''Oo am I?'

The Goblins stared with blank faces.

'Come on, come on,' urged Stinkwart. 'It's obvious, innit?'

Shrugs all round.

'Some kinda tree?' guessed Lardo.

'Nah, nah! Wassa matter wiv you? Look at the nose. It's red, innit? So 'oo am I?'

'A red-nosed tree,' said Lardo. Once his mind was set on a certain course, it never deviated.

'Ah, to heck wiv it!' said Stinkwart, disgusted. 'I'm Rupert, ain't I? Rupert the red-nosed wassit.'

And he tore off his antlers, climbed off the rock and sat down in a sulk.

'I always thort it was Randolph,' said Hog to no one in particular.

It was Eyesore's turn next. He took his place on the rock, wearing what appeared to be an ancient bird's nest on his head. Bits of loose straw curled down to his shoulders. From his pocket, he took a tin bowl and a spoon. He batted his eyelashes, simpered and struck a pose.

'Right,' he said. 'Who am I?'

Another blank silence.

'I'll give you a clue,' said Eyesore helpfully. 'There's porridge in this bowl.'

Still no offers.

71

'I'm a little girlie,' prodded Eyesore. 'I'm a little girlie wiv long yellow hair an' I got a bowl of porridge. Oh, oh, I'm scared of the bears. Who does that remind you of?'

The Goblins were at a loss.

'Goldisocks!' exploded Eyesore at length. 'I'm Goldisocks, fer cryin' out loud. I got the wig an' everythin'. Fancy not gettin' *that*.'

And he flounced off the rock in a huff, tossing his bird's-nest curls petulantly.

'Dis is no good,' burst out Plugugly. He simply couldn't help it. 'Dis is a waste o' time. Dere ain't no way we're gonna win de fancy dress prize unless we can come up wid somefin' better dan dis.'

'What about you, then?' demanded Eyesore, sullenly pulling his nest to pieces.

'Yeah, go on, Plug,' came the chorus. 'Wot's your costume, then?'

'I ain't got one,' confessed Plugugly lamely.

'Well, that's just great, that is,' said Sproggit spitefully. ''E picks 'oles in everyone else's costume, but 'e ain't even got one.'

Plugugly sighed heavily. In fact, he had thought a great deal about his costume. That's why he'd been loitering down in the Wood. He'd been trying to get some inspiration. He knew he wanted to be something spectacular, something that would cause jaws to gape and people to say things like, 'Good ol' Plugugly, trust him to come up with a Good Idea like that.' He could imagine himself receiving the prize from the Great Gobbo himself. He could visualise the thumps on the back, the cheers. He could see the scene. All he needed was the idea.

But he couldn't come up with one.

'Look,' he said. 'Look. I know you done yer best. I'm just sayin' we gotta do better dan dis if we're gonna win de prize. Dat's all I'm sayin'.'

'Know what'd be good?' said Slopbucket with a wistful air. 'Goin' an' buyin' ourselves proper costumes from a proper shop. That'd be good.'

'It would,' agreed Plugugly, ''cept dere ain't no proper costume shop round 'ere. An' even if dere was, we ain't got no money. An' even if we 'ad de money, dey wouldn't serve us, 'cos we's Goblins. An' dat reminds me. Dere's a Witch pantymine on Saturday night. Everyone's talkin' about it. Dere's posters all over de Wood. An' we's banned. I 'eard a coupla Skelingtons read it out. "No Goblins", dey said. Den dey larfed.'

'What's a pantymine?' Lardo wanted to know.

'I dunno,' confessed Plugugly. 'But I wouldn't mind de chance to find out.'

'It comes to somethin', don't it?' said Hog bitterly. 'No costumes, no money, no dinner an' banned from the pantymine. We must be the unluckiest Goblins in the world.'

They sat in a dejected circle.

'What we need is one o' them there things beginnin' with *co*,' said Stinkwart, very suddenly and very obscurely.

'What – you mean like a coconut?' said Lardo hesitantly.

'No, no. Longer. You know. When somethin' 'appens out o' the blue. One o' them flukes o' fate. You call it an amazin' *co* summink. It's on the tip of me teef. You know.'

'Well, person'ly, I ain't expectin' a coconut,' remarked Lardo, pleased with himself for having thought of one and not willing to let it go.

'Look, it's not a coconut, all right?' cried Stinkwart. 'It's – it's like when you got a fancy fer a big fruit cake, an' you ain't got one and then, just like that, there's a knock at the door an' there's yer granny! An' wot's she got in 'er 'and?'

'A coconut?'

'No, no,' began Stinkwart, beside himself with frustration. 'That's not wot I'm getting at –'

But he didn't get any further, because just at that moment there came a tentative knock at the front boulder. The Goblins jumped and looked at each other.

'Who's that, then?' hissed Eyesore.

'Probably Stinkwart's granny,' suggested Hog. 'And we were just talking about her too. What an amazin' coincidence.'

There was a loud clump as Stinkwart passed out on the floor.

'I hope she's brought the fruit cake,' crowed young Sproggit.

'And the coconut,' added Lardo happily.

Plugugly went to answer the boulder. Outside, it was sleeting. A small man with a whuffly moustache stood in a frozen puddle and touched his cap. A short way behind him was a large cart pulled by a bored-looking horse. Written across the side, in big, bold letters, were the words:

GENTLEMAN JOE'S THEATRICAL
COSTUME HIRE COMPANY

'Yeah?' said Plugugly. 'Whatcha want?'

'Sorry ter bovver yer, squire,' said the small man. 'Wonder if you can help me? I'm looking for Witchway Hall. I got an important delivery, see. Think I musta taken a wrong turn.'

'I think you must 'ave,' said Plugugly. 'You're right off track 'ere. Dis 'ere's Goblin Territory. You need a special secret password to go through 'ere.'

As he spoke, the rest of the Goblins came slinking up behind him.

'Wassee want, Plug?' asked Slopbucket.

''E's lost 'is way,' explained Plugugly. ''E's got a delivery ter make to Witchway Hall. I'm tellin' 'im 'e needs ter say de secret password.'

'Wot, you mean "Frogspawn"?' enquired Eyesore.

'Dat's de one,' agreed Plugugly. 'Right,' he added, fixing the small man with a stern stare. 'Wot's de password?'

'Erm – frogspawn?'

'Correck. Right, you go down past de stingin' nettle clump, right, den you take a left, right, by de old cooker an' den a right, right? Or is it left?'

'Straight, innit?' interrupted Hog helpfully.

'Yeah, well, one o' dem. Den you follow de trail down an' around a bit an' den yer in de Wood. De Hall's in de middle somewhere. You can't miss it.'

'Thanks,' said the small man doubtfully. 'Very kind o' you, squire.'

'Dat's all right,' said Plugugly. 'Mind 'ow you go'. He watched him trudge away and climb into the driver's seat.

'By de way,' he called, 'by de way, wassit you're deliverin'?'

'Costumes,' replied the man, and clicked his teeth. The horse raised its eyes to heaven and lumbered off down the slope.

The Goblins looked at each other. They were too shocked to speak for quite some time. At last, Lardo spoke for all of them.

'Now *that*,' he said, 'is what I call an amazing coconut.'

CHAPTER NINE
Rehearsals

In Witchway Hall, a rehearsal was in progress. The current scene was a big, troublesome one, involving Lady Macbeth, half the Pantomime Horse, the lost Babes, Cleopatra, the Pied Piper, Dick Whittington and the fairy. As always, there was a lot of argument going on, mainly around the question of Lady Macbeth's transport. Macabre was flatly refusing to ride half a Pantomime Horse, claiming that she was a serious actress and it would make her look ridiculous. Gaga was prancing around in the wings, practising blowing through her nostrils.

'You've got to,' said Pongwiffy wearily. 'I've ordered the horse suit. I've written it in. Look, it's there in the script. *"Enter Lady Macbeth on half a Pantomime Horse."* That's what Gaga wanted to be and I had to write her in somewhere. You don't want to do Gaga out of her part, do you? She's looking forward to it, aren't you, Gaga?'

Gaga snorted eagerly and pawed the ground.

'Lady Macbeth wouldnae ride half a horse,' objected Macabre. 'It's noo in her character. Anyway, it's noo possible tay ride half a horse. There has tay be a front end. For the reins.'

Pongwiffy sighed. The question of the horse's front end had been bothering her too. She kept pushing it away, hoping that a solution would present itself – but so far, none had. The trouble was, nobody wanted to be zipped into a dark, stuffy skin with an overexcited Gaga at their rear, doing goodness knows what. And who could blame them?

'Ah'm ridin' Rory,' announced Macabre. 'Ah always ride Rory. He's *ma* Haggis an' Ah'm ridin' him.'

Dead on cue, Rory trotted from the wings and stood shaking his orange fringe, doing his best fiery steed impersonation. Macabre climbed on his back and glared down stubbornly.

'All right!' snapped Pongwiffy, exasperated. 'All right, have it your own way. "*Enter Lady Macbeth riding a Haggis.*" Happy now? Don't worry, Gaga, I'll fit you in somehow. Tell you what, we'll give you a whole little scene of your own in front of the curtain. While the scenery's being changed. You can do a funny dance. All right?'

Gaga cantered in small, enthusiastic circles.

'Now, can we get on?' sighed Pongwiffy. 'Please? We've only got until Saturday, you know. Take your places on the stage, twins, and wait for your cue. Remember, you're tied together with rope. You've been kidnapped. You're frightened. Right, fire away, Macabre. Give it all you've got.'

Macabre fancied herself as an actress. She uttered a bloodcurdling cackle and shook her fist before launching into her big speech.

> '*The Babes are mine, there is no doubt.*
> *Ma wicked plan is working out.*
> *Ah'll tie them to this nearby tree*
> *So they cannae escape from me.*
> *Ah'm off tay write a ransom note*
> *And then Ah will come back to gloat. Ha, ha, ha!*'

'Very good, Macabre,' said Pongwiffy. 'Very sinister. Right, you tie the Babes to a tree, then go off to find a pencil. Go on, twins. It's your big moment.'

Agglebag and Bagaggle cleared their throats, clutched each other for mutual support, then spoke in chorus.

> *'Alas! Alack! Oh, boo, hoo, hoo.*
> *Whatever can we poor Babes do?*
> *Oh, for a rescuer to come*
> *And reunite us with our mum.'*

And they looked at each other and giggled.

'Not bad, not bad,' said Pongwiffy. 'Try not to laugh, though. Right, now you lie down under some leaves and go to sleep and have a dream about Cleopatra. Where's Bendyshanks?'

'Here!' shouted the Queen of the Nile eagerly and bounded on. Slithering Steve was draped around her neck, doing his best to look like a poisonous asp.

'Say your bit, then,' ordered Pongwiffy.

> *'I'm Cleopatra from the Nile.*
> *I have a unique dancing style.*
> *So while the Babes enjoy their kip*
> *Sit back and watch me letting rip.'*

Bendyshanks then produced a tambourine and capered around the stage, doing a series of unusual leg-wavings. The twins forgot they were supposed to be dreaming and sat up to watch in fascination. Bendyshanks leapt about until she was purple in the face, then ended up doing the splits.

'So what d'you think?' she said.

'You still need to work on it a bit,' advised Pongwiffy. 'Make it a bit more Egyptian. Try and be more exotic, Steve. Forget grass snake. Think python.'

'I was,' said Steve miserably.

'We'll try again, shall we?' asked Bendyshanks, eager as a puppy.

'No, no. Once is quite enough. We need to move on. Where are we in the script, Hugo?'

'"*Cleopatra exits to rapturous applause,*"' supplied Hugo doubtfully.

'Right. "*Enter the Pied Piper and Dick.*" '

'At last!' cried Ratsnappy and Sharkadder, hurrying on to the stage with Vernon and Dudley at their heels.

'What about the fairy?' piped up Sourmuddle testily. 'I've been waiting for ages. I am Grandwitch, you know.'

'Soon,' hissed Pongwiffy from between gritted

82

teeth. 'She's coming on *soon*. Right, off you go, you two. Say your lines.'

Ratsnappy cleared her throat and stepped forward.

> *'You weren't expecting me, I'll bet.*
> *I'm the Pied Piper, with my pet.*
> *To comb this wood is our intent.*
> *We'll find those Babes, where'er they went.'*

She gave a deep bow and Vernon did likewise. Sharkadder elbowed them aside, swaggered forward with Dudley at her heels and slapped her thigh.

> *'And I am Dick, the hero bold.*
> *Full many a tale of me is told.*
> *I'm here to find those missing mites,*
> *With sword in hand and long green tights.*

'Talking about tights, Pong, when are the costumes arriving? I can't quite get in role unless I look the part.'

'They're due to arrive this evening,' said Pongwiffy to cries of great excitement. 'But you're not allowed to wear them yet,' she added. 'Not until the dress rehearsal tomorrow. Right, let's get on, shall we? Start looking for the Babes. Off you go.'

Sharkadder and Ratsnappy began prowling about the stage, trying hard to avoid trampling over the twins' recumbent forms.

> *'No sign of them! Not one small clue!*
> *Oh, Dick, whatever shall we do?'*

declaimed Ratsnappy, treading heavily on Agglebag's finger. A most unBabe-like word came from beneath the pile of paper leaves.

> *'We must go on, that much is clear,*
> *Although I fear they are not here,'*

Sharkdadder informed her, stumbling over Bagaggle's foot.

Pongwiffy sighed. This was stretching the audience's credulity to the utmost limits.

'You're not supposed to discover them yet,' she explained. 'It's hardly very realistic if you keep tripping over them, is it? Right, Macabre, ready for your entrance?'

Macabre was. Mounted on Rory, she cantered on to the stage, brandishing a home-made cardboard sword.

'Aha! Ah know your cunning plan!
You aim to foil me if you can!
And then you'll make me take the blame.
You hero types are all the same!'

So saying, she dismounted and advanced upon the Pied Piper and Dick, whirling her sword around her head. The two bold heroes flinched and backed away uncertainly.

'Go on,' yelled Pongwiffy. 'Fight! This is a big action scene.'

'There's not enough room,' objected Ratsnappy. 'Not with Ag and Bag lying all over the place.'

'Anyway, she's got a sword,' Sharkadder pointed out. 'We haven't got our swords yet. It's not fair.'

Macabre threw away her sword and adopted a boxing stance.

'Ah dinnae need a sword,' she informed them. 'Ah'll pulverise ye wi' me bare hands. Put yer fists up, ye pair o' softies.'

'That's not in the script, Macabre,' said Pongwiffy wearily. 'You're the baddy. You're supposed to lose, remember?'

But Macabre was enjoying herself. Her fighting spirit was up. She forgot she was supposed to be acting. Fantasy and reality became blurred and she advanced, fists flailing.

Ratsnappy hastily stepped back and tripped over Vernon, who collided with Dudley, who banged into Sharkadder, who fell heavily on to the missing Babes. Everyone went down in a heap and Macabre sat triumphantly on the top.

'There,' she said emphatically. 'That's got *that* sorted.'

'Does the fairy come on now?' enquired Sourmuddle plaintively.

Pongwiffy and Hugo looked at each other and raised their eyes to heaven.

'I think we've done this scene enough for today,' said Pongwiffy. 'Break, everybody. We'll all go home for tea. But I shall expect you back here tonight at seven o'clock sharp to rehearse the final scene. Yes, Sourmuddle, that's you. We're going to do all the songs and dances again as well. Make sure you're on time, because I'm paying the Rhythm Boys overtime.'

There was a united sigh of relief and a surge towards the door. Bendyshanks got there first.

'I say, everyone,' she said, peering out. 'Guess what? It's snowing.'

And, sure enough, it was.

CHAPTER TEN
The Costumes Arrive

Now then. You may be wondering what has been happening to the small man all this time. The one who was bringing the hired costumes, remember?

Well, right now, sad to say, he is lost in the Wood. He was lost in the mountains earlier. And in the bog. He has spent hours and hours going around in circles being lost all over the place – and all because he'd followed Goblin directions.

On top of everything, it had begun to snow. Heavy white flakes whirled from the sky, obliterating the narrow path and dulling all sound. The dark trees were taking on a ghostly, skeletal look.

The small man's name was Ernest Dribble. He hunched miserably in the driver's seat, letting the horse pick its own way, while snow piled up on his hat and icicles formed on his moustache. Even worse – the last straw, this – he was getting the definite feeling that he was being followed. Whenever he slowed down, he heard cracklings and shufflings coming from behind him, and once there was the unmistakable sound of a nose being blown.

It was with a huge sense of relief that he suddenly rounded a corner and came upon a ramshackle building standing in the middle of a glade. Light streamed from the windows and from within came the sound of many voices raised in song, accompanied by a tinkling piano. At last! This must be Witchway Hall.

'Whoa, there, Romeo! Easy, boy!'

The horse ground to a sulky halt. Ernest Dribble climbed down, crunched across to the main doors, banged the snow from his hat and went in.

There was a short pause – then seven short, shadowy forms materialised out of the rapidly whitening bushes and swarmed gleefully over the cart like bees around a honeypot.

Meanwhile, inside the Hall, the final scene was in full swing. The Three Princesses had just finished another graceful dance, and Snoop was kneeling down with a hammer and a mouthful of nails, repairing the large hole in the stage. Everyone was gathered around the piano in the throes of the final song, except for Snow White, who was gloomily pulling splinters out of her foot.

'*If You're Happy and You Know It, Kiss a Priiinnnce,*' warbled the assembled cast enthusiastically. '*If You're Happy and You Know It, Kiss a –*'

'Hold it!' yelled Pongwiffy, raising her hand. 'Where *is* the flippin' Prince? He's supposed to be here.'

Everyone shrugged. Nobody had seen him.

'Perhaps he's snowbound,' suggested Sharkadder. 'It's getting very thick out there. You can hardly see a thing.'

'No excuse!' fumed Pongwiffy. 'No excuse at all. I *told* him. Seven o'clock sharp, I said, and . . . yes, yes, what *is* it?'

She broke off to glare at a little man with a whuffly moustache who had suddenly appeared at her side and was trying to attract her attention.

'Are you Witch Pongwiffy?' enquired the little man, stamping his cold feet and shaking snow from his shoulders.

'I might be,' said Pongwiffy shiftily. She hadn't paid her gas bill for ages and was expecting a summons any day. 'Why?'

'Got somethin' for you,' said the little man, taking a piece of official-looking paper from his pocket. 'You gotta sign.'

'Well, it'll just have to wait,' said Pongwiffy. 'Right now I'm in the middle of a rehearsal. Sit down and don't interrupt. I'll deal with you when we get to the end of this very important scene. Oh, well, if nobody knows where Ronald is, we'll just have to carry on without him, I suppose. But I'm not happy. I'm not happy at all. Right, everybody. One, two, three!'

'If You're Happy and You Know It, Kiss a Priiiince . . .'

Outside Witchway Hall, the snow stopped falling as suddenly as it had begun. A pale moon swam into view, filling the glade with silvery light and making everything seem quite Christmassy. The only thing that ruined the effect was the sight of the Goblins ransacking the costume hampers.

'Cor!' hissed Eyesore, brushing off the snow and throwing back a lid. He reached in and yanked out a pair of silk pantaloons which were intended to grace the snake-like hips of the Queen of the Nile. 'Get a loada these drawers!'

'Look!' whooped Hog, snatching up Sherlock Holmes's deerstalker hat and ramming it on his head. 'Look at me, lads! I'm that there detectin' bloke! That there Shamrock Houses!'

'What about this, then?' gloated young Sproggit, throwing open another lid. 'Swords! Come on, boys, let's muck about!'

With cries of enthusiasm, everyone swooped on the cache of cardboard swords and began to muck about, as only Goblins can. All except Plugugly. He didn't move. He had found something wonderful in one of the hampers.

It was a horse suit.

It came in two halves which zipped together around the middle. It was white with huge red spots. The tail was made of raffia and the head came complete with large white cardboard teeth, pointy ears, a mane sporting a ribbon tied in a chocolate-box bow and a pair of huge, soulful eyes with the longest, curliest eyelashes you've ever seen.

'Whatcha got there, Plug?' asked Lardo.

'A horse suit,' whispered Plugugly.

Impressed by his awed tones, the Goblins dropped their swords and clustered round.

'Cor!' said Slopbucket. 'That's good, innit? Imagine if we went to the ball in that.'

'We can't all fit in,' said Plugugly. 'Dere's only room fer –' Carefully, he counted both bits. 'Two. Yes, two. One at de front and one at de back. An' I'm at de front,' he added firmly.

The two unoccupied front legs trailed limply on the ground as he cradled the head in his arms, stroking the mane and staring deep into the melting eyes.

'You're too fat,' announced Eyesore. 'You'll never fit in 'im.'

'Yes, I will,' said Plugugly. 'An' iss not a him. Issa her. She's got a bow, look.'

Carefully, he stepped into the dangling leg tubes and pulled them up, making sure he straightened all the creases. He then raised the head and lowered it over his own.

'How do I look?' came his muffled voice from inside.

'Good,' conceded Hog, with his head on one side. 'But there's somethin' missin', I dunno what . . .'

'The bum end!' shouted Sproggit, jumping up and down excitedly. 'You gotta have the bum attached, see, else it don't look right. Tell yer what, I'll be the bum.

I'll put the back legs on, an' bend over an' grab Plug round 'is middle, then we can get the final effeck.'

And before anyone could say anything, he'd done it.

The Goblins had to admit that it looked good.

'Zip us up round the tummy, then,' came the muted instruction from the depths of the nether regions.

The Goblins hastened to oblige.

'Cor,' said Hog, standing back and admiring. 'That looks great, that does. Try movin' about a bit.'

The Pantomime Horse hesitated, then its front feet moved cautiously forward. There was a stretching effect in the middle of the body, followed by a sudden squeezed concertina effect as the two back legs careened forward in a shuffling little run.

'Oi!' protested Plugugly, as Sproggit's head cannoned into his substantial bottom.

'Don't go so fast, then,' protested Sproggit from the rear end. 'I can't see back 'ere. We gotta get a rhythm goin'. We gotta count. Er – wot comes after one again?'

'Two,' said Plugugly with the confidence of one who has worked that out earlier.

'Right. 'Ere we go, then. One, two, two, six, two ...'

All this time, Romeo the carthorse had been

standing stolidly between the traces, stamping the snow from his hooves and wishing he was back home in his warm stable, getting stuck into a nosebag. Now, however, he glanced over his shoulder – and did a double take. Hey! What was this? Another horse, no less! And, *phwoaaar!* What a babe! That exotic colouring – that cute bow – and, ooh, those eyes! Those melting, long-lashed eyes!

Eagerly, he shuffled round to get a better look.

Plugugly and Sproggit were beginning to get the hang of walking around in tandem now. It only took a bit of practice.

'Try trottin',' suggested Lardo.

Plugugly and Sproggit tried trotting. The front legs employed a sedate, high-stepping sort of gait, whilst the back legs kicked about in a skittish fashion. The watching Goblins clapped and guffawed. Say what you like, this was entertaining.

It was all too much for Romeo. This wasn't just a crush. This was Love. Yellow teeth bared in a soppy grin, he edged sideways up to his dream girl and playfully nibbled her ear.

'I say,' said Eyesore. 'I fink you got an admirer.'

'Eh?' said Plugugly from inside.

''E fancies you!' crowed Slopbucket, clutching his

95

sides. 'You made a conquest there! Look, boys! The 'orse is in love!'

At this the Goblins laughed so much that they had to hold on to each other for support. Overcome with hilarity, they hooted and pointed and staggered around in the snow, tears streaming from their eyes.

But their glee was short-lived.

At that very moment, sudden light flooded the glade as the doors of Witchway Hall burst open – and out came Pongwiffy with Ernest Dribble scurrying in her wake!

'You should have told me you'd brought the costumes,' Pongwiffy was saying. 'There was I, thinking you were from the Gas Board, and all the while –'

She broke off. She stared. She rubbed her eyes and stared again.

The Goblins, frozen in the light, stared back like rabbits who suddenly find themselves in the fast lane of the motorway.

It was Pongwiffy who broke the spell. Howling with outrage, she launched herself across the glade. With one accord, the Goblins dropped everything they were holding and took to their heels. The front end of the Pantomime Horse, having the advantage of limited vision, attempted to do the same. The back end, however, remained where it was. Sproggit hadn't a clue what was going on and nobody thought to tell him. The consequence was that the front legs did a lot of mad, panicky galloping on the spot, whereas the back legs had about as much forward momentum as a screwed-down table.

'Wot you doin?' squawked Sproggit's muffled voice. 'Wot's happenin'? Why you tuggin' me like that?'

'We bin rumbled!' wailed Plugugly. 'It's dat ol' Pongwiffy! She's seen us! Quick, Sproggit – run! One, two, six – keep in rhythm, for cryin' out loud – five, eight, nine . . .'

Crazily, they veered off into the trees. You might have thought things couldn't get any worse for them – but things did.

THUMP!

A crashing weight landed on top of them. They staggered and only just avoided falling to their knees in the snow.

'Hold it right there, gee-gee!' ground out Pongwiffy, wrapping her arms tightly around the Pantomime Horse's head. 'I said stop, d'you hear?'

'Don't stop!' gasped Plugugly. 'We can shake 'er off . . . keep goin' . . .'

And amazingly, despite the snow and the dark and the fact that they were bent double inside a horse suit with a very angry Witch on their back, they did keep going. And right behind them came Romeo, tugging the cart in his wake. His beloved had gone and he must follow! Hampers full of costumes came crashing down, spilling their contents into the snow as he galloped off in hot pursuit.

And that was the last anyone saw of any of them for quite a while.

CHAPTER ELEVEN
The Great Escape

Time now to move to another part of Witchway Wood, where another dramatic scene is taking place. This one is set in a mysterious cave – and it stars none other than Ronald!

He had come across the cave by chance some weeks earlier when he was plodding past on his way to yet another dreaded rehearsal, daydreaming about his Invisibility Serum and how it would change his life.

Poor Ronald. He hated rehearsals. Pongwiffy never got to his bit and he had spent every night for the past few weeks hanging around in the wings being ignored. It really is time he took a starring role.

The cave was set in a mossy bank and partially hidden by the branches of a willow tree. He had noticed it out of the corner of his eye and gone to investigate. He was struck right away by its possibilities as a secret laboratory in which he could conduct his final experiment.

The cave had several advantages:

1. It would be more private. Things had been getting difficult back at the Clubhouse. The rumour had got round that he was doing secret research in his room and he was getting funny looks.

2. A cave was safer. You never could tell with Magic. Sometimes things could go a bit wrong. Noisy explosions might occur. There could be embarrassing side effects. Best to be on the safe side.

3. Magic worked better in caves. Things *looked* better. It was all to do with atmosphere – shadows, drips, echoes and stuff. Doing it in your bedroom with your teddy looking on just wasn't the same.

So, in the interests of privacy, safety and the look of the thing, Ronald had secretly moved all his paraphernalia to the cave in readiness for the first snowfall. Everything was there – the little jars and test tubes, the Bunsen burner and the crucible and so on, all set up ready and waiting, including a captive toad in a cardboard box with air-holes. Ronald was pretty sure that his serum would work – but he didn't fancy being the first to try it out.

He had just started out for yet another rehearsal when the first flakes began to fall. Fresh Snow, at last! This was what he had been waiting for. Blow rehearsal. Blow princess-kissing. Blow everything. This was his Big Night – and nobody was going to take it away from him.

So, instead of making for Witchway Hall, he had made a beeline for his secret cave. Right now, he was on his knees, adjusting the Bunsen burner, waiting for his mixture to come to the boil. The flame was burning steadily and the serum was beginning to simmer. So far, so good.

The toad watched him unblinkingly from a nearby rock.

'Don't you move, mind,' Ronald warned it. 'Try and escape, and you'll be jolly sorry, I can tell you. I

101

shall place a Spell of Binding on you that'll give you pins and needles for a fortnight. I don't really want to mix two spells up, because it might affect the results. But I will if I have to. What d'you say to that, eh?'

'Ribbit,' said the toad to that. Actually, it could speak excellent English but at this point it didn't want to commit itself.

'You're my guinea pig, you know,' Ronald told it.

The toad turned a pitying look on him. What was this idiot blithering on about? It was a toad. Anyone could see that.

Ronald turned back to the crucible and gave it a stir. The mixture steamed. He sat back on his heels and watched it, cheeks red from heat and nervous anticipation.

'Know what this is?' Ronald asked the toad, who shrugged. 'It's my masterpiece. Extra Strong Invisibility Serum. And it's going to make me rich and famous.'

There was a pause.

'Ribbit?' said the toad, feeling that something was called for.

'Oh, yes. Really. One little sprinkle of this and *pff!* You're gone. Vamoosed. Disappeared. Vanished. Impressive, eh?'

The toad eyed the mouth of the cave and said nothing.

'Ha!' chuckled Ronald. 'I'll show those Witches they can't boss me around. I've got it all planned, you know. When they come looking for me, I'll just coolly sprinkle myself with the serum and vanish before their very eyes. Imagine their faces! And I won't show up again until after the pantomime's over. No more Prince Charming – and there'll be nothing they can do about it. Aha! We've reached boiling point. Get ready, toad. Snow Time!'

Eagerly, he rose to his feet, ran to the cave mouth and snatched up an old bucket which had been placed just outside to catch the falling snow. He hurried back, stepped up to the fire, adopted a suitably dramatic pose, lifted the bucket on high and solemnly intoned the Magic words: 'Oggyoggyoggy! Oi, oi, oi! Come on, you serum!'

Then, with great ceremony, he upended the bucket and tipped the snow into the crucible. There was an almighty sizzling, a bang, a puff of purple smoke – and that was it. The crucible now contained a quantity of thin, colourless liquid with a slight oily sheen. Done. Finished. One Extra Strong Invisibility Serum. Now all he had to do was test it out.

Using an old tea towel, Ronald carefully removed the crucible from the heat, then turned to the toad with an unconvincing bedside-manner smile.

'Right,' he said. 'Sit still. This won't hurt a bit. I'm just going to sprinkle you.'

'Sprinkle yourself, pal, I'm gone,' said the toad. And with a huge leap, it shot over Ronald's head and out of the cave.

'Hey!' shouted Ronald, startled. 'You come right back here!'

Still holding the precious pot of serum, he raced from the cave and out into the snowy Wood.

And that was when things went horribly, horribly wrong. As he stood peering hesitantly around, there came the sound of howling. Crashing footsteps were heading his way. Startled, he looked up – and to his dismay, he saw five screaming Goblins bearing down on him on a collision course!

He gave a horrified gasp, took a step backwards in order to get out of their path – and his heel caught on a half-buried twig. Arms flailing, he tried to regain his balance as his feet slithered away from under him. The crucible flew from his hand. Up, up, it flew. Drops of precious liquid came raining down on the heads of the stampeding Goblin horde – and in a split second, before Ronald's very eyes ... they disappeared! Simply twinkled out of existence. Just like that.

The only evidence of their passing was a line of jumbled footprints making off into the distance, accompanied by receding howls, like the wail of a runaway express train. Then even the howls dwindled away, and once again peace reigned.

Slowly – ever so slowly – Ronald sat up. He spat out a mouthful of snow and gingerly felt himself all over. His eyes flickered towards the crucible, which lay on its side in the snow. With a little moan, he flopped over on to his knees and crawled towards it. With a shaking hand, he picked it up and peered inside.

There was a spoonful left! Oh, thank you, thank you! All was not lost!

Sobbing with relief he staggered to his feet and turned back to the cave, clutching the crucible with its few remaining drops to his chest.

That was when he was hit in the back by a large, red-spotted Pantomime Horse.

CHAPTER TWELVE
The Show Must Go On

I can't understand it,' said Sourmuddle, peering into her crystal ball. 'I should be able to locate them by Magic, but there's not a glimpse of them in my ball, and none of the Search and Find spells work. It's like the whole lot of them have vanished from the face of the earth. Highly mysterious.'

It was the following morning. The Coven, greatly excited by all the drama, had gathered at Witchway Hall for a hastily convened emergency meeting. Also present was Ernest Dribble, looking rather uncomfortable in his role of sole eyewitness to the dramatic events of the night before. There were rather too many pointy hats around for comfort.

The only absentees were Hugo, Sharkadder and Dudley, who were presumably still out trawling the snowy Wood in a hunt for Pongwiffy. Either that or, as Sludgegooey unkindly remarked, home in their beds enjoying a few blissful hours without her.

'Tell us again what you saw, Mr Dribble,' ordered Sourmuddle.

'I told yer,' mumbled Ernest Dribble. 'It were Goblins. Them ones I seen earlier on. They musta followed me. They was over by the cart, muckin' about with the costumes, an' a couple of 'em 'ad the 'oss skin on, an' when they sees us they all makes a run fer it, an' then *she* goes an' takes a running jump an' lands on the 'oss an' they takes off into the Wood an' my Romeo, 'e takes off after 'em! 'E's a bit of a lad when it comes to the ladies,' he added, with a touch of mournful pride.

'Stupid, though,' remarked Sourmuddle. 'Seeing he can't even recognise his own species.'

'That don't stop me bein' fond of 'im,' snivelled Ernest Dribble. ''E's out somewhere in the cold, snowy wastes, eatin' 'is 'eart out, an' I miss 'im.'

He took out a grubby hanky and blew his nose.

'I don't know what you're moaning about,'

107

remarked Ratsnappy. 'You've only lost a lovesick carthorse. We've lost a vital costume and our director, and it's opening night tomorrow.'

Everyone's stomachs flipped over at the thought.

'What are we going to do?' asked Bendyshanks worriedly. 'I mean, supposing Pongwiffy doesn't turn up? Who's going to organise tonight's dress rehearsal and tell us what to do and keep the Rhythm Boys in order and make all the decisions? Somebody's got to direct.'

There was an anxious silence. Even Sourmuddle looked uneasy. Grandwitch she might be, but when it came to the pantomime, Pongwiffy was the undisputed boss.

Bendyshanks asked the one question they were all privately thinking.

'Can we do it without Pongwiffy? Do you think we ought to cancel?'

'*Cancel?*' said a voice from the doorway, making everyone jump. '*Cancel? Is you crazy?*'

It was Hugo.

Eyes blazing, he scuttled down the aisle and up on to the stage. Everybody stared as he climbed on to Pongwiffy's empty chair and gazed sternly around at the assembled company.

'So!' he said scathingly. 'Is zis 'ow ve say sank you to Mistress for all 'er 'ard vork? Vun leetle problem and ve *cancel*? No, I tell you! No, no, no! She 'ave a dream, my mistress. She dream zat zis great show of ours vill pass into ze 'istory books! And now, just ven she need us most, you talk zis sissy cancel talk! Pah!'

There fell a guilty little silence. Everyone looked at each other.

Greymatter cleared her throat.

'Well, if you put it like *that –*'

''Course I put it like zat! So vot if Mistress gone missink? She turn up. Meanwhile, ze show must go on.'

'That's all very well,' said Sourmuddle. 'But who's going to direct?'

'Me,' said Hugo simply. 'Pongviffy, she say to me, "Ugo, if anythink 'appen to me, you must take over and be ze director."'

He crossed his paws behind his back. Actually, Pongwiffy had said nothing of the sort, but it was worth a try.

There was a bit of general muttering. His rousing speech had gone down pretty well on the whole, but the last bit was greeted with a mixed reception. There were some who weren't too happy at the thought of being directed by a Hamster.

'We'll take a vote on it,' decided Sourmuddle. 'Hands up who wants the show to go on?'

Everyone's hand shot up.

'And who thinks they can direct it better than Hugo?'

Hands dropped like leaves in autumn.

'That's it, then,' said Sourmuddle. 'Hugo's appointed as the new director, and everyone has to do what he says except me, because I'm Grandwitch and I can do what I like.'

'But what about the costumes?' asked Sludgegooey. 'Some of them fell in the snow. They're all dirty. And a couple of the swords have gone soggy.'

'Ve vash ze costumes, ve fix ze swords,' said the new director briskly.

'But what about the Pantomime Horse?' piped up Bendyshanks.

'No problem. Ve cut it.'

'But what about Gaga? She doesn't have a part now.'

Everyone looked at Gaga, who had gone very small and sad, quite unlike herself.

'Ve find 'er sumsink else to do,' announced Hugo. 'She can be Usherette. Show people to zeir seats. Viz big, shiny torch. And sell ice cream at ze interval.'

It was an inspired suggestion. Instantly, a gigantic, sunny smile split Gaga's face. A big torch and ice cream! Hey! She could do a *lot* with those. She jumped up on her chair and performed a jolly little dance, then solemnly stood on her head.

'Nice to see her back to normal,' remarked Ratsnappy, and everyone agreed.

'So,' said Hugo. 'Is decided. Tonight, ve 'ave dress rehearsal as planned. And tomorrow night, ve open!'

Smiling and chattering, everybody pushed their chairs back, ready to leave.

'Just a minute,' said Sourmuddle, holding up a hand. Everybody sighed and sat back down again. 'I'm as keen on the pantomime as the next person, but we can't just sit back and let those Goblins get away with it. I didn't get where I am today by letting Goblins get away with things. They have to be caught and punished in a proper manner.'

'She's right, you know,' muttered the Witches. 'They should be.'

'I'm not so bothered about Pongwiffy,' continued Sourmuddle, 'because I'm sure Hugo's right and she'll turn up sooner or later – but we have to get that horse suit back. It's a very expensive costume, and if it's lost or damaged, we have to pay for it.'

Just at that moment the door opened again. This time, it was Sharkadder. For some reason, she was looking terribly pleased with herself.

'Hello, everyone,' she trilled. 'Sorry I'm late. I've been on a very important mission. In fact, I've got the answer to all our problems. Meet Wildman Willy Racoon, famous tracker and bounty hunter and *my cousin*! Step in, Willy, and say hello.'

She stood aside. Behind her, arms folded and short, stocky legs akimbo, stood a Dwarf. He wore buckskin breeches, a fur-lined jacket and a pair of scuffed cowboy boots. On his head was a fur hat complete with dangling racoon tail. He wore a lasso looped over one shoulder and a musket over the other. His face sprouted the biggest, shaggiest mad tangle of a fearsome ginger beard that it is possible for a single face to support. It was the kind of beard things *live* in.

'Howdy,' said Wildman Willy Racoon.

Everyone goggled in surprise at the unexpected visitor.

'Willy's agreed to help us out,' explained Sharkadder airily. 'He's Cousin Pierre's twin brother. Haven't I ever mentioned him?'

'I don't think so,' said Sourmuddle doubtfully. 'I don't think we'll ever get to the bottom of your well of obscure relations, Sharkadder. Pierre's twin, did you say?'

'That's it. Pierre went into catering and Willy here went into – er – wild-manning. Didn't you, Willy?'

'Yup,' said Willy and spat on the floor.

'Yes,' continued Sharkadder. 'He lives up in the wilds of the Misty Mountains. Huntin', shootin' and fishin', isn't that right, Willy? Out in all weathers, sleeping under the stars, communing with nature, washing in icy mountain springs, eating beans and so forth. He came down to visit poor Cousin Pierre when he heard about the accident with the pancake mixer, didn't you, Willy?'

'Yup.'

'Doesn't say much, does he?' said Sourmuddle.

'Ah, well, he's not used to talking, you see,' explained Sharkadder. 'Up there in the mountains, all on his own

with only the stars for company. Eating beans –'

'Yes, yes,' butted in Sourmuddle testily. 'I know about the beans. What I don't know is what he's doing here. We've got enough on our plate as it is without having to entertain your relations.'

'What's he doing here?' cried Sharkadder. 'Why, isn't it obvious? He's going to track down Pong and the Pantomime Horse, of course.'

'Zere you are, zen!' cried Hugo. 'Is all sorted.'

'And my Romeo?' chipped in Ernest Dribble eagerly. 'Can he find him too?'

'Certainly. He can find anything, can't you, Willy?'

'Yup,' growled Willy, adding, 'Ain't no critter can escape ma eagle eye.'

'It's true,' nodded Sharkadder proudly. 'He's quite a legend in the mountains. Show them your scars, Willy.'

The legend needed no encouragement. He rolled up his sleeve and pointed to his forearm.

'See this here? This here's where a mad ole grizzly took a chomp outa ma arm. An' this here's a gorilla's teeth marks. An' this here's where a fork-tongued poison-drippin' rattler sunked its fangs in ma wrist. Last bite that there varmint ever took. Ever eat rattle-snake? Tastes kinda scrumpchuss, all slaaaced up with

114

a messa beans.'

At this, Slithering Steve gave a little shudder and quietly headed for the sanctuary of Bendyshanks's cardigan.

'Thank you, Mr Racoon,' said Sourmuddle briskly. 'I'm sure you're very experienced with wild animals. But this missing Pantomime Horse is quite another kettle of fish. I've tried all my strongest spells, but –'

'Magic! Ha!' Willy Racoon spat contemptuously on the floor again. 'Wildmen don't have no truck with that there sissy Magic. We got our own methods. I does it by sniffin' the wind with ma trusty conk an' inspectin' the ground with ma keen peepers. Ain't no critter can escape –'

'Your eagle eye, yes, you said. But there's another thing.' Sourmuddle peered sharply over her glasses. 'You call yourself a bounty hunter, so I take it you won't be offering your services for free. I'm afraid the funds won't run to –'

'Ah! That's the beauty of it!' cried Sharkadder. 'He's got no use for money, up there in the wilds, have you, Willy? He'll do it for beans! That's what you wildmen live on, isn't it, Willy?'

'Yup,' nodded Willy. 'An' snake. When we can git it.'

Bendyshanks's cardigan gave a convulsive little heave.

'You see?' crowed Sharkadder. 'Beans, that's what he likes. Normally, he charges two big sacks, but seeing as I'm family, we get a discount. One bag of beans and a free ticket to the pantomime. I've told him all about it and he's terribly excited. He's never been to a pantomime, have you, Willy?'

'Nope,' agreed Willy, adding hopefully, 'Will there be dancin' gals, did ya say?'

'Zere certainly vill!' burst in Hugo, thumping on the table in his excitement. 'Dancink girls and princesses and vicked Scotsvimmin and posh fairies, no less! Bring back my mistress and ze missing Pantomime 'Orse by tomorrow night, Villy, and ve vill give you a pantomime you vill never forget! Am I right?'

'Durn right!' came the excited chorus.

Wildman Willy's accent was catching.

CHAPTER THIRTEEN
The Powwow

'That,' said Slopbucket's disembodied voice, 'was the worst night of my life.'

From all around came grunts of heartfelt agreement.

There were five Goblins in the cave. You couldn't see them, of course. Only their voices gave a clue to their whereabouts.

'We'll be for it when them Witches catches up with us,' moaned Eyesore. 'They'll tan our hides for sure. If our hides ever come back again,' he added mournfully.

'It were scary, weren't it?' remarked Hog, with

117

a shiver in his voice. 'Gettin' caught red-'anded like that.'

'Not as scary as comin' over all invizdibibble,' whined Lardo. 'I don't like this 'ere invizdibibbility. Dunno what people see in it.'

There was a pause.

'They don't see nuffin' in it,' Eyesore's voice pointed out. 'That's the 'ole point.'

'All right, all right. I'm just sayin'. I miss meself. I wants me body back, even if it is a mass of bruises. You should see 'em.'

''Ow can we see 'em?' remarked Eyesore. 'They're invizdibibble.'

'That don't stop 'em 'urtin,' said Lardo.

It was true. In fact, all five of them were in a bad way. The long trek home on the previous night had been bad enough with the snow and the darkness to contend with, let alone the added handicap of invisibility. Not knowing where they began or ended meant that they continually misjudged distances and were forever bumping into trees, falling into snowdrifts and tripping over each other's invisible feet.

Goblins, however, have a built-in, primitive, pigeon-like homing instinct which comes to their aid at times of crisis. It works by overriding their brains. Just as well. They would never have got home if they'd relied on those. Even so, it had been well after midnight when they had finally made it back to their cave, where they had fallen in an invisible pile and instantly gone to sleep, hoping that everything would be better in the morning.

And now it was morning and everything wasn't.

'Wot I can't unnerstand is, 'ow did it 'appen?' said Hog for the hundredth time. 'One minute we wuz runnin' away an' the next, we wuz like this. 'Ow come?'

'Magic, innit?' said Slopbucket. 'Gotta be. Issa nasty ol' Witch spell.'

'Nah,' argued Eyesore. 'Wot'd be the point? The Witches wants to *catch* us, don't they? Now then. If you wants to *catch* sumfin', you don't make it vanish, do you? That makes it harder to *catch*, don't it?'

This was sound reasoning, for a Goblin.

'Who then?' pondered Hog.

There was a pause while the Goblins thought about this.

'P'raps it wuz that geezer in the pointy 'at,' said Stinkwart after a bit.

'Wot geezer in the pointy 'at?' enquired Eyesore.

'Remember when we was running across that glade?

An' I wuz in front? There wuz a geezer in a pointy 'at come runnin' outa nowhere, straight into our path. I gotta kinda feelin' we mighta mowed 'im down. I didn't stop to check, mind, 'cos that's when I comed over all invizdibibble, an' everyfin' got confusin'.'

'Sounds like a Wizard,' observed Eyesore knowledgeably. 'Wizards wear pointy 'ats. 'E prob'ly done it outa spite, 'cos we mowed 'im down.'

There was a long pause, whilst the Goblins took this latest suggestion on board.

'P'raps we should find this 'ere Wizard an' throw ourselves on 'is mercy,' suggested Hog after a bit. ''E might take pity on us an' give us a wassit. You know. Wot yer mum gives you when you eats poison ivy.'

'A thump?' ventured Stinkwart, whose mum wasn't known for her bedside manner.

'Nah, nah. There's a word for it. Summin' what reverses the spell. You know. An anti – anti – 'ang on, it's comin' – anti –' You could almost hear his brain struggling – 'dot. Antidot!' he finished triumphantly.

'I got an Aunty Maureen,' remarked Stinkwart unhelpfully.

'Not the same,' explained Hog.

'I gotta niece,' chimed in Eyesore, not to be outdone. 'She's called Denise. I gotta nephew too.'

'What's 'e called?' asked Stinkwart.

'Denephew.'

'No good,' said Hog. 'It's gotta be an Aunty Dot.'

'Why?' argued Stinkwart. 'What can she do that my Aunty Maureen can't?'

''Ow should I know?' said Hog irritably. 'It's just somethin' I 'eard.'

'This isn't gettin' us anywhere,' said Slopbucket. 'All this talk of Wizards' aunties. When 'ave Wizards' aunties ever 'elped out Goblins? Let's face it, lads. We're on our own. We'll just 'ave to sit tight till the spell wears off.'

'Well, let's 'ope it's soon,' put in Lardo. 'I'm 'ungry.'

'Tell yer sumfin' else wot's botherin' me,' said Hog suddenly. 'Where's Plug an' Sproggit? They ain't turned up, 'ave they? I thought they was followin' us.'

'They was!' cried Eyesore. 'I could 'ear 'em gallopin' along be'ind us, crashin' into bushes an' shoutin' at each uvver. I fink they was 'avin' trouble gettin' their legs sorted. An' that daft carthorse, 'e was comin' too, 'cos I 'eard 'im neighin'. An' then – an' then we was invizdibibble an' I dunno wot 'appened to 'em after that. I 'ad enuff problems of me own.'

'Fink we should get up a search party?' asked Slopbucket.

121

'Why?' said Lardo.

'Well – I dunno. Supposin' they're still stuck in the 'orse suit? They might be stufflecated by now. They might be in deadly peril, upside down in a snowdrift with their little legs wigglin'.'

The Goblins thought about this.

'Ah, they'll turn up,' said Eyesore after a bit.

'But wot if they don't?' persisted Slopbucket. 'Shouldn't we go lookin' for 'em?'

There was an even longer silence. Then: 'Nah,' said Stinkwart. 'Cold out there, innit?'

CHAPTER FOURTEEN
Up a Gum Tree

Well!' said Pongwiffy disgustedly. She spoke with difficulty, on account of being suspended high in the air from a branch hooked into the back of her cardigan. 'This is a fine pickle you've got us into, I must say. Now we're *really* up a gum tree.'

They were too.

You may be surprised to hear that there are gum trees in Witchway Wood. But there are. There are oaks, ashes, elms, larches, sycamores, pines and gum trees. The gum trees are tall and thin and tend to be sticky.

The three of them had been up this particular gum tree for quite some time. The Goblins were still hopelessly trapped inside the horse suit. Plugugly was perched perilously astride a bendy branch which he gripped like a vice with his knees. Sproggit was lying stretched out behind him, belly down, hands hooked firmly on to Plugugly's belt, hanging on for dear life.

Above them dangled Pongwiffy, boots feebly paddling the air and hat over one eye.

Down below, Romeo circled the tree, swishing his tail and giving encouraging little whinnies. You could almost see the hearts coming out of his ears.

'Look at 'im!' groaned Plugugly. ''E don't give up, do 'e?'

''Ow can I look?' wailed the muffled voice of Sproggit. 'I ain't got no peep'ole. All I can see is your fat bum. Wot's 'e doin' now?'

'Grinnin',' said Plugugly, with a little shiver. 'Grinnin' up at us wid 'is spooky great teef. 'E loves us, Sproggit. 'E wants to go steady.'

'Shout at 'im,' suggested Sproggit. 'Tell 'im we ain't ready to commit ourselves to a serious relashunship.'

'Oi! Dobbin! Go 'ome! You ain't our type!' bellowed Plugugly, not very hopefully.

Romeo looked up and blew horsey kisses. Right

now, his beloved was playing hard to get – but that was girls for you.

'It didn't work,' Plugugly informed his rear end.

'Well, I suggest you think of something that does,' ground out Pongwiffy from above. 'I've got to get down from here. It might have escaped your attention that I'm being strangled.'

'I ain't goin' down dere,' said Plugugly with a shudder. 'Not wid 'im down below, any rate. Catch me goin' down dere? Brrrr!'

'You got us up,' snapped Pongwiffy. 'You get us down. I really can't afford to hang around here any longer. I've got an important show to put on. I need that horse suit.'

'I's not gettin' down till 'e goes,' repeated Plugugly firmly. 'An' if it comes to it, why don't *you* get us down? Cast a spell or summat.'

'That just goes to show how little you know about Magic,' sneered Pongwiffy. 'You can't just snap your fingers and hope it'll happen.'

(Actually, this is quite untrue. Any Witch worth her salt can snap her fingers and be sure it'll happen. All you need is a good memory and a headful of useful spells. The trouble is, Pongwiffy doesn't have either.)

'Call yerself a Witch?' jeered Plugugly.

'Certainly I call myself a Witch,' snapped Pongwiffy. 'It's just that I haven't got any of my stuff. At the very least I need my Wand. And how am I supposed to make a brew when . . . Oh. Oh dear.'

Suddenly, her voice changed. It now held an element of dread.

'Wot now?' said Plugugly.

'I think it's coming on again.'

Plugugly looked down and braced himself.

'She's right,' he said. ''Old tight, Sproggit. We're fadin'!' And he closed his eyes.

Things are getting complicated, aren't they? Pongwiffy, Plugugly and Sproggit are stuck up a gum tree and now they are becoming invisible. Perhaps we should take a step back to the night before and find out what led up to their current predicament.

There they were, racing through the Wood, with the Pantomime Horse running flat out and Pongwiffy bouncing about on top, grimly hanging on to the ears. When she had first taken that wild leap on to its back, it had been with the intention of stopping it. Now, with the besotted Romeo thundering along behind them, eyes rolling and steam issuing from his nostrils, she changed her mind.

'Faster!' she howled. 'Run, you idiots! Run!'

Luckily, the empty costume cart was proving to be a bit of a handicap to their pursuer. It kept getting stuck between trees, thus slowing him down a bit, otherwise they wouldn't have stood a chance.

Desperately, Plugugly and Sproggit pounded across the same glade that the advance guard of Goblins had raced through less than a minute previously. So great was their panic, and so limited was Plugugly's vision in the horse suit, that he didn't even notice Ronald, who was just picking himself up from his first little encounter.

Pongwiffy didn't spot him either, because her hat was currently down over her eyes.

Yes, they mowed him down. And yes, as you might expect, they got sprinkled with the remaining drops of Invisibility Serum!

Good, you might think. What could be better, at times of crisis, than to become invisible?

Ah. If only it was as simple as that.

The trouble lay in the serum. There just wasn't enough of it. The first wave of fleeing Goblins had received a thorough drenching. Second time round, though, there was only a very little bit left – hardly a big enough dose to work effectively on one person, let alone three.

127

Pongwiffy, Plugugly and Sproggit didn't know this yet – but they soon would.

When invisibility first descended upon them, so blind was their panic that they hardly noticed. Plugugly and Sproggit had got so used to running that their legs just carried on pistoning up and down automatically for a bit. Then Pongwiffy became aware of a sudden, indefinable change. For a moment, she couldn't work out what it was. Then she looked down at herself – and saw fresh air!

'Hold it!' she screamed. 'Something's happened! We've vanished!'

At exactly that same moment, both halves of the Pantomime Horse became aware that something strange had occurred. They could see through the horse suit! They were still wearing it, they could feel it, but it had become transparent!

Even worse – so had they!

'Ahhhh!' shouted Plugugly, screeching to a stop. 'Where am I? I's gone! I can't see meself!'

Sproggit's invisible head once again thudded into the small of Plugugly's invisible back.

'Oooof!' remarked Plugugly conversationally as all the breath was knocked out of him. Down they both went into the snow, bringing Pongwiffy with them. All three flailed around, confused and completely unnerved.

'Where am I?' bawled Plugugly. 'Are you dere, Sproggit?'

''Course I'm 'ere. Where's Pongwiffy?'

'I'm here. Stop kicking me, will you?'

'Can you see me? I can't see me. I can't see you. Can you see you?' wailed Plugugly.

'Of course we can't see you!' snapped Pongwiffy. 'You've vanished. I've vanished. We've all vanished!'

'It's scary!' gibbered Sproggit. 'Wot's 'appenin'?'

As if things weren't bad enough, at that point Romeo came careering around the corner. He had finally shed his cart. One of the wheels had become wedged in a ditch and the traces had broken, leaving him free to pursue his darling to the ends of the universe. Further, if necessary.

He came to a halt, looking puzzled. Funny, there was no sign of her. Where had she gone?

'Ssssh,' hissed Pongwiffy warningly. 'It's him! Don't move!'

They sat in the snow, not daring to move a muscle, as Romeo stood hesitantly looking around. At one point, he stared directly at them – but after a

129

heart-stopping moment or two, he gave a baffled little snort and began to move off into the trees.

'Phew!' said Pongwiffy, feeling invisible sweat break out on her invisible brow. 'That was close. Come on. Let's go while we get the chance.'

Shakily, they clambered to their feet – and at that point, without any warning, *they began to fade back in again*. First, there was fresh air. Then there was the ghostly image of a transparent Pantomime Horse and a see-through rider. Finally they were back, as solid as before.

'Hey!' shouted Plugugly. 'I'm back! Hello, me!'

'Quiet, stupid!' hissed Pongwiffy. 'D'you want him to hear?'

It was all too much for Sproggit, who finally lost his grip and began to scream.

Romeo stopped in his tracks. His ears pricked up and he looked back over his shoulder.

There she was! His beloved! How come he'd missed her? With a wild neigh, he wheeled around – and once again the chase was on. The only difference was that the Pantomime Horse and rider faded in and out like a faulty television set. For a few minutes they would disappear completely, then they would materialise back again. And all the time, Romeo was gaining on them.

'Faster!' bellowed Pongwiffy. 'Go, go, go!'

'Plug!' screamed Sproggit. ''E's right be'ind me, Plug! I can feel 'is breath! I'm gettin' a stitch! I can't run no more!'

Desperate situations call for desperate measures. Plugugly saw the giant gum tree looming before him – and knew that this was their only chance.

'Quick, Sproggit!' he howled. 'Up de gum tree!'

And somehow – they never knew how – they made it.

So. Now we know where they are and how they got there. Many more long, argumentative hours stretch ahead of them. We could stay and keep them company – but we won't. Instead, we'll move forward a few hours and drop in on the proceedings in Witchway Hall, where the dress rehearsal is about to begin.

CHAPTER FIFTEEN
The Dress Rehearsal

In Witchway Hall chaos reigned. At the back of the stage, Vincent Van Ghoul was standing on a stepladder, hanging the first backcloth. This was of Sherlock Holmes's famous Baker Street study. It seemed that the great detective shared Vincent's fondness for the colour red. His study was painful to the eyes. Nobody liked to say so, though, with Vincent being an artist and all. The general consensus was, he'd been paid a lot so it must be good.

Elsewhere, nails were being hammered into cardboard trees. Chairs were being set in rows, with a great deal of scraping. In the orchestra pit, the Witchway Rhythm Boys were going through the overture. The din was unbelievable.

Hugo clapped his paws for silence.

'Right!' he squeaked. 'Leetle bit of 'ush now, if you pliz. All ze cast on stage and stand in line. Time for ze costume parade.'

With a bit of giggling and pushing, the cast filed in and lined up, looking rather self-conscious as Hugo moved slowly along the line.

The Babes were first. They were got up in frilly bonnets and large, matching sleepsuits. Agglebag's was blue and Bagaggle's was pink. Embroidered across the front on each, in large letters, was the word BABE. Each twin was sucking on a large dummy.

'Hmm,' said Hugo doubtfully. 'Perhaps ve should 'ave explained sings a bit more carefully ven ve ordered ze costumes. Oh vell. Too late now. Keep your tummies in and 'ope for ze best.'

Next came the Three Princesses – Snow White, Rapunzel and Sleeping Beauty – all got up in crowns and fancy frocks. In addition, Scrofula was wearing a straw-coloured wig which swept the floor and Bonidle was clutching a hot-water bottle.

'Vot zose stains on your dress, Sludgegooey?'

133

asked Hugo sternly. 'Vot you been eatink in ze dressing room?'

'Beetroot doughnuts,' confessed the fairest one of all.

'Vell, don't. You s'posed to be Snow Vhite, not Slush Grey. 'Ang your 'air over your arm ven you is dancink, Scrofula, it could do somevun nasty injury. Vake up, Bonidle, you is droolink. OK, you vill 'ave to do.'

Bendyshanks was next.

'Hmm. I 'ope you is puttink cardigan over zat lot. Zat a lot of skin you is showink,' said Hugo.

'Ah,' beamed the great queen. 'Well, it's hot in Egypt, you see.'

'Not zat 'ot,' said Hugo firmly. 'Vear a voolly. Zat's an order. Zis is family show.'

Next was Sourmuddle – a vision of loveliness in spangly net. She did a couple of tottery fairy-like twirls, then sank into a creaky curtsy with one eyebrow enquiringly raised.

Everybody clapped politely.

'Ees good,' nodded Hugo. 'Ees very good, Grandvitch. But ze vings is upside down. And I should leave off ze boots.'

Sourmuddle looked shocked.

'Not wear my *boots*? But I always wear my boots. These are my great-granny's boots. They've been passed down from Grandwitch to Grandwitch, these boots.'

'It just zat zey don't quite go viz ze fairy image,' Hugo tried to explain. 'Fairies don't vear steel toecaps.'

'This one does,' Sourmuddle informed him crisply. So that was that.

With a little sigh, Hugo moved on to Sherlock Holmes.

Greymatter's checked cape and deerstalker hat were slightly the worse for wear, having been thrown into a snowdrift by Hog during his mad flight into the Wood.

'Excellent, Greymatter, excellent. You really do look ze part. I see your magnifyink glass is cracked. 'Ow you manage zat?'

'Accidentally, my dear Hugo,' explained Greymatter, who tended to talk in role ever since landing the part.

Hugo moved on down the line, where Sharkadder eagerly waited her turn for inspection. Her pipe-cleaner legs were encased in green tights and a feathered hat was placed at a jaunty angle on her head. She slapped her thigh, blew kisses and cried, 'My public, I love you, I love you all!'

'All right, zat'll do,' said Hugo. 'Your tights is all

135

baggy vere your knees aren't. Pull zem up and stop hoggink ze limelight.'

'I don't see why I have to take orders from a Hamster,' muttered Sharkadder. But she said it quietly. Hugo was proving a very good director in Pongwiffy's absence. Everybody said so.

Next came Ratsnappy as the Pied Piper, clad in a headache-inducing cloak of many colours. She saluted with her recorder and stood to attention.

'Not bad, Ratsnappy. Just a *leetle* tip – try smilink. You ze friend of little children, ya? Zey love your merry music.'

Ratsnappy tried smiling. It didn't work. Her face just wasn't cut out for it.

Macabre was last. She bristled with cardboard weapons, looking quite terrifying in a floor-length tartan cloak. As Hugo approached, she threw back her head and cackled menacingly.

'Very nice, Macabre. Er – per'aps ve can do vizzout ze bagpipes. Zey might get in ze vay durink ze fight scene. Vere is Gaga?'

'She said she'd be a bit late,' said Snow White, absent-mindedly blowing her nose on the hem of her dress. 'She's practising with her torch.'

'Vot you mean, practisink viz 'er torch?'

'Well, she's borrowed all our kitchen chairs,' explained Rapunzel, 'and she's got them set up in rows. And she's making the Familiars be the audience and she's showing them to their seats. And if they don't do what they're told, she – er – practises with her torch. On their heads. It looks rather painful.'

'Fair enough. Right, 'ave I seen everybody? I got a feelink somevun missink.'

'There is,' said Cleopatra, bursting to tell. 'Ronald. He's still in his dressing room. We've told him to come out, but he won't. He says he's got a problem with his costume. He says he doesn't want to be Prince Charming and it's a silly old pantomime anyway.'

'Oh, he does, does he?' growled Sharkadder. 'Right, leave this to me. This is a job for Dick.'

She strode off in the direction of the dressing rooms. A moment later, everyone heard a thunderous banging.

'Ronald! Come out this minute, d'you hear? This is your aunty calling! Do you want a smack? You're not too big to be put over my knee, you know!'

There was a pause. Then there came the sharp sound of a foot connecting vigorously with wood, followed by splintering noises. Then came muffled voices, followed by the unmistakable sound of flesh connecting sharply with flesh. Seconds later,

137

Sharkadder reappeared, looking pleased with herself.

'He's on his way,' she announced. 'It's amazing what a few kind words will do.'

Everybody looked expectantly towards the wings.

Poor Ronald. Things just weren't going well for him lately. As well as losing his Extra Strong Invisibility Serum, he was being made to dress up in a ridiculous Prince Charming outfit and make a fool of himself on stage. The only good thing that had happened to him recently was that he had been awarded his own dressing room. Hugo had explained that this was for two reasons:

1. He was the only male in the cast.
2. Nobody liked him.

Sulkily, he trailed on stage, clutching his reddened wrist. Everybody sniggered as he joined the end of the line.

'What's so funny?' he snarled.

'Your trousers, for a start,' said Snow White.

It was true. Not only were his breeches too big, the elastic had gone. He had had to tie them around his waist with string. Everything else was wrong too. The jacket was too small, the puffy-sleeved blouse was

138

too long in the arms, his cardboard sword was floppy and his crown looked as though it had come out of a Christmas cracker and was perched on top of his sticky-out ears in a very silly way.

'Stand up straight, Ronald,' ordered Hugo. 'Prince Charmink not s'posed to 'ave caved-in chest. 'E supposed to look – 'ow you say? – dashink.'

'How can I?' cried Ronald, stamping his foot crossly. 'Nothing fits! I *gave* you my measurements. You must have written them down wrong. How am I supposed to look dashing in a dwarf's jacket and a giant's trousers?'

'It not my fault you got funny shape. And anuzzer sink. Vy vere you not at rehearsal last night?'

'I – um – got lost in the snow,' mumbled Ronald, going red.

'Vell, you should 'ave been 'ere,' Hugo told him sternly. 'Specially as ve 'ad crisis on our 'ands.'

'Dearie me. Did you?' asked Ronald innocently.

'We certainly did!' put in Cleopatra. 'The Goblins got away with our Pantomime Horse! Pongwiffy's out there somewhere, trying to get it back.'

'We've called in Professional Help,' added the fairy, sounding smug. Calling in Professional Help sounded rather businesslike. Sourmuddle liked to think of herself as the leader of the sort of Coven that, from time to time, might call in Professional Help.

'Oh, really? Who's that?' enquired Ronald.

'Cousin Willy,' burst in Dick. 'Remember Willy, Ronald? The wildman? Cousin Pierre's brother. He's your mother's sister's husband's uncle's grandma's nephew's third cousin twice removed by marriage. Lives up in the mountains. Eating beans.'

'Oh, yes,' said Ronald vaguely. 'Well, that's nice. Cousin Willy, eh? Well, well. How's he keeping these days?'

(Not that he cared. He didn't even remember Cousin Willy. He just wanted to draw the conversation away from the mysterious disappearance of Pongwiffy and the Pantomime Horse. He had a feeling that his role in the matter wouldn't be appreciated.)

'Look,' said Hugo. 'Look. Ve 'aven't got time for all zis. Ve got a dress re'earsal to get on ze road. Clear ze stage, everybody. Is ze orchestra ready?'

Various tootles, twiddles and smashings from the orchestra pit indicated that the orchestra was indeed ready.

'Right, boys!' squeaked the director. 'Off you go. Take it from ze top!'

CHAPTER SIXTEEN
Trackin'

Wildman Willy Racoon knelt in the cave, sniffing intently at the scattered ashes of a cold fire. All around lay a number of mysterious items. A box of matches. A Bunsen burner. The wrapper off a packet of Polos. A cardboard box with holes in. A host of little smashed pots, which rather looked as though somebody had hurled them at the cave wall in a fit of temper.

There was also a piece of many-times-folded paper, which had probably fallen from an inside pocket. It had been cut from a furnishing catalogue and contained a lot of information about chairs!

Willy Racoon prowled around some more. Behind a rock, he found another clue.

A pointy hat! It was rather battered and one of the stars was hanging on by a single thread. It looked as though someone had recently given it a good kicking.

Gingerly, he picked it up and peered inside.

'RONALD THE MAGNIFICENT,' read out Wildman Willy. 'WASH SEPARATELY. Hmm.'

He rolled up the hat and stuffed it into one of the pockets in his buckskins. Then, sucking noisily on a bad tooth, he walked to the cave entrance.

Just outside, the snow appeared to have been churned up by many feet. To add to the mystery, an abandoned copper pot lay to one side, half submerged in a snowdrift. You or I, not being skilled in the ways of the wild, wouldn't have known what to make of it, of course. Not so Willy. To his experienced tracker's eyes, the scene spoke volumes. It all pointed to a Magical experiment that had gone horribly wrong.

It was trusty-conk time again. Willy wiped his large, knowledgeable nose on his sleeve and snuffled at the air like a bloodhound.

'Durned if Ah don't smell Goblin!' he growled to himself.

Two rabbits watching from a nearby bush nudged each other.

'Who *is* that man?' breathed one.

'Don't you know?' whispered the other. 'That's Wildman Willy Racoon, the famous tracker! Ain't nothin' can escape his eagle eye.'

The pair of them watched admiringly as Willy picked up the crucible, examined it, cautiously rubbed a filthy thumb around the rim and held it up.

'Wut in tarnation . . .' began Willy, starting back, his experienced wildman composure deserting him for a moment. He could see through his thumb! It didn't exactly vanish away completely – there wasn't enough serum left for that – but, for a brief moment, it became transparent!

The effect didn't last long. As he watched, the thumb faded back in and became solid again! Cautiously, he wiggled it, just to make sure. Yep. It was back all right, dirty as ever.

Then, suddenly, it all clicked. The clues added up to one thing.

'Ha!' he announced, slapping his thigh in triumph. 'Ah'll be jiggered! Durned if it ain't a case o' invisibility!'

'Amazing!' sighed the watching rabbits. 'How does he do it?'

Willy now turned his attention to the trampled snow. There was a mass of footprints, some overlapping and some going off in confused little circles. It was clear that a major pile-up had taken place. As far as he could make out, there were seven – no, eight – sets of footprints leading off into the trees. Or, to be precise, six sets of footprints – and *two sets of hoofprints*!

The front set was big and rather silly-looking for hoofprints. The back set, which evidently belonged to a more conventional horse, was closely followed by two parallel lines which clearly had been made by a cart. Adopting a cautious, half-stooping gait, the legendary wildman followed the trail across the glade.

The two rabbits watched until he vanished into the trees. Then, in chorus, they both said, 'What a guy!' before skipping off back to their holes to tell their grandchildren.

Watching Willy work was indeed an education. Every broken branch, every overturned twig, every passing breeze told a story. Of course, it helped that there were footprints too.

At one point, the trail split. Without a moment's

144

hesitation, Willy followed the tracks made by the hooves and the cart, which veered off to the right.

The trail went on, winding wildly between the trees. At times, Willy was up to his waist in snowdrifts – but this was routine stuff for someone who lives up in the Misty Mountains, eating beans.

Like a small, relentless snowplough, he plunged deeper and deeper into the Wood. At one point, he came across an overturned cart with one of its wheels firmly wedged in a ditch. From this point onwards, it became clear that the back set of hoofprints was gaining on the front set.

It was some time later, as he rested by a fallen log, eating a handful of beans to keep his strength up, that he heard plaintive cries in the distance.

'Heeeeelp!' came the cries. 'Heeeeellllllp!'

The scene at the gum tree was, in all essential details, exactly the same as when we left it – except that both Pongwiffy and the Pantomime Horse were now per-manently visible. Much to their relief, the effects of Ronald's serum had finally worn off. It had taken a while, mind, and there had been some nasty moments. Fading in and out of sight has the same effect upon the system as riding up and down in a fast lift after a big dinner.

145

At the base of the tree, Romeo still waited patiently, kicking his heels and snorting sweet nothings. All right, so his new girlfriend had strange, foreign ways. Roosting up trees, for a start, not to mention her distressing tendency to fade in and out of sight. But in a way that made her more interesting. Anyway, she was back now, spotty and beautiful as ever.

'Heelllp!' Pongwiffy and Plugugly were bellowing in chorus. 'Heeeeeellllppp!'

There was a stubborn silence from Sproggit's end.

'What's he doing in there?' complained Pongwiffy. 'I don't see why we should be doing all the work. Oi! Sproggit! Help us shout, d'you hear?'

'Can't,' came the muffled squawk from the rear end. 'I've fainted. I can't 'old on no more. I'm finished, I tell yer.'

'No, yer not,' Plugugly told him. 'Yer gonna 'ang on tight. We's all in dis togedder, remember? We's all gonna –'

He broke off. Peering through the mouth hole, he had just spotted something. A small, determined figure in buckskins had suddenly stepped out from behind a bush and was striding towards them, deftly twirling a lasso.

Romeo looked around, startled.

'Whoa, boy,' the stranger was saying soothingly. 'Now then, now then, eeezy does it, eeeeezy does it . . .'

There was a whistling sound, the spinning rope snaked through the air – and plopped neatly over Romeo's head.

Romeo let out an outraged whinny and reared up on his hind legs. What was this? Captured, just as he was about to become engaged? Never!

'What was you sayin', Plug?' came Sproggit's anxious voice.

'Eh?'

'You said we wuz gonna do somethin'.'

'Fall,' said Plugugly tiredly. 'I was sayin', we's all gonna fall.'

With that, Romeo's flailing front hooves lashed out, catching the trunk of the gum tree, which shuddered under the impact.

'EEEEEEEEE . . . .' went Pongwiffy.

'NOOOOOOOO . . . .' went Plugugly.

'AAAAAAAH . . . .' went Sproggit.

And the Pantomime Horse toppled from its branch and came plummeting down on to Romeo's broad back like a sack of potatoes.

And, seconds later, on top of *it* – *plumph*! Down came Pongwiffy.

147

The effect on Romeo was electrifying. He looked around and his ears pricked up. He could hardly believe his good fortune. At last, his darling had relented! Oh joy! Now he could carry her off to his stable and show her his horse brasses. All he had to do was get rid of the pesky Witch and the even peskier Dwarf on the end of the rope.

Nostrils flaring and mane tossing, off set Romeo at a mad gallop, Pongwiffy and the Pantomime Horse helplessly flopping and bouncing about on his back as they were borne off on yet another ghastly stage of their adventure.

And behind, flat on his bottom, clinging grimly to the length of rope, came the legendary wildman, the heels of his boots ploughing up great sprays of snow as he was tugged relentlessly ever onward.

CHAPTER SEVENTEEN
Overture and Beginners

The inhabitants of Witchway Wood tend to be somewhat tribal in their habits. Skeletons stick with Skeletons. Trolls tramp round with Trolls. Ghouls go round in gangs. Tree Demons hang out with other Tree Demons and so on. The only thing that prompts the various factions to bury their differences and mingle is the prospect of live entertainment. Stick up a poster advertising any sort of show and you can guarantee that they'll all come crawling out of the woodwork.

The prospect of a pantomime proved irresistible,

149

particularly on a wintry Saturday night with a huge moon shining on the snow and the smell of Christmas in the air. The Wood rang with the chattering voices of excited theatregoers, all wrapped up warm and making for Witchway Hall, which Vincent Van Ghoul had decked out in red fairy lights for the occasion.

On the edge of the glade, five invisible pairs of Goblin eyes watched from behind a handy clump of snow-covered bushes.

'Come on, then,' hissed Hog's voice. 'Are we goin' in or what?'

'Not yet,' said Slopbucket. 'We don't wanna draw attenshun. We gotta wait till everyone's gone in. Then we'll sneak in at the back.'

'You sure this is a good idea?' piped up Stinkwart, sounding doubtful.

'Wassamatter? You don't wanna see the pantymine?'

'Yeah, yeah, 'course I do. But s'posin' we gets caught?'

''Ow can we get caught? We're invizdibibble.'

There was a pause. Then: ''Ow come we're sneakin' about be'ind bushes, then?' asked Stinkwart, He had a point.

'Traditional, innit?' said Slopbucket. 'We're

Goblins. Goblins always sneak about be'ind bushes. Anyway, stop bein' a wet blanket, Stinkwart. At least we're 'avin an outin'.'

'Oh, yeah,' said Stinkwart glumly. 'I fergot I was 'avin fun. Sorry.'

'There's only one fing I'm sorry about,' chipped in Hog, sounding pious. 'I'm sorry that our good ol' mates Plug an' Sproggit ain't wiv us. Don't seem right, us out enjoyin' ourselves when they're stuck in a snowdrift with their legs wigglin'.'

There was a long, rather guilty silence.

'Ah, they'll turn up,' said Eyesore.

'You keep sayin' that,' Hog reminded him. 'But they 'aven't, 'ave they?'

'Anyway,' said Slopbucket uncomfortably. 'Anyway, we 'ad to get out, didn't we? All that lyin' low wuz doin' my head in.'

Lying low had indeed proved to be more than the Goblins had bargained for. Hour after hour after hour of sitting in a gloomy cave staring at the space where your body should be can get to you.

It had been Lardo who cracked first. He had suddenly shot to his invisible feet, announced that he was feeling claustrophobic and that if he didn't get out of there immediately he wouldn't be

151

responsible for the consequences. Well, he didn't actually use those words. They were much too long for a Goblin. What he actually said was, 'Ahhhhhh! Lemmeoutlemmeoutlemmeout!'

At any rate, he put into words what everyone else had been thinking for some time, and it was the signal for a mass exodus.

If you had been an innocent bystander, you would have seen the boulder door roll to one side, a slight rippling effect in the cold air and five pairs of footprints suddenly appear in the snow. But that's all. As yet, Ronald's serum was showing no signs of wearing off. The Goblins were still well and truly invisible.

Outside, as the long shadows of evening crept across the snow, they stood and debated what to do next.

'Now what?' asked Hog. 'Can't stay 'ere all night.'

'I knows wot we can do,' said Slopbucket suddenly. 'Wot?'

'We can cheer ourselves up an' go on a little outin'.'

'You mean, like, the seaside or summink?' enquired Eyesore doubtfully. Even if he had any swimming trunks (which he didn't), he wasn't sure he could find them at such short notice. Besides, it was hardly seaside weather.

'Nah, nah. Look down there, lads. Whadya see?'

The Goblins looked. Far below, in the darkening Wood, there was a red glow. It lit up the snowy tops of the surrounding trees in a rather festive way. It appeared to come from the general area of Witchway Hall.

'Know what's 'appenin' tonight?' said Slopbucket, his voice all wobbly with excitement. 'The pantymine! What do ya say, lads? Fancy a spot of entertainment?'

'We mustn't!' gasped the others. 'We're not allowed in.'

'Ah,' said Slopbucket gleefully. 'Ah. But they can't stop us, can they? 'Cos we's invizdibibble. Come on, lads. Foller me!'

His footprints set off at a run down the slope – and after a moment, four more sets took off after him.

And that is how the Goblins came to be skulking around in the bushes, waiting for the right moment to slip in and enjoy a night of *Terror in the Wood*.

Backstage, in the dressing room, hysteria reigned as first-night nerves set in. The Babes had lost their dummies. Dick Whittington, having just redone her make-up for the seventeenth time, had suddenly discovered a ladder in her tights and was having a

153

temper tantrum in a corner. Snow White had spilled an entire tin of rouge down herself and was trying to get it off using a cup of cold bogwater and Cleopatra's wig. Rapunzel's lethal hair was tripping everyone up, its owner included. Sourmuddle's wings were giving trouble.

'My wings won't stay on! Who's got the safety pins?'

'There's a ladder in my tights! A ladder, I tell you!'

'I've lost my recorder! How can I play merry music without my *recorder*, for mercy's sake!'

'Has anyone seen my wig?'

'Ouch! Mind where you're putting that sword, Macabre . . .'

Sherlock Holmes hadn't a clue where she'd left her magnifying glass. Sleeping Beauty's hot-water bottle was leaking. Barry was in the toilet, being sick again – and he was only Noises Off!

Suddenly, without any warning, the call came. There was a knock at the door and the announcement came that set hearts pit-pattering and stomachs churning.

'Overture and beginners, please!'

There was an appalled silence.

'Oo-er,' said Bendyshanks. 'That's torn it. Too late to back out now.'

Next door, all alone in his dressing room, Prince Charming stood before his mirror, eyes starting out of his white face and all ten fingers stuffed in his mouth in an attempt to still his chattering teeth. He was currently suffering from a shocking attack of stage fright. Despite all his efforts at keeping his theatrical activities under wraps, somehow his fellow Wizards had got to hear about them and the entire Clubhouse had promised to come along to cheer him on. He had thought the previous night had been the most embarrassing of his whole life. Now he wasn't so sure.

On the stage, peering through a crack in the curtains, Hugo stood alone, watching the seats fill up. It looked like it was going to be a packed house. Mistress would be pleased – if only she was here to see it. Anxiously, he took out a tiny pocket watch and examined it.

Three minutes past seven. Time for curtain-up.

With a little sigh, he put the watch away. It looked horribly like she wasn't going to make it.

CHAPTER EIGHTEEN
Terror in the Wood

Imagine it. The packed hall. The audience rustling and whispering in delighted anticipation. A single spotlight trained on the closed curtains.

Snug in the warm darkness, a row of Wizards are noisily tucking into huge bags of popcorn. A small Thing in a Moonmad T-shirt is absent-mindedly eating his programme. A Skeleton hiccups, and everyone sniggers, apart from those who have had the misfortune to have fallen foul of the overenthusiastic Usherette. They are nursing their sore heads and moaning quietly.

Everybody is present and correct. Pierre de Gingerbeard, the famous chef (twin brother, of course, to our old friend Wildman Willy Racoon), has managed to struggle along, despite his injuries. The Yeti Brothers have taken a rare night off and are sitting munching pizza next to a row of Banshees.

Also present is a Gnome called GNorman; a couple of Mummies, with freshly laundered bandages put on specially for the occasion; a small, portly Genie by the name of Ali Pali, who is trying to sell a carpet to the large Troll sitting next to him; somebody called Mrs Molotoff, who is wearing a lot of fruit on her head and is apparently a seaside landlady; Mr Molotoff, who is called Cyril and is carrying a vacuum cleaner; Ernest Dribble, still grieving for the absent Romeo but not enough to go out there looking for him; one Dunfer Malpractiss (shifty-looking owner of the local Magic shop); and a rather bad-tempered Tree Demon who is refusing to share his fruit drops with *anybody*.

The Royals are there too. Worried little King Futtout sits sandwiched between his vinegar-faced wife and his pouting daughter, who has a face like thunder. Honeydimple hates Hamsters, Witches and Pantomimes, in that order.

One of the Mummies leans over, taps King Futtout

157

on the shoulder and demands that he remove his crown. King Futtout hurriedly does so.

Just along from the royal party sits Scott Sinister, star of stage and screen. He is yawning hugely and ostentatiously looking at his watch, even though it's dark. He wishes to make it very clear that he does not want to be here. He has not brought Lulu.

Suddenly, at the back, in a blast of cold air, the doors creak open, then shut themselves again.

And now, at the very back, where there is standing room only, *there are five invisible Goblins*! But nobody knows that yet.

Down in the orchestra pit, Filth picks up his sticks and plays a drum roll. Arthur plays a series of menacing chords, which are meant to conjure up visions of dark doings and wicked deeds. O'Brian puts his penny whistle to his lips and plays something altogether different, because he's got his music in the wrong order.

Time to begin. The curtains wobbled back, giving everyone a wonderful view of Vincent Van Ghoul's paint-splattered rear end as he bent over making some last-minute adjustments to the vase of plastic poppies on Sherlock Holmes's desk.

The audience gave a united gasp at the redness of it

all. Those who had brought them hastily put on their sunglasses.

'Van Ghoul!' hissed Hugo's voice urgently. 'Get off!'

Vincent turned around, gave a startled little squeak and scuttled out of sight. The audience sniggered and delightedly nudged each other. It was a good start.

On came Sherlock Holmes, Watson perched on his shoulder. Both looked horribly nervous, as anyone would be who had to start the whole thing off. Greymatter raised her trembling magnifying glass, inspected the audience and muttered something.

> *'Mumble mumble mumble do?*
> *Mumble mumble mumble clue.'*

'What's the funny man say, Mummy? shrieked a small Banshee very clearly from the back row.

Greymatter cleared her throat and tried again.

> *'Mumble mumble mumble do . . .'*

'Speak up!' yelled a Mummy impatiently. 'We can't hear you.'

Greymatter glared. 'I *said*, cloth-ears, that I'm Sherlock Holmes, how do you do, I'm searching for a vital clue. And I'll thank you to keep your mouth shut, sonny. Some of us are trying to act up here.'

The audience clapped. This was more like it. There was nothing like a bit of heckling to get everyone into the spirit of the thing.

In command now, the great detective went on to explain the business of the missing Babes and his own personal role in the matter. He did it so movingly that several members of the audience wept into their hankies.

'Is ze rhyming couplets,' muttered Hugo to the Three Princesses who were waiting nervously in the wings. 'Gets 'em every time.'

Throughout Greymatter's speech, Watson nodded encouragingly and made admiring noises, which is, of course, what the Watsons of this world are born to do.

At the very back, the five invisible Goblins were struggling to get to grips with it all.

'Wassappenin'?' hissed Lardo, nudging Hog in his invisible ribs. 'Wot's 'e sayin'?'

'I dunno. Summink about some missin' kiddies.'

'Wot kiddies? Why they missin'?'

''Ow should I know?'

'Sssssh!'

A Zombie sitting in the back row turned around

crossly, intent on telling off whoever was making all the noise. Seeing nothing but fresh air and shadows, he looked puzzled, then turned back to face the stage.

Greymatter finished her speech and stepped to the front of the stage. Hugo pulled on the rope and the curtains closed behind her. The Witchway Rhythm Boys struck up an introductory bar or two, and a large piece of cardboard descended from the wings with words on it. It narrowly avoided decapitating the great detective, who leapt out of the way just in time. To her credit, Greymatter recovered quickly and launched into her song.

We have not heard this before, so we should give it a listen, as Hugo is particularly pleased with this song. It is set to the tune of 'Oh, I Do Like to be Beside the Seaside', and right now Greymatter is giving it her all.

'Oh, I do like to be a great detective,' she trilled, enthusiastically conducting the audience with her magnifying glass, while Watson pointed to the words.

> *'Detecting's the thing I like to do,*
> *There is nothing I like more*
> *Than hunting on the floor*
> *Where I might just find*
> *A puzzling clue, clue, clue . . .'*

161

'Listen to zem!' crowed Hugo. 'It goink vell, ya?' But the Three Princesses were too nervous to talk.

> *'Oh, I do like to be a great detective,*
> *Detecting's my specialiteeee,*
> *I can solve the hardest crime*
> *In a record-breaking time,*
> *Need a detective? Then call for me!'*

The song ended, to rousing cheers. Glowing with triumph, Greymatter and Speks made their exit.

The Woodland Glade scene came next. The curtains parted and the onlookers were treated to yet another faceful of Vincent Van Ghoul's visionary scenery. More gasps of astonishment at the beauty of it all.

The Three Princesses stood in a circle, holding hands. The band struck up something vaguely skippy, and Sludgegooey, Scrofula and Bonidle rolled their eyes and proceeded to thump around a cardboard tree while the audience watched in fascinated disbelief.

At the end of the dance, there was a storm of delighted applause. Dripping with sweat, the Princesses grinned sheepishly and stared uncertainly into the wings, unsure what to do.

162

'Do it again!' mouthed Hugo. 'Go on!'

So they did it again. And got another round of applause.

They would have done it a third time, but the stage was beginning to splinter and Hugo signalled that enough was enough. With a sigh of relief, Bonidle slumped in a pile of paper leaves and promptly went to sleep, as the part demanded.

As soon as Snow White and Rapunzel had rather breathlessly introduced themselves, on marched Sherlock Holmes and Watson. Their earlier triumph had given them real confidence. Greymatter's business with the hanky was particularly compelling viewing and got a cheer.

'Acting at its finest,' whispered one Ghoul to another.

When the great detective had unblocked his nostrils to his satisfaction, he enquired about the Babes and received the information that they had been taken off by force by a Scottish woman on a Haggis.

'I knew ve should have vorked on zat line,' sighed Hugo to Vincent Van Ghoul, who was watching from the wings. 'It just not ze same, some'ow.'

It didn't matter. Out front, the audience were lapping it up. All except the Goblins. They were in a state of bewildered outrage.

''Ear that?' spluttered Eyesore. 'Some Scottish woman's got them kiddies! Poor little nippers.'

'Ssssh!' said Lardo. 'Snow White's talkin'. I don't wanna lose the thread.'

'But some Scottish woman's taken a coupla babies from their mammy ...'

'I know, I know.'

'Sssshhh!'

Up on stage, Snow White was suggesting to Sherlock Holmes that he call in a couple of professional heroes to help on the case.

> *Dick Whittington will help you out,*
> *Of that I'm sure there is no doubt.*
> *I also might suggest to you*
> *You call in the Pied Piper too.*
> *Why don't you give them both a ring?*
> *But now, I think it's time to sing.'*

The Witchway Rhythm Boys hastily put down their cups of tea, snatched up their instruments and played the opening bars of the next song. Snow White, Rapunzel and Sherlock Holmes linked arms and sang from the footlights. Bonidle stayed where she was, sleep-singing.

'Rock-a-bye, babies, gone in the night
Maybe to Scotland, hope they're all right . . .'

Everyone joined in, even the Wizards, who weren't known for their community singing. When the song reached its conclusion, there was hardly a dry eye in the house. The curtains closed, the house lights went up and it was time for the interval. Gaga, clad in her Usherette's uniform (consisting of a natty little hat teamed with a swirly skirt and, rather oddly, yellow wellington boots), hurtled down the aisle bearing a tray.

With one accord, the audience leapt to their feet and swooped on the ice cream.

CHAPTER NINETEEN
More Terror

As intervals go, it was a great success. There had been several interesting scuffles in the ice-cream queue and at one point the Usherette had been required to perform yet more vigorous work with her torch. As the lights went down for the second act, everyone hurried back to their seats, eager to find out what would happen next.

The Goblins, of course, hadn't dared go for ice cream. Not only would they have been trampled in the rush, but there was the distinct possibility that food eaten by an invisible body might well remain on view. Five splodges of chewed-up goo floating in the air didn't bear thinking about. Instead, they had whiled away the interval mulling over the events of the first act. Indignation kept their minds off their empty tummies.

'Wicked, I calls it,' Hog was saying in a hoarse whisper. 'Stealin' 'elpless liddle kiddies away from their mammy . . .'

'What's the world comin' to, I wanna know?' agreed Eyesore. 'We should do somethin'. We should form a search party.'

'Wot, like the one we didn't form when Plug and Sproggit went missin'?'

'Yeah, but this is different. This is liddle *kiddies* we're talkin' about 'ere . . .'

'Sssh. It's startin'.'

There was an ominous roll of thunder, the curtains jerked apart and Lady Macbeth rode on stage, bristling with cardboard weapons and hauling the Babes behind her on the end of a long rope. She reined in centre stage, glared at the audience and uttered a wild laugh, just in case anyone was in any doubt about whether or not she was a baddy.

'Ha, ha, ha, ha, ha, ha, ha, HA!'

The entire audience erupted in a cacophony of boos and hisses.

'It's her!' squawked Lardo, quite beside himself. 'It's that Scottish woman! The cheek of it! She's got the Babes! There they are, look!'

'Get her! The Scottish one! She did it!' howled Hog.

'You leave them Babes alone!' bellowed Stinkwart.

'Yeah!' screeched Slopbucket. 'Stop bullyin' them Babes, you wicked ol' woman, you!'

Luckily, everyone else was making such a noise that nobody noticed the racket from the back.

Enjoying herself, Macabre delivered her big speech with lip-smacking relish, tied the twins to a cardboard tree and strode offstage on a quest for a pencil.

'I don't believe it,' moaned Eyesore. 'They've let her go!'

It was Agglebag and Bagaggle's big moment. They removed their dummies, rolled their eyes at each other and lisped their lines.

> *'Alas! Alack! Oh, boo, hoo, hoo.*
> *Whatever can we poor Babes do?*
> *Oh, for a rescuer to come*
> *And reunite us with our mum.'*

168

'Aaaaah,' snivelled the mothers in the audience. 'Poor little dears. Shame.'

Looking rather pleased with themselves, the twins lay down at the foot of the tree and buried themselves under a pile of red-paper leaves.

This was the cue for Cleopatra's dream sequence. The lights dimmed, the Witchway Rhythm Boys struck up with something snake-charmerish, and Bendyshanks hurtled on stage with Steve coiled dramatically around her neck. The exotic effect was slightly spoilt by the addition of a woolly cardigan, but even so she made the audience sit up.

In ringing tones, she informed everybody that she was Cleopatra from the Nile and that she had a unique dancing style, which she was about to demonstrate.

'Who's this?' whispered Hog, struggling to get a grip. 'What's she doin' 'ere?'

He wasn't the only one. The confused audience rustled their programmes and whispered amongst themselves, not quite keeping up with the subtleties of the plot. Nobody could work out what an Egyptian queen in a woolly cardigan was doing in the Wood at this particular stage in the story.

It didn't really matter, of course. All that mattered was that the dance was entertaining. Bendyshanks gambolled energetically around the stage, pointing her toes and rattling her tambourine, with Steve clinging on for dear life. It was a thoroughly abandoned performance. At one point, she got so hot, she removed her cardigan, hurling it wildly into the audience, where it was caught by Mrs Molotoff's Cyril, who took it home for a souvenir. The audience cheered like billy-o, and it all went straight to Bendyshanks's head. Next to come off was her wig, which was batted around a bit before being neatly fielded by the Thing in the Moonmad T-shirt, who ate it. She would have gone further, but caught sight of Hugo sternly shaking his head. So she contented herself with a final leap or two before sinking into the splits with a tearing sound. She got a nice round of applause, more for enthusiasm than anything else.

With a little yodel, the Pied Piper came bounding on, Rat at heel.

'You weren't expecting me, I'll bet.
I'm the Pied Piper, with my pet.
To comb this wood is my intent
We'll find those Babes, where'er they went.'

'I should jolly well fink so too!' said Slopbucket disgustedly. 'Time someone did summink. Who's this skinny geezer comin' now?'

On strode Sharkadder with Dudley in tow, waving her sword and slapping her thigh and declaring that she was Dick, the hero bold. The four of them then commenced prowling about the stage, pointedly avoiding the pile of leaves hiding the missing Babes.

This was all too much for the Goblins. Why, it was patently obvious where the Babes were hiding. How could anyone not see it? They simply couldn't contain themselves any longer.

'They're behind you!' screamed Lardo, jumping up and down in an agony of frustration. 'You stupid or what?'

'Yeah!' chimed in Hog. 'I can see their liddle tummies, look, pokin' out from them leaves!'

'Behind you!' shrieked Stinkwart. 'Behind you! Behind you! Behind you!'

With one accord, both cast and the entire audience turned around to see where the heckling was coming from.

It should have been all right, of course. After all, the Goblins are protected by their invisibility, right?

Wrong. Whatever the reason – whether it was

overexcitement, the heat of the theatre, the fact that all spells wear off in time or simply plain old bad luck – at this extremely critical moment, just when the Goblins had rashly drawn maximum attention to themselves, *the serum began to wear off*!

'Behind you!' they were screaming. 'Behind you! Behind you! Behi—'

Suddenly, they became aware of all eyes on them. Their voices tailed off. They looked down at themselves, then at each other. They were back again. Hopelessly solid as ever. As visible as visible can be.

'Oooops a dandelion!' said Slopbucket.

On stage, all action had stopped. Dick Whittington and the Pied Piper stood rooted to the spot, their mouths forming identical Os. Aware of the sudden silence, the missing Babes emerged from their pile of leaves and sat up.

You've probably heard the expression 'It Never Rains But It Pours'. Consider what happened next.

The floor began to shake and from outside there came the unmistakable sound of approaching hooves. The door burst open with a crash – and there, framed in the doorway, was Romeo, looking overtired and sulky. Mounted on his back was the small, triumphant figure of Wildman Willy Racoon.

In his hand he held a rope. Tied to the end, looking very much the worse for wear and drooping with exhaustion, was the missing Pantomime Horse. And sitting on *its* back was ...

'Mistress!' whooped Hugo ecstatically, throwing his script in the air. 'You back! Hooray!'

And he ran from the wings, down the stage steps, scuttled up a red-spotted leg, up Pongwiffy's arm and on to her shoulder, where he proceeded to throw his paws around her neck.

'You take over,' he begged in her ear. 'It all too much for me.'

'Cousin Willy!' squealed Sharkadder. 'You see? I told you he'd find them!'

'Well, I never!' gasped the Goblins. 'It's Plug an' Sproggit!'

'Romeo!' cried Ernest Dribble, leaping from his seat. 'Romeo, Romeo! Where's your cart now, Romeo?'

'I dun it!' shouted Willy. 'I got both yer hosses back. Have Ah missed the dancin' gals?'

By now, the word had spread backstage and the entire cast came pouring from the wings.

'What's happening?'

'Pongwiffy's back! With the Pantomime Horse!'

'That's not all! There's Goblins in the theatre!'

'Where?'

'There, look! Up at the back!'

'They've gatecrashed our pantomime!'

'Let's get 'em!'

The pantomime was forgotten as the entire cast poured from the wings and down the stage steps into the auditorium. The Goblins clutched at each other and rolled their eyes in panic in the face of the advancing tide. Then:

'HOLD IT RIGHT THERE!'

The voice had authority. It rang out, clear and strong. Everybody hesitated and looked at the stage. There stood Pongwiffy, face grim and arms akimbo. At her side was the Pantomime Horse, looking rather sheepish (if it's possible for a horse to be sheepish) and swaying slightly in the spotlight.

'Zat's right, you tell 'em, Mistress!' urged Hugo from her shoulder. 'Break a leg!'

'This will not do,' announced Pongwiffy. 'It's always the same, isn't it? Everything always ends in chaos. I come up with these exciting ideas, just to brighten up our humdrum lives a bit, you know, and there's always some disaster. Well, this time, it's not going to happen, see? I'm back now and I'm taking over. Me and Hugo here have written a lovely pantomime and you're jolly well going to enjoy it. Dribble, remove that wretched horse. Everybody else, simmer down. If you're not in the pantomime, get back to your seats. Actors, get backstage and wait for your cue. Wildman Willy, keep an eye on those Goblins and make sure they don't escape. They're under house arrest. I'll deal with them later. But right now, there's a show going on. Do it. NOW!'

Everyone was so surprised, they did it. The audience obediently took their seats and the cast meekly began to shuffle back towards the stage.

'And while everyone's getting themselves settled,' continued Pongwiffy, 'the Pantomime Horse will entertain you. With a dance.'

'Eh?' came two startled voices from inside the horse suit.

'You heard,' muttered Pongwiffy out of the corner of her mouth. 'This is show business. Dance. Or else.' Raising her voice, she shouted, 'We all want to see the horsey dance, don't we, boys and girls?'

'Yes!' came the thunderous response.

'Then, music, maestro, please!'

The Witchway Rhythm Boys looked at each other, shrugged and struck up with a jolly version of 'Yankee Doodle'.

There was nothing else for it. Plugugly and Sproggit took deep breaths, picked up their leaden feet and began to dance. And, what's more, they did it *well*.

As the tune picked up speed, their tiredness fell away and suddenly each found he had a spring in his step and a song in his heart. Legs coordinating beautifully, the Pantomime Horse kicked up its heels and skipped about the stage with its tail swishing and its head held high.

At the end of the routine, its front legs crossed and it gave a deep bow.

The audience went wild.

'More!' they shouted. 'More!'

It would be nice to say that the Pantomime Horse's dance was the highlight of the show. But it wasn't. Not quite.

The fight between Lady Macbeth, Dick Whittington and the Pied Piper proved very exciting, and the goodies triumphed, of course, although the general feeling was that Lady Macbeth won on points. Then, a mysterious fairy turned up and gave everyone three wishes, which was very nice. It was a pity her wings fell off, but most people were polite and pretended not to notice. She was the Grandwitch, after all.

When Sherlock Holmes finally found the missing

177

Babes and everything was sorted out to everyone's satisfaction, the entire cast took to the stage for the final rousing song. The whole thing reached its grand climax when Prince Charming, brick red with embarrassment, trailed on stage and, to the great delight of the watching Wizards and his own everlasting shame, awarded each of the smirking Three Princesses a grudging peck on the cheek.

Yes, of course his trousers fell down. They'd have to, wouldn't they?

When the howls of glee finally began to die down, Greymatter stepped forward and delivered the closing lines.

> *'And now at last our panto's done.*
> *We hope you had a lot of fun.'*

'Hooray!' roared the crowd. 'We did! What a show!'

'Author!' yelled the Thing in the Moonmad T-shirt. And everybody else took up the cry.

'Author! Author!'

It was music to Pongwiffy's ears. She walked on stage, Hugo sitting proudly on her hat.

'Thank you!' she cried. 'Thank you, one and all. As some of you may know, this pantomime has had

178

its fair share of problems. But I think for once I can safely say that everything ended happily ever after.'

The cheers rose to fever pitch.

'Hugo,' said Pongwiffy, 'I think this is my finest hour.'

And, so saying, she stepped over the edge of the stage and fell like a stone into the orchestra pit.

CHAPTER TWENTY
Christmas Eve

'S nowing again, I see,' said Pongwiffy. 'You'll have to shovel the path, Hugo. After you've cooked my supper.'

'Ya, OK,' said Hugo. He was standing on a stepladder, putting the finishing touches to the Christmas tree. The Broom stood below, handing up the tinsel.

'I want a proper invalid supper, mind. Maybe a little soup, or a lightly poached egg.'

'Ya, ya, OK.'

'Shouldn't those mince pies come out of the oven

now? Actually, skip the invalid stuff. I'll just make do with those.'

'You 'ave to vait. Zey not ready yet.'

'But I'm hungry!' wailed the invalid. 'I haven't eaten a thing since teatime. I've got to keep my strength up.'

''Ave some leftover skunk stew. Zere's a big pot of it under ze sink.'

'I don't fancy it,' grumbled Pongwiffy. 'It's months old. There's green speckly bits in it. I want mince pies and I want them *now*.'

'Ya, ya, OK, *OK*! Vait a minute, vill you? 'Ugo, do zis, 'Ugo, do zat. 'Ugo, don't forget to 'ang up my stockink, 'Ugo, put anuzzer log on ze fire, 'Ugo, pop out and buy some more Christmas cards. You not sink I got enough to do?'

'Ah, but I've got a broken leg.'

'Zat not my fault.'

'Yes, it is. You said, break a leg. And I did.'

'I keep tellink you! Break a leg is old theatrical sayink. It not mean you got to go and do it!' Pongwiffy had, indeed, broken a leg. It was the left one. Right now, she was sitting in her favourite rocking chair with her leg heavily encased in plaster and a crutch lying across her lap. On Christmas Eve too.

A knock came at the door and the Broom swept

over to open it. A flurry of snowflakes blew into the hovel along with Sharkadder, who was carrying a large sack over her shoulders.

'Surprise! Hello, Pong. I've brought you your Christmas present.'

'Really?' Pongwiffy looked more cheerful. 'What's that, then, Sharky?'

'Well, you're not supposed to open it until tomorrow, but as you're poorly, I'll let you. Here.'

She dug into the sack and withdrew a parcel wrapped in old newspaper.

'Oh,' said Pongwiffy. 'Gift-wrapped, I see.'

She unwrapped it and held up a large, shapeless, sludge-coloured cardigan.

'It's hand-knitted,' explained Sharkadder. 'I hope you like the colour.'

'Oh, I do, I do. Sludge. Lovely. Just like the other hand-knitted sludge-coloured cardigans you've given me for the last fourteen Christmases.'

'I thought you could wear it to the big Christmas lunch at Sourmuddle's tomorrow,' explained Sharkadder. 'Twelve o'clock prompt, mind. Don't forget. Everyone's invited. We're all bringing something. Cousin Willy's bringing beans and Cousin Pierre's made us a lovely Christmas pudding.'

'I've got some nice leftover skunk stew,' began Pongwiffy, but Sharkadder shook her head.

'Oh, no, Pong. You're the guest of honour, on account of the wonderful job you did with the pantomime. We've raised loads of money, you know. Anyway, you've got a poorly leg. How *is* it feeling?'

'It hurts,' said Pongwiffy with a sniff. 'It hurts a *lot*. There's only one thing that's cheering me up.'

'And what's that?'

'I don't hurt as badly as the Goblins,' said Pongwiffy with a little chuckle.

'I was going to ask you about that. I know Sourmuddle said you could decide on their punishment, to make up for all the suffering they caused you. So what did you do with them?'

'I turned them over to Gaga,' said Pongwiffy with malicious pleasure. 'She practised on them with her torch.'

Over in the Wizards' Clubhouse, the Wizards sat in overstuffed armchairs before a roaring fire. A row of stockings was pinned hopefully to the mantelpiece. There was a general air of seasonal festivity. Boxes of chocolates, heaped bowls of candied fruit and little glasses of

183

smoking green stuff were very much in evidence.

The door opened quietly and Ronald slipped in, trying to make himself as inconspicuous as possible. He had kept himself to himself since the night of the pantomime. He couldn't face all the teasing and jokes at his expense. He had made the excuse of a bad cold and had stayed in his chilly attic room, eating his meals off a tray.

However, it was Christmas Eve and the sound of clinking glasses and rumbling laughter had finally drawn him down to the lounge. He rather hoped that his acting debut would have been forgotten by now. He would just slip quietly in and warm his hands before the fire for five minutes . . .

'Hey!' shouted Frank the Foreteller. 'If it isn't Prince Charming! Where've you been keeping yourself, Your Royal Highness?'

'I've had a cold, actually,' muttered Ronald.

'Oooh dear, sorry to hear that. Probably caught something from all that princess-kissing, eh?'

He gave a wink and everybody but Ronald fell about in paroxysms of wheezy laughter.

'Look,' said Ronald bitterly. 'Look, I don't want to talk about it, all right? I'm not going to spend my whole Christmas being the butt of your jokes. Now, if you'll excuse me, I shall retire to my room . . .'

'Hang about, hang about, keep your hair on. What d'you think, gentlemen? Shall we give it to him now?'

'Yes, go on,' urged Dave the Druid. 'Let him have it. He needs cheering up.'

For the first time, Ronald became aware of a large, gaily wrapped parcel sitting in the middle of the lounge.

'For me?' he said.

'For you,' chorused the Wizards.

'We had a whip-round,' explained Fred the Flameraiser.

'Go on,' urged Gerald the Just. 'Open it.'

So Ronald opened it. He ripped off the fancy paper, removed the top of the box and peered inside. What he saw caused a lump to form in his throat and tears of gratitude to well up in his eyes.

'Oh,' he said. 'Oh. Thank you so very, very much. It's just what I always wanted.'

It was a chair. A chair of his very own. It had a carved back. It had a cushion with tassels on. It had a plaque with his name on. Ronald the Magnificent, it said.

It rather seemed that Christmas wasn't going to be so bad after all.

Far away, somewhere in the Lower Misty Mountains, lies Gobbo Towers, home of the Great Gobbo. Tonight, there is something special going on. A fancy dress ball, no less.

The Great Gobbo sits on a raised dais at one end of the great hall. You can tell this is the Great Gobbo, because his braces are made of gold thread and he wears a crown over his bobble hat. He is also being fed grapes by a bevy of Goblin handmaidens in pink bikinis, just like Lardo described.

The floor is packed with Goblins of all shapes and sizes. They have been dancing the night away to hideous sounds provided by the Goblinaires – an enthusiastic trio whose instruments consist of a burglar alarm, a dustbin lid and a blackboard (for scraping the fingernails down).

The time has now come to judge the fancy dress competition. The Great Gobbo claps his hands for silence and runs his eyes over the massed ranks before him. It is not a promising sight. There is only so much you can do with twigs and birds' nests. The place is packed with Randolph the red-nosed wassits and Goldisockses.

Only one Gaggle of Goblins stands out from the rest. At least their costumes are original.

They are covered in bruises. At least three have black eyes and two have cauliflower ears. Bandaged limbs and sticking plaster are much in evidence. It all looks terribly realistic.

The Great Gobbo crooks his finger. The bandaged ones start and, uttering things like, 'Who, us? Does he mean *us*?', hobble painfully to the dais, where they stand awestruck before their great leader.

The Great Gobbo picks a grape pip out of his teeth and surveys them in silence for a moment. Then he speaks.

''Oo you s'posed ter be, then, lads?'

The one with the badly dented saucepan on his head clears his throat nervously.

'As you can see, Great Gobbo, we has made a group effort. We has come as a Gaggle o' poor, innocent Goblins who, through no fault o' deir own, has got tangled up with a loada spiteful ol' Witches. We has come as a dreadful warnin' to you all. We calls ourselves the Dreadful Warnin' Boys. Sir.'

'I like it,' said the Great Gobbo. 'It's different. It's new. It don't involve twigs. I award you first prize.'

He waved his hand and a huge hamper was

187

ceremoniously brought on and dumped at the feet of the incredulous winners. When the lid was raised, it was found to contain a year's supply of tinned nettle soup!

'Oh, wow!' gasped Plugugly, quite overcome. 'Dis is too much! Some Christmas dinner iss gonna be dis year, lads.'

It was only when they got home that they realised they didn't have a tin opener. But that's another story.

Time now for the happy ending. What could be nicer than Witchway Wood on this Christmas Eve, with the snow falling gently down on the houses of the sleeping inhabitants. Even Pongwiffy is asleep. She is lying in a sea of mince-pie crumbs, dreaming of riding a red-spotted Pantomime Horse around a vast stage, with loud cheers ringing in her ears.

Beside her, on the pillow, Hugo is curled up in the tea cosy he likes to use as a sleeping bag. At the end of the bed hang two stockings. One is the size of a postage stamp. The other is outsize and has a note pinned to it. The note reads: 'BROKUN LEG. GIVE JENERUSLY'.

Right now, both stockings are empty. But not for

long. From far away, there comes the unmistakable silvery tinkle of bells. They are coming nearer . . .

Time to leave now.

Turn the page for another
Pongwiffy adventure!

even more

Pongwiffy

stories

The Spellovision
Song contest

WHAT'S ON
SPELLOVISION

6.00   **Zombie Decorating**
The Zombies paint a room – and watch it dry.

7.00   **The News** with Sheridan Haggard
The Skeleton with the Golden Voice brings you all the Witchway news.
Followed by the weather, presented by our glamorous Zombie weather girl, Brenda.

7.30   **Gnome and Away**
GNarleen's in love with GNorman, who's secretly going out with GNometta, who's got a secret crush on GNeville …
Repeated tomorrow at 12 noon

8.00   **Familiar Fortunes**
Tonight the Toad family try for the big prizes.

9.00   **Goblins in Cars**
Those crazy Mountain Goblins are racing more beat-up old cars. No rules, no skills, just lots of crashes.
Repeated Friday at 10.30 pm

10.00   **Fiends**
Six Fiends sit and drink bogwater and talk about each other's problems.
See Pick of the Week: page 24

DON'T FORGET – TOMORROW NIGHT

THE GREAT SPELLOVISION SONG CONTEST!

Get your entry forms
NOW for the

SPELLOVISION SONG CONTEST

SONGS MUST BE ORIGINAL

FABULOUS PRIZES TO BE WON!

ANYONE CAN ENTER – EXCEPT GOBLINS

CHAPTER ONE
A visit to Sharkadder

'Moon's up. I think I'll go out,' announced Witch Pongwiffy to Hugo, her Hamster Familiar.

'OK,' said Hugo, not even looking up. He was comfortably settled in the tea cosy, nose deep in a very small book. A saucer full of chopped carrot was within easy reach. The kettle was boiling, ready to pour into a thimble of cocoa.

'You coming?' asked Pongwiffy, taking her hat from its hook.

'No. I is readink.'

'Who said you could read? You're supposed to be

working for me, not reading. What is it, anyway? A book of stamps? Hmm? Little sticky stamps? Is that why you've had your nose stuck in it for days?'

'No. Is *Ze Little Book of Hamster Vit and Visdom*. Is collection of clever Hamster sayinks.'

'Oh yeah? No wonder it's small. OK, OK, only joking. Tell me one.'

'*Hamsters might be small, but zey haf great big hearts*,' Hugo read out.

'Rubbish!' said Pongwiffy. 'If your hearts were big, there wouldn't be room for the rest of the stuff. Your tummy and lungs and daft little kidneys. What else?'

'*Hamsters are better zan cats.*'

'Hamsters are better than cats?' scoffed Pongwiffy. 'What kind of saying is that? That's not wise or witty.'

'Is true though,' said Hugo firmly.

'Why? How are they better?'

'In every vay. Hamsters better lookink, tougher, got better personality. See zis scar?' Hugo pointed to his ear. 'A cat did zat. Boy, voz he sorry.' He turned a page of his book and gave a little snigger. 'Listen. Zis good vun. *If ignorance is bliss, vhy are cats so miserable?*'

'Hmm,' said Pongwiffy. 'Is there a *lot* of anti-cat stuff in the book?'

'Loads,' said Hugo. 'Vant to hear more?'

'No. I'm bored with cats.'

'How about zis, zen? *Blue are ze violets, red are ze roses. Hamsters are furry, viz little pink noses.*'

'Good grief! Is that the best you lot can come up with?' said Pongwiffy, unimpressed. 'I'm off. Perhaps I'll take the Broom and fly over to Sharkadder's.'

The Broom, which had been quivering hopefully in a dark corner, came flying out and started attacking the door enthusiastically.

'OK,' said Hugo, head back in his book. 'Bye, zen.'

'Sure you won't come?'

'Huh? Oh. No. Zis is gripping stuff.'

'About as gripping as the elastic on my oldest pair of knickers,' sneered Pongwiffy. Which was a rude thing to say, but we'll forgive her because she was disappointed that Hugo wasn't coming.

Out she went, with the Broom whizzing eagerly round her in little circles, keen to be up and away.

Pongwiffy's hovel – Number One, Dump Edge – stood on the edge of a huge rubbish dump. The beauty of it was that the view from her window was constantly changing. There was the rusty cooker and the broken mangle and the three-wheeled pram and the pile of mouldering old mattresses, of course. They'd been there for years. But every week, fresh junk magically appeared, adding fascinating new smells and textures. As Pongwiffy was always boasting to anyone who would listen, she never got bored.

She stood in her doorway, closed her eyes, and breathed in the familiar smell of rotting rubbish. Tonight, it had subtle new overtones. There had obviously been a new delivery. Should she go and pick over it now, or save that pleasure for later?

Her mind was made up by the Broom (Woody), which had been cooped up for too long and was now fly-crazy. It kept jumping up at her in an annoying, puppyish way, then nipping round and banging into the back of her knees, trying to get her to climb on.

'All right,' she said. 'Stop your nonsense, we're going, we're going.'

Seconds later, they were airborne. They skimmed over the trees, enjoying the cool night breeze. Below lay Witchway Wood – dark, silent and strangely empty.

'Seems quiet down there tonight,' shouted Pongwiffy over the wind. 'No smoke from the chimneys. Looks like everyone's out. Hey! It's not the last Friday of the month, is it? I'm not missing a Coven Meeting, am I?'

The Broom didn't reply. It could only speak in

Wood. Besides, it wasn't the brightest Broom in the cupboard. It *never* knew what day it was.

'Actually, it's Tuesday,' mused Pongwiffy. 'I remember now, because yesterday was Monday, when I always water the toadstools under my pillow. Strange how quiet everything is, though ...'

Witch Sharkadder stood on her step, locking the door. She was dressed up to the nines – hair a mass of tortured curls, spiderleg eyelashes, lipstick (Mad Mildew), perfume (Oppression, French, very posh), freshly sharpened nails, the works. Her Familiar, a one-eyed cat called Dead Eye Dudley, was glaring sullenly out of the window, clearly put out at being left behind. Her Broom, name of Ashley, was propped against the drainpipe. A green ribbon was tied in a floppy bow around its stick.

Everyone winced as Pongwiffy came hurtling down into the flower bed, boots ploughing up the neat row of delicate crocuses that had just begun to show their shy little heads.

'Oh,' said Sharkadder with a little sigh. 'It's you, Pong. What a pity, I'm just off out.'

'Lucky I caught you, then,' said Pongwiffy, climbing off her Broom, which took one look at Ashley's ribbon and fell about laughing. (To your ear and mine, this would sound like straightforward rustling.)

'But I'm going out,' repeated Sharkadder, popping her key in her handbag.

'That's all right. I'll come with you. Where are you going, anyway?'

'Visiting.'

'Well, I can see that. Who?'

'Oh – just a friend,' hedged Sharkadder, snapping the bag shut. 'I can't stay here talking to you all night – I'm late as it is.'

'What friend?' persisted Pongwiffy. 'A better friend than me?'

'No, of course not. You're my best friend, you know that.'

'Who, then?'

'Nobody special.'

'*Who?*'

'Well – Sourmuddle, if you must know.'

'Oh *really*? Nobody *special*, eh?' Pongwiffy sneered. Sourmuddle was only Grandwitch, boss of the Witchway Coven. She was certainly special.

'She's having a sort of small select gathering,' mumbled Sharkadder, going a bit pink.

'*Really?*' Pongwiffy's eyebrows shot up in surprise.

203

Sourmuddle wasn't known for her hospitality. She usually took her meals at other Witches' cottages. It was one of the advantages of rank. 'Like who?'

'Well – me. And I think Macabre will be there.'

'Is that all?'

'Well – the twins. And Ratsnappy.'

'Anyone else?'

'Greymatter. Oh, and Gaga.'

'What about Sludgegooey and Scrofula?'

'Um ... yes. I believe so.' Sharkadder had reached the carefully-looking-the-other-way stage.

'And Bonidle and Bendyshanks?' enquired Pongwiffy sternly.

Sharkadder looked down and twiddled her high-heeled shoe.

'Probably.'

'That's not a small select gathering,' Pongwiffy pointed out. 'That's the whole Coven!'

'Erm – yes.'

'Everyone except me!'

'Erm – yes.'

'Well, that's just terrific!' sulked Pongwiffy. 'I was wondering where everyone was. And now I know. There's a thundering great party at Sourmuddle's and I'm not invited!'

'It's not exactly a *party*.'

'What, then?'

'Oh, all right, if you must know. Sourmuddle's got one of those new spellovisions and we're all going round to watch it. It's not that she doesn't *want* you, Pong. But you know how small her parlour is and, quite frankly, your smell in an enclosed space is . . .'

'Never mind my smell. Go back a bit. She's got a *what*?'

'A spellovision.'

'And what's that, when it's at home?'

'Surely you must have heard of *spellovision*!' Sharkadder pretended to be amazed, although, in fact, she had only just heard about it herself. 'It's *quite* the new thing. It's a sort of square box and you sit and watch it.'

'What's the point of sitting and watching a box?' asked Pongwiffy. 'I've got a box at home. I keep coal in it, along with my spare socks. I've never felt the need to sit and watch it, though.'

'No, no. This is different. It's – a new sort of Magic. Invisible pictures come through the air and get caught in the box. Sourmuddle says it's got a screen. You twiddle knobs and the pictures come alive and you watch them.'

205

'What are the pictures of?'

'I don't know, do I? That's why I'm going to Sourmuddle's to find out.'

'Well!' said Pongwiffy, highly miffed. 'I think I'll just come along too. I don't see why I should be left out.'

'Oh, don't go all huffy. If it's any consolation, the Familiars aren't allowed to come. No room, see. So you're not the only one.'

'That's different. I'm a Witch. It's discrimination, that's what it is, and I shall say so in no uncertain terms. In fact, I shall give Sourmuddle a piece of my mind.'

'Suit yourself,' said Sharkadder with a shrug. 'But don't bring me into it.'

CHAPTER TWO
watching spellovision

'So I called in on Sharkadder and she mentioned she was about to come over to you and I was wondering if I could come in and watch your spellovision, please?' begged Pongwiffy humbly. It was easy to *talk* about giving Sourmuddle a piece of her mind, but a bit different when she was there in the flesh, glaring on the doorstep.

'Don't blame me,' said Sharkadder disloyally. '*I* didn't ask her.'

Sourmuddle peered over the top of her glasses.

'It's very crowded in the parlour,' she said.

'I'll make myself small.'

'It's stuffy too. I'm not sure I can accommodate you.'

'It's my smell, isn't it? My smell's not welcome. All right. Just this once, I'll squirt myself with Sharkadder's perfume.'

'What, at ten pounds a bottle? Not likely,' said Sharkadder unhelpfully.

'Then I'll sit by the window.'

'There aren't enough peanuts,' said Sourmuddle.

'I don't mind. I'm not hungry. Look. I'm getting on my knees and begging.' Pongwiffy sank to her knees and wrung her hands in supplication. 'Please! Oh pretty please! Pleasepleasepleasepleasepleaseple asepleasepleasepleaseplea—'

'All right,' said Sourmuddle grudgingly. 'But you'll have to keep quiet. This is a momentous occasion and I'm not having you spoiling it.'

'I'll be good,' promised Pongwiffy, which was rather like a monkey promising not to eat bananas.

The parlour was hot and crowded. Every available seat was taken, apart from the rocking chair, which was reserved for Sourmuddle. Witches Macabre, Greymatter and Agglebag and Bagaggle, the twins, were squashed on the sofa. Bonidle snoozed in an armchair, flanked by Ratsnappy and Sludgegooey, who perched on the arms. Bendyshanks and Scrofula sat on upright chairs that had been brought in from the kitchen. Gaga hung from the curtain rail, because she preferred dangling to sitting.

They all faced a large, mysterious, square box with a grey screen, which sat in pride of place on Sourmuddle's best coffee table.

'Oh,' said Bendyshanks, rising hastily. 'It's Pongwiffy. I'll open the window.'

Agglebag and Macabre squeezed up even more to make room for Sharkadder, and Pongwiffy picked her way over to the open window and stood obediently in the draught.

Out in the starry garden, she noticed Woody had pulled off Ashley's ribbon and was waving it around in a confrontational sort of way.

'Right,' said Sourmuddle, coming in from the kitchen with a very small bowl. 'Nuts first. Pass them round, would you, Ratsnappy? I think you'll find there's exactly one each. Except for Pongwiffy, who wasn't invited.'

The bowl was passed round and everyone except Pongwiffy carefully took a nut. There was a lot of exaggerated lip-smacking and smarmy cries of 'Delicious!' and 'My, that hit the spot!' Buttering up Sourmuddle was in everyone's interest.

'Good,' said Sourmuddle. 'Never let it be said that I'm mean with the catering.' She walked over to the square box and put her hand on one of the knobs.

'Well, you all know why you're here. I've got one of these newfangled spellovision sets. Only for research, you understand. As Grandwitch, it's my responsibility to keep up with any new fad that comes along. Anyway, it's the very latest thing and I thought you'd like to see what all the fuss is about. Remember, you saw it here first. Can everybody see?'

'Yes!' came the excited chorus. Pongwiffy couldn't, but thought she might be pushing her luck to say so. Out in the garden, things were getting interesting. Ashley had got its ribbon back and was being chased round the water barrel by Woody.

'Ready?' said Sourmuddle. 'Here we go, then. Prepare to be amazed.'

She pressed the knob. A thrilled gasp went up as important-sounding music swelled and the screen flickered into life!

A smooth-looking Skeleton, wearing a smart bow tie, sat behind a desk with a pile of papers before him.

'Oooh!' gasped the watching Witches, craning forward excitedly. 'Look at that! Just like real life!'

'*Hello and welcome*,' said the Skeleton in a rich,

golden-brown voice. *'I am Sheridan Haggard and you are watching the midnight news, brought to you from the Witchway news desk. Here are the main points. The Wizards have announced the date of their Annual Convention. It will take place on . . .'*

'Move your hat, Greymatter, I can't see,' complained Pongwiffy.

'Ssshhh!' hissed everybody.

'. . . and will be staying as usual at the Magician's Retreat, Sludgehaven-on-Sea. A Wizard was quoted as saying, "We like it there. The sausages are good." '

'But I can't *see!*' insisted Pongwiffy, bobbing around, attempting to find a gap in the forest of pointy hats.

'Once more and you're out!' snapped Sourmuddle.

Pongwiffy subsided.

'Earlier today,' continued Sheridan Haggard, *'a daring masked Troll attempted to rob a small Gnome of his lunch. Young GNelson Pondworthy was out fishing when the attack occurred. The Troll swallowed a cheese sandwich, a strawberry yoghurt and half a carrot before being bravely beaten off with a fishing rod by have-a-go GNelson. His mother, Mrs GNorma Pondworthy, said, "My boy is a hero."*

'The Banshee jumble sale, held last week, raised a

record nine pence. It will go towards topping up the tin of tea bags, which is getting perilously low ...'

'Gnome muggings!' scoffed Pongwiffy. She just couldn't help it. 'Jumble sales! Wizard Conventions! Ha! As if anyone cares.'

Rather to her surprise, nobody said a word. They were all hunched forward, eyes glued to the screen, hanging on to the Skeleton's every golden-brown word.

Out in the garden, the Brooms had come to blows. Ashley had had enough and was attacking Woody with its stick. Woody was defending itself by trying to brush Ashley away. Other Brooms had gathered in a circle and were rustling wildly, egging the combatants on. It was quite exciting. Pongwiffy wished she was out there, cheering from the sidelines.

'Sales of spellovision sets are rising hourly, due to unprecedented public demand,' Sheridan Haggard announced. *'From tomorrow, The Daily Miracle will be printing details of forthcoming programmes in place of the usual crossword puzzle. Order your copies now to beat the rush. That is the end of the news. And now a word from our glamorous weather girl. Brenda, over to you.'*

The scene changed. A bored-looking female Zombie in a bright pink suit teamed with green hair and big brass earrings stood before a badly drawn map of Witchway Wood. She was chewing pink bubblegum and holding a fistful of cut-out cardboard clouds.

'*Oh. Is it me? Right. Yeah,*' said Brenda the glamorous weather girl. She reached into her mouth, took out the gum and used it to stick the largest cut-out cloud slap bang in the middle of the map, where it obscured pretty well everything.

''*S gonna rain,*' she said. '*Probubly. As if I care.*'

She vanished, and Sheridan Haggard filled the screen again.

'*Thank you, Brenda. Well, that's it from me. Stay tuned for tonight's film,* Gnome Alone, *a comedy for all the family about a young Gnome who gets left alone only to find himself at the mercy of two wicked Brownies who . . .*'

'Not *more* Gnomes,' complained Pongwiffy. She'd had enough Gnomes for one night. Her boredom threshold as far as Gnomes were concerned was very low. She was Gnomed out.

Night beckoned through the open window. To her disappointment, the Broom fight was over. The Brooms had lost interest and were wandering around sweeping up a few twigs and grass cuttings. Woody was currently bashing at the garden gate, desperate to be up and away. Ashley was licking its bristles over by the rain barrel. There was no sign of the green ribbon. Who had won or lost wasn't very clear.

In the parlour, nobody spoke. On the screen, to the accompaniment of jaunty music, a family of Gnomes were packing suitcases and throwing fishing rods into a cart, obviously off on a fishing trip. The dialogue went like this:

FATHER: *Let us go on a fishing trip.*
MOTHER: *Oh yes. It will be fun.*
TEENAGE BOY GNOME: *I will take my rod.*
TEENAGE GIRL GNOME: *We will catch some fish.*
ALL: *It will be good.*

Pongwiffy gave a loud, ostentatious yawn. She had been involved in quite a few theatrical ventures in her time. She knew a bad script when she heard one.

'Is it me,' she enquired, 'or does anyone else find the acting wooden? I mean, *look* at them. I've seen gateposts with more personality.'

Silence. It was very clear that everyone else found it enthralling.

'Hello? Anyone listening?'

No one was, apparently.

'No one's bored, then? Personally, I am. I'm bored stiff. There was a Broom fight outside just now, did anyone notice?'

More silence.

'Shall we turn it off now and have a cup of bog-water? I could tell you all about this new spell I've been working on. It's very easy. You take a bucket of coal and mix it with treacle, by hand. Then add . . .'

'Shhhhh!' came the furious, hissed chorus. On screen, the Gnome family were in the fascinating process of locking up the house.

FATHER: *I have a key. I will lock up the house.*
MOTHER: *Yes. Then we will go on our holiday.*
TEENAGE GIRL GNOME: *It will be fun.*
TEENAGE BOY GNOME: *Yes. Let us go.*

Pongwiffy gave up. She slipped through the open window and left them to it. Woody came bounding up to meet her. She straddled the stick and they took off on a nice long flight to Crag Hill and back, which they both enjoyed.

Hugo was still up reading when they got back.

'Hi. Haf good time? Vot you do?' he asked.

'I've been watching spellovision,' said Pongwiffy.

'Vot zat?'

'You haven't heard of *spellovision*? I thought everyone knew. It's a Magic box and you turn it on and watch rubbish.'

'Vot sort of rubbish?'

So Pongwiffy told him all about it.

'... and there are altogether too many Gnomes,' she finished. 'Nothing of interest for Witches. It's just another fad. I'm sure it won't catch on.'

CHAPTER THREE
Quite the New Thing

Spellovision did more than catch on. It took over. Before the week was out, almost everybody in the Wood had a spellovision set. If you stood on Crag Hill and looked in the direction of Witchway, you would notice a cold, bluish glow in an empty sky through which no Broomsticks flew.

Nobody went out at night any more. Nobody went herb gathering or shopping. The Skeletons stopped having picnics. The Trolls stopped playing rockball. The Wood was empty of all but the rabbits and foxes. As for the Witches – they were well and truly hooked.

If a Witch went scurrying by, you could be sure that she'd be on her way home with a last-minute takeaway before slumping on the sofa and growing square eyes. Nobody cooked any more. Nobody did any spells or any housework. Wands lay abandoned in dark corners. Nobody even picked up a crystal ball to talk to a friend.

Pongwiffy went round to Sharkadder's to complain about it. They sat in the kitchen. Well, Pongwiffy sat. Sharkadder hovered by the door in a strange half-crouch, trying to conceal a large wooden crate that had arrived that morning and which she hadn't yet had time to unpack. Dudley sat glaring down from the top of the dresser, drumming his claws and mumbling insults under his breath.

'It's ridiculous,' said Pongwiffy, through a mouthful of fungus sponge (Sharkadder's speciality). 'Nobody goes anywhere any more. I just walked here and the Wood is practically empty. Everyone's in bed asleep because they were up all night watching stupid spellovision. Lovely cake.'

'Mmm,' said Sharkadder vaguely, adding, 'although I don't know why you've got such a thing about it. What's wrong with spellovision?'

'Everything! It's full of rubbish and it stops people doing things. It's taking over the world. Even *The*

Daily Miracle's full of it. I mean, look.' She pointed at the paper, which was spread on the kitchen table. 'A huge story about that smarmy newsreader, splashed all over the front page.'

'Sheridan Haggard,' said Sharkadder rather dreamily.

'Yes, him. The colour of his stupid limousine, the name of his dog, where he goes for his holidays, where he buys his daft ties. As if anyone cared.'

'What *is* the name of his dog?' enquired Sharkadder casually.

'Ribs. Why? What does it matter?'

'I don't know. It's interesting.'

'No it isn't. Nothing about Sheridan Haggard is remotely interesting. He's just some Skeleton.'

'But you must admit he does have a lovely voice. Like velvet . . .'

'Velvet, my bum!'

Sharkadder looked shocked, as well she might.

'And look at this!' shouted Pongwiffy, really worked up now. 'Here's a photo of that weather girl, wotsername, Brenda. She used to be the receptionist up at the Wizards' Clubhouse. I didn't think it'd be possible to sink any further.'

'Mmm. I like those little clouds she sticks on, mind . . .'

'And look! They've even done away with the crossword! The whole back page is about tonight's programmes. *6 pm. Embalming with the Mummies. 7 pm. The News, with Sheridan Haggard. 8 pm. Zombie Decorating.* Good grief!'

'Actually, *Zombie Decorating*'s quite good,' said Sharkadder.

'What d'you mean, good?'

'Well, these Zombies paint a room. Then they sit and watch it dry. It's very – soothing, isn't it, Duddles?'

'How do you know all this?'

'Dudley and I watched it over at the twins' last night. They've got an extra-wide screen.'

'Really?' said Pongwiffy sharply. 'You didn't tell me.'

'Oh, I just popped in for a moment. I didn't stay long. I wanted to catch the news. Then I watched *Zombie Decorating* for an hour. Then there was *Gnome and Away*. Well, I couldn't miss that, could I?'

'What's *Gnome and Away*?'

'It's a soap opera. It's on every night.'

'A *soap* opera?' Pongwiffy, a born soap avoider, was appalled. 'What, they sing in the *bath*? What do they wear? Flannels?'

'No, no! It's nothing to do with soap. It's about these Gnomes, you see, who –'

220

'Enough with the Gnomes!' Pongwiffy hurled the paper into a corner. 'I don't want to know about Gnomes. It amazes me why anyone does. I'm a Witch. I'm interested in Witchy things. I thought you were too.'

'I am, I am!' protested Sharkadder. 'It's just that GNarleen's in love with GNorman, who's secretly going out with GNometta, who's got a secret crush on GNeville and . . .' She caught Pongwiffy's eye. 'Well, anyway, it's good,' she ended lamely.

'*Good!*' spat Pongwiffy. '*Good!* What I want to know is, what happened to old-fashioned entertainment? Playing charades, or singing songs round a piano? All this sitting in front of a box watching Gnomes, it's not healthy.'

'It's not just Gnomes. There's *Goblins in Cars*. I watched it at Macabre's. There's this tribe of crazy Mountain Goblins and they've got hold of these beat-up old cars and they race them.'

'I didn't know Goblins could drive.'

'They can't. That's the whole point. They bash into each other. It's hilarious. Macabre loves it.'

'I see,' sneered Pongwiffy. 'Car-driving Goblins bashing into each other hilariously. I see.'

'And, just for your information –' Sharkadder

looked proud – 'Cousin Pierre's doing a cookery programme. Ten o'clock tonight, live from the Gingerbeard Kitchens. It's called *Pierre's Pantry*. Tonight, it's marzipan frogs.'

Despite herself, Pongwiffy was impressed. Pierre de Gingerbeard, the famous Dwarf chef, was Sharkadder's cousin, twenty-four times removed. He was an excellent cook. His marzipan frogs were amazing. She knew. She'd tasted them.

'All right,' she conceded. 'So maybe, just occasionally, there might be something worth watching. But mostly, it's rubbish. If I want to watch rubbish, I can look out of my window. You'd have to be mad to spend good money on a talking box.'

'Mmm.'

'Why are you crouching by the door like that? Why don't you come and sit down?'

'It's all right. I like crouching.'

'What's in that crate you're trying to hide?'

'Hide a crate? Me?' twittered poor Sharkadder. 'Whatever can you mean?'

'Stand aside,' ordered Pongwiffy sternly. 'I want to see it.'

'No,' said Sharkadder.

'In that case, let me guess. Could it be a new

222

cauldron, by any chance? Or a job lot of fish heads for Dudley? Hmm? Or – this is just a wild stab, mind – *could it be a spellovision?*'

'Oh, all right!' cried Sharkadder, stamping her foot. 'So what if it is? I can have a spello if I want.'

'*Spello!*' mocked Pongwiffy. '*Spello!* What kind of a daft name is that? And you stood there agreeing with me and all the time you're standing in front of one.'

'I wasn't agreeing with you.'

'You weren't disagreeing either.'

'Oh, shut up.' Sharkadder's temper was up now. 'I was being polite, that's all. But quite frankly, I've had enough. You've finished the sponge so you can go. I've got some unpacking to do. And don't bother to come round later either. Dudley and I will be watching spello, won't we, Duddles?'

'Aye,' agreed Dudley. 'I likes the cat-food adverts.'

'All right, then,' said Pongwiffy, highly miffed. 'See if I care.'

'I don't care if you care or not.'

'And I don't care whether you care whether I care. So there.'

A little silence fell. The clock ticked. Dudley swore under his breath.

223

'So,' said Pongwiffy stiffly. 'Does this mean we're breaking friends?'

'I don't know. Probably. I'll think about it. Now go.'

'Shall I see you at the Coven Meeting on Friday?'

'Haven't you heard? It's cancelled. There's a new show starting called *Fiends*. It looks terribly good from the clips, doesn't it, Duddles? It's all about this group of Fiends who sit and drink bogwater and talk about each other's problems . . .'

Pongwiffy went home.

CHAPTER FOUR
A Fascinating Find

It had been raining, just as Brenda the weather girl had predicted. Mind you, it often rained in Witchway Wood, so the odds were in her favour. When Pongwiffy arrived back at the Dump, the dampness had brought out the smells in force. A fox, made brave by her absence, stood nosing at an old cabbage that had escaped from a sack of rotten vegetables.

'Mmm,' murmured Pongwiffy. 'There's nothing to beat the smell of home ... Oi! You! You leave that alone! What's here is mine!'

The fox gave her a dirty look and slunk off, its eyes red in the moonlight.

'That's right!' jeered Pongwiffy. 'Clear off back to your daft den and don't come back!'

And just to make absolutely sure the fox got her point (and because she was in a bad mood anyway), she aimed a kick at the cabbage. It flew from the tip of her boot, sailed up and over the mountains of junk and landed with a . . .

. . . *plink*.

Now, cabbages can land with a *thump* or, occasionally, a *splat*, depending on how mouldy they are. But they never land with a *plink*. Unless the thing they land on *plinks*.

'Funny,' said Pongwiffy. Her eyes narrowed. Slowly, she raised her head and sniffed the air.

Now, as you know, smell is Pongwiffy's speciality. Smell fascinates her. She's good at it. Not only does she have her own unique odour, carefully honed over many years, but she actually has a very highly tuned nose. What came to it now was a new smell. It was faint, but it was there. The smell of varnish. And wood. With faint overtones of metal. There was something new in the Dump – something she hadn't smelled before.

Using her nose as a guide, Pongwiffy left the path and began wending her way towards the source.

It didn't take her long to find. It lay half under the broken ping-pong table. It was covered with a thick layer of dust, but the shape was unmistakable.

'Oooh,' said Pongwiffy, picking it up. 'A guitar.'

It was. All but one of the strings were broken and two of the pegs were missing, and the neck wobbled, but it was still a guitar.

Pongwiffy stood, turning it over in her hands. Using her sleeve, she gave it a brisk little rub. The moon glinted on polished walnut. Experimentally, she plucked at the string.

Plink.

It really was a rather satisfying sound. She did it again.

Plink. Plink, plink. Plink, plink, plink, plink, plink, plink, plink ...

'Vot in ze vorld you got now?' said a voice from behind. It was Hugo and he was clutching his *Little Book of Hamster Wit and Wisdom*.

'It's a guitar,' said Pongwiffy happily. 'I've just found it. Good, isn't it?'

'It only got vun string?'

'Yes. So? That's all you need to go *plink*. Listen.' *Plink.* 'See?'

227

Hugo looked less than impressed.

'Oh, come on!' cried Pongwiffy. 'It's great! Just look at it. It's an antique. Probably quite valuable.'

'Zen vhy it in ze Dump?'

'Well, obviously, it got thrown away by mistake. See here, look. It's got lovely patterns carved on the neck. A sort of raspberryish design. Who knows what famous person might have played this? It may even have belonged to Wild Raspberry Johnson himself.'

'Who?'

'Surely you've heard of him? Wild Raspberry Johnson, the famous Wandering

Woodsman? Or Rasp, as we fans affectionately refer to him. He sort of rasps when he

sings. He's got a gravelly sort of voice. Shame he's not around any more.'

'He gone? Vhere he go?'

'Dunno. He's a Wandering Woodsman. Probably wandered off. He was good, though, in his day.'

'Ven zis singing Raspberry play guitar, 'e can do more zan *plink*?'

'Of course!' scoffed Pongwiffy. 'But then, so will I. I just need to get it fixed, that's all. I'll take it along to the Witchway Rhythm Boys – they'll do it. It'll cost me an arm and a leg, mind. But it'll be worth it. Then I have to learn to play. But that'll be easy, because I'm very musical.'

'You are?' Hugo sounded surprised.

'Oh yes,' boasted Pongwiffy. 'It's in the blood. What's with all the questions, anyway? Every time you speak, you ask a question. Why?'

'*A vise 'Amster alvays ask questions. Many a truth falls from ze most unlikely lips.*'

'Is that a quote from your stupid book?'

'Suppose it is?'

'Are you implying that my lips are unlikely?'

'Suppose I am?'

'Are you going to speak in questions for evermore?'

'Suppose I do?'

'I'm going in,' announced Pongwiffy, bored now. 'I can't be bothered to play silly games with you. I'm going to have a good look at my guitar.' She smiled down at her new treasure and gave it another little rub. 'You know, it's funny I should find this now. I was just saying to Sharky that all the good old ways of amusing ourselves have gone. Hey! We could build a porch on the hovel. Then I can sit out in my rocking chair on hot evenings, looking out over the Dump, with a glass of iced bogwater, playing my guitar. When I've learned, of course. But that shouldn't bother me, because I'm a natural . . .'

Chattering away, cradling the guitar in her arms, she marched back to the path, with Hugo trotting in her wake. He kept a firm grip on *The Little Book of Hamster Wit and Wisdom*. He had a feeling he was going to need it.

CHAPTER FIVE
Goblins in Cars

It was a Tuesday night, and the Gaggle of Goblins who lived in a cave on the foothills of the Lower Misty Mountains should have been out hunting. (Traditionally, they always hunt on a Tuesday. Traditionally, they never catch anything. They are probably the worst hunters in the entire world, but that doesn't stop them trying.)

However, on this particular Tuesday, most of them were laid up with a very nasty dose of the Squidgets. This is a malady common to Goblins, brought on by eating fermented nettle soup. Goblin digestive systems can handle nettle soup with no ill effects as long as it's fresh. But when it starts to ferment, that's when the problems start. Symptoms include embarrassing noises, headaches, runny noses and itchy ears. The only cure is to lie down and groan until it goes away.

Five of the seven Goblins in the Gaggle were afflicted: Stinkwart, Slopbucket, Hog, Eyesore and Lardo. Only Plugugly and young Sproggit were unaffected. This is because they were fighting each other at suppertime and didn't notice the others finishing up the soup until it was too late. Just as well. A black eye is nothing compared to the Squidgets.

So. Plugugly and Sproggit had gone off hunting as usual, leaving their stricken comrades moaning in the cave. They said they'd be gone all night, so everyone was quite surprised when they came rushing back after only an hour or so, bursting with exciting news.

'Whassup?' croaked Eyesore, squinting at the dazzling moonlight that streamed into the cave. 'Ooh, me head. Shut the boulder, I can't stand the glare.'

'Yeah,' agreed Slopbucket, clutching his bucket. 'We's sick, remember? You is s'posed to come in on tippy toes wiv a bunch o' grapes, not all this runnin' an' shoutin'. What's all the fuss about anyway?'

Groaning, the sickly Goblins struggled to a sitting position.

'We just seen sumfin' *good*,' burst out Plugugly.

'Was it a doctor?' asked Hog, scratching his ears like mad. 'A doctor in a white coat, wiv a stifflescope an' a big bottle o' anti-Squidget pills? That'd be good.'

'Nope,' said Plugugly. 'Better. Seen it wiv our own eyes, didn't we, Sproggit?'

'Yeah,' agreed Sproggit, nodding eagerly. 'Wiv our own eyes. Go on, Plug. Tell.'

'Well,' said Plugugly, drawing it out for dramatic effect. 'W-e-e-ll, me 'n' Sproggit was checkin' de traps down in de Wood . . .'

'. . . an' it was all quiet,' chipped in Sproggit.

'Yeah. It was. Nobody about. "Funny," I says to Sproggit.'

''E did,' Sproggit assured the company. 'That's just what 'e said.'

'"Funny," I says. An' we happens to be passin' dat ole Witch Macabre's cottage at de time, an' I says to Sproggit, "'Ere! What's dat funny blue light comin' out de winder?"'

'That's what 'e said,' corroborated Sproggit, nodding vigorously.

'Yeah,' continued Plugugly. 'So we tiptoes up to de winder, right, Sproggit?'

'Right. We tiptoes up. An' we looks in, an' we sees it.'

'Sees *what*?' came the united chorus. For the moment, the Goblins had forgotten their illness and were sitting up, all ears. They had been confined to a cave for the last week or so, remember. This was heady stuff.

'It were a Big Magic Box,' explained Plugugly. 'And dere was movin' pictures on it. And guess what de pictures was? *Goblins in Cars!*'

There was an electrified silence.

'What – *real* cars?' breathed Stinkwart, unable to believe his ears.

'Yep.'

'What – Goblins in *cars*?'

'Yep.'

'You mean – *real* cars wiv *Goblins* in 'em?'

'Yep. Dey was drivin' dem,' Plugugly elaborated. 'Dey was racin' dem round an' round. Dey went, *vroooooom! Vrooooom! Eeeeeeeeeek!*'

Plugugly raced his hand to and fro in the air, simulating as near as possible the sight and sound of the racing cars. Sproggit, wild with excitement, joined in. They smacked palms in mid-air, miming a crash.

'*Piaaaoooooow!*' they cried. '*Boom! Ouch!*'

'Sometimes dey crash,' added Plugugly, by way of explanation.

'They do,' affirmed Sproggit. 'It's great.'

The rest of the Gaggle sat struggling with this for a bit. Goblins are not quick on the uptake. It was too much information in one go. Their brains were overloading.

'So, this Box,' said Stinkwart after a bit. 'It's Magic, you say?'

'Must be,' said Plugugly. 'Movin' pictures, what else? An' you know what? Dey all got 'em. De Witches, de Trolls, de Skellingtons – everyone. Everywhere you goes, dey all got a Magic Box so dey can watch *Goblins in Cars*.'

''Cept us,' added Sproggit, sounding bitter.

'Who were the Goblins in the cars?' Eyesore wanted to know. 'Do we know 'em?'

'Yep,' said Plugugly crossly. 'We knows dem all right, an' we doesn't like dem. It's dat outlaw Gaggle up in de Misty Mountains. De ones wiv de levver jackets. De Grottys. Dey gatecrashed our cave warmin' dat time, remember? An' now dey is on de

Magic Box. You shoulda seen dem showin' off. Just 'cos dey got cars.'

There was a lot of teeth-gnashing and resentful thumping of fists into palms at this. (Goblins are very competitive. The Annual Inter-Gaggle Punch-Up is a highlight in the Goblin calendar. The Grottys win every time. It is a sore point.)

'Them Grottys!' growled Hog. 'Wiv their cars an' – an' their jackets! Grrr!'

'Think they're tough!' sneered Lardo.

'They *are* tough,' Slopbucket reminded him. 'They won the Punch-Up Cup three years runnin'.'

'Sixty-five years runnin', weren't it?' disputed Eyesore.

'Three, six, seventy-nine, who cares?' said Slopbucket carelessly. 'We can't count anyway.' Which was true.

'Since when 'ave they 'ad cars?' asked Hog, sick with jealousy. 'Last time I heard, they only 'ad one little old rusty tricycle between 'em. 'Ow come they got cars now?'

''S not fair! 'S not fair!' shouted Lardo, and the others joined in as soon as they got the hang of the words.

'Know wot?' said Plugugly suddenly. 'I fink I feel an idear comin' on.'

The chanting trailed off into a respectful silence.

All eyes were on Plugugly. Goblins rarely got ideas.

'I bet I know what it is!' Sproggit said, nearly exploding with excitement. 'I bet you're gonna say *we* oughter get one o' them Magic Boxes an' bring it back up 'ere to the cave an', an', an', *watch* it every night, like everyone else. Am I right?'

'No,' said Plugugly, to everyone's surprise. 'Dat's not it. What do we want an ole Magic Box for? We dunno where to get one an', anyway, we ain't got no money so we'd 'ave to steal it. An' den dey'd find out we done it and take it away again. An' even if we did manage to keep it, knowin' our luck, somefin' 'd go wrong. We'd drop it or break it or de Magic'd turn on us or somefin'. We'd best steer clear o' Magic Boxes. Dey ain't a Goblin Fing.'

Actually, this was rather wise of Plugugly. Goblins and Magic are like bacon and chocolate sauce. They just don't go together.

'So what's the idea then?' asked Stinkwart. 'What *do* we want?'

'I'll tell you what we wants,' said Plugugly slowly, importantly, aware that all eyes were on him. 'We Wants A Car.'

CHAPTER SIX
Obsession

Pongwiffy sat in her rocking chair, practising her guitar. The Witchway Rhythm Boys had done a good job (at a very steep price!). They had replaced the strings and fixed the neck. All the pegs were present and correct. It had been glued and waxed and buffed. Even Hugo had to admit it looked good.

Pongwiffy loved it with a passion. She carried it everywhere. She slept with it. She even *cleaned* it. Apart from eating, it was her favourite occupation.

She had moved on from *plink*ing. Her new method of playing now consisted of sweeping her hand across the open strings, producing a horrible discord that clashed with itself, let alone whatever she happened to be singing.

Well, singing is a kind term. Pongwiffy's voice was a sort of tuneless honk that careered off on its own sweet way, regardless of melody, rhythm or anything at all, really.

The worst of it was, she thought she was good.

> *'One Witch went to woo,'*

honked Pongwiffy, strumming her discord.

> *'Went to woo a Wizard,*
> *One Witch and her Wand*
> *Went to woo a –*

'AND WHERE HAVE THE PAIR OF YOU BEEN, MAY I ASK?'

Hugo and the Broom were standing in the doorway, attempting to sneak in without being noticed.

Pongwiffy carefully placed the guitar on the kitchen table, currently strewn with scribbled-on bits of paper (lyrics for her songs), stood up and looked stern. The Broom drooped and made abject little circles on the floor with its bristles. Hugo stood his ground.

'*Well?*'

'Novhere,' said Hugo shortly.

Things hadn't been too good between the three of them recently. Hugo and the Broom were getting very tired of Pongwiffy's new hobby. Hour after hour, night after night, she sat crooning away, asking what they thought and forcing them to join in the chorus. Her obsession was becoming more than they could bear, which is why they had accepted an invitation from Vernon, Ratsnappy's rat Familiar, to go round and watch *Familiar Fortunes*, the new game show everyone was talking about.

'Yes you have. The two of you have been watching spellovision round at Ratsnappy's, haven't you? Don't tell me fibs because I know. I heard Vernon invite you when he thought I wasn't listening.'

'OK. Is true,' admitted Hugo, with a shrug. 'Ve go out to get avay from ze *plink*ink. Vot else ve supposed to do? I not even got nussink to read since you hide my book.'

'I didn't hide your book, *actually*,' said Pongwiffy. This was true. She hadn't. She had thrown it away.

240

Hurled it far into the rubbish dump when Hugo wasn't looking.

'Anyway,' she continued, 'anyway, I don't *plink* any more! I haven't *plink*ed for days. That just shows how much interest you take. I've been experimenting with my technique and I sort of hit the strings now. I call it thrumming. Like this.'

She snatched up the guitar and demonstrated.

Thrummm!

'*Plink, thrummm*, votever, is horrible,' said Hugo. 'You not *fun* any more. Togezzer, ve used to make good Magic. Now you make bad music. I bored, I go out.'

'Well, you shouldn't!' scolded Pongwiffy. 'You're my Familiar. Your job is to help me in *all* my undertakings. *All*. That means listen to me practise. Tell me how good I am. Give me support and encouragement in my new career. You!' She turned to the Broom, which was dithering uncertainly in the background. 'Get in the cupboard. You're grounded.'

'Vot new career?' asked Hugo. A little wrinkle of anxiety crossed his furry brow.

'My new career as a singer-songwriter. I should have done it years ago. My old mum used to say I sang like

241

a lark. Or was it a shark? Do sharks sing? Does it tell you that in your *Little Book of Wisdom*? Hmm?'

'How I know? You hide it.'

'No I *didn't*, I tell you. Although you couldn't blame me if I had, because, let's face it, you've been neglecting your duties recently. Of course –' she paused, considering – 'of course, I won't need a Familiar any more if I swap Magic for music.' She stared at Hugo for a long moment, then gave a snort of laughter. 'Oh, take that daft look off, I'm only kidding. I've missed you actually. Put the kettle on and make us both a nice cup of bogwater. I'll sing you my latest song. It's about you – listen.

> *'My Hamster lies over the ocean,*
> *He left on a silly wee raft,*
> *Forgetting to take any paddles,*
> *Which just goes to show that he's –'*

'Votch it,' warned Hugo. But he grinned a bit. He hopped on to the draining board and began busying himself with kettle and teacups.

'So. What's it like out in the Wood tonight?' asked Pongwiffy.

'Quiet. Everysink cancelled due to lack of interest.'

'It's getting worse,' observed Pongwiffy grimly. 'Everybody's spellovision mad. Obsessed, that's what they are. Know what obsession is, Hugo? It's when people can't stop talking about one thing to the point where they become utterly boring. Now, shut up and listen to this. It's a song about my cauldron.

> 'You are my cauldron, my rusty cauldron,
> You cook my dinner, it tastes OK.
> The bits of rust-o I eat with gusto,
> Please don't take my cauldron away . . .'

Sharkadder was passing by, hurrying to get back to the evening spellovision feast. If Pongwiffy was obsessed with her guitar, Sharkadder was utterly addicted to spellovision. She simply couldn't drag herself away from it. The only reason she was out now was because her cupboards were bare. She had finally run out of absolutely *everything* and was forced to go shopping for the first time in ages. She was doing it on her own too. Dudley was laid up with a bad back and her Broom claimed bristle rash, although really they were both perfectly well and just wanted to stay at home and watch *Familiar Fortunes*.

So. There was poor Sharkadder, struggling under

the weight of four enormous shopping bags, three of which consisted entirely of tins of cat food. The handles were cutting into her fingers. She was wearing brand new spike-heeled boots with pointy toes and her feet were killing her. Every few steps, she had to stop and put everything down. To make it all a thousand times worse, each dwelling she passed had spellovision on.

Several times she had been tempted to knock and ask if she could come in and watch, but, desperate though she was for spello, she was even more desperate for a cup of bogwater and knew that nobody would offer her one. Hospitality was at an all-time low since the advent of spellovision. Nobody could be bothered to leave the sofa.

It was during one of her rests that she heard the sound of distant honking coming through the trees.

'Oh, the grand old Witch of Rhodes,
She had ten thousand toads,
I said, please will you give me some?
I notice you have loads.
That Witch, she said to me,
"Those toads do not come free,
Go catch your own, you lazy crone!"

244

Fa lala lala lee . . . Come on, you two,
join in the chorus!
Oh, fa lala lala leee . . .'

It was horrible, horrible singing, but it was music to
Sharkadder's ears.

'Ah,' said Sharkadder. 'Of course! Pong'll be pleased
to see me.'

And she limped off in the direction of Number
One, Dump Edge.

Hugo opened the door.

'*Fa lala lala leeee . . .'* Pongwiffy was warbling
cheerfully in the background.

'Oh,' said Hugo. 'It you. You got zat bad old cat viz you?'

'No,' said Sharkadder humbly. 'Dudley's home
watching spellovision. I was just passing, and I was
wondering if Pong was busy.'

'Ya. She sink.'

The background honking broke off.

'Who is it, Hugo?' called Pongwiffy.

'Vitch Sharkadder. Viz lot of shoppink.'

'Really? Sharky? Oh *good*!'

Pongwiffy appeared in the doorway, guitar in hand
and best welcoming smile on her face.

245

'Hello, Pong,' said Sharkadder slightly guiltily. It was the first time she had seen Pongwiffy since their row. 'Can I come in for a minute and rest my feet? It's these new boots. My toes feel like they've been sharpened.'

'Come in?' cried Pongwiffy heartily. 'Of course you can come in. Old pal, old mate, old buddy.'

'Really? I thought you weren't speaking, after the words we had about You Know What.'

'Oh, pooh! Long forgotten. Hugo, get out another cup – we've got a visitor.' Pongwiffy peered down hopefully at Sharkadder's bags. 'Is there cake in any of those bags? By any chance?'

'Yes, there is. A chocolate one, which I'm saving for –'

'Good,' interrupted Pongwiffy approvingly. 'Plates, Hugo! Any biscuits?'

'Well, yes, some jammy ones I'm planning to have tomo—'

'We'll have them too. Hugo'll do it. Come on, I'll play you my guitar.' She led the way into the squalid hovel.

'I noticed the guitar,' observed Sharkadder, following behind with the bags. 'Is it new? You never mentioned you played.'

'Didn't I? Oh yes,' said Pongwiffy carelessly. 'I'm

rather good actually. Not quite in Wild Raspberry's class yet, but then, we have different styles.'

She began rummaging in Sharkadder's shopping, sorting out the things she liked.

'Er ... Wild Raspberry?' enquired Sharkadder, puzzled.

'Yes. I take it you're not a fan.'

'I prefer gooseberries myself,' said Sharkadder, confused. 'Especially in a flan.'

'Ah!' Pongwiffy emerged with a cake box and waved it triumphantly. 'Here we are – Hugo, get slicing. Sit down, Sharky, and I'll play you the song I wrote about you.'

'About me?' said Sharkadder, surprised and flattered. She sank gratefully into the nearest chair. 'Really? You've written a song about *me*?'

'Oh yes. It's one of my better efforts. I call it "Nose Song".'

Pongwiffy threw herself into her rocking chair, played her horrible discord – *thrummmmmm!* – took a deep breath and burst into song.

'Of all the witches in the Wood,
There's none like good old Sharky.
She wears a lot of lipstick

In unusual shades of khaki.
I love her very dearly
And I'm glad I have a friend
With a nose so long and pointy
That you cannot see the end.
Poi-nty!
Poi-nty!
Her nose is long and pointy
And you cannot see the end.'

Thrummmmmm!

'Why, thank you, Pong,' said Sharkadder. 'Nobody's written a song about me before. I'm really touched.' She scrabbled in her handbag for a hanky and dabbed at her eyes.

'You see?' said Pongwiffy. 'I look around me and observe interesting things like people's noses, then compose songs about them. I wouldn't have written that if I'd been watching spello, would I?'

'You're right,' agreed Sharkadder humbly. 'You wouldn't. I'm terribly grateful, Pong.'

'So you liked it.'

'I loved it. Lovely words. Very – rhymey.'

'Lyrics. They're called lyrics, because they're set to music.'

'Oh, right. How does the tune go? Will you sing it to me again?'

Pongwiffy obliged. Then they had tea and cake while Hugo wrote the lyrics out neatly because Sharkadder wanted a copy to take home. Then Pongwiffy sang it a few more times, and Sharkadder joined in, in a shrill, wobbly soprano. Then they demanded more tea and cake, followed by biscuits. Then they talked about writing a second verse and called for more paper and ink.

That was when Hugo went to bed.

Much, much later, Dudley and the Broom were surprised when the door burst open and Sharkadder came flying in, scrabbled around in a drawer and emerged with an ancient harmonica before rushing out again, slamming the door behind her.

Well, they were surprised for half a minute. But it took no time at all before they settled back to watching spellovision.

CHAPTER SEVEN
Gossip

Malpractiss Magic Ltd is a wandering shop that comes and goes as it pleases. This can be a bit inconvenient sometimes. However, you can usually catch it between the hours of midnight and dawn by the stream under the old oak tree. Some nights you might have to wait a bit while Dunfer Malpractiss, the owner, finishes serving the last customer in another dimension. But he and his shop generally turn up. He has a lot of regular customers in Witchway Wood.

This particular night – Friday – he was late, and a

queue was forming by the patch of empty space where the shop currently wasn't.

At the front was a female Skeleton with a blonde wig and a net shopping bag. She was avidly reading the latest article in *The Daily Miracle* about Sheridan Haggard (his favourite brand of soap and where he bought his bow ties).

Behind the Skeleton stood two large Trolls. They were discussing the latest programme to appear on their screens – a DIY show with a Troll slant entitled *Changing Bridges*. Both agreed it was much better than *Zombie Decorating*, which was getting a bit samey.

Behind *them* was a group of Witches: Bendyshanks, Ratsnappy and Scrofula. Guess what they were talking about? Right.

'It's undemanding, that's what I like about *Gnome and Away*,' Witch Bendyshanks was saying. 'No plot to speak of. All the characters are the same. Restful viewing, that's what it is. Like floating in warm treacle.'

'You can have too much treacle, though, can't you?' mused Witch Ratsnappy. 'I like the adverts myself. Better plots.'

'That's true,' nodded Scrofula. 'Although Barry and

I like *Fiends*. And *The News*, with Sheridan Haggard, of course.'

'Oh yes,' agreed Bendyshanks and Ratsnappy. 'That goes without saying.'

'Such a lovely voice, hasn't he?' sighed Bendyshanks. 'I could listen to him all night.'

All three Witches had run out of things that you can munch in the dark on a sofa, and had come out to stock up. Unlike Sharkadder, who spoiled Dudley dreadfully, they had brought their Familiars along to help carry the bags – Bendyshanks's Snake (Slithering Steve), Ratsnappy's Rat (Vernon) and Scrofula's bald Vulture, Barry. They too were talking about spellovision.

'Did you see *Familiar Fortunes* last night?' Vernon was asking.

'Too right I did,' said Slithering Steve. 'What's with that Toad family? Talk about thick.'

'Where do they find 'em, eh?' agreed Barry, adding wistfully, 'I wonder how you appear on it?'

'That'd be something, wouldn't it?' sighed Steve. 'To be on spellovision.'

'That'd be something, all right,' nodded Vernon. 'We'd be famous then, eh?'

They laughed.

Just at that moment, the air gave a wobble and the Magic Shop appeared. It was rather like a caravan with a big cutaway section at the front where Dunfer served his customers. The blind shot up and there was the man himself, sucking on his moustache and leering unpleasantly over the till. The blonde Skeleton folded her paper, took out a shopping list and began pointing to various items on the shelves. The queue shuffled forward a fraction.

'I wish she'd hurry up,' said Bendyshanks. 'I want to get home. That weather girl, Brenda, said it might rain. Mind you, she always says that.'

'At least we're not missing anything good,' remarked Ratsnappy. '*Goblins in Cars*, that's all.'

'We don't like *Goblins in Cars*,' chorused two more voices. Agglebag and Bagaggle, the twin Witches, had joined the end of the queue.

'Me neither,' agreed Bendyshanks, Ratsnappy and Scrofula. 'Loada rubbish.'

(Witches and Goblins don't get on. *Goblins in Cars* was the one programme the Witches didn't bother watching, apart from Macabre, who had a violent streak, and Sharkadder, who would watch anything.)

'Here,' said Ratsnappy. 'Has anyone seen Pongwiffy lately?'

'*I* heard she's come over all musical. Learning the guitar, I heard,' said Scrofula.

'Really?' said Bagaggle with a little frown. 'Did you hear that, Ag?'

'I did, Bag,' said Agglebag. 'I bet she's not as good as us.'

'Fat chance, Ag,' said Bagaggle. The twins played violins and mistakenly considered themselves very good at it.

'Sharkadder's been going round there most evenings, I heard,' contributed Scrofula.

'I thought they weren't speaking,' said Ratsnappy.

'Oh, they're all friends again now, apparently. Sharkadder's taken up the mouth organ. They're writing songs together.'

'Fancy,' said Ratsnappy. 'Seems a funny thing to do when you could be watching spello. Although I must say it's ages since I practised my recorder ...'

In Number One, Dump Edge, Pongwiffy and Sharkadder were practising their new song. It was called 'What Shall We Do with a Rude Familiar?' and was intended to have a rollicking, seafaring sort of feel.

'Poke 'em in the dark with a sharpened chair leg
Early in the morning!'

they carolled merrily. Pongwiffy played her discord again, several times. Sharkadder sucked and blew her mouth organ, producing a series of wheezy chords. Then they both sat back and smiled at each other happily.

'That's three songs we've co-written,' said Sharkadder. 'Three whole songs and we've only been at it for three days and nights. We're getting good, aren't we?'

'Good?' cried Pongwiffy. 'We're better than *good*. We're staggeringly, amazingly brilliant. Of course, I was writing good stuff *before* you started coming round, but I must say we make a good team. It's fun doing things together again, isn't it?'

'It is,' agreed Sharkadder. 'I'd forgotten.'

'Better than watching spellovision. Go on, admit it.'

'I do,' said Sharkadder. 'You're absolutely right, Pong. There's nothing like old-fashioned, home-grown entertainment. Can we sing "Nose Song" again? It's still my favourite. And can I do another mouth organ solo between verses?'

'By all means,' said Pongwiffy graciously. 'After three. One, two, three.

255

'Of all the Witches in the wood –'

But just at that point, there came a knock on the door. This time, there was no Hugo to answer it. Rather tiresomely, he had gone missing again for the third night running. So had the Broom.

'Oh, bother!' cried Pongwiffy, jumping to her feet. 'Who can that be? Hold that note, Sharky, I'll be right back.'

It was Ratsnappy, standing on the doorstep, holding a recorder in one hand and a large paper bag in the other.

'Hello, Pongwiffy,' she said. 'Can I come in? I just happened to be passing by with my recorder and this bag of delicious doughnuts.'

'I see,' said Pongwiffy, folding her arms. 'Nothing on spellovision?'

'Well – to be honest, I've been getting a bit bored with spello lately. I fancy a change. I heard you and Sharkadder were having musical evenings and I was hoping you might let me join in.' She held up the bag. 'They're *jammy* doughnuts.'

'Ah.' Pongwiffy loved jammy doughnuts. 'Funnily enough, I was thinking that the one instrument lacking was a recorder. In you come, Ratsnappy. Make yourself at home. Sharky! We're a trio!'

They had hardly got settled when there came another knock on the door. This time it was the twins, armed with their violins and two more paper bags. It was common knowledge that the way to Pongwiffy's heart was through her tummy.

'Bag and I have come for the musical evening,' announced Agglebag.

'We've brought our violins,' added Bagaggle.

'Hmm,' said Pongwiffy. 'What's in the bags?'

'Toffees,' chorused the twins.

'In you come,' said Pongwiffy.

And that was only the beginning . . .

CHAPTER EIGHT
Plans

Witch Macabre and her Familiar, a Haggis called Rory, sat slumped on the tartan sofa, eyes glued to the screen. *Goblins in Cars* was on. A number of old, beat-up vehicles were screeching around a dusty racetrack, backfiring and shedding various bits – wing mirrors, bumpers, doors, exhaust pipes, wheels and so on – as they took the corners at ludicrously high speeds.

Each car was driven by a demented Grotty who didn't care about anything except going *fast*. Forget danger, rules, pain, all that stuff. Speed was the thing.

The race didn't appear to have a start, a finish, or any rules whatsoever. Engines regularly burst into flames. Every so often one of the drivers would take it into his head to screech to a halt, turn round and go the other way.

There were a *lot* of crashes. Not enough for Macabre, though.

'Aye!' bawled Macabre. 'That's it! Put yer sissy foot doon, Number Five! Aim for Number Three! Go on, go on! Faster, faster, bit left, straighten up, ye fool – och, blast! Missed. See that, Rory?'

'Aye,' scoffed Rory. 'Flippin' amateurs. Pass us a shortbread. Or have ye eaten them all?'

'Aye,' confessed Macabre. 'Ah think Ah might have at that.'

'Your turn to go to the cupboard,' said Rory.

'Ach, nooo!' wailed Macabre. 'That means Ah'll havtay *mooooove*!'

The sofa was away from the window, so neither of them noticed that they were not alone. Outside in the chilly night, who should be crouching in Macabre's toadstool patch, noses propped on the window sill, jaws dropped, eyes on stalks, goggling at the amazing Magic Box, but – the Goblins! They were over the Squidgets and had come to see for themselves whether

259

or not Plugugly and Sproggit had been exaggerating about *Goblins in Cars*.

'See what I mean?' whispered Plugugly. 'Ain't it just – just de *best* fing you ever sawed?'

'Yeah,' breathed Hog, Lardo, Eyesore, Stinkwart and Slopbucket. Their boggling eyes were riveted on the flickering screen.

'Told ya, didn't we?' squeaked Sproggit. 'It's just like what we said, ain't it? About the Magic Box an' everyfin' – oof!'

He broke off as Slopbucket smacked a hand over his mouth.

From inside the room, there came a sudden noise like a miniature hailstorm. Macabre had stood up and was emptying her lap of the evening's biscuit crumbs. As she did so, there came a strange, muffled cry from outside and a sort of urgent, disturbed, flapping noise, but when she moved to the window to investigate, there was nothing to be seen. She put it down to a night bird, drew the curtains and hurried to the kitchen on a quest for more shortbread.

Some time later, the Goblins arrived back at their cave. Plugugly heaved the boulder shut behind them. Then, quietly, with none of their usual fuss or argy-bargy, they all sat down in a circle.

They hadn't uttered a single word all the way home. Not one. Not even 'ouch' when they walked into trees. It was as though they were in a trance. They didn't argue or push or anything. Each was lost in his own thoughts. Well, thought. There was only room for the one thought, because it was such a big, overwhelming one. The thought was this:

CAR. WANT ONE.

Plugugly broke the silence.

'So now you know,' he said.

The Goblins nodded.

'Goblins in cars, just like we said,' added Sproggit.

More nods, and some drooling.

'C-a-a-r,' whispered Eyesore, drawing the word out slowly as though testing the feel of it in his mouth.

'*Vroom, vroom*,' agreed Slopbucket faintly.

'Eepy, beep,' added Lardo dreamily, hands stretched before him, turning an imaginary steering wheel.

'Eeeaaaaaaaaaw – *bang*!' contributed Hog, eyes closed as he relived one of the more spectacular crashes.

'C-a-a-a-r,' drooled Eyesore again. 'Want c-a-a-a-r.'

'Yes,' said Plugugly. 'We know dat, Eyesore. De fing *is*, 'ow is we going to get one? Dat's what we got to fink about.'

'C-a-a-a-r. C-a-a-a-a-r. C-a-a-a-a-r,' droned Eyesore, rocking to and fro.

'He's got stuck in a groove. Someone sit on 'is 'ead,' said young Sproggit.

Lardo obliged, and Eyesore's unhelpful contributions to the discussion became blissfully muffled.

'Come on,' said Plugugly. 'Fink. 'Ow do people get cars?'

'Buy 'em from a car shop?' suggested Hog.

'No car shops round 'ere,' said Plugugly. 'Besides, we 'asn't got no money.'

'Let's nick one,' suggested Lardo. Loud snores came from beneath his posterior. Eyesore was asleep.

'Oh yeah,' said Plugugly. 'An' what 'appens when dey find it gone? Den what?'

Blank faces all round.

'Dey'll come lookin' for *clues*, won't dey?' continued Plugugly, on a roll now. '*Clues* what will show who dunnit. An' straight away, dey'll see a dirty great big one.'

'What?' everyone asked.

'Us drivin' round in it. No point in 'avin' a car you can't drive round in.'

'Oh yeah,' said everyone, seeing the light. 'Right.'

'Seems like every plan we come up with 'as got a fatal flaw,' sighed Slopbucket. 'Can't buy one, can't steal one. I dunno.'

'P'raps someone'll give us one for a present,' said Hog.

'Who?' came the chorus.

'Santa?'

'Nah. Won't fit in the stockin',' Stinkwart pointed out.

'All right, the Tooth Fairy, then.'

'She only leaves *pennies*, stupid,' jeered Slopbucket. 'Since when 'as the Tooth Fairy left a car under yer piller? Stupid, you are.'

'Say that again,' said Hog crossly, 'an' I'll punch you really 'ard an' knock all yer teeth out and you can put 'em all under the piller an' maybe we'll get enough to buy a car after all.'

'Oh yeah?'

'Yeah!'

'Quiet, or I'll knock yer 'eads togevver,' threatened Lardo.

'Oh yeah?' (Slopbucket and Hog)

'Yeah!' (Lardo)

263

'Dere's only one fing we can do,' said Plugugly slowly, away in his own world, not even listening. 'It'll be hard, mind. But if we all work as a team, we might jus' pull it off.'

'Yeah?' said everyone. 'What?'

'We'll make one,' said Plugugly.

CHAPTER NINE
They're playing Music!

'Beg pardon, Snoop? They're doing what?' bellowed Grandwitch Sourmuddle. She was watching *Fiends* on spellovision. The volume was up full because she was a bit deaf.

'Playing music in Witchway Hall, Mistress. And singing,' bawled Snoop.

Snoop was Sourmuddle's Demon Familiar. He was small and red, with horns. Right now, he was toasting currant buns over the fire, using the prongs on his pitchfork. Sourmuddle hadn't bothered to go out for her meals for some time. In fact, she didn't even go into the kitchen. These days, she was rooted in the parlour, where she could adjust the volume to ear-splittingly loud and eat buns. (Buns, she had discovered, were ideal spello food, being too big to lose down the side of the sofa and more filling than peanuts.)

'What?' howled Sourmuddle. 'Speak up! They're doing *what*?'

Snoop reached out and turned the volume down.

'Singing. If that's what you call it. More like a cat's concert, if you ask me.'

'What d'you mean, singing? Who said they could sing?'

'No one, I reckon,' said Snoop, with a shrug. 'Why? Do you need permission to sing?'

'Most certainly, if you do it in Witchway Hall,' said Sourmuddle firmly. 'Everything that goes on in there needs my permission. If you want to *breathe* in there, you need my permission. Who was there?'

'I don't know. I didn't stop to count. I was just passing. On my way home with the buns.'

'Well, you should have checked,' scolded Sourmuddle, wagging her finger. 'Whoever was there is breaking the rules. All bookings are supposed to go through me. Fetch the Bookings Book. I need to look into this.'

It took a while for Snoop to come up with the Bookings Book. Both he and Sourmuddle had become rather lax with the housework lately. Somehow, there never seemed to be a long enough gap between programmes to deal with it. Newspapers, magazines and mail just got dumped on the kitchen table, along with dirty coffee cups and screwed-up bun bags.

'You need to clear this place up a bit,' grumbled Sourmuddle from the sofa. 'I've just noticed what a tip it is. Come on, where's that book?'

'I'm looking, I'm looking, all right?'

Finally, he found it in the bread bin of all places. He handed it to Sourmuddle with bad grace, then threw himself on to the sofa and settled down to *Fiends*.

Sourmuddle brushed off the crumbs, flipped the book open and ran a finger down the page. 'Nope. Just as I thought. Nothing down for tonight. Turn the spellovision off, Snoop.'

'Huh?'

'Turn it off.'

'*Huh?*'

'The spello. Turn it off.'

'Turn it *off*?'

'That's right.'

'But we never turn it off.'

267

'Tonight, we do.'

'But *Familiar Fortunes* is on next.'

'You've seen it – it's a repeat. Turn it off, we're going out.'

'Out? Out where?' said Snoop, confused. Going out was a thing of the past, unless you were on the bun run.

'Where d'you think? To Witchway Hall. If there's illegal singing going on, I want to know *A*, why it hasn't been registered in the Bookings Book in a proper manner and *B*, why I haven't been invited. Now, where's my hat?'

Pongwiffy's musical evenings had proved unexpectedly popular – so much so that it was no longer possible to fit everyone into Number One, Dump Edge, which was a very *small* hovel and not really geared up for visitors. Every night for the past week, more and more wannabe band members had turned up on the doorstep, keen as mustard, waving bags of confectionery and begging to be let in. Musical evenings at Pongwiffy's were becoming the new In Thing.

'I'm sorry, you can't come in,' Pongwiffy would explain airily on the doorstep to the latest supplicant. 'I'm running out of space. Besides, we've got enough singers. I'm restricting it to people who can play an instrument.'

'But I *can!*' the eager Witch would cry. 'Look! I've brought my castanets/triangle spoons/comb and paper/bagpipes/Panamanian hip flute! And a bag of sherbet lemons. Oh, please!'

In the end, Pongwiffy always relented. She was a Witch of Dirty Habits who didn't get many visitors. It was a novelty, having all these people coming round with food bribes, begging to be let in the hovel instead of weeping to be let out.

'Oh, all right then,' she would say, rolling her eyes to heaven. 'If you *must.*' But she could never resist adding with a sarcastic little smirk, 'Although I thought you'd rather be at home *watching spellovision.*'

To which the sheepish visitor would generally respond with, 'Oh no! I wouldn't, really I wouldn't. I'd much sooner be here. I saw Sharkadder/Sludgegooey/ the twins yesterday and they said it's fun. Oh, *please* let me in. I've brought a trifle . . .'

Finally, when the number of band members swelled to twelve, it became clear that Pongwiffy's place really was too small. Nobody seemed to be using Witchway Hall these days, so it made sense to gather there.

Right now, they were in the middle of rehearsing a

new song. Eleven chairs were arranged in a semicircle facing the twelfth, on which sat Pongwiffy, loudly strumming her all-purpose discord. Attempting to play along with varying degrees of success were: Agglebag and Bagaggle (violins); Ratsnappy (recorder); Bendyshanks (castanets); Scrofula (cowbell); Sludgegooey (comb and paper); Sharkadder (harmonica); Bonidle (triangle); Gaga (spoons); Greymatter (tambourine) and last and most certainly not least, Macabre on bagpipes.

The rehearsal was a bit of a shambles. Nobody seemed to know quite where they were in the new piece. It had been written jointly by Pongwiffy and Sharkadder and was entitled 'Witchway Stomp'. It featured a long harmonica solo and Pongwiffy's discord, played quite fast.

Ratsnappy, who could only play if she had the music, had lost her score and was crawling about on the floor, searching. Sharkadder had stopped playing owing to a serious lipstick build-up in the holes of her harmonica. Sludgegooey's comb-and-paper combination was giving her trouble (disintegrated paper, toothless comb). The twins appeared to be playing a different piece altogether, although none of that mattered because Macabre's bagpipes drowned everything else out anyway.

270

The rhythm section was totally out of control. Gaga was sitting directly behind Scrofula and kept clonking her on the head with a spoon. Scrofula was hitting back with her cowbell. Bendyshanks hadn't quite got the hang of her castanets, but she was a queen of rhythm compared to Greymatter on the tambourine.

'Hang on, hang on!' Pongwiffy shouted over the cacophony. 'Stop! This isn't working. Sharky, what's happened to your harmonica? I can't even hear you.'

'Sorry,' called Sharkadder, poking around with a hairgrip. 'Lipstick stopped play. I'm just digging it out.'

'Well, hurry up. How can we keep in time if people keep dropping out just when they feel like it? Gaga, keep your spoons to yourself. Greymatter, please don't sing. You've got a voice like a toad with indigestion. Macabre, not so loud – it's giving us all headaches. Right, everybody, let's start again. Is anybody listening to me? Right. From the top. One, two – *oooooooer*!'

There was a bang, a green flash, and a very disgruntled-looking Sourmuddle appeared in their midst, holding a smoking Wand. Snoop materialised at her side, clutching the Bookings Book. Green smoke drifted around the stage, causing a lot of coughing.

'And what's all this about?' demanded Sourmuddle. 'Of course, I know I'm only *Grandwitch*, nobody *important*, but maybe *somebody* might inform me as to exactly what's going on?'

'We're having a musical evening, Grandwitch,' explained Greymatter. 'Pongwiffy started it.'

'I see,' said Sourmuddle frostily. 'And why, may I ask, is it not entered into the Bookings Book?'

'We didn't think it was necessary,' admitted Pongwiffy. 'I mean, nobody's using the Hall these days, are they? All that space going begging. We thought we'd use it, that's all.'

'*We* did, did *we*?' snarled Sourmuddle. 'Funny how *we* never got round to mentioning these musical evenings to *me*.'

There was a guilty silence. It was true. Nobody had thought to mention the nightly gatherings to Sourmuddle.

'We hadn't seen you, that's all,' Pongwiffy hastened to explain. 'You're always cooped up indoors watching spello. We weren't trying to keep you out on purpose.'

'I should think not,' said Sourmuddle. Adding, 'Especially as I'm such a talented pianist.'

'You are?'

273

'Oh yes. Of course, I haven't played for years, but it's like riding a Broom. You never forget.'

And to everyone's astonishment, Sourmuddle climbed down into the orchestra pit, where the old piano had its permanent home. She whisked off the dust sheet, sat on the stool, opened the lid, cracked her knuckles, paused for a moment with her fingers suspended over the keyboard and her eyes closed – then lowered her hands and played.

She had a slapdash, who-cares-about-the-odd-wrong-note sort of style – but that didn't matter, because the tunes she played were jolly, romping, tinkley-tonkley ones, the sort that people sing standing on tables whilst hilariously showing their knickers. For the next ten minutes, the admiring Witches crowded round and tapped their feet. When she finally played the last, triumphant chord and smashed the piano lid down, everyone burst into spontaneous applause.

'Wow!' gasped Pongwiffy. 'That was *good*, Sourmuddle. And I'm talking as one musician to another. You can really tickle those ivories, can't she, girls?'

The assembled company couldn't have agreed more.

'And there was me thinking *I* was good,' said Pongwiffy.

'Were ye?' said Macabre rather unkindly. 'Nobody else was. Ye're rubbish, actually. Hands up who thinks Sourmuddle should be bandleader from now on?'

Everyone's hand shot up, apart from Pongwiffy's. Even Sharkadder's.

'Well, thanks very much,' said Sourmuddle briskly. 'A very wise decision. I'm sure I'll live up to the confidence you have placed in me.'

'Hey, hang on!' complained Pongwiffy, hurt. 'Whose idea was it, having musical evenings, in the first place?'

'Too bad. I'm Grandwitch and what I say goes. Right. Everyone bring your chairs down here and regroup round the piano. I'm taking over.'

'Don't take it to heart, Pong,' whispered Sharkadder. 'I think you're wonderful.'

'So why vote for Sourmuddle, then?'

'Well, I don't want to get into her bad books, do I? And neither do you. Look at it this way. If you don't have to be leader and worry about what everyone else is doing, you can concentrate on playing your discord, can't you? And we can still write our songs together.'

Pongwiffy thought about this. Actually, if the truth be known, she was quite relieved that Sourmuddle was taking over. Under her own control, things had been a bit . . . well, chaotic, really.

275

'All right,' she conceded. 'Sourmuddle can be leader, I suppose. But I'm still chief songwriter. And I just hope nobody forgets that this was my idea in the first place.'

'What are you talking about?' enquired Ratsnappy, as they moved their chairs round the piano.

'The fact that the musical evenings were my idea,' explained Pongwiffy.

'Were they? I'd forgotten.'

By the end of the evening, though, Pongwiffy had to admit that things were improving under the musical leadership of Sourmuddle. Sourmuddle had a good, solid left hand that maintained a steady beat. People didn't get so mixed up. Also, they behaved better. Gaga stopped playing Scrofula's head with her spoons. Scrofula kept her cowbell to herself. When Sourmuddle said to play a solo, solos got played. When people were told to sing up during the chorus, they sang up. To everyone's relief, Sourmuddle took Greymatter's tambourine away and sent her into a corner with instructions to write poetry.

They ended the evening with a vigorous, almost recognisable rendition of that old favourite, 'When the Stoats Go Marching In'.

'Hey!' shouted Pongwiffy, all cheerful again. 'We're

getting good. You know what? They ought to put *us* on the spello! We're a bloomin' sight better than most of the tripe they have on.'

Instant silence. You could have heard a pin drop. Everyone was thinking – hard. Finally, Sourmuddle spoke.

'Pongwiffy,' she said slowly. 'I don't often go along with your ideas, which, quite frankly, are usually bonkers. But this time, I think you just might have something ...'

CHAPTER TEN
An Important meeting

At Spellovision Centre, in a grand boardroom full of polished wood and potted plants, an important meeting was taking place. The head of the studio, a portly Genie by the name of Ali Pali, was addressing his team, which consisted of five members: the Star, the Cameraman, the Soundman, the newly appointed Head of Glamour and the Everything Else Boy, who was currently in charge of the tea trolley.

Clearly, the Studio Head wasn't best pleased. He sat at the top end of a long table, arms folded, scowling beneath his turban. Beside him was a flipchart, showing a graph with a steeply descending line. Before him was a pad, a feathered pen and inkpot, and several sharpened pencils.

'. . . and so, as you can see, the ratings continue to slide,' he was saying, in tones of deepest gloom. 'Not good. Not good at all. In fact, worse than not good.'

'That'd be bad, then,' said the Head of Glamour, who was none other than Brenda the weather girl.

'Well, I hope you're not blaming *me*,' drawled the Star, Sheridan Haggard, in his rich, golden-brown voice. '*I'm* still popular enough, if my fan mail's anything to go by. Aren't I, Ribsy? Isn't Daddy a star?' He patted the small bundle of bones on his lap. This was Ribs, Sheridan's adored pet dog, who ate from a silver bowl and wore a bejewelled collar.

Ribs wagged his skeletal tail and gave a little woof.

'I am not *blaming* anyone,' Ali Pali told him wearily. 'I am just stating a fact. People are switching off. In the beginning, we could palm them off with any old rubbish, even *Zombie Decorating*. Novelty value, you see. But now, alas, boredom is setting in. Which is why I've called this meeting. We must decide which programmes get the chop, and come up with some new, exciting ideas quickly, before I start losing money.'

The Cameraman – a pale Vampire called Vincent Van Ghoul – stuck up his hand.

'Mr Pali?' he said.

'Yes, Vincent?'

'I think we should cut *Goblins in Cars*. Nobody watches it. It came bottom in the viewers' poll.'

'Yeah. Vince is right – it's rubbish,' agreed the Soundman, a small, bad-tempered Tree Demon wearing earphones.

'Apart from anything else, it's dangerous to film,' added Vincent. 'They're crazy, those Grottys. Drive straight at us, don't they, TD?'

'I thought *I* was mad,' growled the Tree Demon.

'We should stop giving them cars,' continued Vince. 'It's irresponsible. Mindless violence. What if little kiddies see it?'

'Very well,' said Ali Pali. He took a pencil and made a note on his pad. 'Cut *Goblins in Cars*. Any more suggestions?'

'Well, of course, personally, *I* feel it would make sense to extend *The News*,' said Sheridan Haggard, never backward in coming forward. 'After all, it's me they want. By the way, will this take much longer? I have a skull polish at three. The limo's outside with the engine running.'

'Yes, well, of course, it would be. And at my expense, no doubt,' snapped Ali Pali, slamming down his pencil, which broke. Everyone stared. It was rare for him to lose his composure. The situation was clearly critical.

'Nice cup of tea, Mr Pali?' suggested the Everything Else Boy.

The Everything Else Boy was a small, furry, energetic Thing in a Moonmad T-shirt. It had started out in spellovision as the tea boy, but people took advantage of its enthusiasm and its career had taken off. It was now make-up artist, set designer, production assistant, casting director and a whole host of other things too numerous to mention. But it liked making tea most. You knew where you were with tea. Plus, you got to wear a frilly apron.

'Good idea,' agreed Ali Pali. 'Tea would be good.'

The Thing raced to the trolley and started crashing about with cups.

'Sixteen sugars for me,' said the Head of Glamour, who had a large, dirty foot on the table and was painting her toenails pink.

'No tea for me. I only ever drink champagne,' announced Sheridan Haggard airily. 'And Ribs will have a bowl of fizzy mineral water, with half a slice of lemon.'

'What about *Zombie Decorating*?' went on Ali Pali, ignoring him. 'Chop or no chop? Vince? TD? What do you think?'

'Chop,' chorused Vincent Van Ghoul and the Tree Demon.

'And personally, I think we're overdoing the Gnomes,' added Vincent. 'There are Gnomes in nearly every programme.'

'But Gnomes are cheap,' Ali Pali, ever the businessman, reminded him. 'Desperate to get into showbiz, Gnomes. You know what they say. There's Gnome Business Like Show Business.'

'Yeah, but they can't act,' the Tree Demon pointed out.

'Does that matter, though? *Gnome and Away* is still very popular,' mused Ali.

'Not as popular as *The News*,' Sheridan Haggard slipped in smoothly. 'They're calling me The Skeleton with the Golden Voice. It was in yesterday's paper. I take it you all saw the article?'

There was something very annoying about Sheridan Haggard. Vincent Van Ghoul and the Tree Demon caught each other's eye.

'Of course,' said the Tree Demon sourly, 'of course, *you* were actually second choice. Boss here tried to

282

get Scott Sinister to read the news, but he was too expensive. Right, boss?'

'Ahhhh,' said Ali Pali, glibly sidestepping the question as the Thing in the Moonmad T-shirt came rushing up with a tray full of steaming mugs. 'Tea. Excellent.'

'Did you?' enquired Sheridan Haggard in tones of rich indignation.

'Did I what?' asked Ali Pali, sipping his tea.

'Did you try to get Scott Sinister?'

'Now, why would I do that when I have you at half the price, Sheridan? Besides, he's away on location, as you well know, since you are currently renting his castle.'

This was true. Scott Sinister, the famous film star (and, incidentally, Pongwiffy's dreamboat), was currently off making *Return of the Avenging Killer Poodles V.* Sheridan Haggard was renting Scott's holiday retreat, in order to be near the studio.

'I said no tea,' complained Sheridan Haggard, flinching as a chipped mug was dumped before him. 'Where's my champagne?'

'I can't afford champagne,' snapped Ali Pali sharply. 'Not after your last pay rise. You are costing me a fortune, Sheridan, with your exotic celebrity lifestyle, your fancy ties and your fancy car and your expensive drinks. I'm a hardbitten business Genie. You'd better be worth it. You'd better hope your popularity lasts.'

'Ooh,' said Sheridan to the room in general. 'Get *him*.'

'I am just saying. And while we're on the subject, I'm not paying out for your entourage any more. Your butler and your chauffeur and your minders. You have to get rid of them.'

'But who will do all the work?' cried Sheridan, horrified. 'I am a *professional newsreader*! I must have *some* help. What will my fans think?'

'Hmm. Well, I'll think about it. All I am saying is, don't push your luck. Now then. Back to business. Ideas for new programmes. Head of Glamour? Any suggestions?'

'You what?' said Brenda, beginning on her second foot.

'You have just been made Head of Glamour, Brenda. You are meant to cover the female angle and come up with glamorous ideas.'

'What, now? While I'm doin' me feet?'

'Never mind, dear,' said Sheridan Haggard spitefully. 'You stick to what you're good at.'

'What about Luscious Lulu Lamarre, the actress?' suggested Vincent Van Ghoul. 'Couldn't we get her? She could do an hour's special. Singing and dancing and showing her talents. Right, TD?'

'Cor, yeah,' said the Tree Demon, brightening up.

Sheridan Haggard frowned. He didn't want famous actresses stealing his thunder.

'Sadly, we can't afford her,' sighed Ali Pali, and Sheridan relaxed. 'Besides, I ask myself, do we *need* a star? What do the viewers really *want*? Yes, thank you, Sheridan, I know they want you. But what else? Know what I think? I think they want programmes with the common touch. They want to see people just like them on spello.'

'So,' said Vincent reflectively. 'You're saying we need a programme that'll appeal to everybody.'

'Exactly. And preferably cheap. So don't suggest sending people off to faraway islands or quiz programmes where we give away money.'

'What about a sporting event?' suggested Vincent thoughtfully. 'A marathon, or something?'

'Hmm. Not everyone likes sport. But a competition of some sort – that's a good idea. Something like ... like ...'

Everyone blinked at the sudden flash of green light,

followed by a thick cloud of evil-smelling smoke. Ali Pali choked on his tea, Brenda spilled her nail varnish and Ribs clattered down from his master's lap and hid under the table.

'Singing Witches,' finished off Pongwiffy, briskly stepping out of the green murk. She tucked her Wand away and stared around at the startled company, who were busily choking and mopping up spills. 'That's what you need.'

'Oh,' said Ali Pali, wiping his streaming eyes. 'It's you, Pongwiffy. And that ridiculous Hamster.' He sounded glum.

'Hey,' said Hugo, from Pongwiffy's hat. 'Votch it.'

(It should be explained that there is quite a bit of history between Pongwiffy and Ali Pali. Their paths have crossed before. They have a wary respect for each other's talents, but are not what you would call good friends. The same can be said about Vincent Van Ghoul, the Tree Demon, Brenda and the Thing in the Moonmad T-shirt, all of whom have had previous dealings with Pongwiffy.)

'You're darn right it's me. How's it going, Pali? I might have known you'd be behind this spellovision racket. It's your sort of thing, isn't it? Always got an eye open for the main chance. And look who's here!

Vincent Van Ghoul and the Tree Demon, wouldn't you know. Well, well, well. Hey, you!' She pointed at the Thing in the Moonmad T-shirt. 'I'll have a mug of tea, if there's one going.'

'What are you doing here, Pongwiffy?' demanded Ali Pali wearily. 'This is a private meeting. You can't just come barging in.'

'I've come with a message from Grandwitch Sourmuddle. She says we Witches want to be on spello and you've got to come and make pictures of us singing or she'll want to know the reason why.'

'I'll tell her why,' said Ali Pali. 'Because nobody would watch it, that's why.'

'Witches would,' pointed out Pongwiffy reasonably.

'But not all viewers are Witches, are they? What about the rest of the viewing public? Can you see anyone else tuning in to hear Singing Witches? Vincent. You're a Vampire. Would you?'

'I'd sooner lie on a sunbed eating a garlic sandwich,' said Vincent Van Ghoul.

'But we're good!' argued Pongwiffy. 'Better than the other rubbish you show. Tell them, Hugo. Aren't we good?'

'It's not a question of good or bad,' explained Ali Pali. 'It's a question of what the viewers want.

If you really want to know, I am *looking* for new programmes. If I thought Singing Witches would make people switch on, I'd be most happy to send the crew along. But, sadly . . .'

'Shh,' said Pongwiffy. 'Stop yapping. My Familiar wants a consultation.'

Hugo had dropped on to her shoulder and was tugging at her earlobe. Pongwiffy inclined her head, and he proceeded to hiss in her ear. As he talked, a grin began to spread across her face.

Sheridan Haggard, the only one who didn't know Pongwiffy, said, in his most pompous golden-brown tones, 'My dear madam, I don't know who you are, but I really don't think . . .'

'Didn't you hear?' said Pongwiffy, staring at him coldly. 'We're consulting.'

Sheridan subsided. The Thing shoved a mug of tea into Pongwiffy's hand. She took a loud slurp, then listened some more, nodding and grinning as Hugo whispered. Another minute or so dragged by. And then, 'Got it!' cried Pongwiffy triumphantly. She thumped on the table. Ali Pali's inkpot crashed to the floor. 'A Song Contest!'

'What?'

'A *Spellovision* Song Contest. It's brilliant. Everyone

gets the chance to enter an original song.' Again, Hugo whispered in her ear. 'Well, everyone except Goblins, of course. And you film it while it happens and then the public votes for their favourite.'

Hugo whispered again.

'Better still,' continued Pongwiffy, 'there could be specially selected juries. And a really good prize for the winners, like a big silver cup and a week's all-expenses-paid holiday at Sludgehaven-on-Sea. You could get someone famous to present it.'

'Well, of course, I suppose I *could* –' began Sheridan Haggard, but he was cut off by Pongwiffy.

'I mean *really* famous. A *proper* star. Not some minor celebrity with a daft voice.'

'Now, look *here* . . .'

'Scott Sinister, for example. He's a friend of mine.'

This wasn't strictly true. By no stretch of the imagination was the famous star Pongwiffy's friend.

'Ha!' sneered Sheridan Haggard. 'A likely story!'

'But the money!' fretted Ali Pali. 'The studio's been losing money hand over fist. All those prizes . . .'

'Ah,' said Pongwiffy uncertainly. 'Yes. Well. I expect I'll think of an idea of how you can solve that. Won't I, Hugo?'

'Ya,' said Hugo, who was tired of whispering. He

spoke to Ali directly. 'Easy. You make it pay for itself. Charge ze advertisers. Zey pay big money to get zeir product on zat night. And get live audience to come and votch. Charge zem too. Offer special deal on spello sets. Lots of publicity. Lots of pizzazz!'

'He's right, you know,' said Vincent Van Ghoul to the Tree Demon. 'It could work.'

'*She's* right, you mean,' Pongwiffy corrected him. 'This is *my* brilliant idea, you know. So what do you think?'

She directed the question at Ali Pali, who was currently sucking his flashiest medallion and staring into space. He gave a little start and came back to earth.

'What do I think? I'll tell you what I think.' He held out his hand. His mouth split, revealing a lot of white, shiny teeth. 'Pongwiffy, allow me to congratulate you. It *is* a brilliant idea. An *inspiring* idea. In fact, I wish I'd thought of it myself.'

'You do?' said Pongwiffy, preening a bit. (Flattery didn't come her way often.)

'I do. Perhaps we can put our differences behind us and you would consider becoming my Head of Programming – and your Hamster, of course?'

'I'll think about it,' promised Pongwiffy, 'but I

don't hold out too much hope. I'm not sure I can fit it in. My music is all-consuming. I've given you the grand idea; it's up to you to work out the details. As long as we Witches win, I don't care. Now, you'll have to excuse me. I've got a song to write.'

CHAPTER ELEVEN
Sheridan Haggard, Newsreader

It was the following evening. Sheridan Haggard sat at the dining table, reading the latest article about himself in *The Daily Miracle*. He was wearing a crimson silk kimono embroidered with skeletal dragons. Gold-framed reading glasses perched on the bony ridge between his eye sockets. Expensive rings flashed on his metacarpals (finger bones to you). Ribs sat on an expensive Persian rug, chewing a bone, of all things.

'Listen to this, Thing,' commanded Sheridan. 'There's another big piece about me in the paper.'

The Thing in the Moonmad T-shirt was currently clearing away the supper dishes. Its job as Everything Else Boy had recently expanded to being Sheridan's entire entourage. It was chief cook and bottle-washer, chauffeur, valet, skull masseur, minder – well, you get the idea. By replacing Sheridan's posse of grovelling attendants with the Thing, Ali Pali had neatly solved the problem of how to save money and keep Sheridan happy at the same time.

Right now, the Thing was in butler mode. It wore a dark suit and a bow tie. At its master's command, it obediently set down its tray and adopted a polite listening pose.

'*Sheridan Haggard, the Golden Voice of spellovision, will be opening Wraithways, the new supermarket, shortly before midnight tonight*,' read Sheridan Haggard. '*Large crowds are expected. The popular newsreader has really caught the public's imagination, with his velvet tones and polished charm. It is hoped he will be bringing along Ribs, his charming little dog, a firm favourite with the kiddies. Hear that, Ribs? Children love you.*'

'Woof,' said Ribs, worrying his bone.

'Will I need the chauffeur's hat, boss?' asked the Thing. It had a lot of hats and small props. It was the only way it could remember who it was supposed to be.

'Most certainly,' agreed Sheridan. 'Clear away the dishes, set out my white shirt and opera cloak, then bring the limo round. Go on, hop to it. I can't be late. I'm an important man. After I've opened the supermarket, I have to be back in the studio in time for *The News*. I live for those bulletins, you know. It's only before a camera that I become truly alive.'

The Thing scooped everything on to the tray and hurtled out through the door.

Sheridan rose to his feet and stretched luxuriously. This was the life! Champagne and caviar on tap. A chauffeur-driven limousine. Flattering articles in the paper. Cheering crowds whenever he showed his skull in public. A huge salary and an enormous expense account which enabled him to rent a grand castle. And all because he happened to have a rich, golden-brown voice.

Lucky or what?

A short time later, dressed in frilly shirt and sweeping cloak, Sheridan stood before the castle gates, Ribs in his arms, waiting for the Thing to bring up the limo.

As always, a small crowd of diehard fans was there

to witness his departure. The Skeleton with the blonde wig was there, holding a bunch of wilting daisies. There was a Troll family, consisting of Mum, Dad, Grandma and two small, shy Troll toddlers. Dad had a camera. The toddlers clutched autograph books.

'Go on, Gravella, ask him!' hissed the mother Troll, giving the girl toddler a shove. You could tell she was a girl because she was wearing a pink sun bonnet. She took her thumb out of her mouth, toddled forward and thrust out the book. Ribs liked children. He wagged his tail and gave a happy little woof.

'Pleathe, thir, can I have your autograph?' whispered little Gravella shyly. The dad Troll readied his camera.

Sheridan looked down from his great height.

'Not now, small girl,' he said haughtily. 'I'm not in the mood.' And he stared pointedly up at the moon, tapping his foot impatiently.

Tears welled up in little Gravella's eyes. She flushed, looked around uncertainly, then walked back to her family and buried her face in the folds of her mother's frock.

There came a low purring, a glint of moonlight on polished chrome and the long black limousine slid up to the gates. The Thing was at the wheel, wearing leather driving gloves and a chauffeur's hat perched at a jaunty angle. It jumped out, leaving the engine running, and scuttled round to open the back door. A rich smell of leather wafted from the interior.

Sheridan folded his tall frame and climbed in, placing Ribs on a special cushion. The door clicked shut and the Thing hopped back in the driver's seat. The Skeleton with the daisies moved forward hesitantly, holding out her flowers, then leapt back with a startled cry as the car pulled away. The bunch of daisies fell to the ground and was thoroughly mashed by the back wheel.

'So tedious,' sighed Sheridan, as the limousine picked up speed and the little group of fans receded into the distance. 'No respect for privacy. Have they never heard the phrase, *A Skeleton's home is his castle*?'

'Ain't strickly *your* castle, though, is it, boss?' observed the Thing, steering efficiently around the trees. 'Belongs to Scott Sinister.'

'Ha!' Sheridan let out a short, derisive bark. Ribs looked up anxiously, then went back to crunching the jewels off his collar. 'Don't mention that name to me.'

'What, Scott Sinister?'

'I said don't mention it!'

'Why not?' enquired the Thing innocently, honking at a rabbit.

296

'Because the man's an overrated charlatan, that's why.'

'Oh, I dunno,' argued the Thing, nudging the car on to the main trail, which wound through Witchway Wood. 'He was good as the daddy in *The Mummy's Curse*.'

'I didn't see it,' sniffed Sheridan.

'He was good. 'Course, he dropped off a bit after *Return of the Avenging Killer Poodles IV*. But they say the next one's gonna be a cracker. And that leadin' lady of his, that Lulu Lamarre, she's a bit of all right an' all.'

'Look,' said Sheridan through tight jaws, 'I said I didn't want to talk about him. The only good thing about Sinister is his castle, which I must admit is quite comfortable. But then, so it should be, with the excessive rent he's charging. Drive faster, we're late.'

'He's a proper star, though, isn't he?' persisted the Thing, who was indeed a fan. 'You gotta admit it. Why, he's got the whole world at his feet – *oi!*' Brakes were suddenly applied, the limo slowed to a crawl, and the Thing wound down the window and leaned heavily on the horn. 'Out of the way, losers!'

Seven figures were directly ahead, trudging along the middle of the road. They halted and stared over their shoulders, caught in the glare of the headlights like startled rabbits.

'Now what!' exploded Sheridan.

'Goblins,' said the Thing with a grin, hunkering down and revving the engine. 'Hold tight, boss. I'll scatter 'em.'

It pressed the accelerator and the limousine leapt forward, sleek, smooth and deadly as a car-shaped panther.

The Goblins scattered all right. With wild little squawks and howls, they dived for the bushes. Horn blaring, the limousine carved a path through them and vanished in a cloud of dust and exhaust smoke.

There was a short pause. Then, one by one, seven Goblin heads emerged from the bushes.

Now, you would expect them to be furious, wouldn't you? Mown down like that, without any warning. But they weren't. Oh no. Their faces wore the same trance-like expression as when they had been watching spellovision through Macabre's window.

As one, they faced the point in the distance where the limousine had vanished. Then, slowly, as one, they said, in tones of deepest admiration and envious wonderment, *'Phwoarh!'*

CHAPTER TWELVE
Songwriting

'We haven't seen each other for a bit, have we, Hugo?' observed Pongwiffy. She was sitting in her rocking chair, guitar cradled in her arms, waiting for Sharkadder to come round to visit. 'Not since music took over my life.'

'Mmm,' mumbled Hugo. He was sitting in the chipped sugar bowl, frowning down at a tiny pad of paper and pulling on his whiskers. A pencil stub was in his little pink paw.

'I mean, we *see* each other,' continued Pongwiffy,

'around and about. But we haven't had a proper chat for ages.'

'Mmm.' Hugo tapped his teeth with the pencil.

'So. How *are* things? What have you been up to? I expect you're getting a bit bored with all this time on your paws. What with us not doing any spells and you having nothing to read now your daft little book's lost. I expect you'd probably like me to give you a task to do. Like put the kettle on.'

Hugo looked up, brow furrowed. 'Vot?'

'I said put the kettle on. Sharkadder'll be here any minute. I expect she'd like a cup of bogwater before we get started. We're working on our original song tonight. For the Song Contest. Nothing like bogwater to oil the brains.'

'You put it on. I busy.'

'No, you're not. You're sitting in a sugar bowl,' Pongwiffy pointed out. 'If that's busy, I smell like a rose garden.'

'I write,' said Hugo, waving his pad. 'See? I busy.'

'Oh,' said Pongwiffy. 'I *see*. It's *writing* now, is it? And what are you *writing*, may I ask? A letter to your stupid rodent relations? The world's first Hamster novel? What's it called? *The Boring Adventures of Fluffy*?'

'If you must know,' said Hugo stiffly, 'I is composink a sonk.'

'I *beg* your pardon?' Pongwiffy frowned. 'A *song*? I thought *I* was the songwriter around here. Why are *you* writing a song?'

'Vhy you sink? 'Cos ve is entering ze Sonk Contest, of course.'

'*We*, meaning?'

'Ze Familiars.'

'The *Familiars*?' Pongwiffy let out a rude cackle. 'Entering the Song Contest? Don't make me laugh!'

'And vhy not?' snapped Hugo.

Pongwiffy stopped laughing. You had to be careful with Hugo. He had a short fuse.

'Everyvun else is. Ze Trolls, ze Gnomes, ze Banshees, ze Skeletons . . .'

'Gosh. Really?'

'Oh ya. It very popular. Zere goink to be strong competition, I sink.'

Pongwiffy didn't know whether to be pleased or worried. It's always nice to have ideas that are popular. On the other hand, strong competition meant that the Witches might not necessarily win.

Just then there came a knock at the door, followed by a shrill, '*Cooooeeee! Only meeeee!*' And in came

301

Sharkadder, wearing a long purple cloak and matching purple ankle boots. She was carrying a purple lace parasol, a purple handbag, a special purple drawstring bag in which she kept her harmonica and a large cake box. Much to Hugo's disgust, Dead Eye Dudley was with her, swishing his tail and glowering at everyone.

'Hello, Pong, sorry we're late,' said Sharkadder, looking around for somewhere to sit. It was a choice between the sofa, which was currently sprouting a fine crop of mushrooms, or a three-legged chair on which had been dumped a half-finished plate of skunk stew, a collection of dirty socks and a wide-open tin displaying the warning: *Fishin Maggots. Kepe Furmly Clozed.*

'Have a seat,' said Pongwiffy.

'I'm trying to – I'm just picking off maggots. My, it's disgusting in here. I brought Dudley along because he wants to write a song with Hugo.'

'No I don't,' growled Dudley.

'Yes you *do*, Duddles. Remember what Mummy said? You have a lot of musical talent. There's no reason why you and Hugo shouldn't work happily together, just like Pong and me.' She beamed at Pongwiffy and added, 'The Familiars are entering the Contest, did you hear?'

'I heard,' said Pongwiffy.

'I told Dudley they should do one of his sea shanties.'

'Over my fluffy body,' sneered Hugo.

'Ah, shut yer gob, small fry!' spat Dudley.

'Say zat again, fleabag!' Hugo shot out of the sugar bowl and squared up.

'Small fry! Squirt! Daft little fur ball!' obliged Dudley.

'Mangy old vindbag! Mummy's boy! You sink you tough? I keel you!'

'Is that so? Listen, sonny, if 'twasn't for my bad back . . .'

'Listen to them teasing each other,' said Sharkadder fondly. 'It's a good thing they don't mean it.'

'I suppose we'd better get on,' said Pongwiffy. 'You've brought a cake, I see. Put the kettle on while I tune my guitar.'

With a little sigh, Sharkadder went to deal with the kettle while Pongwiffy pretended to fiddle with the tuning pegs. In the background, Hugo was poking Dudley with the pencil stub, while Dudley tried to flatten him with his paw.

'I must say that things have improved now Sourmuddle's taken over,' remarked Sharkadder over her shoulder. 'At least she's keeping everyone in order.

Things were getting a bit out of hand before, don't you think?'

'True,' admitted Pongwiffy. 'Thank badness she took those spoons away from Gaga.'

'Absolutely. And stopped Greymatter singing. Now Sourmuddle's in charge, you and I can concentrate on what we do best. Which is being creative and coming up with the winning song.'

This was true. Sourmuddle had lost no time in getting everyone organised. Everybody now had a proper role in the band and it was working much better. The line-up went like this:

Sourmuddle – band leader and piano
Pongwiffy – guitar and writer of winning song
Sharkadder – harmonica and co-writer of winning song
Ratsnappy – recorder
Twins – violins
Macabre – bagpipes (but not so loud)
Bendyshanks – backing vocals / percussion
Sludgegooey – backing vocals / percussion
Scrofula – backing vocals / percussion
Bonidle – drums
Gaga – backing dancer
Greymatter – mouthing the words

'Mind you,' said Pongwiffy, 'I'm still not sure about Bonidle on drums. Drummers aren't supposed to fall asleep between verses, are they?'

'She snores very rhythmically, though,' pointed out Sharkadder. She took two chipped mugs of bogwater to the cluttered table and found room between the piles of scribbled-on paper. She removed the stew, socks and maggot tin from the three-legged chair, drew it up to the table, spread out a clean purple hanky and sat down carefully.

'Aren't we having the cake?' asked Pongwiffy hopefully.

'Work first, cake later,' said Sharkadder firmly. 'We have to take this seriously. You said so yourself.'

'Oh, absolutely,' agreed Pongwiffy hastily. She didn't want anyone thinking she didn't take songwriting seriously. Although a bit of cake would have been nice.

In the background, the door slammed. Hugo and Dudley had taken their argument outside.

'Right,' said Sharkadder. She opened her bag and took out her harmonica, a clean pad and a nicely sharpened pencil. 'First things first. Are we absolutely sure we can't do "Nose Song"?'

'No. I keep telling you. It has to be a *new* original song.'

'All right,' sighed Sharkadder. 'OK. New song. Are we starting with the tune or the words?'

'The words,' said Pongwiffy. Tunes were all the same to her, but she had a fine appreciation of words, being a talkative type.

'I agree,' said Sharkadder. She wrote WORDS on her pad and underlined it. 'What should our song be about, do you think?'

Pongwiffy considered. Until now, most of her songs were rude ones about Hugo or boastful ones about the superiority of Witches. She had a feeling these were specialist interests. Witches would relate to them, of course, but the general public would want something a bit more – well, general.

'I'm not sure it has to be *about* anything,' she said. 'I think it just needs to be easy. Something you sing in . . . places where people sing.'

'Like in the bath, you mean.'

'Don't say that word,' said Pongwiffy with a shudder. 'I mean, something undemanding. With lots of repetition.'

'You mean meaningless?'

'Well – yes. Meaningless, but catchy.'

'Right.' Sharkadder wrote it down. '*Meaningless – but catchy*. Like what?'

'I dunno.' Pongwiffy cast about desperately. 'Like . . . I dunno . . . bing, bang, bong or something.'

'Bing, bang, bong,' nodded Sharkadder, scribbling away. 'OK. I've got that.'

'Or bong, bang, bing,' improvised Pongwiffy. 'Just as a variation.'

'Good idea. Or – this is just a suggestion, mind – what about bing, bong, bang?'

'Not bad,' agreed Pongwiffy. 'Not bad at all.'

'Or,' added Sharkadder excitedly, '*or* even banga-langa binga-linga bonga-longa bing bong? Or is that going too far?'

'No, no,' said Pongwiffy. 'I think we can use it. Write it down.'

'*Or*,' suggested Sharkadder, really getting carried away now, '*or*, how about binga-linga banga-langa bonga-longa rum dum, rama dama root toot, ding dong do?'

'Mmm. Getting a bit fancy now. But maybe it'll slip in somewhere. Stick it down, just in case.'

'We're getting on well, aren't we?' said Sharkadder happily. 'It's fun collaborating, isn't it, Pong? Don't you agree?'

'I would if I knew what it meant,' said Pongwiffy. 'Shall we have the cake now?'

CHAPTER THIRTEEN
The Competition

It wasn't only in Number One, Dump Edge, that preparations for the Song Contest were under way.

The Wizards' Clubhouse (think pointy turrets and lashings of gold paint) stands on top of a hill in the Misty Mountains range. Despite erratic local weather conditions, the Wizards get excellent spellovision reception. In pride of place in the lounge is a set with the biggest screen you have ever seen.

Wizards love spellovision. They have taken to it like flies to a jam sandwich. They spend most of their waking hours slumped in armchairs waiting for the next meal anyway, so watching spello is the ideal way of passing the time. Nobody does the crossword puzzle now. Nobody reads. Nobody makes wise, Wizardly comments in loud voices. Conversation is a thing of the past.

Well, it was until Sheridan Haggard announced the forthcoming Spellovision Song Contest on the news. That got them talking all right.

'... *and specially selected juries will vote for the winner,*' explained Sheridan in his golden-brown voice. '*Each team is invited to submit a specially composed song. This can be performed by a soloist, or it can be a group effort. The contest is open to all, except Goblins. Entry forms are available from Spellovision Centre, at the address displayed below on your screens.*

'*The idea for a Spellovision Song Contest originally came from Witch Pongwiffy of the Witchway Wood Coven. A host of fabulous prizes awaits the lucky winners ...*'

And Sheridan went on to explain about the fabulous prizes, while the Wizards paid close attention.

'... *a silver trophy, a bag of gold, a recording contract and a week's all-expenses-paid holiday in Sludgehaven-on-Sea. All of which will be presented –*' Sheridan paused and smirked at the camera – '*by none*

*other than myself. So, get that form filled in and sent off
without delay.*

'*And now, sport. The hockey match between St
Banshee's and Harpy Girls High got off to a bad
start when —*'

The sound cut off, leaving Sheridan mouthing
soundlessly like a stranded carp. Dave the Druid –
a short, plump wizard with a big beard and
half-glasses – stood before the screen, obviously keen
to say something. There were a few protests.

'Turn it up!'

'Hey! I was watching that!'

Dave held up a hand.

'Did you hear that, gentlemen?' he asked. 'A Song
Contest! What about that for an idea?'

'It's clever,' observed Gerald the Just, a hawk-nosed
Wizard with a reputation for being fair. 'It gets
everyone interested, there's the element of competition,
and the studio won't have to pay the performers
because everyone wants to be on spellovision. Shame
the Witches came up with the idea first. But it's clever.
You have to hand it to them.'

'Let's hope they don't win as well,' came a voice
from thin air. It belonged to Alf the Invisible,
who was supposed to take reversing pills, but kept

forgetting. 'That'll be something else they can throw in our faces.'

'They won't win. Not if I can help it,' declared Dave the Druid, eyes glinting with the light of battle. 'I don't know about you lot, but I reckon I can hold a tune. I come from the valleys, I do, and we're known for our singing. And it can't be *that* hard to come up with a song. If someone would have a bash at the words, I can set them to music. Any volunteers?'

A lone hand hesitantly rose and hovered in the air. The Wizards turned and stared at the owner.

The owner was the youngest Wizard there. His name was Ronald and he happened to be Sharkadder's nephew. Three disadvantages, and that's without even mentioning his spots. He went pink as everyone fell about laughing.

'Think of yourself as a bit of a wordsmith, do you, young fellow?' sneered Frank the Foreteller, who loved baiting Ronald.

'I'll give it a go, certainly,' said Ronald.

'Hmm. Well, let's hope you come up with the goods. I've a feeling this Song Contest will be popular.'

He was right. The moment that the contest was announced, everyone wanted to be in it. Ali Pali could hardly open the studio door for entry forms.

The Trolls were into hard, heavy rock music. The hard, heavy rocks weren't a problem. The music bit was more difficult. Trolls aren't known for their singing talent. However, a youngster named Cliff Rigid had come up with some lyrics that sounded promising.

The Banshee Girls' Choir was entering a jolly little ditty entitled 'Oh Woe!' The Zombies were working on some sort of comedy number. Xotindis and Xstufitu, the two Mummies who lived in the Wood, were singing a duet. There was a rumour that a lone Werewolf named Roger would be entering a ballad or something. Four Vampires had formed a barbershop quartet. If you went for a walk in the Wood at any time, day or night, you would hear snatches of song and bursts of drumming, twanging, scraping and honking issuing from caves, sheds, castles and underground holes.

The Familiars rehearsed in an old, ruined barn on the edge of the Wood. You already know Hugo and Dudley. You have also met Snoop, Rory, Vernon, Steve and Barry. The others are: Speks (Greymatter's Owl); Bonidle's Sloth (who has no name because Bonidle can't be bothered to give him one); Filth (Sludgegooey's Fiend); IdentiKit and CopiCat (twin Siamese cats belonging to the twins) and, last but not least, a large posse of Bats that hangs around Gaga.

They were gathered in the dimly lit barn. The Bats hung in a neat line from a shadowy rafter. Barry perched on the handle of an old rake. Vernon and Steve sat on a crate that had once held apples. IdentiKit and CopiCat had made themselves comfortable in a pile of straw. The Sloth was asleep on an ancient tarpaulin. Rory the Haggis was leaning against a rusty old plough. Filth the Fiend wasn't there because he was the drummer with the Witchway Rhythm Boys and already had a rehearsal.

Snoop was in a corner, cleaning his nails with his pitchfork, sulking because he wasn't in charge. It didn't seem right, bearing in mind that his mistress was Grandwitch. However, although Snoop was a good organiser, his talents were sadly lacking in the musical department, and he had been elbowed to one side by Hugo, who was currently standing on a soapbox, holding a tiny sheaf of papers in his paw.

'So what have ye got there, wee Hugo?' asked Rory.

'Is vords,' explained Hugo. 'Vords for our sonk. I hope you like.'

'I very much doubt *I* will,' muttered Speks, who, like his mistress, considered himself a bit of a poet. Greymatter was the intelligent Witch in the Witchway Coven. Speks often helped her with the crossword. (*One Across. Night bird with a reputation for wisdom. Three letters, beginning with O and ending with L.* That sort of thing.)

'Give him a chance,' protested Vernon. 'You haven't heard it yet. Might be good.'

'Ar. An' fishes might use umbrellas,' sneered a voice from the doorway. Dudley sauntered in, sat down and awarded Hugo a challenging glare.

Very sensibly, Hugo ignored him. He could fight Dudley any time. Right now, there was work to be done.

'Sonk is called "Oh I Do Like to Be a Vitch Familiar".'

'Sounds promising,' remarked Barry politely.

'Sounds rubbish,' scoffed Dudley.

'Fire away then, wee Hugo,' said Rory. 'Let's hear it.'

Hugo took a deep breath and burst into squeaky song.

> *'Oh, I do like to be a Vitch Familiar,*
> *I do like to help viz all ze spells.*

314

I don't even mind when zey go wrong, wrong, wrong,
Causing a great big bang and a terrible
pong, pong, pong . . .'

Yes. The Music Express had arrived in Witchway Wood all right, and everyone wanted to climb aboard.

CHAPTER FOURTEEN
car problems

Much to his annoyance, Sheridan Haggard was being stalked by Goblins. Or, to be precise, his car was. Everywhere he went, there they were, gathered in a silent little cluster, open-mouthed and staring. Quite often, he noticed, they were carrying stuff – a bath, an old chair, bits of assorted ironmongery.

Whenever he left the limo unattended, they would creep out from behind trees and surround it. The second his back was turned, there they would be, crouching down, poking at the wheels, pushing the windscreen wipers to and fro, playing with the mirror and, worst of all, laying their grubby hands on the paintwork!

'It's intolerable!' Sheridan raged to the Thing. 'The nerve! I won't put up with it, I tell you!'

Of course, Sheridan didn't know what lay behind the Goblins' disturbing behaviour. For the past few nights, they had been making regular raids on Pongwiffy's Dump in order to collect items that fell under the general heading of Car Stuff.

They had had long discussions about the essential components that made up a car. So far, all they had agreed on was wheels, seats, doors, windows and, of course, fluffy dice. And probably some other bits and bobs. Then they would join them all together. Somehow.

To their great dismay, *Goblins in Cars* was no longer on spello, so they didn't even have that as a reference any more. Examining Sheridan's limo just might give them some clues.

(The Goblins weren't the only ones who were fed up about losing *Goblins in Cars*. As we know, it was Macabre's favourite programme. When it got taken off, she had thrown a boot through the screen and vowed never to watch spello again.)

Funnily enough, people didn't seem to be watching spellovision so much these days. Making music seemed to be the current fad. Not that the Goblins cared *what* everyone else was into. Car assembly was their thing.

Anyway, Sheridan had a dilemma. He didn't want to stop using his limousine, which was one of the top perks of being a famous newsreader. But he didn't want it swarmed over by Goblins every time he left it unattended. He couldn't leave the Thing to mind it because who would open doors, pour champagne, fluff up his cushion, wipe his brow and sharpen his newsreading pencil?

In the end, he decided to try leaving Ribs to guard it. This would have worked fine if Ribs had had a guard-dog-type disposition. But he didn't. He was a mild, jolly little dog who liked everybody. Even Goblins.

The limousine was currently parked outside the spellovision studios where Sheridan was reading out the first news bulletin of the evening. The moment he disappeared inside, with the Thing hot on his heels, seven squat shapes crept from behind the bushes and clustered around the car. Ribs instantly perked up, stood on his hind legs and smiled toothily through the window, bony tail wagging like mad.

'Ah, look at him,' said Plugugly, staring through the glass, a soppy smile on his face. 'Dere's a good little doggy. Hello dere, little feller. Who's a nice little doggy den? Who's got a pretty sparkly collar? Coooeeee, doggy, doggy, doggy.'

'Wot, is there a dog in the car or summink?' asked Lardo, who had been bending down, studying a tyre.

'Yes. He got a waggy tail, look!' Plugugly tapped on the glass. 'Hello, little doggy.'

'Woof,' said Ribs, jumping up and slobbering all over the window. Quite how he managed to slobber, considering he was made entirely of bones, is something of a mystery – but slobber he did.

'I *fink* I see where the smoke comes out,' shouted Hog, who was lying underneath the limousine, peering up at its underside. 'There's a pipe fing. I'll see if it's hot. *Ow, ow, ow, me finger!* Yes.'

'Can you see where it's comin' from, though?' Slopbucket wanted to know.

'No,' admitted Hog. 'It's too dark.'

'Well, we need to find that out, don't we?' said Eyesore. ''Cos it's the smoke what makes it go, I reckon.'

'Know what I reckon?' chipped in Stinkwart. 'I reckon there's a little horse in here. Under this bit.' He rapped on the gleaming bonnet.

319

'How's it make the smoke, though?' asked Eyesore.

'Perhaps it's smokin' a pipe,' said Stinkwart.

'Horses don't smoke pipes, do they?' enquired young Sproggit.

'Trained specially, I expect,' said Stinkwart, unwilling to let the smoking-horse idea go. 'Trained to go an' stop and smoke a pipe.'

'It's a very quiet horse,' observed Slopbucket. 'You don't hear it neighin' or anyfing.'

'Or coughin',' added Lardo. 'It'd cough, wouldn't it? If it smoked a pipe. I don't reckon there's a horse in there at all. It's sumfin' else makin' it go. A baby dragon, perhaps. What d'you reckon, Plug?'

But Plugugly wasn't paying attention. He was too taken with Ribs, who was now bouncing around on the back seat, crashing playfully into the window.

'Nice little doggy,' cooed Plugugly. 'Is oo hungry? Does oo want a bone?'

''E's got a bone,' remarked Sproggit. 'If 'e was that hungry, 'e could eat his own foot.' He gave a little snigger.

Just at that moment, there came an enraged cry. Sheridan had finished reading the news and had spotted them through the studio window, which overlooked the car park.

'Hey! You there! What have I told you? *Get away from my car!*'

'Oops,' said Slopbucket. 'Time to skidoodle.'

And with one accord, they took to their heels. Well, six of them did. Plugugly was still besotted with Ribs and didn't notice.

'Poor little doggy,' he was crooning, as Ribs thrashed around, beside himself with excitement. 'Did dey leave oo on oo's ownio? Did dey? I wouldn't, not if you was mine. Dere, dere, never mind ...'

He broke off as he found his arms gripped firmly by Hog and Lardo, and was dragged off into the night.

Abandoned, Ribs gave a sad little whimper as his new friend was borne away. Without much hope, he launched himself at the window one last time. His bony back leg landed accidentally on the door handle. There was a click and, to his surprise, the heavy door swung open.

Freedom!

With a happy little woof, Ribs jumped out and merrily scampered off in pursuit of Plugugly.

The moonlight streamed in as the Goblins rolled the boulder to one side and squeezed into their cave. There wasn't much room, because of all the Car Stuff. It rose in a vast, teetering pile, slap bang in the middle.

There was one broken cartwheel. One old pram. One supermarket trolley. Two nude deckchairs (i.e. no cloth, frame only). One rotten garden bench. Four broken kitchen stools. One overstuffed armchair with a spring sticking up through the seat. A bundle of forks. A roll of garden wire. String. A box of candles. A collection of rusty saucepans. One large tin of turquoise paint. One collapsed umbrella. Three bottomless buckets. A set of taps, both hot and cold. The grill from a camping stove. A broken anglepoise lamp. One parrot cage. One large tin bath. One mangle . . .

No. I can't bear it any more. Imagine it for yourselves.

'Here we all are, then,' said Stinkwart. ''Ome again. Back to the pile.'

'We got enough stuff now, ain't we?' asked Sproggit. 'Ain't it time we started?'

'Yeah!' came the united chorus. 'Yeah! Let's make the car! Let's make the car! Let's make . . .'

'All right,' agreed Plugugly. He sounded a bit reluctant, though. 'We'll start. Even if I is still feelin' sad an' not at my best. Don't fink I has forgiven you for pullin' me away from dat little doggy. I liked dat little doggy, I did. I wish I had a little doggy of my own.'

'You'll like 'avin' a car though, won'tcha?' soothed Stinkwart. 'Come on. You know you will.'

'True,' agreed Plugugly, cheering up. Rolling up his shirtsleeves, he stepped towards the huge junk mountain that soared up into the shadows and spat on his palms. 'You is quite right, Stinkwart. I *will* like dat. So what is we waitin' for? Come on, boys! Let's make a car!'

CHAPTER FIFTEEN

The Song

Over now to Witchway Hall. Pongwiffy and Sharkadder are about to unleash their lovely new song on the Coven.

'I'm feeling a bit nervous, aren't you?' whispered Sharkadder, applying a fresh coat of prune lipstick with a shaky hand. 'How do I look?'

'Fine,' mumbled Pongwiffy, without looking. To tell the truth, she was feeling a bit queasy. They were running late because Sharkadder kept changing her mind about what to wear – plus, they had had a lot to carry. So Pongwiffy had used one of her unreliable transportation spells, which got them there in double-quick time but left their tummies lagging three minutes behind in the process.

The Coven was all ready and waiting. Excitement was in the air. Witches like nothing better than the opportunity to criticise.

'I must say I'm looking forward to this,' remarked Bendyshanks to Ratsnappy as the composers took their seats and nervously organised themselves with music stands, guitar, harmonica, glasses of water, flask, emergency sandwiches, throat sweets and lyrics, copied on to a sheet of paper in Sharkadder's neat hand. 'I wonder what they've come up with. If it's awful, let's boo.'

'I hope it's a nice ballad,' said Sludgegooey. 'I love a nice, romantic ballad, me.'

'Ballad!' scoffed Macabre, overhearing. 'We dinnae need that sissy stuff. We need somethin' dark an' dramatic, wi' words that reflect the true Witch experience. Damp caves an' blasted heaths an' cauldrons full o' heavin' murk.'

'But only Witches would like that, wouldn't they? We need a song that'll appeal to everyone, don't we?' mused Scrofula. She raised her voice and shouted, 'What's it called, Pongwiffy?'

'"Banga Langa Bing Bong Boo",' said Pongwiffy and Sharkadder together. There were a few raised eyebrows at this, and a certain amount of muttering.

'Why?' asked Greymatter politely.

'Why not?' said Pongwiffy, plucking a string and fiddling with a peg as though she knew what she was doing.

'Let's save the questions for later, shall we?' said Sharkadder briskly. 'Trust us, Greymatter, we know what we're doing. We've been writing songs together for ages now, haven't we, Pong?'

'Oh yes,' said Pongwiffy. 'We're very experienced.' And she swept her hand over the strings. *Thruuuuuuuuummmmmmm.* 'Right. That's me tuned up.'

'Get a move on, then,' said Sourmuddle, who was sitting at the piano with her arms folded. 'Let's hear it. I hope it's good. We want to win this contest.'

'On my count, Sharky,' said Pongwiffy. 'One, two, three!'

And together, over Pongwiffy's horrible thrumming, they burst into song.

> *'Well, here's a little ditty*
> *We're sure you'll want to sing.*
> *It isn't very witty*

And it doesn't mean a thing,
But we know you're gonna love it,
Of that we have no doubt,
'Cos once it's lodged inside your head
You'll never get it out!
Oooooooooooh ...
Banga-langa binga-linga bonga-longa,
bing, bong, boo,
Rooti-tooti, that's a beauty, rama-
dama ding, dong, do,
Twiddle-twaddle, nod your noddle,
see if you can do it too,
Banga-langa binga-linga bonga-longa,
bing, bong, boo!'

Pongwiffy played her discord one last time, Sharkadder gave her harmonica a long, vigorous suck, then there was silence. A long, long silence.

'So what do you think?' asked Pongwiffy hopefully.

More silence.

'Would you like to hear it again?' offered Pongwiffy.

All eyes were on Sourmuddle, who was sitting with her head on one side and her eyes closed. She was the Grandwitch. Nobody liked to venture an opinion until she had spoken. Suddenly, she opened her eyes, gave a brisk little nod and said, 'It'll do.'

'She likes it!' shrieked Pongwiffy.

'She likes it!' trilled Sharkadder. They both leapt to their feet, linked arms and did a celebratory little jig.

'I'm not saying it's great music, mind,' added Sourmuddle. 'In fact, musically speaking, it's rubbish. But it's rubbish with universal appeal. The sort of thing people hum in the bath. Am I right?'

It didn't do to disagree with Sourmuddle. With one accord, everyone else decided that they liked it too.

'It's catchy, I'll say that,' agreed Scrofula.

'Aye. It wasnae what Ah was expectin', but Ah must say Ah'm pleasantly surprised,' nodded Macabre.

'Sing it again,' ordered Sourmuddle. 'Without the harmonica solo this time. Pongwiffy, don't thrum so much.'

'I like to thrum,' said Pongwiffy, hurt. 'It's what I do.'

'Well, do it quieter,' ordered Sourmuddle.

So Pongwiffy and Sharkadder sang it again. And again. By the third time, everybody knew the words and was singing along. Even Bonidle roused herself enough to clap along and Gaga started dancing on the piano until Sourmuddle made her stop. There followed a noisy, cacophonous hour while those with instruments tried to work out what they would play and the singers practised getting the tune right. Then they tried it again.

And again.

And again.

And very slowly they began to improve.

CHAPTER SIXTEEN

'How Do Dey Make Cars Anyway?'

Goblins are just not practically minded. They have trouble doing up their own bootlaces, so it isn't surprising that building a car from scratch was proving a tad challenging.

Right now, most of them were gathered worriedly around the huge pile of junk, scratching their heads and talking about wheels. The problem wasn't how many were needed. They had already agreed on that. One on each corner and a spare on the back. Seven. Easy. No, the problem was that the wheels they had collected didn't match. They had: one

'Oi, Plug?' sniggered Sproggit. 'I said bum. 'Ear me? Tee hee.'

The Goblins collapsed anew with mirth.

'I heard,' sighed Plugugly. He had so hoped that, somewhere along the line, inspiration would come and the way forward would miraculously become clear. But it hadn't.

'So why ain't you laughin'?'

''Cos,' said Plugugly, ''cos dis is *serious*. Dis isn't a game we is havin'. Car buildin' is *serious*, right? We gone to all dat trouble gettin' all dis stuff an' tryin' to look at how cars is fitted togedder an' now we has got to de hard bit an' if we don't stop messin' about an' – an' *pull togedder* an' work out how to do it, we has wasted our time. I can't do it by myself. We has *all* got to do it. Right?'

This was probably the longest, most solemn speech he had made in his entire life. The rest of the Gaggle listened to it with respectful incomprehension.

'Right,' said Sproggit. 'Still – *bum*,' he added, with a little snort, setting the Goblins off again.

Plugugly looked at them writhing around helplessly. Then he looked at the huge pile of junk. Briefly, he closed his eyes, and the vision came to him. The vision that haunted his dreams. The one

333

where he was bowling along a road at the wheel of a shiny limousine, the twin of Sheridan Haggard's, *exactly* like it except just a fraction bigger, with the sun shining and the windows open. Off to the seaside, with a posh picnic in the boot. Wayfarers pointing and crying out with amazement as he passed ...

He opened his eyes. Lardo was looking down his own trousers for his hat. Hog had climbed on to the seat of the armchair and was bouncing up and down, making chicken noises. Sproggit was poking Stinkwart with the collapsed umbrella and Eyesore and Slopbucket had placed buckets over their heads and were charging each other head first.

Why had he ever thought it would work? Why?

'I dunno,' he said sadly. 'How do dey make cars anyway?'

Nobody even heard.

He heaved a deep sigh, threw down the hose and the string, kicked the lemon grater into a corner and walked out of the cave.

Outside, just to bring him down even more, as well as getting dark it was damp. A thin, depressing drizzle was slowly turning the scrubby slopes of the Lower Misty Mountains into a mudslide.

Plugugly turned up his collar, thrust his hands

into his pockets and trudged off down the slope. He needed to be alone for a while, to get over his disappointment. Actually, he wasn't sure he would *ever* get over it.

Why did things never work out right for Goblins? Why did other people get all the brains and all the luck? Why was it always *somebody else* who found a mysterious ring or Magic lamp or lucky stone or something and got three wishes? Why? Why, for instance, couldn't he have a pet, like that nice little dog? At least it would be company. And he could take it for walks and train it to bite Sproggit, who was really getting on his nerves these days.

He aimed a dejected kick at a small pebble lying in his path.

And that's when he heard it. A jolly little sound, coming from somewhere off in the distance.

'*Woof!*'

Plugugly stopped. Had he imagined it?

'*Woof! Woof!*' No. It was coming closer. Could it be?

He rounded a clump of prickly bushes – and suddenly his arms were full of wagging, wiggling bones!

'Doggy!' cried Plugugly, drowning in happiness and slobber. 'My little doggy!'

*

'Faster!' instructed Sheridan Haggard. 'Faster, *faster*! Put your foot down!'

'I am,' said the Thing, screeching around a corner on two wheels. 'It's a bendy road, boss. Calm down, why don'tcha?'

'Calm *down*?' boomed Sheridan, all righteous indignation. 'A pack of Goblins have stolen my beloved pet and you're telling me to *calm down*?'

'You don't *know* they stole him, though, do you? You didn't see 'em actually do it.'

'Of course they did it! They were messing around with the limo again. I saw them!'

'Yeah, but the doors were locked. I know 'cos I did it myself. Ribs must have opened it himself, from the inside.'

'He's a *dog*, Thing, not a locksmith or a trained octopus! No, it's quite clear what happened. Those wretched Goblins managed to force the door open and they've stolen him for his lovely jewelled collar. Oh, Ribsy, my poor little Ribsy! Why did I leave you?'

Sheridan began to sob. Large tears trickled down his smooth cheekbones. (This may surprise you. But then, Ribs can slobber and both of them can eat and drink. Skeletons have their own mysterious ways of doing things, and that's that.)

'Hold tight, boss!' advised the Thing, crashing the gears and narrowly avoiding a rock. 'We're going up the mountain. Lot o' potholes. One coming up right n—'

As it spoke, there came the unmistakable sound of a skull crashing into a hard roof, followed by a very rude, un-newsreader-like word.

'Oops,' said the Thing. 'See what I mean?'

Up in the cave, it suddenly dawned on the Goblins that Plugugly was missing.

'Where's he gone?' asked Hog.

'Who cares?' sniffed Lardo. He was down in the dumps because he still hadn't found his hat. The others shrugged their shoulders and looked blank.

'When did we see him last?' pondered Hog. 'Anyone remember?'

''E was makin' that speech,' said Stinkwart. 'About bein' serious about sumfin'. 'E sounded a bit fed up. I didn't take it seriously, though.'

'*He's* fed up?' sulked Lardo. 'Huh. At least he ain't lost 'is hat.'

'Fink we should go and look for 'im?' (Hog)

'Why?' (Sproggit)

'I dunno. We're s'posed to be makin' the car, right?

It was his idea. Why should we do all the work while he slopes off?'

'Oh. Right!'

So the six of them set off to look for Plugugly. Slipping and sliding down the muddy slope, they were soon swallowed up by shadows.

No sooner had they vanished than two headlights stabbed the darkness and Sheridan's sleek limousine came purring up the track, coming to a halt directly outside the Goblins' cave.

The driver's door shot open and the Thing scrambled out, pausing only to dispose of its chauffeur hat and don a pair of minder-type dark glasses to make itself look tough before racing round to open the passenger door at the back. After a brief pause, Sheridan emerged. He unfolded his bony frame with a series of little clicks and pops, then stared around grimly in the fading light, taking in the depressing surroundings.

'Ribs?' he shouted. 'Are you there, boy?'

Silence. Without another word, Sheridan stalked towards the cave with the Thing hurrying at his heels.

Rather to their surprise, the front boulder was rolled to one side. Beyond lay total darkness. Sheridan bent down and squinted in.

'Hello there!' he called, his golden-brown voice bouncing off the walls. 'Anybody in?'

Silence.

'There's no point in hiding, you know,' boomed Sheridan threateningly. 'I know you're in there. Send out the dog, then come out yourselves with your hands up. I'm making a Skeleton's arrest. I shall count to three.'

More silence.

'One – two – three! That's it, I'm coming in!'

'Hang on, boss. Could be a trap,' advised the Thing, in its role as bodyguard.

'Oh. Do you really think so?'

'Could be.'

'In that case, you go first.'

'Right,' said the Thing stoutly. 'Here I go. Stay right there.'

And it marched into the cave.

'What can you see?' called Sheridan.

'Nothing,' shouted the Thing. 'I'm feeling my way round the edges.'

'Is it safe?'

'Well, I don't think there's anyone at home.'

'In that case, I'm coming in. Wow! It's very dark. I can't see a thing . . .'

A cave in total darkness is hazardous enough, what with low bits of ceiling to bang your head on and half-buried rocks to trip over. It is made doubly dangerous when it contains a huge, tottering, precariously balanced mountain of rubbish.

As you might expect, Sheridan walked slap bang into it!

If you had been standing outside, you would have heard a startled cry – then a rumbling, slithering effect, followed by dramatic crashing and tinkling noises as the huge edifice came tumbling down.

Then silence.

'An' dat's when I found de Lucky Wishin' Pebble,' gabbled Plugugly happily as the Gaggle hurried back up the slope with Ribs racing around their ankles. 'Just as I was rememberin' about de little dog and wishin' he was mine. An' I kicked it, just like dat, an' den suddenly, dere 'e was! De little dog, wot I love. Just as I was feelin' sad about de car an' wishin' sumfin' good would happen. An' den I kicked it again an' wished I' ad someone to tell about it an' you lot shows up! Den I kicked it again!'

'An' what happened?'

'Well – nuffin'. But at least I got a doggy.'

340

'I wants to borrow the Lucky Wishin' Pebble,' whined Lardo. 'I wants me hat back.'

'I fink it only works for me,' Plugugly told him sadly. 'Sorry.'

'What we gonna call the doggy?' asked Slopbucket. 'Needs a name, don't 'e? What's a good name fer a dog?'

'Puss?' suggested Hog.

'Fluffy?' (That was Stinkwart's offering.)

'Mr Stuart Prichard?' (Sproggit, being particularly weird.)

'Who?' said everybody, staring at him.

'Mr Stuart Prichard. That's the name of my gran's dentist.'

'Well, it's not a good name for a little doggy,' said Plugugly firmly. 'If you fink I's gonna call my little doggy Mr Stuart Prichard, you is mad. No, I know what I is gonna call him. I is gonna call him Fang de Wonder Hound. I is gonna teach him tricks an' everyfin'. Now, if only we had a car, everyfin' would be jus' perfect – *hold it*!'

He came to a sudden stop. Everyone piled up behind, like dominoes. Fang the Wonder Hound stopped racing around like a mad thing and came to sit at Plugugly's feet, panting up lovingly into his

341

face. For once, Plugugly didn't notice. Something had caught his attention.

'Look!' he gasped, pointing with a trembling hand. 'De Lucky Pebble *did* work anudder time after all!'

Sure enough, there, outside the cave, stood the car of their dreams. Fang the Wonder Hound recognised it immediately, and proceeded to bite the tyres.

'It's exackly like the uvver one!' marvelled Hog. 'The one that Skellington's got. Same colour, everyfin'! That's some Pebble you got there, Plug.'

'I know,' said Plugugly proudly. He fingered the wonderful stone deep in his pocket, reached down and gave his new pet a fierce, loving hug. For once, all his dreams were coming true.

Hardly daring to believe their own eyes, the Goblins crept forward and ran their hands over the limousine's gleaming surface. Experimentally, Eyesore pressed the handle on the driver's door. Instantly, it swung open, revealing a rich, leather interior and a set of keys hanging from the ignition.

'It's open!' breathed Hog.

'So what are we waitin' for?' squealed Sproggit, wild with excitement. 'Let's go for a drive! Let's go to Sludgehaven-on-Sea! Right *now*!'

There was a sudden silence.

'*Can* we drive?' asked Eyesore doubtfully.

'No,' came the chorus.

'Do we care?'

'No!'

'Then let's go!'

Overcome with emotion, young Sproggit threw his hat in the air, sank to his knees in the dirt and hugged the fender.

'Best push the boulder over,' said Slopbucket. 'Don't wanna come 'ome an' find we bin robbed.'

'Right,' said Hog. 'They might nick our stuff.'

'We ain't got any stuff,' observed Lardo. 'Except our huntin' bags. And they got holes in.'

'What about the Car Stuff?' Eyesore said.

'We don't need that now we got a proper car, though, do we?' said Stinkwart.

'Eyesore is right,' said Plugugly. 'We doesn't want people snoopin' about. Supposin' someone tells Pongwiffy? We'll be for it. Or what if a bear comes along lookin' for somewhere to move in?'

Everyone agreed that it made sense to roll the boulder back in place. Nobody thought to check inside first, of course. That's Goblins for you.

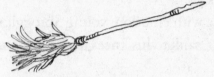

CHAPTER SEVENTEEN
Robbed!

I don't believe it!' wailed Pongwiffy. 'I've been robbed!'

She was standing, looking out over the rubbish dump with Sharkadder. It was a bright, sunny morning – the first morning she had seen for some time. Nights had been taken up with rehearsals and the days spent catching up with eating, sleeping and shouting at Hugo.

'It's a bit depleted, I'll give you that,' agreed Sharkadder.

'Depleted? It's a shadow of its former self! Stripped bare of all the choice bits! The bath, the mangle, the shopping trolley – gone, all gone!'

344

'We're talking about a rubbish dump here, Pong,' remarked Sharkadder. 'I don't know why you're getting quite so worked up.'

'Because it's *my* rubbish dump. Mine. I've been so busy lately I just haven't thought to check on it. And somebody's been here helping themselves while my back's been turned. Who, I wonder? Who'd be stupid enough to tangle with me?'

'Actually, I think I can help you there,' said Sharkadder. She stooped down and poked a long green talon at something lying by her boot. 'Look. A clue.' Gingerly, she picked up the grubby item and held it out. 'A Goblin hat, if I'm not very much mistaken.'

'Typical!' raged Pongwiffy. 'Sneaky little tea leaves! How dare they! Well, they'll be sorry. Just wait till I get my hands on them. In fact, I'll do it right now, while the mood's on me. I'll just go and get my Wand. Coming?'

'No,' said Sharkadder, 'and neither are you. Now is not the time, Pong. We've got to focus on the Contest. Just think – tomorrow night! Only thirty-six hours to go. And I haven't even started putting my make-up on.'

'Gosh,' said Pongwiffy, startled. 'Is it? Is it *really* tomorrow?'

'Yes. Isn't it terrifying? In a sort of deliciously exciting way? I simply can't wait to see myself on spello. I can't decide what to wear. Lilac or puce? Shoes or boots? Hat or no hat? Whenever I think of it, I come over all of a flutter. I just know our song will win, don't you?'

'Sure to,' agreed Pongwiffy, adding, 'although I've got a feeling the Familiars'll be strong contenders. Hugo's very competitive. And they say the Banshees are good. And then there are the Wizards. You know how they like to get one over on us . . .'

'Oh, stop being doomy!' cried Sharkadder gaily. 'Have faith! Of course we'll win, with our brilliant song.'

'You're right,' said Pongwiffy, cheering up. 'It *is* a good song, isn't it?'

'It's perfect. We'll win, and then we'll get presented with the cup and I'll be on spello and get to meet Sheridan Haggard and we'll get a lovely holiday and – oh, I'm so excited I could *burst*! I do think a Spellovision Song Contest is one of your best ever ideas, Pong, I really do! Come on – let's go and practise!'

'All right,' said Pongwiffy. 'But those Goblins are really for it when I catch up with them.'

Ali Pali sat in his office with his feet on his desk, studying the latest viewing figures. There was good news and bad news.

The bad news was that the viewing public was getting fussier by the hour. No longer could people be palmed off with a load of Gnomes. In fact, Gnomes were currently out of favour. Anything featuring Gnomes caused people to switch off in droves. People didn't seem to be interested in Fiends much, either, or in celebrity Dwarf chefs, or in instructive documentaries about embalming.

The only programme that continued to enjoy undiminished popularity was *The News*. People always tuned in for that. It had become even more popular since the announcement about the forthcoming Spellovision Song Contest. Every news bulletin ended with Sheridan reading out the latest entrants.

The Spellovision Song Contest. Here, at last, was good news. Oh yes. Very good news indeed.

These days, the talk was of nothing else. In cottages, caves and castles, the excited contestants would switch on *The News*, then sit on the edge of their seats in great excitement, waiting for their own name to be read out in Sheridan's rich, honeyed tones. When it came, they would go pink and either nudge their fellow watchers or hug themselves, if they were alone.

Pongwiffy's Hamster had been right. A Spellovision Song Contest was a magnificent idea. It held universal appeal. Spellovisions were selling like hot cakes. Desperate advertisers were sending bundles of used notes through the post in the hope of bribing Ali Pali to show their advertisement at peak time, when the whole world would be watching.

Ali hoped he was going to make a *lot* of money.

CHAPTER EIGHTEEN

Trapped!

Sheridan Haggard sat on the rotten garden bench, skull in hands, attempting to recover from his ordeal. It had taken ages for the Thing to dig him out from beneath the avalanche of rubbish. He still felt shaky.

'Feelin' better now, boss?' enquired the Thing. It was of a practical disposition, was the Thing, and possessed of exceptional energy, which is why it made such a good Everything Else Boy. It also possessed a useful box of matches. As well as extracting both itself and Sheridan from the sea of junk, it had located a

350

couple of candle stubs stuck in niches in the walls, so at least they were no longer in darkness. It was now scuttling about tidying up – a thankless task owing to the sheer volume of rubbish, but, then again, the Thing specialised in thankless tasks.

'I feel *terrible*,' groaned Sheridan. 'I'm covered in filth, my skull aches and I'm suffering from shock. Quick! Champagne! Failing that, mineral water.'

'No water here, boss,' said the Thing cheerfully. 'I've checked. No grub either.'

'In that case,' said Sheridan, attempting to rise in a wobbly way, then sitting back down again, 'I shall leave immediately. Assist me to my feet and help me outside. I require fresh air.'

'Can't be done, boss,' said the Thing. It pointed to the heavy boulder that blocked the opening. 'See? Someone's stuck the stone back. We can't get out. You'd need a lot o' muscle power to shift that baby.'

Whistling cheerily, it waded around in the sea of rubbish, collecting up armfuls of miscellaneous tat, totally unfazed by their grim situation.

'Are you telling me,' began Sheridan, voice trembling with indignation, 'are you *seriously* telling me that we are *stuck here*? Without food and drink? In a *Goblin cave* that for some mysterious reason

351

contains the world's biggest scrap heap, which has recently *collapsed on my head*?'

'Yep.'

'But – this is *preposterous*! How did that boulder get there?'

'Someone pushed it, I s'pose,' said the Thing with a shrug.

'Who?'

'Didn't see, did I? I was pulling you out from under the junk at the time. But whoever did it took the limo. I heard it leave.'

'The limo?' Sheridan, white already, went even whiter with shock. 'They've taken *my limo*?'

''Fraid so.'

'Well, I'm not having it!' announced Sheridan. He rose to his feet, swayed a bit, then tottered over to the cave mouth. He set his shoulder bone to the boulder and pushed with all his might. His slight weight made no impression whatsoever.

'Give up, boss,' said the Thing. 'You're too flimsy. You'll do yourself an injury.'

Sheridan strained ineffectually for another few seconds, then gave in. Gasping, he staggered back to the bench, buried his skull in his hands again and groaned with despair.

'Cheer up,' advised the Thing. 'It could be worse.'

'How?' moaned Sheridan in hollow tones.

'Well, at least we got matches an' there's plenty o' chair legs an' that. We can light a fire if we get cold.'

'Oh yes,' said Sheridan, heavily sarcastic. 'That's a *good* idea. Let's start a *big fire* in a *cave we can't get out of.* Oh, what *fun*, do *let's*.'

'All right,' said the Thing a bit sniffily. 'No need to be sarky.'

'There is *every* need!' shouted Sheridan. His golden voice had acquired a tinny, not-so-golden edge. 'Don't you realise how serious this is? I am *the newsreader*! In less than one hour I am meant to be at my desk reading the midnight bulletin! Not trapped in a stinking Goblin cave drowning in tin trays and old prams, watching you *tidy up* like some kind of demented Cinderella!'

'I can't help it,' argued the Thing. 'I gotta keep busy. It's my nature.'

'Well, I forbid it! Stop it this instant and think of a plan to get us out of here! Make it quick. I've never liked small spaces. Come on, come on! I'm already going stir-crazy! Arggh! The walls, the walls! *The walls are closing in!*'

Sheridan reached out and clutched the Thing in a panicky grip.

'Calm down, boss! Take deep breaths!' advised the Thing, smacking at the bony hands.

'Get me out! Get me out!' howled Sheridan, breaking into a cold sweat. He stumbled over to the walls and began feeling them for cracks.

'I can't, boss. There ain't no way out. All we can do is wait until they send out a search party.'

Sheridan suddenly stood stock-still. There was a glimmer of hope in his eye sockets.

'Ah,' he said. 'A rescue party. Of course. They'll be sure to come looking when I don't turn up, right?'

'Sure to. You being such an important person an' all. See? Now you're thinking on the bright side.'

'Yes,' said Sheridan. He took out a large white hanky and mopped his streaming brow. 'Yes, you're quite right, Thing. I mustn't overreact. They'll send out a search party. There's one on its way right now, I imagine?'

'Sure to be,' soothed the Thing. 'And as soon as we hear 'em coming we'll yell out and they'll rescue us. Before you know it, you'll be reading out all about yourself on the news. It'll be in the paper too, I shouldn't wonder. Think of the publicity. *Famous Celebrity Newsreader In Goblin Cave Rescue Drama*. I can see the headlines now.'

'Yes,' muttered Sheridan. He was calmer now, but still a bit twitchy. 'Yes, you're right. Of course. In fact, this is probably quite a good career move. But what about poor Ribs? We still haven't found him, have we?'

'He'll be fine. Probably found his own way home by now. That, or gone wild and living with wolves.'

'I suppose you're right,' sighed Sheridan.

'I know I am. There. Feelin' better now?'

'A little.'

'So can I get on with the tidyin'?'

'*No!* Leave it, d'you hear? You take your orders from me. And right now, your job is to keep me amused. Take my mind off things. Entertain me until the rescue party arrives.'

'Fair enough,' agreed the Thing amiably. 'What do you want? I Spy? Charades? Fancy a sing-song?'

'Oh, *bother*!' cried Sheridan, curling one hand into a bony fist and smacking it into the other. 'What did you have to say *that* for?'

'What? What did I say?'

'*Sing*. Now you've gone and reminded me that it's the Spellovision Song Contest tomorrow night and I'm presenting the trophy to the winner! I

355

simply *have* to be there. I say! You don't think there's the slightest chance that we'll still be here tomorrow, do you?'

'No,' said the Thing, crossing its fingers behind its back.

'Tell the truth. I can take it.'

'Yes, then.'

'Aaargh!' wailed Sheridan. 'I can't take it! I can't! The walls are moving in again! The walls! *Stop the walls!*'

'I'm kidding, I'm kidding! Calm down! 'Course they'll find us. Any minute now, I expect. Tell you what. Sit down and I'll read to you. How's that?'

'Read what? We haven't got any books.'

'That's what you think.' The Thing reached into its pocket, withdrew something the size of a matchbox and waved it triumphantly. 'See? A book. Found it amongst all the rubbish.'

'Really? What's it called?'

'*The Little Book of Hamster Wit and Wisdom*,' read the Thing, squinting at the tiny writing.

'Hmm. Odd sort of thing to turn up in a Goblins' cave. Still. I suppose it's better than nothing. Fire away.'

'Right. Shouldn't take long, it's very small. Are

you sitting comfortably? Then I'll begin. *What kind of Hamsters live at the North Pole? Cold ones.* Ha, ha, get it? That's good, that is. Here's another one. *If at first you don't suck seed, suck, suck, suck again . . .'*

CHAPTER NINETEEN

Setting Up

The Spellovision Song Contest was going to be held in Witchway Hall. It was the only place big enough to hold the huge number of contestants taking part and their armies of supporters. (The Hall might not look like much from the outside, but the interior has the useful design feature of being able to magically expand into the fourth dimension. When necessary, it can accommodate vast crowds.)

Vast crowds were what Ali Pali confidently expected. Vast crowds and record-breaking viewing figures.

Right now, he sat by himself in the front row,

tapping numbers into his calculator and keeping an eye on the camera crew, which was busy setting up.

Everything was going to plan. The Tree Demon was scuttling about with a big furry microphone on a stick. Vincent Van Ghoul was ducking and bobbing around the aisles, staring through the viewfinder of his spellovision camera, trying out different angles. Brenda was directing a couple of Gnomes where to put the scoreboard. The Witchway Rhythm Boys were in the orchestra pit, setting out their music stands.

There was only one niggling worry. Sheridan Haggard and the Everything Else Boy had gone missing. Nothing had been seen or heard of them since the evening news bulletin the night before. They hadn't turned up for the midnight news, which was highly unusual.

Ali had rung Sheridan's crystal ball to demand an explanation – but Sheridan wasn't answering. Ali had sent a runner round to the castle. The runner had come back saying that the place was all locked up and the limo gone from the garage. No note of apology, no sign of foul play, nothing.

'Any news, boss?' asked Vincent Van Ghoul, squinting through his camera.

'No,' said Ali. 'Nothing.'

'I shouldn't worry,' said Vincent. 'He'll turn up. Catch Sheridan missing something like this. He's probably at the tailor's having a posh suit made for the occasion.'

'You may be right,' said Ali Pali. 'But I'm a businessman. I can't afford to take chances. This contest must go off without a hitch. Everything is riding on it. My reputation, as well as my bank balance.'

'Then you'll be pleased to know I've got everything under control,' broke in a new voice. An all too familiar odour was in the air. Ali Pali whirled round, startled. Pongwiffy was sitting in the seat directly behind him.

'Oh,' said Ali. 'It's you. What do you mean, under control?'

'Meaning,' said Pongwiffy smugly, 'meaning that you can forget about Sheridan Haggard. I've come up with someone much better. I've written to my very good friend Scott Sinister, telling him to come along to present the prizes.'

'Really?' Ali Pali's beam went from ear to ear. 'But this is wonderful news! He's really coming?'

'Oh yes,' said Pongwiffy. 'He'll come all right. In fact, he'll be delighted.'

360

Actually, this wasn't quite true. Scott Sinister was less than delighted when Pongwiffy's missive dropped through the letterbox of his luxury trailer. It said:

deer scott,
i no you will be pleezed to hear frum me agin.
yes, it is i, pongwiffy, yore number wun fan. hav
you seen this new spellellovishun lark theyve got
now? persnally i reckon it needs livening up. it is
mi idea to haf a song contest wich i no evrywun
wil enjoi espeshully as you are presentin the priz
to the winers who will of cors be we witches.
congratulashuns on reseeving this onour.
see you in witchway hawl nex saterday nite.

yore frend and admirer

pongwiffy
x x x x x

ps I dont trust that skellington who is renting yore
cassel. shifty eye sockets.

CHAPTER TWENTY
The Contest Begins

The lights dimmed. Filth the Fiend played a drum roll. The audience settled back into their seats as a magnified voice boomed forth from nowhere.

'Ladies and gentlemen, viewers at home, welcome to the Witchway Wood Spellovision Song Contest! Please give a big hand to the head of Spellovision Enterprises and your host for this evening – the genial Genie, *Mr Ali Pali*!'

The Witchway Rhythm Boys launched into something jaunty, the lights came back up and the audience cheered wildly as Ali, plump paunch tightly encased in a glittery jacket, came running onstage, waving and smiling. He jogged to a halt by a large board on which were written the names of all the contestants placed alphabetically, like this:

Contestant	Song	Score
1. Banshees	'Oh Woe!'	☐
2. Familiars	'Oh, I Do Like to Be a Witch Familiar'	☐
3. Ghosts	'A Haunting We Will Go'	☐
4. Ghouls	'Here come the Ghouls'	☐
5. Gnomes	'Gnome, Sweet Gnome'	☐
6. Mummies	'All Wrapped Up and No Place to Go'	☐
7. Trolls	'Trollhouse Rock'	☐
8. Vampires	'That's a Very Nice Neck, By Heck!'	☐
9. Werewolf	'A Change is Gonna Come'	☐
10. Witches	'Banga Langa Bing Bong Boo!'	☐
11. Wizards	'The Long and Winding Beard'	☐
12. Zombies	'Whoops, There Goes Me Arm!'	☐

Vincent Van Ghoul moved in for a close-up. Ali, smiling a dazzling smile that would have given a piano keyboard a run for its money, waited for the applause to subside, then said, 'Thank you, one and all. Well, what a wonderful occasion this is. First, a big hand for the Mistress of the Scoreboard – your very own weather girl, the lovely Brenda!'

To more jolly vamping from the Rhythm Boys, Brenda slouched onstage wearing a lurid pink evening gown. Her green bird's-nest hairdo looked as though it had been kicked into place by some couldn't-care-less eagle. Chewing, she took up her station next to the scoreboard.

'Isn't she gorgeous?' beamed Ali Pali. 'Now then. As this is our first ever Song Contest, I will briefly explain how it works. The acts will appear in alphabetical order. When all the songs have been performed, the voting will take place. The votes will be cast by twelve specially selected juries to ensure no cheating. Each jury has ten points to divide as they please, with the proviso that they are not allowed to vote for their own song. The points will be totalled by Brenda at the end.'

The audience, bored by all this mathematical talk, was beginning to doze off. But they jerked awake again as Ali raised his voice.

'And now, the big surprise of the evening – an unexpected guest! I know that a lot of you were expecting our popular newsreader Sheridan Haggard to be here this evening. Sadly, he is indisposed.'

'Boo!' shouted Sheridan's disappointed fans.

'The Skeletons have withdrawn from the competition in protest,' continued Ali, 'but never mind, *we* don't care, because we have a *real* treat in store. Ladies and gentlemen, let's give a big Witchway welcome for that great star of stage and screen – *Scott Sinister*!'

Gasps, startled squeaks, and an outbreak of thunderous cheers broke out as the popular star strolled on from the wings. As always, he wore his black velvet cape and trademark sunglasses. He waved a languid hand, acknowledging the applause. Someone threw a bunch of flowers onstage. Scott picked them up, sniffed them, then presented them to Brenda, who glamorously kicked them into the orchestra pit.

Backstage, Pongwiffy looked up smugly from the monitor. (This is a special spellovision that shows the events going on out front.)

'You see?' she said. 'I knew he'd come. Do anything for me, he will, because I'm his biggest fan.'

(In truth, Scott hadn't wanted to come, not one little bit. But he knew better than to turn down a request from Pongwiffy, who can get quite spiteful when things don't go her way. Scott knows this. He has crossed her before.)

'Scott will be awarding the fabulous prizes to

tonight's winners,' announced Ali, to more cheers. Scott nodded and smiled and waved and blew kisses.

'All right, that'll do,' said Brenda. 'You can shove off now.'

Scott was happy to oblige. Live appearances were more exhausting than film work, which consists of a lot of hanging around. By simply walking on, he had already done more work in one evening than in the past six weeks. He hurried back to his dressing room to recover.

Back onstage, things were beginning to happen.

'And now!' Ali was shouting. 'The moment you have all been waiting for – the first song! This is the entry from the Banshees and features the Banshee Girls' Choir singing "Oh Woe!"'

The choir shuffled on, red-eyed and miserable-looking. There were six of them, all wearing trailing white nightgowns and sporting the regulation Banshee hairdo – long, wild and uncontrollably frizzy. Being professional weepers, they all carried large, businesslike handkerchiefs. The tallest – presumably the leader – raised her hanky to her nose and had a jolly good blow. This was evidently the signal to start.

366

Oh woe!' wailed the Banshees. *'Oh woe!*
Misery, doom and dismay,
Let's all sob in our hankies,
That's the Banshee way.
Let's whine and wail and whinge, girls,
Let's all get depressed,
Let's howl and shriek for the whole of the week,
'Cos that's what we do best . . .'

There was quite a bit more   of this sort
of thing. Banshees are
good at depression.
The interminable
song finally
ended in a
welter of
sobs, breast
beating
and hair
tearing –
and that
was just the
audience!
The choir
drooped

offstage, wringing out their sodden hankies.

After a moment's pause, Ali Pali bounced back on.

'So there we have it! Thank you, ladies. A truly tragic start to the contest. And now, the Familiars, with a song entitled "Oh I Do Like to Be a Witch Familiar".'

Hugo, wearing a tiny bow tie and clutching a miniature conductor's baton, hurried onstage. He was followed by the rest of the Familiars in varying degrees of stage fright. Snoop, Rory and Vernon looked boldly confident. IdentiKit and CopiCat looked smug. Speks looked unsettled, as though he would much rather be elsewhere, bringing up a pellet. Barry and Slithering Steve were both dying of shyness. Dudley brought up the rear, looking sullen. Overhead, Gaga's bats flapped about as they always did. Nobody knew what they were feeling.

Bonidle's Sloth had fallen asleep in the dressing room.

Hugo took up his position centre stage and waited until everyone had formed a relatively tidy group. There was a bit of nervous throat clearing. Rory blew the fringe out of his eyes. Then Hugo raised his baton . . . and the song began.

CHAPTER TWENTY-ONE
Rescued

Sheridan Haggard sat slumped with his skull in his hands as the Thing continued to read extracts from Hugo's book by the dim light of the last, guttering candle. The funny thing was, it was a very small book and yet it never seemed to end.

'*You can lead a Hamster to its wheel but you can't make it run,*' the Thing informed him. The only response was a low moan.

'*What would we do in a world without Cats, apart from be happy?*' continued the Thing. '*Even a Hamster can be big in the pictures. What do you*

get if you cross a Cat with a skunk? Dirty looks from the skunk.'

'Stop!' groaned Sheridan, rocking to and fro.

'What's blue and furry? A cat holding its breath. Musical Hamsters fiddle with their whiskers. Cats have feelings too – but, hey, who cares? What is the best way to keep Hamsters? Don't return them. A wise Hamster . . .'

'No more!' screamed Sheridan, leaping to his feet. 'I can't take any more of this rodent rubbish! Shut up, shut up, shut *up*!'

'OK,' said the Thing, sounding a bit hurt. 'Just trying to keep you amused, boss.'

'Well, don't. It's driving me out of my mind. Oh, what are we to *do*? We must have been in here for hours. Hours and hours. What time do you think it is? I've missed the midnight news, haven't I? Do you think they'll have sent the search party yet? That candle's about to go out, isn't it? Then we'll be in the dark! I don't like it in the dark! The walls will close in and we won't see them coming! Mummeeeeeee . . .'

Outside, a short way down the slope, a passing farmer on a cart clucked to his donkey, and it obediently ground to a halt. The farmer's name was Burl Bacon. The donkey was called Gervaise. Neither of them possessed a spellovision, which is why they were probably the only living creatures in the world who were neither performing in the Song Contest, watching it live nor glued to the spello.

Burl and Gervaise were currently on their way home from market, which had been cancelled owing to disinterest, although nobody had told them. Their cart was piled high with unsold baskets of eggs. It was now getting dark and they were taking the short cut home through Goblin territory.

The reason Burl stopped was because he heard something – something that sounded suspiciously like a hollow scream, coming from a cave set into the hill, just up the slope a bit.

'Hear that, Gervaise?' said Burl slowly, chewing on a straw reflectively. 'That there hollow screamin', comin' from behind that there boulder?'

Gervaise said nothing, because he was a donkey.

'*Heeeeeeelllllp!*' came the faint cry. '*Let me ouuuut!*'

'Reckon someone's trapped in that there cave, Gervaise,' reflected Burl, nodding wisely. 'That's what Oi reckons, at any rate.'

'*Arrrrgh! The walls! Heeeeeeeellllllp!*'

'Ar,' went on Burl, agreeing with himself. 'That's what 'appened, shouldn't wonder. Shouldn't wonder if someone 'adden gone an' got theirself trapped.

371

Now then. 'Ere's a dilemma. Shall us pay no mind an' go on back 'ome? Or shall us amble over an' take a little look?'

'*Heeeeeelllllllllp! Let me ouuuuuuuuuuut . . .*'

'Ah, sufferin' cowpats, us'll be charitable,' decided Burl. 'Righty-ho, Gervaise. In yer own time.'

Slowly, the cart creaked up the slope. When they reached the front boulder, Gervaise clopped to a halt. Unhurriedly, Burl removed his straw hat, scratched his head, replaced his hat, cleared his throat, removed the straw from his mouth and said, ''Ello?'

'At *last*!' cried the unseen owner of the voice. Up close, it sounded rich, but wobbly. Anybody but spellovisionless Burl would have recognised it instantly, despite the wobble. 'Oh, at last you're here! Where have you *been*?'

'Oi been to market,' Burl told him, after a bit of thought. 'But it were cancelled. Ar.'

'What? You're not the search party?' wailed the voice. You could hear the hysteria bubbling away just below the surface.

'Nope,' agreed Burl. 'Don't reckon Oi am.'

There came the sound of muffled voices conferring. Then: 'Did you just say you've been to market?' asked the voice.

'Ar,' agreed Burl.

'Meaning . . . *it's Saturday*?'

'Ar.'

'What time on Saturday?' asked the voice urgently.

'Eight o' the clock,' guessed Burl, looking up at the sky in wise-old-farmer fashion.

'Eight o'clock in the morning?'

'Nope. Evenin'.'

'Eight o'clock *Saturday evening*? Then it's *started*!' cried the voice, wild now. 'Whoever you are, listen carefully. My name is Sheridan Haggard. You will have heard of me. I am the famous spellovision newsreader and I have been trapped in this cave for a night and a day. I am due to present an award at a very important event, which has already started. My car has been stolen. And I will personally *mangle* whoever is responsible, I tell you that. Oh yes. I'll take him by the throat and I'll . . .'

The voice, which was rising in pitch, suddenly broke off. There was a bit of mumbling. Then it resumed. It was clear that the owner was barely under control.

'Forgive me if I sound a little strange. My brain has gone missing, owing to a combination of starvation, dehydration, claustrophobia and a surfeit of rodent sayings. Just get me to a camera and I'll be fine. You will be rewarded. I can promise you that.'

Burl Bacon looked around at his baskets of unsold eggs. A reward would certainly come in handy.

'Ar. Fair enough,' he agreed, and reached for a length of rope he kept in the cart for just such an emergency as this.

It was the work of minutes – fifty of them, to be precise – to lasso the boulder, attach the other end to the cart and get Gervaise to do the donkey work. As soon as the boulder was dragged to one side, a skeletal figure came staggering out into the moonlight, supported by a short, hairy Thing.

'My oh my,' said Burl, staring at the bony one in mild surprise. 'You *'ave* been in there for a long time.'

Neither of the ex-prisoners said a word. The Thing helped the trembling Skeleton to the back of the cart. Unresisting, the Skeleton climbed in and folded itself into a narrow space between the baskets of eggs. The Thing came round to the front.

'Shove over,' it ordered shortly.

'Eh?'

'I said, shove over. Got to get boss back to civilisation. All right back there, boss? Relax. We'll make it yet.'

374

'Now, 'old your 'orses,' objected Burl. He pointed an indignant finger at Sheridan, 'He never said nothin' about needin' a lift. He said if Oi got him out o' the cave Oi'd get a reward. He said . . .'

The Thing jumped on to the driver's seat, snatched the reins and gave Burl a brisk shove. To his surprise and annoyance, Burl suddenly found himself sitting in a clump of thistles, watching his own cart go swaying off into the distance, pulled by his own donkey.

He removed his straw hat and threw it into the dirt.

'Darn it,' said Burl. 'Ar.'

CHAPTER TWENTY-TWO
The Best Song

In Witchway Hall, the Witches sat in their dressing room watching the proceedings out front. The atmosphere was very tense. Soon, it would be their turn – and the nerves were really beginning to kick in. There was a lot of nail biting and compulsive peppermint sucking. There was nervous twiddling and fiddling with instruments. There was mass sweating and much complaining about the heat.

'My lipstick is melting,' complained Sharkadder. Tonight she was a vision in mauve. Mauve feather in mauve hair, mauve cheeks, mauve eyelids, mauve gown, mauve fingernails, mauve lipstick. She couldn't move for mauve.

On the monitor, four smarmy-looking Vampires in elegant evening dress were bowing low, having just finished a polished rendition of 'That's a Very Nice Neck, By Heck!', performed in close harmony. Their supporters were cheering loudly, but it wasn't everybody's cup of tea. A large section of the audience had shown complete indifference and talked throughout.

'Very professional,' admitted Sourmuddle. 'You've got to give credit where it's due.'

'I have reservations about the lyrics, though,' remarked Greymatter. 'Too much gore by half. Non-Vampires won't go for it.'

'I must say the standard in general is higher than I expected,' admitted Sourmuddle grudgingly. 'The Mummies were good. And the Ghouls.'

'I think the Familiars are far and away the best so far,' put in Scrofula. 'They were my favourites, anyway. I was really proud of my Barry. He sang his little heart out, did you notice?'

'An' ma Rory,' added Macabre. 'Had me in tears, he did. When he sang his wee solo.' She blew her nose loudly.

'They certainly gave it their all,' agreed Sludgegooey. 'Except for Dudley, who looked rather cross, I thought.'

'Anyway,' said Ratsnappy, 'we'll have our work cut out to beat them. It was a good little song your Hugo came up with, Pongwiffy.'

'I know,' said Pongwiffy. She had mixed feelings about Hugo's song. On the one hand, she was proud that he'd written it. On the other, she could have done without the competition. 'Of course, I taught him everything he knows,' she added.

'It'll be embarrassing, though, won't it?' fretted Bendyshanks. 'If the Familiars win. Imagine. They'll get all those prizes and go on holiday. We'll never live it down. Steve'll be insufferable.'

There came a chorus of agreement. It would indeed be humiliating if the Familiars won.

On screen, it was now the turn of a lone, slightly mangy Werewolf with patched dungarees and a banjo. Sweating heavily and showing the whites of his eyes, he perched on a stool in the middle of the stage and checked his tuning. The camera zoomed in for a close-up. A bead of sweat trickled down his nose.

'Look at him,' sniffed Scrofula. 'He's going for the sympathy vote.'

'It's us next, Ag,' quivered Bagaggle.

'I know, Bag,' quavered Agglebag.

And they reached for each other's hands and squeezed them tight.

It appeared that the Werewolf had forgotten the words to the first verse. The audience started an unsympathetic slow handclap.

There came a bang on the door and a Gnome stuck its head round.

'You're next, ladies. Everybody ready?'

'We're on!' gasped Sharkadder. 'Help!'

Nobody made a move. They were all rooted to the spot with fear. Even Sourmuddle choked on her throat lozenge.

'Come on, girls,' said Pongwiffy, always good in an emergency. She picked up her guitar and marched to the door. 'Deep breaths. We know we're good. Let's blow them away!'

'How are you doin', boss?' called the Thing over its shoulder. They were crawling along beneath the trees at a snail's pace.

'It's uncomfortable,' complained Sheridan, rattling around miserably. 'I'm not used to this uncouth form of transport. And it's *slow*. Can't you get that animal to move any faster? We'll never get there at this rate. Oh, if only we had the *limo* …'

At exactly that moment, something rather unexpected happened. There came a droning noise from behind, accompanied by a cloud of dust. Tyres screeched, a horn blared, there were the sounds of loud howls and demented barking – and around the bend came the limousine, with Plugugly hunched over the wheel, wearing a large pair of pink plastic comedy sunglasses with attached false moustache.

The rest of the Goblins hung on for dear life as they cornered on two wheels. Slopbucket was holding a bunch of balloons. Eyesore was wearing a Stetson. Lardo was clutching a goldfish in a plastic bag. Sproggit had a straw donkey in one hand and a stick of rock in the other. Stinkwart was wearing a beret and had a string of garlic wrapped around his neck. Hog was eating an enormous ice cream and offering licks to Fang the Wonder Hound, who had his head stuck out of the sunroof. Dozens of takeaway pizza boxes littered the back shelf, along with fishing rods, a set of golf clubs, a couple of tennis rackets, a large straw sombrero and a novelty ashtray inscribed *A present from Sludgehaven.*

Gervaise reared, plunged and lurched to one side as

the limousine, horn still blaring, flashed by with only centimetres to spare and zoomed off into the distance. The cart's off-side wheel trembled on the verge of the ditch, then miraculously righted itself. Gervaise took a few tottery steps towards the middle of the track, then stopped, breathing heavily.

There was a pause – then Sheridan's irate skull popped up from between the egg baskets. (Amazingly, they had all remained steady and none of the eggs was smashed.)

'My limo!' he shrieked. 'Did you see that? Goblins, driving *my limo*! *And they've got Ribsy!*' He pointed with a trembling digit. *'Follow that car!'*

CHAPTER TWENTY-THREE
More Contest

Ladies and gentlemen, time now for the next song –
"Banga Langa Bing Bong Boo!", performed
by – The Singing Witches!'

Vincent Van Ghoul moved in for a close-up as the
curtain rose on the Witchway Coven, all neatly in
place, looking terrified but determined to give it their
best shot.

It was a very different outfit from the rowdy rabble
who had turned up at Witchway Hall that first night
for a bit of a sing-song and a laugh. Nobody was
messing about now. Sourmuddle ran a tight ship. She

was in this contest to *win*. She sat bolt upright at the piano, sleeves rolled up, cracking her knuckles. It was clear she meant business.

She nodded at Greymatter, who poked Bonidle with a stick. Bonidle jerked awake, caught Sourmuddle's glare and started to tap an erratic beat on the drum. Sourmuddle played an interesting little twiddly bit on the piano, followed by a series of chunky chords played over an old-fashioned honky-tonk left hand.

At this point, Gaga, the official backing dancer, erupted from the wings and began wildly cavorting about. She had given a lot of thought to her stage costume. It consisted of yellow wellingtons and a grass hula skirt, teamed with a warm red jumper with a hole in the sleeve and a badly knitted frog on the back. A diving helmet was her chosen headgear. She looked – well, interesting.

Gradually, in response to glares from Sourmuddle, the rest of the instruments came in. Ratsnappy's reedy recorder. The twins' scratchy violins. Macabre's overwhelming bagpipes. Then the backing singers.

'*Ooby dooby doo*,' crooned Bendyshanks, Sludgegooey and Scrofula, breaking into the synchronised shuffle routine they had worked out earlier. '*Do wap, do wap!*'

It was a long introduction. Pongwiffy and Sharkadder grew visibly more tense as they waited for their big moment while Vincent ducked around them with his camera and the Tree Demon clonked them on the head with his microphone. Pongwiffy looked grouchy and miserable and appeared to be threatening the Tree Demon out of the corner of her mouth. Sharkadder, in contrast, went in for ear-to-ear smiling, so they didn't match very well.

But none of this mattered when they began to sing. It didn't matter that Pongwiffy sounded like a walrus in distress or that, on occasion, Sharkadder's shrill soprano wobbled out of orbit and off into another space and time. What mattered was the *song*.

The audience loved it.

> *'Well, here's a little ditty*
> *We're sure you'll want to sing . . .'*

began Pongwiffy. In the auditorium, there was an instant stir of interest. Everyone sat up, ears pricked.

> *'It isn't very witty*
> *And it doesn't mean a thing . . .'*

warbled Sharkadder. Several people in the front row leapt to their feet and waved their arms in the air.

> *'But we know you're gonna love it,*
> *Of that we have no doubt ...'*

honked Pongwiffy. People were clapping along in time to the rhythm now. Feet were tapping. A couple of Fiends began dancing madly in the aisle.

> *''Cos once it's lodged inside your head*
> *You'll never get it out!'*

contributed Sharkadder. *'Ooooooooooooh ...'* they both went, along with the backing singers. Then:

> *'Banga-langa binga-linga bonga-longa,*
> *bing, bong, boo ...'*

And the place went crazy! *This* was what the audience had come for. Oh yes. Forget the ballads and the clever stuff. What everyone wanted was a daft, jolly song with meaningless words that you could pick up in two minutes flat. Something that was easy to stomp your feet along with, or scrub your toenails to when you were lying in hot, soapy water. Something that made you feel *happy*. Something that put a soppy grin on your face. That's what they had come for. And that was exactly what they got.

There was a riot when the song finally reached its triumphant end.

'Witches! Witches!' chanted the audience, stamping their feet. 'Encore! Encore!'

'I think they liked it,' said Pongwiffy to Sharkadder out of the corner of her mouth.

'I think they did,' agreed Sharkadder, grinning and bowing low.

'More!' raved the audience. 'More! More! More!'

They weren't allowed more, though. One go at your song, that's all you got. To loud boos, Ali Pali hurried onstage, signalled for the curtain to be brought down, then began to explain the rules yet again. This was a contest. Each act performed the song once, and once only. There were still two acts to go – the Wizards and the Zombies. Then, and only then, could the specially selected juries cast their votes. So if the Witches could kindly get offstage and everyone could take their seats again, perhaps things could move on. At this point, a Gnome scuttled up and whispered in his ear.

'Correction,' amended Ali, speaking directly to

camera. 'There is only one more act. The Zombies have withdrawn because they've all got sore throats.'

'Sore at losing, more like!' heckled Pongwiffy, from behind the curtain. Zombie supporters in the audience blushed and hung their heads. They knew it was true.

The Wizards, however, were made of sterner stuff. Under the leadership of Dave the Druid, they had worked hard on their song. There was no way they would step back and let the Witches win without a fight. 'The Long and Winding Beard' would be given an airing, like it or not. (Ronald, of course, was particularly keen, because he had written the words.)

Wisely, the Wizards didn't bother with instruments. Their strength was in song. They concentrated on the vocals. Dave the Druid had done a good job. He had set Ronald's words to music. Over the past two weeks, he had made the Wizards struggle out of their armchairs and practise scales and do breathing exercises. He had taken them walking and stopped them eating too many sausages. He had divided everyone up into basses and tenors and falsettos and explained all about harmony. He had worked on pitch, tone and timing. He was a stickler for diction too. Every word was crisp and clear. End consonants were particularly emphasised.

'The longga andda windingg beardda,'
sang the Wizards.
'Is always in the jammm,
It'ss often fullll of toastttt
And egggg and bitss of hammmm.
I'll never shave it offf,
For that's the way I ammmmm ...'

The Witches stood in the wings, listening.

'They're *quite* good,' decided Sourmuddle, adding mysteriously, 'though I've never been one for male-voice choirs since I got bitten by one.'

'They're very good, actually,' sighed Sharkadder. 'Ronald wrote the words, you know. Talent runs in our family, as well as beauty.'

'They're not a patch on us, though,' said Pongwiffy, oozing confidence, now her bit was all over. 'We'll win. I'll bet my Wand on it.'

'I'm not so sure,' fretted Sharkadder.

'Beyond any shadow of doubt,' said Pongwiffy firmly. She hugged her guitar. 'A song like that? And talent like ours? No question.'

At this point, let's just pop back and see how the car chase is coming along.

Dramatic incidents don't happen much in the life of a cart-pulling donkey, and Gervaise had decided to get into the spirit of things. Right now, he was galloping after the limo at an alarming rate, with the Thing fighting to hang on to the reins. Sheridan Haggard was poised precariously on the swaying cart, a basket of eggs in each hand.

'Wot's 'appenin'?' bellowed Plugugly, wrenching the steering wheel hard left and missing the ditch by half an air molecule. 'Who's dat chasin' us?'

They zoomed round a corner and past a holly tree. All Slopbucket's balloons burst in a flurry of sharp pops. Fang the Wonder Hound was barking crazily and attempting to wriggle out through the sunroof. Several twigs and low-lying branches were lodged in his rib cage. The wind whistled through his bones.

'I can't see!' screeched Eyesore. 'There's egg all over the back window!'

'Oh no!' wailed Sproggit. 'Flyin' chickens!'

'That ain't no chickens!' bawled Hog. 'It's that Skellington! 'E wants 'is dog back! 'E's throwin' eggs at us!'

'Give 'im the dog!' screeched Stinkwart. 'Push it out the sunroof!'

'Don't you dare!' warned Plugugly, letting go of the

steering wheel and shaking his fist. 'You leave Fang alone, you – you *wicked* Goblin!'

'Log pile comin' up!' screamed Eyesore, covering his eyes. 'Plug! Watch the road!'

Plugugly swivelled round and grabbed the wheel. The car lunged to one side. More eggs splattered the windscreen.

'Watch out!'

'Arrrrgggh!'

'Faster, Plug! Go faster!'

Oh yes. The car chase is coming along nicely.

CHAPTER TWENTY-FOUR
And the Winner Is...

I n Witchway Hall, the votes were beginning to come in. Backstage, dressing rooms fell silent. Trembling contestants clustered around the monitors or hid in corners with their hands over their faces.

Only Scott Sinister was uninterested in the whole business. The monitor in his private dressing room was on, but he wasn't even watching. Bored out of his mind, he reclined on a couch with chunks of cucumber balanced on his eyelids, dreaming of the moment he could hand over the trophy, make his excuses, hopefully avoid that awful Pongwiffy and hurry off back to his rich and famous lifestyle.

Out front, Vince's camera was trained steadily on Ali Pali, who stood next to the scoreboard armed with earphones and a clipboard. Brenda, clearly underwhelmed by the whole thing, was reading a magazine.

'Yes, folks, I've just heard that we're now ready to hear the votes of the Troll jury,' announced Ali. He raised his head and addressed the air. 'Hello, Trolls, are you there?'

After a worrying moment or two, the air rang with a loud fit of coughing. Then a gruff, disembodied voice with an odd echo, which made it sound like it was coming from under a mountain (which it probably was), replied, 'Yer, Ali, 'ere we are.'

The Tree Demon held up a board saying *CLAP*. Obediently, the audience clapped.

''Ere are the votes of the Trollish jury,' the voice went on. 'The Banshees – nuthin'. Too depressin'.'

'Banshees – no points,' Ali solemnly relayed to Brenda, who popped a bubble and slotted a big zero into the scoreboard.

Backstage, the heartbroken Banshees howled and wrung their nighties.

'Familiars – not bad at all. Good solo from the Haggis.

Three,' continued the Trollish voice. Faint cheers could be heard coming from the Familiars' dressing room.

'Familiars – three points,' Ali told Brenda pointlessly.

'Ghosts – quite effective. Two.'

'Ghosts, two points.'

'Ghouls – borin'. One.'

'Ghouls – one point,' interpreted Ali.

'Gnomes – four. Quite appealin' we thought that was.'

'Gnomes – four points.'

'It's taking for ever,' complained Pongwiffy, never known for her patience. 'Can't they speed it up a bit? Just give us the trophy, take our photograph with Scott, let us sing our song again and eat any celebration cake that's going, then go home. We're off to sunny Sludgehaven tomorrow, and Hugo and I haven't even packed yet. That's if I decide to take him. I still haven't really forgiven him for entering the contest without permission.'

'Shhh,' hissed everyone. More points were being awarded. In fact, they were coming in thick and fast now. Ali and Brenda were finding it hard to keep up. Moreover, they were becoming increasingly odd.

'Mummies – seven,' intoned the Troll voice. 'Vampires – thirteen. Werewolf – twenty-three. Witches – eighty-five.'

'Yesssssss!' went up the excited cry from the Witches, and Gaga did a celebratory pirouette.

'I'm sorry, I'll have to stop you there,' Ali told the air sternly. 'That is more than ten points in total.'

'What?' said the disembodied voice.

'Ten points,' explained Ali wearily. 'Each jury gets *ten points*, remember? I've been through it a million times. I thought we were all clear.'

At this, there was a bit of invisible whispering, if there is such a thing. Then: 'We're Trolls,' said the voice. 'We'll have as many points as we likes. We liked the Witches' song. It's catchy. We *wants* to give it eighty-five. And we liked the Wizards' song as well, though not quite as much. So we give that eighty-two and a half.'

Backstage, a loud '*hoorah!*' came from the Wizards' dressing room.

'You can't do that,' argued Ali. 'There have to be rules.'

'Yeah, well, we've just changed 'em,' the disembodied voice informed him. 'We don't like the scoring system. We want more points.'

'It's too complicated,' snapped Ali.

'No it ain't. A hundred an' fifty's a good top mark, not too big, not too small. While we're about it, we'll upgrade the Familiars to twenty-seven and a half, just because we're Trolls and we can. An' finally, we gives

395

the talented Troll group Cliff and the Chips the top mark of *one hundred an' fifty*. That concludes the votes of the Trollish jury. Wanna make somethin' of it?'

'You see?' Sourmuddle scolded Pongwiffy. 'You shouldn't count your chickens. The Wizards have got nearly the same as us.'

'How many more juries to go?' asked Sharkadder, who had gone sweaty with nerves. Streaks of mauve make-up trickled down her flushed cheeks.

'Lots.'

'Well, I can't watch any more. I'm going to lie down. Tell me when it's over.'

Meanwhile, back with the Goblins, the eggs were coming thick and fast. They came whistling overhead from behind, falling in an arc over the roof and bursting open on the windscreen in runny yellow splats. Plugugly stabbed blindly at a random button on the dashboard in a desperate attempt to activate the wipers. The heater came on and the eggs began to scramble.

'I can't see!' bawled Plugugly, wrenching the steering wheel. 'How close are dey? I can't see! I can't – *Ow!*'

Everyone gasped, jerked upright and bit their tongues as they went down a pothole. Sproggit's stick of rock went up his nose.

'I dunno how close, do I?' cried Eyesore. 'I keep *tellin'* you, I can't see!'

'Well, stand up an' look out de sunroof! Hold on, goin' right!'

Tyres screamed as the limo swerved hard to the left.

'Ooooooh!' wailed the Goblins, in chorus.

'Slow down, Plug!' begged Slopbucket. 'We don't want to be on this road. We can shake 'em off if we get on the back roads.'

This was an amazingly sensible suggestion for a Goblin. Slopbucket came up with it by accident, probably because his brains were being shaken up. It is a great pity that nobody took any notice.

'Faster!' shrieked Sproggit, gnawing the stuffing out of his straw donkey. 'Fasterfasterfaster! Yahoooo!'

'Which shall I do?' screamed Plugugly. 'Go fast or go slow?'

Nobody heard. They were all howling too loudly. They had seen something in front: the silhouette of a large, familiar building. It was still some way off in the distance – but it was coming ever closer.

'Oh well,' said Plugugly with a shrug. 'I'll do both!'

And the limousine went into a wild spin as he pressed both pedals at the same time.

In Witchway Hall, things were balanced on a knife-edge. The Troll jury's refusal to conform had set the tone for the rest of the juries who, to Ali's rising despair, ran roughshod over the rules and awarded haphazard points to whoever they liked. The scoreboard was now bizarre in the extreme. It said:

Banshees	*0*
Familiars	*197½*
Ghosts	*152*
Ghouls	*151*
Gnomes	*158*
Mummies	*179*
Trolls	*150*
Vampires	*188*
Werewolf	*156*
Witches	*199*
Wizards	*199*

Imagine the tension. All but one of the juries had now voted. Each had given their own song top marks, apart from the Banshee jury, who awarded 'Oh Woe!' zero points because they liked to make themselves miserable.

It was now the turn of the Mummy jury. Out of respect for their great age and the fact that most of them had royal connections, they had been left until last.

Ali Pali, annoyed that he had lost control of the scoring, but determined to see things through to the bitter end, strode to the centre of the stage and addressed the audience.

'And now, ladies and gentlemen and viewers at home, it's time for the votes from our final jury tonight. Coming live from a pyramid in Egypt –' Ali paused to fiddle with his headphones – 'sorry, I stand corrected, yes, sorry, coming *dead* from a pyramid in Egypt, we welcome the Mummy jury. Hello? Hello? Is that the Mummies? Mummies, are you there?'

'Good evening, Ali,' creaked a dry, ancient voice. It reminded you of sand and wind and embalming fluid. 'This is Pharaoh Nuff the Third, spokesman for the Mummy jury. Viewers at home, greetings. Before we give you our votes, we would like to make a comment. In our ancient wisdom, we feel we must point out that the original scoring system was much fairer than the one introduced by the Trollish jury, which is, quite frankly, ludicrous.'

'Hear hear,' agreed Ali. 'That's just what I said. Thank you, sire. At last, someone with sense. A round of applause for Pharaoh Nuff the Third, ladies and gentlemen.'

'Never mind all that,' continued the dry voice, somewhat testily. 'Let's just get on, shall we? In the interests of ancient justice, we shall revert to the first system. So, with no more ado, here are the results of the Mummy jury. Banshees – no points. Familiars – three points . . .'

'Oh no!' groaned Pongwiffy, backstage. 'One hundred and ninety-seven and a half plus three. That makes – um – how much does that make?'

'Two hundred and a half points,' said Greymatter grimly. 'That takes them higher than us. If we get zero, we're done for!'

At this, several Witches fainted. Nobody noticed, so they sheepishly came to again and joined the tense crowd round the monitor.

In his dressing room, Scott Sinister gave a little sigh, removed the chunks of cucumber from his eyes and reached for the trophy. Any minute now, he'd be on.

'Ghosts – zero,' went on the dry voice out front. 'Ghouls – zero. Gnomes – one point. Mummies – well, much as we would like to, we cannot vote for our own. Very well done, though, Xotindis and Xstufitu, you did us proud. Trolls – zero. Vampires – two points. Werewolf – one point.'

There was an excited buzz. The moment everyone was waiting for had arrived.

'That leaves three points,' continued the dry voice. 'We could have awarded one and a half each to the Witches and the Wizards, which would have resulted in an unsatisfactory tie. So, in our ancient wisdom, we have decided to award all three points to . . .'

You really don't need to be told what happens next, do you? You've seen it coming.

There came the sound of squealing brakes and a screaming engine, mixed in with howling voices – and, to everyone's horror, a large section of the right-hand wall of the auditorium imploded under the impact of a large, black, smoking, egg-splattered monster, which, in another life, had once been a gleaming limousine. Bricks and plaster sprayed down upon the audience as the ruined car tore across the hall, missing the front row of the stalls by a whisker. With a loud *crump*, it embedded itself in the opposite wall.

That caused plenty of commotion in itself.

Things got even crazier when the passenger door fell off and a Gaggle of howling Goblins poured out, like dirty water from an unblocked pipe.

At this point, the cart arrived through the hole in the wall, adding a wild-eyed donkey, a dishevelled

401

Thing, a Skeleton with a grudge and a lot of eggs to the already volatile mixture.

Loads of things happened then. Dressing room doors crashed open and the various contestants came rushing out and made for the stage.

Pongwiffy spotted the Goblins.

Fang the Wonder Hound spotted Dudley.

Age-old enemies suddenly spotted each other and decided to break whatever wobbly truce was currently in place. With all those eggs around, it was a shame to miss the opportunity.

Ali Pali was running about in circles, trying to regain a semblance of control – but it was a losing battle. Brenda tucked up her pink evening dress and waded in amongst it all, seizing Gnomes and glamorously banging their heads together.

Through it all, Vincent Van Ghoul continued to film, while the Tree Demon ran here and there with his microphone, capturing the whole shocking thing on tape. Determinedly, the Witchway Rhythm Boys played on.

We won't dwell on the fight between Sheridan Haggard and Scott Sinister, which happened much later on. Something about non-payment of castle rent. The Thing tried to break it up, but failed.

We don't want to hear how everything got too much for poor Sharkadder, who came over all emotional and cried, then stamped her foot and blamed Pongwiffy.

Neither do we want to know what a spectacle Brenda made of herself. Or what Fang the Wonder Hound did to Dudley, aided and abetted by Hugo. Or how the Witches and the Wizards got into a slanging match, which ended in them going outside and having a Magical showdown, which resulted in Witchway Hall burning down.

We *really* don't want to know what Pongwiffy did to the Goblins. It's too disgraceful and would make a very unpleasant ending to the whole sorry affair. Suffice to say, it did for her guitar.

The fact remains that it happened, and everybody involved later felt rather ashamed of themselves and just looked sheepish when they passed each other in the Wood.

And what did the viewers at home make of all this?

They disapproved, of course. All that mess and mayhem and not even a clear result.

But they all agreed it was great spellovision.

CHAPTER TWENTY-FIVE
The end

'Moon's up. I think I'll go out,' said Pongwiffy to Hugo, a day or two later.

They had just finished supper. Hugo had cooked a really nice pie. Through the broken window, the moon sailed high and the stars were coming out. Pongwiffy had her feet on her plate and was picking at her toenails with a fork. Hugo was doing the crossword puzzle, which was back in *The Daily Miracle* by popular demand.

It was a cosy scene. Everything had settled back to normal. Pongwiffy had made the Goblins return every last bit of rubbish, so the Dump was restored to its former glory. In fact, it was even better than before, being now full of discarded spellovisions. Nobody was interested any more. Like most new fads, it had burnt itself out.

Fang the Wonder Hound, now known as Ribs again, was back with Sheridan, who had moved out of Sinister Towers and was said to be writing a book now that his job as newsreader was no more. (However, it must be said that Ribs sometimes goes missing in order to visit his old friend Plugugly, who is always thrilled to see him.)

'So vhere you go?' asked Hugo.

'I thought I'd pop out and get rid of the guitar.'

'Ya?' Hugo was surprised. 'I thought you say it antique? Zat maybe it belong to zat old Raspberry man?'

'Yes, well, maybe. Who cares? I keep tripping over it. And there's only one string left and the neck's gone all unstuck again.'

'Oh, right,' nodded Hugo. 'No more music, zen?'

'No. I'm bored with music now. It was fun for a while. But I think I've probably gone as far as I can with my guitar playing. Which is – well, if I'm being honest, nowhere, really.'

There was a longish pause while Hugo just sat tight.

'You're supposed to say, *Oh no, Mistress*,' Pongwiffy reminded him. 'That's what you're *supposed* to say.'

'*A vise Hamster knows ven to keep his mouth shut*,' quoted Hugo.

There was another longish pause. Then they caught each other's eye and burst into laughter.

'You're right,' said Pongwiffy, wiping her eyes and blowing her nose on the tablecloth. 'I wasn't very good, was I? Come on, pardner. What say we both go out and dump the guitar.'

So that's what they did. It arced over the rubbish dump and fell on the far side with a *plink*.

'Good riddance,' said Pongwiffy, dusting her hands. 'Let's get the cauldron out and do some Magic, eh? What do you say?'

'Ya!' agreed Hugo. And together they went back into the hovel.

On the far side of the tip, an old tramp happened to be passing by. The broken guitar fell at his feet.

'Well, durn me,' said a low, rasping voice. 'If that don't beat all. Whoever woulda believed it? After all these years.'

And Wild Raspberry Johnson bent down, picked it up and wandered slowly on.

Turn the page for another
Pongwiffy adventure!

even more

Pongwiffy

stories

BACK ON TRACK

WITCHWAY WOOD O'LUMPICK GAMES
READ CAREFULLY!

The Witches proudly announce that the very first O'Lumpick Games will be held in three weeks' time. You are cordially invited to join in. Yes, YOU. The Games are open to all.* You are required to form teams who will compete against each other in seven exciting events (see below). Each team may enter one contestant only per race. An exception is made for the Three-Legged Race , which needs two,** and also for the Relay Race, which needs four.

In the true O'Lumpick spirit, the Games will be played FAIRLY. Yes, really! Magic is Strictly Banned. So is Cheating, Skullduggery, Back-stabbing and Fighting. Mingling is compulsory. So is Good Sportsmanship, even if you lose, which you probably will.

The best three contestants in each event will be presented with medals by popular star of stage and screen Scott Sinister, who will also provide the commentary.

Please complete the following in your best handwriting. YOU HAVE THREE WEEKS TO GET FIT!

TEAM NAME ....

EVENT	CONTESTANT NAME(S)

Three-Legged Race ....

Egg and Spoon Race ....

Weightlifting ....

High Jump ....

Sack Race ....

Toss the Caber ....

Relay Race ....

*N.B. Except Goblins.   **N.B. Three-legged monsters are not eligible.

CHAPTER ONE
A Typical Evening

It was evening, and a typical scene was taking place in Number One, Dump Edge, Witchway Wood. Supper was over and Witch Pongwiffy was slumped in her armchair, eating toffees and watching Hugo, her Hamster Familiar, wash up.

The only sounds were of clinking plates and a bit of tuneless humming from Hugo and a lot of vigorous, noisy chewing from Pongwiffy.

Suddenly, the chewing stopped.

'*Gugo!*' said Pongwiffy, urgently but indistinctly. '*Gugo gy geeg!*'

Was this some sort of new language?

Hugo turned and looked at her. Pongwiffy was sitting bolt upright, pointing at her mouth with a strange expression. Sort of alarmed but sheepish at the same time.

'Vot?'

'Gy *geeg*! Gy *geeg* ga gug goo gegger!'

Her teeth were stuck together.

'Vot, *again*?'

'Nng.'

Pongwiffy rolled her eyes and waited for help. Hugo dried his paws on a tiny tea towel.

'It ze last time I do zis,' he warned.

He scrabbled in a drawer, took out a fork and a small hammer and advanced briskly on Pongwiffy, who quailed. With a hop and a jump, he was on her shoulder.

'Turn head,' he instructed. 'Open up.' Pongwiffy turned to face him and nervously bared her teeth. He positioned the fork and brandished the hammer. 'Ready?'

'Nng. Nnnnnggggggg . . .' There was a sharp crack. '*Ah!*' Pongwiffy gave a cry as her newly freed jaws sprang open. 'Ooh, that's better. What a relief.'

'Vot I tell you 'bout eatink toffees?' scolded Hugo, clambering down.

'But they're all I've got left. I've eaten all the crunchy ones and the soft centres.'

'*Zat whole bag of sweets?* But I only got zem zis morning!'

'So?'

'Zat so greedy,' tutted Hugo. 'After great big supper too.'

Pongwiffy had indeed had a big supper. Four greasy helpings of skunk stew, no less. And now, on top of all that, she was eating sweets.

Or would be, if she hadn't run out.

Hopefully, she fished around in her cardigan pocket and, with a glad little cry, produced something green, fluff-covered and frog-shaped.

'Ooh, look. A *Hoppy Jumper.*' She peered down, picked off

the fluff, popped it in her mouth and crunched. 'Yum. I love these, I do. I could sit here and eat 'em all night.'

'I thought you goink out,' said Hugo. 'You say you goink to visit Sharkadder.'

'Did I? Well, I'm not. I've broken friends.'

'Oh ya?' Hugo didn't sound all that surprised. Witch Sharkadder was Pongwiffy's best friend. They argued a lot, though, so they frequently weren't speaking. One day best friends, the next, worst enemies. It was hard to keep up.

'She wouldn't answer the door,' explained Pongwiffy. 'Last time I called. I know she was in there, though. Crunching sweets in the dark. Didn't want to share, I reckon. So I'm not speaking. She just doesn't know it yet.'

'So go round and tell 'er,' advised Hugo.

'How can I *tell* her if I'm not speaking?'

'Write note.'

'Can't be bothered. Too far to walk.'

'Fly zen, if you so lazy. Take Broom.'

The Broom, who had been mournfully drooping in a corner, straightened up and looked desperately keen, like a puppy who's been promised a walk. It hadn't been flown for ages and it was terribly bored, just hanging around collecting cobwebs. A brisk fly would be just what the tree doctor ordered.

'Don't want to,' said Pongwiffy. 'I want to lie around and eat sweet things. Like cake. Fetch me some cake.'

The Broom went back to mournful drooping. Hope dies quickly in Broom World, especially if you belong to Pongwiffy.

'No cake,' said Hugo. 'All gone. You eated it.'

'So make another one. Make a sponge cake, it'll soak up the grease. Basic science.' She gave a loud, rude belch and rubbed her stomach, which was inflated to the size of a small balloon.

'Exercise,' advised Hugo. 'Zat vot you is needink. You in bad shape.' He began poking around in the food cupboard which was empty apart from three jars of skunk stew labelled *Last Week*, *Month-Old* and *Vintage*. 'You not fit. Just lie about eatink rubbish.'

'And what's wrong with that?'

'Everysink. You should be like 'amsters. Alvays on ze go, 'amsters. 'Specially ven it comink up to ze Rodent Olympic Games.'

'The what?'

'Ze Rodent Olympics. Held in my home town, 'amsterdam. Boy, do ve train 'ard. Is big sing.'

'A big *sing*? What, like opera?'

'No, no. *Sing!*'

'Oh, *thing!*'

'Ya. Is like big Sports Day. High spot of ze year.'

'*Is* it now?' Pongwiffy gave a theatrical yawn.

'Ya. Ve play games.'

'Do you *really?*'

'Oh, ya. Rats, mice, guinea pigs, 'amsters. All join in.'

'I didn't think you got on with mice and guinea pigs. I thought you usually fought, that's what you said.'

'Not ven it ze Olympics. On zat day ve have truce. Got to be nice to each uzzer. It all about teamvork.'

'Teamwork?' sneered Pongwiffy. She didn't care for teamwork. Witches aren't known for their cooperation.

'Ya. Rats gotta team. Mice gotta team. 'Amsters gotta team. Everyvun compete against each uzzer, see? Ze best team vin.'

'It'd be quicker to fight, wouldn't it? Get it over and done with?'

'Not ven is *Sport*,' explained Hugo. 'Sport different. Sport got rules. Got to be fair. No fightink, no cheatink.'

'No *cheating*?' Pongwiffy sounded shocked. 'Are

419

you serious?'

'Ya.'

'You mean – no *Magic*?'

'Certainly not.' Hugo was scandalised.

'Well, it doesn't sound like a Witch thing,' said Pongwiffy. 'Playing fair and being nice. All that effort when you can just wave a Wand.'

'Ah, but zat not ze *point*. Ze point is . . .' Hugo gave up. Pongwiffy was scrabbling through her pockets again and had stopped listening. 'Ah, never mind. Vere ze sugar?'

'How should I know? Why? Isn't there any?' asked Pongwiffy innocently, and instantly came out in green spots. (This always happens when she tells fibs. It's very inconvenient.)

'You eated it, didn't you?' said Hugo.

'I might have had a couple of handfuls, I can't remember.'

'Green spots,' said Hugo, pointing.

'All right,' said Pongwiffy sulkily. 'All right, so I did.' The green spots faded.

'You such a fibber,' said Hugo, shaking his head.

'Oh, stop lecturing me. I don't want want to be lectured by a Hamster. Leave me alone, I've got tummyache.'

'You better get better,' warned Hugo. 'Is Coven Meeting midnight tonight.'

'I think I'll have to cancel. I'll send you along with a sick note. Oooooh.'

'Vot, *again*?'

'Yes, *again*. Just shut up and make cake.'

'Can't,' said Hugo. 'Run out of cake stuff. No sugar, no eggs, no flour, no nussink.'

'Well, I'm not sitting here all night with nothing to munch on. You'll just have to go along to *Sugary Candy's* and get me more sweets. I'd go myself if I didn't feel so poorly. Don't look like that, it won't hurt you. Get me a mixed bag, heavy on the *Hoppy Jumpers*. I'll have some *Bat Splatz*, and a couple of *Bog Bars*. Oh, and some *Minty Stingeroos* . . .'

CHAPTER TWO
Sugary Candy's

Sugary Candy's was the name of the new sweet shop
in Witchway Wood. It had only recently opened,
but was already attracting a huge amount of custom.
It was designed to look like a charming gingerbread
cottage, with painted sweets stuck on the walls and a
twist of pink candyfloss emerging from the crooked
chimney. It had a pointed roof and an old-fashioned
door with a quaint shop bell. But instead of poky little
windows there was one great big one. The display was
truly a sight to behold.

Sweets! Great big jars of them arranged in rows,

all different shapes and colours. Green froggy ones, crimson ones shaped like little mouths, black bat-shaped ones that flapped in your mouth and large staring ones like eyeballs that blinked when you bit into them. There were humbugs and gobstoppers and big pink balls of bubblegum. There were huge red lollipops with faces on. There were toffees and sherbet dips and striped sticks of rock and – oh, everything under the sun. It would take far too long to describe all those sweets. You just need to know that temptation-wise, they were off the scale. They had exciting names too, written on the labels. It made them fun to buy.

As well as the giant jars of sweets, there were trays of chocolate. Big brown bars, piled high. *Slime Slabs. Mocklit Fudge. Bog Bars.*

It would have been good if *Sugary Candy's* was owned by somebody called something like Mr Twinkle or Arthur Applecheek – a merry old fellow who loved little children. It wasn't, though. It was owned by the Yeti Brothers – large, hairy, hard-headed business types who didn't love anybody.

The Yetis specialised in bad food. It was cheap and it was greasy, cooked carelessly in dirty kitchens and dumped any old how on grubby plates. Their names were Spag Yeti and Conf Yeti, and they owned a great number of greasy spoon cafes, burger bars and pizza houses in far-flung locations, all of which they ran simultaneously although nobody knew how, seeing as there were only two of them. They also did the catering for important events like parties and weddings. (Same bad food, but cut up small and served on shiny platters.) Rumour was that the Yetis cloned themselves, but it was more likely that they just ran very fast. Or took short cuts through dimensions known only to Yetis. Or possibly had a lot of identical hairy cousins with the same names.

Spag and Conf's decision to open a sweet shop was proving to be a very good one. The residents of Witchway Wood had little in common, but apparently were united in their love of lurid confectionery. *Sugary Candy's* gave them exactly what they wanted. It was pricey, mind. But, oooh. It was worth it.

Here is a typical scene. The customer can be a Skeleton, a Witch, a Banshee, a Troll, a Vampire, an anonymous hairy thing, take your pick. This is how it would go.

SPAG YETI:	Yeah? What you wanna?
CUSTOMER:	A large bag of *Tooth Rotters*, please. Oh, and some of your delicious *Molar Manglers*, they're my favourites. And throw in a dozen *Gloopy Guzzlers*, and fifteen of those big red lollipops and ten *Jumbo Lumpos*, the ones with the pink sprinkles. And a giant packet of *Bat Splatz*.
SPAG YETI:	That-a be one month's salary, please.
CUSTOMER:	*(Hands over salary)* Thank you so very much, see you tomorrow.

(Customer leaves, poor but happy. Spag rings up the till, rich and even happier.)

Business was *good*.

This particular night, Spag stood behind the counter, stuffing money into the overflowing till. There was a long queue trailing out of the door. At the front was a Werewolf, followed by two Skeletons, a family of Trolls, a small Thing in a Moonmad T-shirt, a Gnome (named GNorman, currently reading the paper), a sour-faced Tree Demon and a solitary Vampire in a beret, who was licking his lips and eyeing up a jar containing the red sweets shaped like little mouths.

Three Witches stood at the back. Sludgegooey, Ratsnappy and Bendyshanks. They had come for their night's supply.

'What are you getting?' Sludgegooey asked Ratsnappy, who was breathing heavily because she had just walked up a short, gentle slope.

'Don't know yet,' gasped Ratsnappy. 'Can't talk. Still puffed out from that climb.'

'I usually have *Minty Stingeroos*, but I'll think I'll try those stripy yellow ones for a change.'

'What – *Beezi Kneezies*?' chipped in Bendyshanks, who had a swollen cheek. 'Take my advice, don't. I had those the other night. Hard as nails. Broke a tooth. I'm in agony, actually. It was a real struggle to get here. But I couldn't miss my sweet run. I'm getting *Bat Splatz*, they're softer on the gums.'

'I haven't tried those yet,' admitted Sludgegooey.

'Oh, you must!' cried Bendyshanks. 'They flap about your mouth, then explode and all this lovely green melty gooey stuff comes out.'

'Melty gooey stuff's not good for teeth, is it?' said Sludgegooey, not in a disapproving way but because she was interested.

426

'Takes the mind off the pain,' explained Bendyshanks.

'Oh, right. I was thinking of *Hoppy Jumpers*.' Thoughtfully, Sludgegooey eyed the rows of jars.

'Oh, don't have them,' advised Bendyshanks, the expert. 'They play havoc with the tummy, especially after a big greasy meal. And don't have those blinking eyeballs, they're horrible.'

'I hope this won't take long,' groaned Ratsnappy. 'My back's killing me from the walk up that hill. I had to lie down halfway up. Vernon had to come and give me extra special perspiration.'

'It's artificial respiration, isn't it?' asked Sludgegooey.

'All I know is I was sweating a lot.'

'I know what you mean. It's hard on the knees, walking. My knee keeps clicking. Listen.' Sludgegooey bent a knee, which dutifully clicked. 'See? I'd be tempted to bring along a chair, except I'd have to carry it.'

'You should get Filth to carry it,' said Ratsnappy.

'I would, but he's out rehearsing.'

I should explain here that Sludgegooey's Familiar is a Fiend called Filth. He is small and hairy and plays drums with the local band called the Witchway Rhythm Boys. He says 'yeah, man' a lot, even when he means 'not likely'. He is always neglecting his

427

duties and sloping off to rehearsal. Sludgegooey puts up with this because she thinks he is creative, although she does find his habit of air drumming at the table annoying.

'You should make him,' said Bendyshanks. 'That's what you employ him for. He gets away with too much, your Filth. I'd make Steve.'

'Ah, but Steve can't *carry* a chair, though, can he?' Sludgegooey pointed out. 'It's easy to say when he can't even *do* it.'

This is true. Slithering Steve, Bendyshanks' Familiar, is a small grass snake. He has his talents, but they don't include chair carrying.

'He would if he could,' said Bendyshanks a bit huffily. 'He's willing. It's hard to carry a chair without arms.'

'Some chairs have got arms,' remarked Ratsnappy, who was thinking about sweets and losing track a bit.

'We're talking about Steve's limitations,' said Sludgegooey.

'And Filth's,' added Bendyshanks firmly.

'Oh, *right*. Yes, well, all the Familiars have those, don't they? I have to admit my Vernon can be very sneaky. You have to check your change. And his cooking's terrible. I'm living on takeaways.'

'Me too,' said Sludgegooey. 'Can't be bothered to cook up a brew. Run out of herbs and whatnot. Can't go out picking, not with my clicking knee. How much *longer* is that idiot going to be?'

At the front of the queue, the Werewolf was being indecisive about his purchases. He was already weighed down with loads of paper bags full of sweets and was now wondering if he could manage a family-sized bar of fudge as well.

'Is that real chocolate?' asked the Werewolf, pointing.

'Eez-a chocolate-*flavour* chocolate,' said Spag. 'Called mocklate.'

'What's in it?'

'How should I know? I sell it, not-a make it.'

'Well, yes, but I was just wondering . . .'

'Look,' said Spag. 'You wannit? Or you donna wannit?'

'I *want* it,' explained the Werewolf. 'I just don't know if I can carry it. Do you deliver?'

'Oi!' shouted Sludgegooey. 'Get a move on, fur face, there's folks waiting.'

'There are,' said a dry voice from behind, adding firmly, 'but I'm not one of them. Out of the way, coming through.'

CHAPTER THREE
Sourmuddle Jumps the Queue

The queue shuffled hastily to one side. This was Grandwitch Sourmuddle, Mistress of the Witchway Wood Coven, over two hundred years old, sometimes hard of hearing, often short of temper and definitely not to be crossed.

She came waddling up the line with Snoop in tow. Snoop was a small, red, officious Demon, generally considered by the other Familiars to be a bit above himself. He scampered along at her heels, bossily waving a tiny trident.

'Why is that old woman pushing in?' demanded a

small Troll of his parents, who looked embarrassed and told him to shush.

Sourmuddle reached the counter and elbowed the Werewolf to one side.

'Marshmallows,' she demanded. 'The ones I always have.'

'Alla-outa, sorry. Been a run,' explained Spag, adding, 'but I gotta *Swampswallows*. Same as Marshmallows, but different colour. Orange-a.'

'What? Speak up.'

'ORANGE-A. YOU LIKE-A.'

'Excuse me?' piped up the Werewolf. 'I was here first, you know.'

'No, you weren't,' said Sourmuddle, who could hear fine when she wanted. 'Single-celled organisms were here first. They were brainier than you, though. They'd know better than to argue with *me*.' Casually, she fingered the Wand hanging from a string around her neck.

'But you jumped the queue. She did, didn't she?' The Werewolf appealed to onlookers, but was met with a lot of blank stares. Everyone was tired of his faddy ways and would be glad to see the back of him. Besides, Grandwitch Sourmuddle versus a Werewolf? No contest.

'She's allowed,' called Bendyshanks from the back. 'She's Grandwitch Sourmuddle and she can do what she likes.'

'Quite right,' agreed Sourmuddle. 'I can. Is that you, Bendyshanks? Come on up to the front, you can be next.'

'Can I bring Ratsnappy and Sludgegooey with me?'

'Are they there too? Yes, come on up, Witches go first. Anyone want to argue with that? No? Good. All right, Mr Yeti, I'll take the *Swampswallows*, but they'd better be good.'

The queue sighed resignedly as Bendyshanks, Sludgegooey and Ratsnappy pushed their way to the front, looking smug.

'Well I never!' sulked the Werewolf, then caught Sourmuddle's eye and went quiet.

'I'm glad I saw you three,' went on Sourmuddle, as Spag began shaking squashy orange balls into a set of weighing scales. 'I'm changing tonight's arrangements. We're not flying to Crag Hill, we'll have the Meeting in Witchway Hall.'

The Witches always held their Meetings on Crag Hill, unless really bad weather conditions prevented it. Well, they did until the last few weeks. Up until then they flew to Crag Hill even if there were storms brewing or blizzards threatened. But lately, they hadn't been so keen. It was just such an effort, dusting the Brooms off and getting ready with the extra vest and looking for the umbrella when you could be lying around scoffing sweets in front of the spellovision. Nobody could be bothered. An excuse could always be found.

'So what's the excuse?' asked Bendyshanks. 'Is it a good one?'

'My Broom's not well. Nasty case of stiffbristle. I've got it soaking in a bucket of warm water.'

'Stiffbristle's catching, isn't it?' asked Ratsnappy, vaguely alarmed. 'I'd better check on mine. I haven't taken it out of the cupboard in ages. I heard it banging on the door a few days ago but I was in the middle of a takeaway curry and couldn't be bothered to get up.'

'You don't have to get up, though, do you? To open your Broom closet,' said Sludgegooey. 'You can just lean across from your chair.'

'I wasn't in my chair. I was in bed,' explained Ratsnappy. 'I have all my takeaways in bed.'

'So what you're saying is, you don't do any exercise at all?'

'Nope. Vernon does it for me. I make him do ten

434

press-ups every night and every morning. I feel ever so much better after watching him.'

'So why are you doing your own shopping, then?' enquired Sludgegooey.

'Oh, I wouldn't trust him with *that*. He'd come back with the wrong things. He's only a Rat, you can't let him make those kind of decisions. Especially about sweets. I like to choose my own. I'm going to have some of those *Swampswallows*, like *you*, Sourmuddle.'

'An excellent choice,' said Sourmuddle, snatching an enormous paper bag from Spag and thrusting it into Snoop's little red arms. 'Here. Don't drop 'em. I take it they're on the house, as usual?'

Spag swallowed. This went against everything he stood for. But this was Grandwitch Sourmuddle, who did as she liked.

'Yeah. I guess so.'

'Very kind, much appreciated. Now. What else do I fancy, I wonder . . . ?'

It was at this point that Hugo arrived, swinging a tiny wicker basket. He joined the back of the queue, behind the Vampire.

'Hello,' said the Vampire in hollow tones. His name was Vincent Van Ghoul, and he always wore a beret and a smock with red paint splashes because he was a bit of an artist in his spare time.

''Ello,' said Hugo.

'Taking a while,' said Vincent, sucking his teeth. 'Long queue.'

'Ya,' said Hugo. Hamsters and Vampires having little in common, he couldn't think of anything else to say.

'Still working for Pongwiffy, then?' asked Vincent.

'Oh, ya.'

'Haven't seen her around lately. Nothing wrong, I hope? Stiff neck? If she's got a stiff neck, I could pop round and take a look. I'm good with necks.'

'No, no, neck not stiff. Problem is vot she put down it. Too much rubbish food.'

'She shouldn't mix colours. Tell her to eat red things. That's my advice.'

'OK.'

'Strawberries. Beetroot. Tomatoes are good.'

'OK.'

'Only red.'

'OK.'

The queue shuffled forward a bit. Sourmuddle, Snoop, Sludgegooey, Bendyshanks and Ratsnappy pushed their triumphant way back along the line, loaded down with paper bags. Sourmuddle paused and stared down at Hugo.

'Ah,' she said. 'Hugo. Where is your mistress?'

'Back in ze hovel, lyink down,' said Hugo. 'She not feelink so good.'

'Well, tell her I expect to see her at the Meeting tonight. She's missed three in a row.'

'Ya, well, she not feelink . . .'

'I don't want to hear excuses. Tell her to be there. Midnight sharp. And spread the word amongst the Familiars. All your Witches are to attend. There's been too much bunking off recently.'

'OK,' said Hugo. And the queue shuffled forward.

CHAPTER FOUR
Late

Despite Sourmuddle's warning about punctuality, almost everyone was late to the Meeting. At midnight sharp, thirteen chairs were drawn up to the long trestle table in Witchway Hall, but only three were occupied.

Sourmuddle sat at the top end, looking grim. Arranged before her was a register, her Wand and a half empty bag of *Swampswallows*. Snoop was crouched on the back of her chair, holding a large watch and making tutting noises.

At the far end of the table sat Witches Agglebag and

Bagaggle, the identical twins, with their Familiars on their laps. They were two Siamese cats called IdentiKit and CopiCat, and they were exceedingly snooty, although no one knew why as all they seemed to do was sit around posing and demanding cream. The twins had a large bag of *Bat Splatz* which they were sharing between them with a lot of rustling and whispered consultation.

'Midnight,' said Sourmuddle. 'Where is everybody?'

'Coming,' said Agglebag.

'But slowly,' added Bagaggle.

'We called in for Greymatter, but she's watching spellovision and eating chips with chocolate sauce.'

'Sharkadder's trying to hide her spots. She's had another outbreak.'

'We passed Bendyshanks coming back from the dentist.'

'And Ratsnappy, lying down halfway up the hill.'

'Scrofula and Bonidle'll be late. Scrofula's pushing Bonidle in a wheelbarrow.'

'We don't know about Macabre. Rory's refusing to let her ride. He says she's got too heavy . . .'

'Enough!' shouted Sourmuddle. 'I said midnight sharp, not breakfast time tomorrow!'

The door swung open to reveal Ratsnappy, bent

double and gasping. She tottered in and flung herself into the nearest chair. She was accompanied by Vernon, who was small and sulky and looked like he'd had quite enough of doing his mistress's press-ups for her.

'Can't speak,' wheezed Ratsnappy, pulling a grubby hanky from her pocket along with a load of sweet wrappings and mopping her brow. 'Can't breathe. Got a stitch.'

She was closely followed by Bendyshanks, who had a bandage tied around her face and was groaning loudly. Then came a little group – Sludgegooey (with clicking knee), Gaga (chewing enthusiastically on a mouthful of bubblegum) and Macabre, who stood with arms akimbo and fiercely announced, 'Mutiny in the ranks! Ah had tay *walk*! Rory refused tay carry me, can ye believe!'

All four had their Familiars with them. Bendyshanks had Slithering Steve draped around her neck. Sludgegooey had Filth, who for once wasn't rehearsing. Gaga, as always, was surrounded by a little swarm of Bats. They zoomed excitedly around her head, neatly avoiding the sticky pink bubbles she kept blowing. Macabre's Haggis, Rory, remained outside, cropping the grass and sulking. He was large, shaggy and ginger, with two sharp horns. His orange fringe hung low over his eyes. He was fed up because Macabre had just given him an earful.

'Sit down and be quick about it!' snapped Sourmuddle. 'You all get triple black marks for lateness.'

'I couldn't help it, it's my tooth,' moaned Bendyshanks.

'Anyway, we're not last,' pointed out Sludgegooey. 'Bonidle and Scrofula are still at *Sugary Candy's*. They've run out of sweets.'

'Well, they're no having any o' mine,' said Macabre, firmly patting her bulging sporran. Her chair creaked ominously as she sat down. She had put on a bit of weight recently, as Rory would tell you. Well, all the Witches had. Their tummies were very much in evidence.

'I thought it closed at midnight,' said Sourmuddle.

'It does. They're trying to break in. Well, Scrofula's throwing bricks at the window. Bonidle's snoring in the wheelbarrow. I think they'll be a while.'

'No, we won't,' said a voice. 'We're here, so there.'

Witch Scrofula stood in the doorway, panting heavily, holding the handles of a rickety wheelbarrow containing Bonidle and her Familiar, who was a Sloth.

He didn't have a name because Bonidle couldn't be bothered to give him one. Both were snoring loudly.

'You each get triple black marks,' snapped Sourmuddle. 'No, fourple. Make a note, Snoop.'

'But I was wheeling Bonidle,' protested Scrofula.

'Fiveple black marks. For answering back.'

'No luck breaking the window, then?' enquired Sludgegooey.

'No,' sighed Scrofula. 'Waste of time, wasn't it, Barry?'

The Vulture perched on the rim of the barrow nodded sadly. This was Barry, Scrofula's Familiar. He was moulting again, and not feeling too well.

'*Ah* could have told ye that,' said Macabre. 'Magically reinforced glass, ah reckon. Tried it mahself, with a batterin' ram. *Everybody's* tried it. It's unbreakable.'

'Yes, well, we know that *now*,' snapped Scrofula crossly. She upturned the barrow and decanted Bonidle and the Sloth on to the floor. Neither woke up.

'Prop her up in a chair,' ordered Sourmuddle. 'This is a formal meeting.'

The twins jumped up and helped Scrofula hoist Bonidle into a chair. She just slumped there, with her eyes closed. Then her hand slowly rose and floated towards the twins' bag of *Bat Splatz*.

'Get off,' said Agglebag, snatching it away. 'Buy your own and stop sleep stealing.'

'So who's left to come?' enquired Sourmuddle.

'Greymatter – arrrgh! Sharkadder – arrrgh! – and Pongwiffy,' groaned Bendyshanks, clutching her jaw. 'Arrrgh!' she added, just in case anyone was in any doubt about her pain.

'We'll start without them,' decided Sourmuddle. 'I want to get away early. My Broom's sick, I need to change its water. And I have to call in for a takeaway. We don't have time to cook, do we, Snoop? Too busy nursing poor Stumpy. Are we all ready? Hail, Witches!'

'Hail!' came the response. There came a sudden, sharp rattling on the roof as a small cloud released a barrage of hailstones before scooting off in a northerly direction. This always happens at the start of Coven Meetings.

'Right,' continued Sourmuddle. 'First things first. Whose turn was it to bring the sandwiches?'

'Greymatter's, but she isn't here,' came the chorus.

'Oh. Well, we'll start with News. Anyone got any new spells they'd care to share with us?'

There was a lot of shrugging, followed by rustling as the Witches reached for more sweets. The twins huddled over their bag, keeping a sharp eye on Bonidle. Nobody wanted to share anything, that was clear. Crazed by sugar, Gaga was swinging from the rafters, in pink bubble heaven.

'Here comes Greymatter,' said Bendyshanks. 'Don't forget to give her some black marks. Arrrgh!'

'I don't deserve black marks,' said Greymatter, marching in briskly and shaking hailstones from her hat. She had a piece of paper in one hand and a pencil was tucked behind her ear. Her Familiar – an Owl named Speks – sat on her shoulder.

'Yes, you do,' said Sourmuddle. 'You're late.'

'Ah, but that's because I was composing a poem about chips.'

Everyone looked impressed. Greymatter was the clever one. She knew a lot of long words and wrote poetry. She was good at crosswords too.

'Let's hear it, then,' said Macabre. She reached into her sporran, selected a sweet and popped it in her mouth. 'Anyone like *Porridge Balls*?'

'I do,' said Scrofula hopefully.

'Aye, they're lovely, aren't they?' said Macabre, and meanly put them away.

'Read us your poem, then, Greymatter, and we can get on with the News,' ordered Sourmuddle.

'*Ode To Chips*,' said Greymatter. 'Ahem. Chips, chips, I really love chips, more than ships, whips, parsnips, tulips, paperclips or pillowslips. Especially with dips.'

A little silence fell.

'That's not as good as your usual ones,' remarked Scrofula eventually. 'It's just a list of words with 'ips' at the end.'

'Yes, well, I haven't felt in a creative mood recently,' said Greymatter. 'You have to feel serene and settled to write poetry. My brain isn't working as well as it should be. I haven't been sleeping.'

'That's because you eat chocolate-covered chips in bed,' said Scrofula.

'You're right,' admitted Greymatter. 'I do. And very lovely they are too. By the way, I couldn't be bothered to make sandwiches, but I've brought along a bag of *Gloopy Guzzlers*. Anyone want one?'

Everyone did.

Witch Sharkadder came hurrying along the moonlit track that led to Witchway Hall. She was late because she had been trying to disguise the latest nasty crop of sweet-induced spots that had exploded on to her face. She had run the gamut of all her make-up, but nothing did the trick, so she had resorted to wearing a black net veil and a large pair of dark sunglasses. It wasn't a good look, particularly with her pointy hat. Her long, sharp nose stuck out, straining at the veil. It was only a matter of time before it bored a hole through.

Dead Eye Dudley, her cat Familiar, came loping along in her wake. He was large, battered and piratical-looking with one glaring yellow eye and a permanent sneer.

'Come on, Duddles,' trilled Sharkadder. 'Don't hang about. We're very late, you know.'

She rounded the bend and came across Hugo sitting on a tiny log, swinging his little legs and looking resigned.

'Oh,' said Sharkadder. 'It's you. Where's Pong?'

Hugo pointed to a nearby bush. It was shaking a bit, and there were groaning noises coming from it.

'She's turned into a bush?' enquired Sharkadder. It wasn't such an odd question. Witches often turn themselves into things, just to see what it feels like. It could be anything – a jar of pickles, an old sofa, a scarecrow, a knitted hat. A bush wasn't so strange.

'No,' said Hugo. 'She behind it. She poorly.'

He looked past Sharkadder, spotted Dudley and pulled a rude face.

'I'll scupper ye,' growled Dudley. 'I'll hoist ye from the main brace, see if I don't. By yer tiddly little *knees*.'

Hugo and Dudley didn't get on.

'Shush, Dudley, this isn't the time,' scolded Sharkadder. 'Pong? Are you all right?'

There was a pause. The bush trembled again and Pongwiffy came crawling out from behind it, looking green.

'Oh dear,' said Sharkadder. 'You *do* look rough.'

'I feel rough,' said Pongwiffy, climbing to her feet and reeling about, clutching her stomach. 'I've never felt so rough in my life.'

'Something you've eaten?'

'*Everything* I've eaten.'

'Told you,' said Hugo. 'Shouldn't have eated all zose *Hoppy Jumpers*. Told you.'

'I know you did, Hugo, and you were right. I should have listened.'

'*I* could have told you about *Hoppy Jumpers*,' said Sharkadder. 'They thump around in all the sloshy stuff you've eaten, don't they? Sort of squishing it down. Squish, splosh, sloppity squish . . .'

'Yes,' said Pongwiffy, going even greener. 'They do.

447

But I'd like you to stop talking about it now. Why are you wearing that?' She pointed to Sharkadder's veil.

'A slight rash,' mumbled Sharkadder.

'It's worse than that, isn't it? The tip of your nose has bored through. It's covered in pimples.'

'I know,' admitted poor Sharkadder wretchedly.

'It's like a knobbly parsnip. A raw, lumpy parsnip with . . .'

'I know, I *know*. I haven't been out for a week. I've been too embarrassed to answer the door.'

'I'm aware of that. I came round. I expect you heard me shouting.'

'Well, I'm sorry, Pong. I just didn't want anyone to see me. Even you.'

'I'm not surprised, I've never seen anything like it. That's some nose, that is. Have you been sandpapering it?'

'*No!* Look, are you coming, because we're late for the Meeting.'

'I'm coming,' said Pongwiffy grimly. 'Sick as I am, I'm coming.'

'Well, come on then.'

'You go on. I'll be there in a minute. Something I need to do . . .'

Looking green again, Pongwiffy dived behind her bush.

When she finally emerged, Hugo was still sitting on the log. He was watching something. Silhouetted against the moon, a lone squirrel was running around the branches of a tree. It twirled and leapt and swung and somersaulted, chittering happily to itself.

'See zat?' said Hugo. 'Zat vun fit squirrel. He run, he jump, plenty exercise, eat healthy nuts, 'ave fun.'

'Hugo,' said Pongwiffy, 'I have taken your point and learnt my lesson. From now on, things are going to be different. Let's get to that Meeting. And while we're walking, you can tell me all about that *thing* you were on about. The Rodent Oh Something or other. Exactly what happens . . . ?'

CHAPTER FIVE
Pongwiffy's Idea

I'm still waiting,' said Sourmuddle, drumming her fingers. 'Waiting for News. Come on, I'm getting irritable now. No new recipes? Anyone zapped any Goblins? Spied on any Wizards?' She broke off as Sharkadder came hurrying into the Hall with Dudley at her heels. 'Ah, there you are, Sharkadder. Sixple black marks for being late.'

'There's no such word as sixple,' pointed out Greymatter.

'There is if I say there is,' snapped Sourmuddle. 'Sixple, sevenple, twenty-twople, whatever I say.'

'I couldn't help it,' protested Sharkadder. 'I had problems getting ready.'

'That's an interesting *bee-keeping* look, Sharkadder,' remarked Sludgegooey, referring to the sunglasses and the veil. Everyone sniggered.

'Yes, well, I have a slight rash,' mumbled Sharkadder.

'That's no excuse,' said Sludgegooey. 'I've got a knee that clicks. I got here before you, though.'

'So did I, even with ... arrrrgh! Toothache.' (That was Bendyshanks.)

'What about my back, then?' (Ratsnappy.)

'I don't think any of you realise quite how long a poem takes, particularly when one isn't in the mood ...'

Everyone began shouting, apart from Gaga, who was experimenting to see what happens if you blow bubbles when standing on your head. (Nothing pleasant.)

'Here I am. Sorry I'm late.'

A voice came suddenly from the doorway. Everyone looked around.

'Oh,' said Sourmuddle sourly. 'It's you, Pongwiffy. A hundredple black marks for being last. Sit down, we're doing News.'

'I will,' said Pongwiffy. 'I *will* sit down, but not until I've made a very special announcement.'

'Is it News?'

451

'More important than News. I want you to take a good look at me.' She struck a pose. 'What do you see?'

The Witches took a good look at Pongwiffy. Some put on their spectacles. There was a little silence.

'You,' said Bendyshanks eventually.

'But a bit worse than usual,' added Sludgegooey. 'Wheezing a bit. Even dirtier, if that's possible. And smelling to high heaven, that goes without saying.'

Everyone nodded. That about summed it up.

'Ah,' said Pongwiffy. 'But what you see before you is the *Old* Pongwiffy. The *New* Pongwiffy is about to come. Prepare for a huge change.'

There was a general sigh of disappointment.

'That's *it*?' demanded Sourmuddle. 'That's the announcement? That you're *changing* yourself? What's so special about that?'

It was pitifully easy to turn yourself into something different. All the Witches could do it, with a wave of the Wand and a muttered incantation. They could become a mermaid, a kangaroo, a steamroller, anything. Simple transformation. It wasn't the sort of thing that deserved a special announcement.

'Ah, but I'm not using *Magic*,' explained Pongwiffy. 'I'm talking about a *real* change. I'm going to do it properly. No short cuts. I took a long look at myself

452

before I came here tonight, and I didn't like what I saw. And I can't tell you how poorly I was on the way. Hugo knows, so does Sharky.'

'She was,' agreed Sharkadder loyally. 'Poor Pong.'

'So,' announced Pongwiffy, 'I've made a decision. I'm going to get fit.'

Now, that was a word you don't hear often in Witch circles. It caused shock, bewilderment and a certain amount of rude laughter.

'You can laugh,' said Pongwiffy sternly. 'Oh, you can *laugh*. But you won't, not when you see the new me.'

'Will it have washed its cardigan?' shouted Scrofula. 'The New You?'

Everyone fell about.

'I'm not talking about surface dirt,' said Pongwiffy irritably. 'I'm not talking about *smell*. I *could*, all night long, in fact I'd love to, but I'm not. I was discussing it with Hugo on the way here. He said something. What was it you said, Hugo? About treating the body as a wimple?'

'Temple,' said Hugo. 'Treat body like *temple*.'

'I think you'll find a wimple is a medieval headdress worn by . . .' began Greymatter, but Pongwiffy waved her quiet.

'Temple, wimple, pimple, whatever. The main thing is, I'm getting back on track. I'm going to start looking after myself and get healthy. I'm going to stop eating junk and go for things like – like – um –' Hugo whispered in her ear. 'Like cauliflower. And grapes.'

'That's good, is it?' asked Bendyshanks doubtfully. 'Cauliflower and grapes?'

'Certainly. Fruit, vegetables and lots of exercise.'

'All right,' said Sourmuddle suddenly. Snoop was tapping at the watch. 'That's enough of you. Let's move on to News –'

'Wait a minute, wait a minute! I haven't finished.'

'Is this a different part of the special announcement?'

'Yes.'

'Is it more interesting than the first part?'

'Yes.'

'Well, get a move on, we haven't got all night.'

Pongwiffy took a deep breath and stared around the hall. 'The thing is,' she announced sternly, 'we've *all* got to change, not just me. I've seen the light, you see. It took a lot of suffering behind bushes and an athletic squirrel, but finally I've seen it.'

'What's she on about?' sighed Scrofula. 'Bushes, lights, squirrels, what's she on about? *Can* I have one of your sweets, Macabre?'

There was an instant rustle as everyone suddenly remembered their sweets. They were getting bored with Pongwiffy, who was taking far too long to get to the point.

'You see? That's just what I'm talking about!' cried Pongwiffy. 'All this rubbish we're eating! The sweets and the greasy stuff. Oh yes, it *tastes* nice, I know that, but just look at us. Tummyaches, spots, toothache. Running out of breath if we walk as far as the garden gate. Clicking knees, backache.' She whirled, pointing an accusing finger. 'Macabre's gone up three kilt sizes. Greymatter hasn't written a decent poem for weeks. We've stopped making brews. The Brooms never get taken out. Is this what the Witchway Coven has come to? A bunch of decrepit has-beens who spend all their time pigging out on *sweets*, like a load of half-baked *Gretels*?'

It was a rousing speech and there was a lot of truth in it. There came a series of guilty crunching noises as the Witches hastily disposed of the sweets in their mouths, then a hail of rustling as they tried to hide the bags. Even Sourmuddle decided against taking another *Swampswallow*.

'All we're doing,' went on Pongwiffy, 'all we're doing is making the Yetis rich and ourselves unhealthy. So it's time for a change. If I can do it, we all can. But it won't be easy, so we need something to aim for. So here's the idea. We hold a Sports Day.'

There was a long, startled silence.

'What did she say?' demanded Sourmuddle after a bit. 'Did she say – *Sport?*'

'I did. I'm speaking of a great big sporting contest that'll be talked about for years to come. Hugo was explaining it to me. Apparently, in Hamsterdam, where he comes from, they hold something called the O'Lumpicks.'

'Not O'Lumpicks. *Olympics*,' said Hugo. 'Rodent Olympic Games, very popular. 'Amsters, rats, mice, guinea pigs, veasles, ferrets. All join in.'

'Sounds daft,' jeered Dudley. 'Load o' little furry critters running about. Daft.' Vernon gave him a glare, and he shut up.

'And the point of it?' enquired Sourmuddle.

'Well, like I said, it'll give us a goal to aim at, won't it? While we're getting fit. And not just us Witches either. We'll throw it open to all. Everyone who lives in the Wood. Skeletons, Trolls, Wizards, Vampires, Zombies, Ghouls – everyone except Goblins. We have to draw the line somewhere.'

'Why would we *do* that, though?' mused Ratsnappy. 'Throw it open to all?'

'Ah, well, you see, this is where it gets interesting. Apparently, Hugo was explaining to me, as well as making you fit, an O'Lumpicks has got a Noble Purpose.'

'*Olympics*,' said Hugo.

'The whole idea is to meet and mingle. We get to discover all the things we have in common.'

There was a bewildered silence.

'What, that we hate each other, you mean?' asked Ratsnappy eventually.

'Well ... yes. But we pretend we don't.'

'Let me get this right,' said Scrofula slowly. 'Are you saying we have to be – *nice*?'

'Right. We have to behave in a sporting manner. No fighting.'

There was a rumble of disbelief. What a very novel idea. This would take some getting used to.

'I havenay got anything in common wi' a Wizard, Ah'll tell ye that,' said Macabre stoutly, to wide agreement.

(Witches and Wizards have a different style of Magic. Stinky brews versus flashy illusion. They don't mix. Witches and Wizards try to keep well apart. Although there is some intermingling. Sharkadder's nephew is a Wizard. His name is Ronald and occasionally she has him round for tea. More about Ronald later.)

'We're *Witches*,' said Ratsnappy. 'We don't *want* to mingle. Witches are superior, everyone knows that. Everyone else is riff-raff.'

There was another rumble of agreement.

'So we'll prove it,' said Pongwiffy firmly. 'We'll get fit and prove it by winning every single event.'

'Like what?'

'I dunno.' Pongwiffy waved a vague hand. 'Everything. There'll be lots of races and stuff. Running and jumping. I haven't thought it through yet. I'll have to form a Sports Committee and iron out the details.'

'Will there be prizes?' Macabre wanted to know. 'Because Ah dinnay intend tay rouse mahself unless there's a prize at the end.'

'Certainly there'll be prizes,' promised Pongwiffy rashly. 'There'll be gold medals. And silver and bronze for the runners-up. But we Witches'll be going for gold. We'll train and train until we're the fittest Coven in the world. Undisputed champions of the Witchway Wood O'Lumpick Games.'

'*Olympic*,' said Hugo.

'Why bother to train?' interjected Bendyshanks,

fingering her sore mouth. 'We can win everything using Magic. Simple speed spells. Strength pills. I've got a recipe for kangaroo potion at home. Three drops and I can clear the house. Not with this toothache, mind.'

'That's not *sporting*, though, is it?' said Pongwiffy. 'That's cheating.'

'Where does it say Witches can't cheat?'

There were nods of agreement all round. Witches have a very casual attitude to cheating.

'Not when it's *sport*,' said Pongwiffy. 'The whole point is to eat well and get fit. Magic doesn't come into it. Magic is banned.'

There was a shocked gasp at this.

'Ah've nivver heard such a thing!' exploded Macabre.

'There's got to be a level playing field, you see,' said Pongwiffy.

'There isn't a level playing field around here,' pointed out Ratsnappy. 'Just trees and thickets and bogs and bumpy little pathways.'

'I've thought of that,' said Pongwiffy. 'We'll use the palace gardens. We'll pull up the rose bushes and mark out a running track on the lawn. We'll have to chuck out all the old statues, of course, they'll be in the way. And maybe chop down a few trees.'

'The King won't like it,' remarked Sourmuddle thoughtfully. 'Very nice this year, his roses. Credit where credit's due, he's got a good garden.'

The King's name was King Futtout, and he did indeed have a lovely garden. He spent a lot of time in it, to stay out of the way of his wife, Queen Beryl, and their daughter, Princess Honeydimple. The palace grounds stretched right to the borders of Witchway Wood and were surrounded by a high wall, to keep out undesirables.

'All in a noble cause,' said Pongwiffy airily. 'He'll agree, I'll see to that. If he doesn't, we'll do it anyway. Come on, Sourmuddle. What do you think?'

'I must say I'm struggling with the idea,' said Sourmuddle. 'It's all a bit newfangled for me.'

'You don't want to get fit, then?'

'What's the word I'm looking for?' Sourmuddle thought briefly. 'No.'

'Well, I must say, I'm shocked. You wouldn't like to run everywhere? So you could be even more punctual?'

'I'm over two hundred years old. Why run? Besides, I'm Grandwitch. It's not dignified, is it, Snoop? We don't *run*, do we?'

'Certainly not. The very idea,' snapped Snoop, breathing out a cross little puff of smoke.

460

'So you're saying we can't have an O'Lumpicks? You can't say we can't, you *can't*!' Pongwiffy sank to her knees and wrung her hands. 'Don't say we can't. Oh please, oh please! I'm really *keen*!'

'I haven't decided. I'm not sure about the whole mingling thing. Or the playing fair. Or the sport, come to that. But I confess that getting Futtout annoyed has a certain charm.' Sourmuddle gave a dark little chuckle. 'It's been a while since we rattled his cage.'

'It'd be very good publicity too. For the Coven, I mean.' Pongwiffy was being crafty here. Sourmuddle was never averse to good publicity. 'I mean, I know we're good at being *Witches*, everyone knows that. But this'd be something different, wouldn't it? Something that'd benefit the whole community. And we'd be the hosts, so we'd run it our way. We'd make ourselves popular and get fit and win all the gold medals at the same time. We can't lose.'

'Would I get my name in the paper, do you think?' asked Sourmuddle.

'Sure to!' promised Pongwiffy. 'You can go on spellovision too, and talk about it on all the chat shows. Just imagine it! Marching around with our flag at the Grand Opening Parade. A spectacular display of Witch pride. Traditional costumes. The band playing. Everyone cheering.'

'Opening Parade?' cut in Scrofula. Everyone perked up. It's a dull person indeed who doesn't like the idea of a parade.

'Oh yes, there has to be one of those, doesn't there, Hugo?'

'Zere does,' agreed Hugo. 'Parade first, zen Games, zen ze medals. Zat how it go.'

'All the teams march in under their own flag,' explained Pongwiffy. 'But because we're running things, we go first. So we get the biggest cheer.'

Barry the Vulture asked the question that all the Familiars were dying to ask. He wasn't feeling quite so unwell now. All the Familiars were sitting up, looking interested. Steve had wriggled out from beneath Bendyshanks' cardigan. Rory had come in from outside, and Filth had stopped air drumming. Dudley looked a bit sulky, though. Hugo was getting far too much attention in his opinion.

'Permission to speak?' asked Barry the Vulture. 'On behalf of the Familiars?'

'Go on, then, but make it quick,' said Sourmuddle. Familiars weren't encouraged to speak at Coven Meetings.

'Can *we* be a team? Instead of just running around making tea?'

There came an explosion of laughter from the Witches.

'Ah dinnay *think* so,' cried Macabre. 'The very *idea*!'

'Ha, ha, ha!' chortled Greymatter. 'Familiars competing against Witches! Oh, my splitting sides!'

Pongwiffy caught Hugo's eye.

'Yes, they can,' she shouted. 'We've got to do this right. The Games are open to all. Even Familiars.'

The laughter cut off. There was a shocked silence. Hugo whispered in her ear.

'And they can have their own flag,' announced Pongwiffy.

'I bet it's a daft one,' said Macabre, who still hadn't forgiven Rory for making her walk.

'Them's fightin' words,' growled Dudley. 'Us can make a better flag than you landlubbers, I knows that!'

'Don't be cheeky, Dudley,' Sharkadder reprimanded him. 'Just be glad Pongwiffy's given you permission. This is a Witch Meeting, you're not supposed to interrupt. What was that you were saying about traditional costumes, Pong?'

'That's what we wear before we change into our

shorts. I thought you could design them, Sharky. With your good fashion sense.'

'We have tay wear *shorts*?' howled Macabre.

'Of course. A healthy diet, a noble mind, team spirit and shorts, that's what the O'Lumpicks are all about. Hey, you know what else I thought? We could get Scott Sinister to be the commentator and present the medals at the end. And you know what else? We could . . .'

Hugo sat quietly on Pongwiffy's hat, listening to her rant on. A Sports Day, held in the palace grounds. A Grand Opening Parade. Races. Medals. Competition. Everyone in shorts. Everyone getting together to find out what they had in common. Scott Sinister, the famous film star, to present the prizes. It was an ambitious plan. It could be fun, or it could be a recipe for disaster.

However it worked out, one good thing had come out of it. From now on, Pongwiffy would be eating healthily. He could finally throw away those jars of mouldy skunk stew.

CHAPTER SIX
Plugugly Drools

At exactly the same time as Pongwiffy was outlining her big idea, Plugugly the Goblin was standing stock-still with his nose flattened against the window of *Sugary Candy's*. He had been there for some time.

It was the first time that Plugugly had seen the new sweet shop. He rarely ventured down into Witchway Wood for fear of coming face to face with a Witch. Goblins are sworn enemies of Witches. Well, they're sworn enemies of everybody actually. But they are particularly wary of Witches, who automatically zap them on sight. (Zapping is painful, involving a green flash, a short, sharp scream and flaming trousers.)

However, it was the last Friday of the month, and the Witches would be tied up with their Coven Meeting. Plugugly had been told this by a Thing in a Moonmad T-shirt who he happened to have bumped into earlier, when out wandering the mountains with his empty hunting bag.

Usually, Plugugly hunted with the rest of the Gaggle. A Gaggle, you should know, consists of seven Goblins who do everything together – eat, fight, and sit around plotting stupid things mainly. But on this particular evening, Plugugly was alone. This was because he'd had a big argument with the others. It had been about hats. More specifically, whose hat was best. Like all Goblin arguments, it had come to nothing, but the general agreement seemed to be that out of all their hats, Plugugly's was the silliest.

Plugugly was fond of his headgear, which was an old saucepan he'd found in a dump. He thought it was a bit helmet-like and made him look like a knight of old. It didn't. It just made him look like a Goblin with a saucepan on his head.

Anyway, it all ended with him seizing his hunting bag and stomping out in a fury.

'Ow!' the Thing in the Moonmad T-shirt had said, picking himself up. 'Watch where you're going!'

'I is in a *hurry*,' Plujugly had snapped. 'I is goin' *huntin'*.' He waved his bag, which had the Traditional hole in the bottom. (Goblins always persist in cutting that Traditional hole, although they sometimes wonder why they never succeed in catching anything. It is one of their stupidest Traditions, although they have others that come close.)

'Why? It's not Tuesday.'

(This is another Tradition. Goblins always hunt on a Tuesday. Everyone knows this, including the prey, which is why they never catch anything and live on stinging nettle soup.)

'It isn't?' said Pluggly doubtfully. He had no calendar and relied on his fingers to count. He often got it wrong.

'No,' scoffed the Thing. 'It's *Friday*. The last Friday of the month. The Witches' Coven Night. Don't you know *anything*?'

'I know I'll bash you up,' said Pluggly crossly.

'Oh, oh, I'm so scared!' jeered the Thing, and went skipping off, leaving Pluggly to reflect upon his words.

So. It was the last Friday of the month. The Witches

467

would be tied up with their Meeting. That meant there would be no Witches wandering around the Wood, although he'd need to keep an eye out for Trolls. Worth the risk? Probably.

Plugugly made for the Wood. He knew he wouldn't catch anything with a *face*, because he never did. Faces tend to have brains behind them. Even really tiny brains belonging to small, dim mice are more than capable of outwitting a Goblin.

But, reckoned Plugugly, there might be toadstools. Or, if he was lucky, some of those red berries you could add to nettle stew. They made it look pretty, although you always felt funny afterwards. Anyway, whatever he got, he would take it back to the cave and scoff it in front of everyone. Without sharing. That'd learn 'em.

The moon was out and the sky was splattered with stars, so it wasn't too dark under the trees. Nevertheless, Plugugly kept his saucepan pulled well down over his eyes to protect him from low branches. Of course, that meant he couldn't actually *see* them, so his passage through the woods was accompanied by a series of loud ringing noises. *Clang! Ping! Dong!* You could hear him coming a mile away. Lots of little fluffy things sat smugly in their holes, nudging each other and sniggering.

Plugugly hadn't ventured down into the Wood for some time, so he was very surprised when he came across *Sugary Candy's*, sitting slap bang in the middle of a glade. More than surprised. Goblinsmacked. That's the same as being gobsmacked, but worse, as you will see.

Dazzling light blazed from the window of the beautiful gingerbread house, the glistening sweets shining like jewels in the moonlight. The window was chock-a-block with big, multicoloured jars and mountains of heaped chocolate bars. The shop might be closed, but Spag and Conf knew the value of advertising their wares twenty-four seven and always left the shutters open and the lights on.

Slowly, Plugugly pushed back his saucepan so that he could get a proper eyeful.

Plugugly had only ever eaten sweets once in his life. On one never-to-be-forgotten occasion, the Gaggle had attended a fancy dress party at the Great Gobbo's palace. They had eaten wonderful things there. Jellies. Cakes. Pink wobbly stuff. Brown sticky stuff. Best of all, handfuls of delectable sweets from deep bowls. Oh my, what a night that had been.

The shop window drew Plugugly like a magnet. His feet left the ground, and before he knew it he was standing with his nose glued to the glass, mouth open and drooling, well and truly goblinsmacked.

That was how the Gnome called GNorman found him.

'What are you doing there, Plugugly?' enquired GNorman. He was on his way home to supper, a copy of *The Daily Miracle* tucked under his arm.

Plugugly didn't even look round.

'Oi! You!' shouted GNorman. 'Plugugly! What are you doing?'

Plugugly gave a faint moan and continued to drool.

'No point in looking,' said GNorman. 'They're closed.'

Slowly, Plugugly dragged his eyes away. He turned. His eyes were glazed and his mouth hung open. He was slavering really badly.

'Sweeeteeeeeeez,' drooled Plugugly.

'Yes, I know,' said GNorman impatiently.

'Sweeeeeeteeeeeeeezzzzzzz . . .'

'That's right, sweets, that's what they sell.'

'Sweeeeeeeeeeeeeeeeeeeeeeee . . .'

Plugugly was obviously stuck in a groove. His brains were jammed. GNorman picked up a fallen branch and hit him on the saucepan very hard.

CLAAAANG!

'Ow,' said Plugugly crossly. 'Dat hurt.'

470

'Had to be done,' said GNorman. 'You should thank me. I asked you what you're doing here in the Wood, where you're not supposed to be?'

'Nothin'. Just lookin'.'

'There's no point. They're closed. The door's got a magic padlock on it. And you can't break the window, if that's what you're thinking. Everyone's tried, it's hopeless.'

'Bet I can,' said Plugugly.

'Go on then. Let's see you do it.'

Plugugly marched back some way from the shop, lowered his head and ran full tilt at the window. He collided with it, rebounded and fell flat on his back.

BOING!

'See?' said GNorman. 'Not even a little crack.'

'But I want *sweeeeeties*,' moaned Plugugly. He sat up, clutched his head and rocked to and fro. 'I *want* dem. I do, I do, I *do*!'

'Well, you'll have to pay for them like everyone else,' said GNorman. 'Come back when they're open, and bring lots of money.'

'But I hasn't got no money!'

'So get a job and earn some.'

'What job?'

'I don't know, do I? Look in the paper.'

'But I can't *read* de paper.'

'How pathetic,' sighed GNorman. 'I don't know, can't even read the paper. You Goblins are *hopeless . . .*'

His voice suddenly cut off. That was because Plugugly's hand was around his neck.

Plugugly's Gaggle lived in a damp cave on the lower slopes of the Misty Mountains known as Goblin Territory. Their names were Hog, Lardo, Slopbucket, Stinkwart, Eyesore and Sproggit. They didn't like living where they did – it was a desolate place, full of rocks, rain and rubbish. But sadly, they were stuck there. A long time ago they had fallen foul of a Wizard who had banished them there for ever as a punishment, so there wasn't anything they could do about it. No matter how far they hiked, in the end they always ended up back in the cave, so they never bothered going far.

They were sitting around in sullen silence, wishing there was something to eat, when the boulder that served as a front door came crashing back and Plugugly burst in and announced, with great triumph, *'I has got a Gnome!'*

He had too. Poor little GNorman was tucked tightly under his arm, legs wiggling.

'Can we eat it?' asked Eyesore hopefully.

'*You* can eat it,' said Plugugly, adding, 'Dat's up to you. But *I* isn't. *I* is goin' to eat ... *sweeeeeteeeez!*'

There was a united gasp. Sweeties? What was this?

'Where you gonna get sweeties from?' enquired Hog. 'There ain't no sweetie trees round 'ere last time I looked.'

'Ah,' said Plugugly, 'I know. But I has seen somethin' very excitin'! Dere's a new shop! Down in de Wood! Dere's lots o' sweeties! Big jars of 'em! Like what we had at de Great Gobbo's party dat time, but *better*! I saw dem!'

'Liar,' said Stinkwart. 'There ain't no sweet shop in the Wood.'

'Dere is!' insisted Plugugly. 'If you doesn't believe me, ask *him*.'

He set GNorman on a small rock. The rest of the Gaggle crowded round.

'Look what you've done to my paper,' said GNorman crossly, trying to straighten out the creases. 'Do you have to be so *rough*?'

'Tell dem,' said Plugugly, giving him a poke. 'Tell dem about de new shop.'

'All right, all *right*. There's a new shop. It's called *Sugary Candy's*. The Yetis own it. It sells overpriced sweets. Can I go now?'

'Oh no,' said Plugugly. 'You isn't goin' nowhere. I has got plans for you.'

'What?' asked GNorman, a bit alarmed. 'You can't eat me, I don't taste nice.'

'Niver does nettle soup, but we eats that,' remarked Slopbucket.

'We isn't eatin' de Gnome,' said Plugugly firmly. 'Dat's not de plan.'

'What is, then?' piped up Lardo.

'Ah,' said Plugugly. All eyes were upon him. He was enjoying the attention. 'Ah. Well, see, I bin finkin'. Dere's dis sweetie shop, right? An' we likes sweeties, right? So I was finkin' we can get some money, see, and den – *we can go to de new shop an' buy some!*'

'Oh yeah?' That was young Sproggit, sounding highly sarcastic. 'Oh *yeah*? And where we gonna get money from? Livin' round 'ere? Ain't no *banks* to rob, is there? 'Cept mud banks!'

Everyone howled with laughter at the thought of a bank in Goblin Territory.

'I know *dat*,' said Plugugly. 'I know dere isn't no banks. And dere isn't no buried treasure an' nobody never gives us no pocket money. And nobody's nan's due for a visit. So dat only leaves one fing. We has got to get a job.'

A silence fell.

'A job?' said Eyesore after a bit. 'You mean – like, *work*?'

'Dat's right,' said Plugugly. 'We does a job an' dey gives us money. Dat's how it works, right, Gnome?'

'What job?' asked Eyesore.

'Ah. Dat's where de Gnome comes in.'

Everyone stared at GNorman.

'He's already in,' observed Stinkwart. 'You brought him, under yer arm, just now.'

'No, no. I know he's *in*. He's in de *cave*, I know dat. What I mean is, he can read out de jobs in de paper.'

'I don't see why I should,' snapped GNorman. 'I'm not a reading machine, you know. You can't put a penny in the slot and make me read.'

'We can poke you wiv a sharp stick and make you blub like a *babby* though,' said Lardo, and everyone sniggered.

'Ain't no banks to rob round 'ere,' said young Sproggit, in the hopes of regaining the comedy crown, but his time was gone and he was ignored.

'Go on, Gnome,' said Plugugly.

'That's what I'd *like*,' said GNorman. 'I'd *like* to *go on 'ome*.'

Everybody else was trying to be funny, so he

475

thought he might as well. Sadly, his little play on words fell on stony ground. Goblin humour is very basic. Witty Gnomish puns go over their heads. The sort of thing that makes a Goblin laugh is someone falling over a cliff.

'Get readin',' said Plugugly. 'Or else.'

GNorman sighed. It seemed there was no getting out of it. He sat down cross-legged, took a pair of spectacles from his pocket, hooked the ends around his pointy ears and said firmly, '*Sit*. You have to sit when you're being read to.'

Obediently, the Goblins sat. GNorman opened the paper to the Situations Vacant page. The Goblins watched his every move. This reading business was a complete mystery to them. They were in awe.

'Right,' said GNorman. 'Here goes. TREE FELLERS WANTED. APPLY AT WOOD YARD.'

'Dat's no good,' said Plugugly. 'Dey only want tree, an' dere's seven of us. What else?'

'MILKMAIDS WANTED. IF COLD HANDS, DO NOT APPLY.'

'None of us are called Hans,' remarked Slopbucket. 'Does that mean we can apply?'

'None of us are milkmaids, though,' said Stinkwart doubtfully.

476

'Funny name for a milkmaid, ain't it? Hans?' reflected Hog. 'They're usually called Betty.'

GNorman was getting tired of all this.

'It's *Cold Hands*! Not called Hans. They want milkmaids with hands that are *not cold*.'

'Not called what?' said Hog, confused.

'Anyway,' said Plugugly, 'anyway, we is not girls an' cows doesn't like us. Carry on.'

'GARDENERS WANTED AT PALACE. APPLY KING FUTTOUT.'

'We ain't workin' for King Futtout,' cried Lardo. 'Remember when he chased us outa his orchard that time? Like them apples *belonged* to 'im, or summink?'

'They did,' pointed out Stinkwart. 'It was his orchard.'

'Oh yeah,' said Lardo. 'I see what you mean.'

'Carry on,' said Plugugly to GNorman. 'We isn't gardenin' for royalty, dey doesn't like us. What else?'

'VAMPIRE WANTS HEADLESS HORSE-MAN. MUST HAVE FULL COACH DRIVING LICENCE.'

'Nope. Can't drive coaches, got heads, and Vampires...'

'Don't like you, yes, I thought that might be the case,' said GNorman wearily, adding, 'You're being very fussy, you know.'

'Go on,' insisted Plugugly. 'What else?'

'Not much. This is the last one. WANTED. LIVE-IN NANNY FOR NEW BABY BOY. APPLY MR AND MRS STONKING, STONKING TOWERS. BIG BAG OF GOLD FOR THE RIGHT PERSON.'

There was a long silence. After a bit, Sproggit asked what they were all thinking, 'What's all that about then?'

CHAPTER SEVEN
The Stonkings

The Goblins know nothing about the Stonkings. Not being privy to the gossip grapevine in Witchway Wood, they are never up to date with the news. It will be down to GNorman to bring them up to speed.

It is the following day. Right now, the Stonkings are sitting on the stout reinforced balcony of their big flashy house. The house sits atop a hill overlooking Witchway Wood. In the distance are the Misty Mountains. They have an enviable view. Down below, there is a big garden with big sunshades, a big ornamental fountain and a big barbecue with an ox-spit. There is also a garage containing a great, big, shiny red motorbike because the Stonkings are keen bikers.

They are also Giants. Did I mention that?

Bigsy Stonking has his shirt off and is enjoying the rays of morning sun, which glint off the gold medallions nestling in his chest hair, the gold rings on his fingers, the gold chains around his wrists, the gold hoops in his ears and the single, big gold ring through his nose.

His wife, Largette, is wearing a heavily stained pink bathrobe and a massive pair of sunglasses. She has her hair in curlers and is painting her toenails red. It would be an idyllic scene if it weren't for the sound of angry roaring coming from somewhere inside.

'THIS IS THE LIFE, EH, PETAL?' thundered Bigsy. Giant speech has to be written in capital letters, because it is VERY LOUD.

'IT WOULD BE,' agreed Largette, 'IF BABY PHILPOT WOULD JUST GIVE IT A REST FOR TWO MINUTES. TALK ABOUT STRESS. LOOK AT THE MESS I'M MAKING OF MY NAILS.'

'RELAX, PETAL. STICK COTTON WOOL IN YER EARS. I DO.'

'I'VE GOT NO TIME TO MYSELF AT ALL. I LIKE TO LOOK NICE, BIGSY.'

'I KNOW YOU DO, PETAL.'

'I HAVEN'T EVEN HAD TIME TO TAKE MY CURLERS OUT.'

'I KNOW, I KNOW.'

'LISTEN TO HIM, BIGSY. HE NEVER STOPS. HE WANTS FEEDING AGAIN.'

I should explain that the Stonkings have only just moved into this very large, flashy remote house. The house has to be large, flashy and remote for these reasons:

1. They are Giants.
2. They are seriously rich and can afford to throw their money around.
3. They have a brand new baby boy who does nothing but ROAR.

Let me tell you a bit about Giants in general. Never confuse Giants with Ogres. They are quite different. Bigsy and Largette Stonking do not have two heads. Well, they do, but not two *each*. They do not rampage around in seven league boots, waving clubs with nails in. They don't kick down mountains or juggle sheep. They're not *that* big, or that bothered. Even if they were, they wouldn't have found the time, not with the new baby, who is very demanding.

No, Ogres they are not. But that isn't to say they

aren't big. I mean, *really* big. To put it into perspective, you would probably come up to Bigsy's knee. The Stonkings would have trouble fitting into your house. Unless you live in a cathedral.

Most Giants live somewhere they call The Big Country, a long way from Witchway Wood. There is only one town in The Big Country. Predictably, it is called Giant Town. Almost all Giants live there, mainly because it has a Giant supermarket called Vasto's which always has special offers.

Giants tend not to travel much. This is because everything in The Big Country is the right size for them – big. Nowhere else in the world caters for them properly. Everywhere is too small and everything is horribly fiddly. There are very few houses they can comfortably fit in. Only really rich Giants settle elsewhere, mainly because they *can*. They can afford to have new, big furniture made and get big food imported from home.

Bigsy Stonking can afford it. He has plenty of cash to throw around. His family owns Vasto's.

To tell the truth, there was another reason why the Stonkings moved, apart from wanting to show off. Neither of them liked their mothers-in-law. Largette didn't like Bigsy's mother, and Bigsy didn't like Largette's. Neither of the mothers liked their son-in-law, daughter-in-law or each other, so it was all very fraught at family barbecues. This is how it went, when they talked about moving.

Largette: I'M TELLING YOU NOW, I'M NOT HAVING YOUR MUM INTERFERING, BIGSY. NOT WHEN OUR BABY ARRIVES. SHE WAS BAD ENOUGH AT OUR WEDDING.

Bigsy: I KNOW, PETAL, I KNOW.

Largette: SHE WAS RUDE ABOUT MUM'S HAT.

Bigsy: I KNOW. (A pause.) YOUR MUM WAS RUDE ABOUT 'ERS FIRST, THOUGH.

Largette: THAT'S BECAUSE IT WAS HORRIBLE. ANYWAY, I'M NOT HAVING HER COMING ROUND BEING BOSSY AND TELLING US WHAT TO DO. I WANT TO MOVE FAR AWAY, BIGSY. I WANT A BIG HOUSE ON TOP OF A HILL. SOMEWHERE QUIET. JUST US, WITH A NURSERY FOR OUR NEW BABY.

Bigsy: AND YOU SHALL 'AVE ONE, PETAL. BIGSY'LL BUY YOU ONE.

He was as good as his word. He purchased the big house on top of the hill, bought big flash furniture and big flash sunshades and the barbecue and everything they needed to make life comfortable. And then Baby Philpot arrived.

The Stonkings weren't prepared for Philpot.

You should know something about Giant babies. When they are first born, they are surprisingly small. Bigger than a human baby, of course, but still quite small. Their lungs are big, though, so they roar really loudly. They do this for three weeks. That's all they do – roar, drink milk, eliminate milk and roar again. They never sleep.

Baby Philpot was just like all Giant babies – angry. He never, *ever* stopped roaring. Not ever. He was permanently purple in the face. He never smiled. He never slept. Just roared.

He was doing it now.

'IT'S YOUR TURN TO GIVE HIM HIS MILK,' said Largette. 'MY NAILS ARE STILL WET.'

'IN A MINUTE,' said Bigsy.

'WELL, GO ON THEN.'

'I WILL, I WILL. IT'S JUST THAT 'E NEVER SEEMS TO WANT IT.'

'HE'S A BABY, BIGSY. HE'S GOT TO HAVE MILK,

484

IT SAYS SO IN THE BABY MANUAL. NOTHING BUT MILK FOR THE FIRST THREE WEEKS. THREE BUCKETS A DAY, THAT'S WHAT HE'S SUPPOSED TO HAVE.'

'BUT HE SPITS IT BACK IN YER FACE! I CAN'T GET IT DOWN 'IM.'

'WELL, YOU'LL HAVE TO TRY. IT'S YOUR TURN,' said Largette crossly.

'YEAH, YEAH, ALL RIGHT.'

'GO ON THEN.'

'I'M GOING, I'M GOING.'

'PUT HIM IN HIS PRAM, TAKE HIM FOR A WALK. HE MIGHT NOD OFF.'

'OH YEAH. SINCE WHEN HAS HE NODDED OFF?'

'NEVER,' admitted Largette with a sigh. There was a heavy silence.

'BIGSY?' said Largette.

'WHAT?'

'I'M TIRED OF BABY PHILPOT. DOES THAT MAKE ME A BAD MOTHER?'

'WELL – YEAH,' said Bigsy. 'BUT THAT'S NORMAL, AIN'T IT? DON'T BEAT YERSELF UP.'

He was right. Giants don't make the best parents. Well, not for the first three weeks, when their babies are small, sleepless and permanently furious.

But that stage only lasts for three weeks, thank goodness. When Giant babies are exactly three weeks old, they produce their first tooth and immediately go on to solids. (That means food that you can chew as opposed to drink.) They stop roaring then, and just eat. They eat continuously, and that makes them grow. And I mean *grow*. They become walking, talking toddlers in a matter of days. Then they thump about and say cute things and become much more agreeable. Their parents start liking them then.

'I JUST HOPE THERE'S A GOOD RESPONSE TO THE ADVERT,' went on Largette.

'THERE WILL BE, YOU'LL SEE.'

'BECAUSE I NEED HELP, BIGSY. I CAN'T DO IT ALL.'

'I KNOW, PETAL. AND YOU WON'T 'AVE TO, NOT WHEN YOU GOT THE NANNY.'

Bigsy stuffed cotton wool back in his ears, closed his eyes and thought wistfully about the big, flashy red motorbike that he never got to ride now he was a father. Largette gave a little sniff, and despondently eyed her toenails.

Inside the house, the baby roared.

CHAPTER EIGHT
The Sports Committee

'Right,' said Pongwiffy briskly. 'Let's get started. You fetch the fungus sponge, Sharky, and somebody put the kettle on.'

It was the first meeting of the Sports Committee. There were eight of them squashed around the table in Sharkadder's kitchen – four Witches and four Familiars. Pongwiffy, Sharkadder, Greymatter and Macabre accompanied by Hugo, Dudley, Speks and Rory, who stood outside with his head through the window.

'I didn't make a sponge,' said Sharkadder. 'We're

not supposed to be eating cake, are we? If we're getting fit?'

'You didn't make a *sponge*?' Pongwiffy was aghast. Sharkadder's fungus sponge was famed far and wide for its delectable deliciousness.

'No. But there's good news. I have prepared a delicious bowl of healthy fruit and vegetables, which we can nibble on.'

'What sort of fruit and vegetables?'

'Sliced lemons tossed with sprouts.'

'Mmm,' said Pongwiffy. 'Well, maybe later, if we're desperate. Ready with your pen, Greymatter? You have to write everything down. Write Witchway Wood O' Lumpick Games in big black letters.'

'*Olympic*,' said Hugo tiredly.

'First, we've got to write down a list of what games we're having. There's got to be a running game, a jumping game, a game where you throw things, a game where you lift things and a relay race at the end. Write it down. Now, moving on . . .'

'Wait a minute there!' That was Macabre, who had only got on the Sports Committee because she threatened Pongwiffy with violence. 'Ye cannay decide just like that!'

'Yes, we can,' argued Pongwiffy. 'We're the experts

488

here, me and Hugo. Hugo's *done* a Sports Day. He's done a whole O'Lumpick, haven't you, Hugo?'

'*Olympic.*'

'Stop correcting me, I like O'Lumpick better. Anyway, that's what you do on a Sports Day. Run, jump, throw things . . .'

'I have a question about running, Pong,' said Sharkadder, sticking her hand up. 'Where do we run? In a circle? In a straight line? Over a cliff? Do we all run at the same time? If we trip up, can we start again? Where do we stop? Who says? How do we know? Does everyone have to wear shorts? Can we wear high heels if we like?'

'That's a hundred questions,' said Pongwiffy irritably. 'We'll be here all day and all night if we ask a hundred questions about everything. This meeting is just to get things started. We'll sort out the details later.'

'Bad idea,' argued Greymatter, who was frantically scribbling away with her tongue out. 'Sharkadder's quite right. We have to do things properly right from the start.'

'No, we don't,' insisted Pongwiffy. 'All we need right now is a broad plan of action. Details are boring, details can wait.'

'No, they *can't* . . .'

Let's just break off a minute and examine the Sports Committee while they're arguing.

Pongwiffy and Hugo had enjoyed selecting the Sports Committee. They had held auditions, and asked everyone to make a small speech about why they wanted to be on it. Everyone was keen, apart from Sourmuddle who announced that they could do what they liked as long as she got her picture in the paper.

Everyone else turned up to audition. Some of the speeches were rather good, and it's a shame we don't have time to hear them. In the end, Pongwiffy chose Sharkadder because she was her best friend, Greymatter for her writing skills, and Macabre because she had to (the threat of violence, remember?). The ones who weren't chosen – Gaga, Ratsnappy, Bendyshanks, Sludgegooey, Scrofula, Bonidle and the twins – were terribly disappointed and more than a little resentful, but there was little they could do but trail off home and wait to be told what would happen next.

'Look,' said Pongwiffy. 'It's my idea and we're doing things my way.'

'Ah'll tell ye what we're gonnay do,' said Macabre, whose blood was up. She thumped the table with her fist. 'We're gonnay write doon suggestions. We're all gonnay ha' a say, that's fair. Like, Ah want Tossin' the Caber.'

'And what is that?' enquired Pongwiffy through politely gritted teeth.

'It's where ye take a Caber an' toss it.'

'And what is a *Caber*? Can we buy one? Do you know of any *Caber* shops?'

'Ah think a sharpened tree'll do the trick. Write it doon, Greymatter.'

'You know, I rather like the idea of the Egg and Spoon,' observed Greymatter, pausing in her scribbling. 'It's a jolly sort of race, isn't it? All that tripping up and losing your egg. It's hilarious. I mean, this is the O'Lumpick *Games*. Games implies enjoyment. It's meant to be fun.'

'I thought Sport was meant to be taken seriously,' remarked Sharkadder.

'So it'll be a funny Egg and Spoon Race which we take seriously.'

'Fair enough,' said Pongwiffy, who quite liked the idea of a seriously funny Egg and Spoon Race. 'Write it down.'

'Don't forget Veightlifting,' put in Hugo. He flexed his little furry muscles. 'I sink I vin zat, no contest.'

Across the table, Dudley exploded into helpless laughter.

'Don't be rude, Dudley,' Sharkadder reprimanded him. 'He's a guest in our house.'

'Shouldn't there be a Sack Race?' enquired Speks. 'There has to be a High Jump . . .'

'And what about a Three-Legged Race? There has to be one of those . . .'

Everyone was shouting at the top of their voices at once.

'All right, all right, that's enough!' shouted Pongwiffy. 'Caber Tossing, Egg and Spoon, Sack Race, Three-Legged, Weightlifting, High Jump and Relay. That's seven Games. Should be plenty, there won't be time for any more.'

'How will it work, though?' mused Greymatter. 'Everybody can't enter for everything. It'd be chaos.'

'Explain, Hugo,' said Pongwiffy vaguely. She wasn't sure herself how it would work.

'Is simple,' explained Hugo. 'Vun from each team enter each event.'

'So how do we decide who does what?' persisted Greymatter, who had a tidy mind and liked to get things straight. 'In the Witches' team, I mean? Suppose everyone wants to be in the same thing?'

'We'll get Sourmuddle to make a ruling,' said Pongwiffy. 'Everybody has to go along with her decision. That's fair, isn't it?'

'Nobody else had better Toss the Caber, that's all Ah know,' said Macabre. 'Ah thought of it and Ah'm tossin' it. Or things'll get nasty.'

'No, they won't,' said Pongwiffy sternly. 'Nastiness doesn't go with the spirit of the O'Lumpicks. We're a team. We have to support each other and pretend we don't care, even if we do. Now, let's move on. We've got to think about publicity. Hugo and I thought of asking Vincent Van Ghoul to do some posters.'

'I don't know,' demurred Greymatter. 'All that red. Does it give the right message, do you think? It's a Sports Day, not a gore fest on a battlefield.'

'He's cheap, though,' pointed out Pongwiffy. She was right. He was. 'I'll pop along and see him tomorrow.'

'What about telling the King we're holding it in his garden?' enquired Sharkadder. 'Who's doing that?'

'I am,' said Pongwiffy. 'I'll go along after I've seen Vincent.'

'I've just thought of something,' said Sharkadder. 'Who'll be the judge?'

'Hmm.' Pongwiffy frowned. She hadn't thought about that.

'Got to have judge,' chipped in Hugo firmly. 'Say who vin vot.'

'He means who wins what,' translated Pongwiffy.

'Ya. Zat vot I *say.*'

'No, you didn't,' sneered Dudley. 'You can't talk proper, we all knows that.' Sharkadder gave him a sharp tap on the tail, and he subsided.

'He's right, though,' went on Pongwiffy. 'Come on, everyone, think. Who's going to be the judge? Although, actually, *I* wouldn't mind. Perhaps I'll compete and be a judge as well. Then I'll be certain to get a gold medal.'

'You can't do zat,' chipped in Hugo. 'Zat not sporting. Has to be somebody who not *in* it.'

'Sourmuddle could be the judge,' suggested Sharkadder. 'Then all of us Witches will get gold medals.'

Hugo gave a heavy sigh.

'No,' he said wearily. 'Look, I keep *tellink* you ...'

'We know, we know,' interrupted Pongwiffy. 'It's got to be fair, we know. It's just that it takes a bit of getting used to. Like eating greens instead of cake.'

'Talking of that, *do* have a delicious lemon sprout,' said Sharkadder. There was a little pause while she passed them round. Everybody took one. Even Dudley, who was a cat and didn't like them. Rory took two. The Familiars were taking the healthy eating thing as seriously as anybody.

'So who do we get to judge?' said Pongwiffy, crunching noisily.

'Vot about ze King?' piped up Hugo. 'He not competink, right? Give him sumpsink to do.'

'Hugo,' said Pongwiffy, 'you are a little genius. Futtout can be the judge. He'll be thrilled. Right, I think that's everything for now. I shall visit Scott to tell him he'll be commentating and giving out the medals. I expect I'll be gone some time. We're old friends, Scott and me, he's sure to offer me refreshments. I expect I'll get something to eat at the palace too. Cake with royal icing, I expect.' Hugo gave her a little poke. 'Oh. Right. Sorry, forgot. Got to be healthy. I'll order salad.'

'You, you, it's all aboot you,' complained Macabre. 'What are the rest of us doing while you're off visiting artists and kings and film stars?'

'Greymatter can write out the list of Games. And design the entry forms. We'll need lots of those, we're sure to have millions of competitors. And she can hammer out the rules too, as she's so keen on detail. And contact *The Daily Miracle* and the spellovision people.'

'What about me?' asked Sharkadder. 'I want an important job, because I'm your best friend, remember.'

'You can start designing the costumes for the Grand Parade. And you can come up with the team flag, Macabre.'

'Suppose Ah don't want tay do the flag?' protested Macabre. 'Suppose Ah want tay do something else?'

'Tough. You wanted to be on this committee, so commit.'

'Ah'll give you *commitment*! Ah'll commit mah fist to your *nose* . . .'

'Anyone for another sprout?' put in Sharkadder brightly.

Nobody was.

CHAPTER NINE
Nanny plugugly

The Goblins sat in a circle in the cave, surveying the results of their latest hunting trip. Well, let's be clear. Not so much a hunting trip as a *stealing* trip. It had taken them all day, but now they were back with their spoils.

The spoils consisted of six items. These were: a large blue spotty frock (stolen by Lardo from a washing line); a straw bonnet with flowers on it (snatched from a little old lady's head by Sproggit); a white starched apron (snipped by Eyesore from the waist of a tearful milkmaid); a wicker basket (wrenched from the hand

497

of a small girl by the gallant Slopbucket); a big glass medicine bottle with a screw top (found by Hog in a skip); and lastly, a stick.

The stick was Stinkwart's contribution. He hadn't been paying attention when GNorman was explaining what a nanny should have in order to look like a nanny. He had wandered around in a daze all day and finally decided on a stick rather than come back with nothing.

'You done good,' said Plugugly approvingly. 'It's all good. 'Cept for the stick.'

Stinkwart looked mutinous and muttered something.

'Wot?' said Plugugly. 'Wot did you say?'

'He said wot's wrong with a stick,' interpreted Sproggit.

'Everythin',' said Plugugly firmly. 'Nannies don't have sticks. Did de Gnome say anythin' about nannies havin' sticks? No.'

Stinkwart muttered something else.

'Wot?'

'He said the Gnome didn't say nuffin' about them *not* 'avin' sticks,' said Sproggit.

'He didn't say nuffin' about dem not 'avin' *tractors*, or – or *telescopes*, or – or – or – *accordions*, did 'e?'

cried Plugugly. 'That's daft, that is. We gotta fink about wot nannies *do* 'ave, dat makes 'em nannyish. A frock, an apron, a bonnet, a basket an' a big bottle o' baby medicine, dat's wot de Gnome said. Not a *stick*. It'd frighten de little baby, walkin' in wavin' a great big *stick*.'

'Ah, shut up,' said Stinkwart, and went into a deep sulk.

'The thing is,' said Lardo suddenly, 'the thing *is*, we can't *all* be nannies, can we? We ain't got enough nanny fings.'

'You're right, Lardo,' agreed Plugugly. 'Dere's only one of everythin'. Dat means only one of us can be de nanny. An' you know wot? I fink it should be me.'

'I don't see why,' growled Stinkwart. 'You didn't get none o' the nanny stuff.'

'Dat's 'cos I was getting' rid of de *Gnome*,' cried Plugugly. 'I 'ad to take de *Gnome* back, didn't I? I done more dan my fair share! I found de sweetie shop. Anyway –' his eye fell on the voluminous blue spotted frock, 'anyway, I fink dat frock'll fit me best. I fink it's my size.'

'You don't know that,' said Stinkwart.

'Yes, I do.'

'Try it on, then.'

'I will,' said Plugugly. 'Shut yer eyes. No peekin' 'til I say.'

Everyone obediently closed their eyes. There followed several minutes of rustling noises. Then ...

'All right,' said Plugugly. 'You can look now.'

Six pairs of Goblin eyes opened – and six Goblin jaws hit the floor.

'Ooooooh,' breathed Hog. 'Get *you*, Plug!'

Plugugly was transformed. The frock fitted him perfectly. So did the flowery bonnet, tied under his chin with a large bow. The apron gave him a motherly, capable air, and the basket added a charming touch.

''Ow do I look?' simpered Plugugly, and patted his bonnet.

'I 'ardly knows you wivvout yer saucepan,' admitted Lardo.

'I 'ave to say the bonnet suits you,' agreed Eyesore. 'An' the dress is your colour an' all.'

'Really?' Plugugly swished his skirt. He wished he had a mirror.

'You can't just *look* like a nanny, though,' remarked Stinkwart, still put out about the poor reception of his stick. 'You gotta *talk* like a nanny. Bet you can't do that.'

'Why, you rude, *naughty* little boy!' trilled Plugugly

in a falsetto voice. 'Anudder word from you, and I is puttin' you straight to bed widdout any supper!'

The Goblins cracked up at this. They rolled around the floor, clutching their stomachs and sobbing with mirth, all except Stinkwart. It was so funny, hearing Plugugly talk like that.

'Say somethin' else, Plug!' begged Sproggit. 'Go on, say somethin' else!'

'All good children got to wash der hands before teatime!' Plugugly advised them, and was rewarded with another blast of merriment. It wasn't often he got the chance to shine.

'Do anuvver one, Plug!' urged Hog, wiping his eyes.

Plugugly reached into his basket, pulled out the big glass bottle and waved it around.

'Line up an' take

your medicine like good little children!' Vigorously, he shook the bottle and waited for more laughter. There was a bit, but not much.

'Come along, come along!' he tried again. 'Everybody in line!'

Silence.

'That's not so good,' said Stinkwart. 'The bottle don't slosh. You can tell there's nuffin' in it.'

'Dat's right,' said Plugugly. 'It is empty. I know dat. But it won't be on de day. We'll fill it wiv baby medicine.'

'We ain't got any medicine,' pointed out Lardo.

'So we'll use pretend medicine. Like – like –' Plugugly cast his eyes around, looking for inspiration. They fell upon the rusty bucket of nettle soup by the front boulder. It contained the Goblins' food for the day. 'Like nettle soup.'

'Pretend medicine won't *work*, though, will it?' said Stinkwart triumphantly. 'They'll know you're not a real nanny if the medicine don't work. They'll know that right away. Think you're so clever. Givin' out pretend medicine, ha.'

'It might work,' said Plugugly crossly. Stinkwart was really getting on his nerves.

'No, it won't.'

'Well, dat's all you know, Stinkwart. You fink nannies 'ave big *sticks*. You don't know nuffin' about nuffin'. Anyway, I'm de nanny an' I know best, so shut up.'

'You needs a name,' observed Lardo. 'Whatcha gonna call yerself?'

Plugugly reflected. It was a good point. He needed a lady name. A nannyish name. Nanny Plugugly didn't have the right ring.

'I fink,' he said finally, a bit shyly, 'I *fink* I would make a good Susan.'

The Goblins considered this.

'Try it,' advised Lardo. 'We'll tell you. Go on, be Susan.'

'Good mornin',' trilled Plugugly, and dropped a little curtsey. 'I is Nanny Susan an' I has come to look after your little babby. Is dat de dear little feller? Wot a beauty. I do believe he has your eyes. Pass 'im to me, 'e needs windin'.'

The Goblins stared in amazement.

'Cor!' said Hog. 'That's good, that is. 'Ow d'you know all this stuff, Plug?'

'I dunno,' said Plugugly. He was as surprised as the rest of them. 'Seems to come natural, like. I musta bin a nanny in unudder life.'

503

'Well, that's it, then,' said Lardo. 'Plug'll be the nanny. And the rest of us can take it easy an' wait for 'im to bring 'ome the bag o' gold.'

'Suits me,' snarled Stinkwart. ''Long as 'e's not in the cave, suits me.'

Plugugly lost his temper then, and there was a bit of a fight.

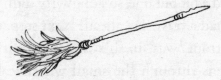

CHAPTER TEN
Three Visits

Pongwiffy had three visits lined up, so she took the Broom. It hadn't been flown for ages and it went a bit mad. Both she and Hugo were decidedly windblown when they arrived at the red-spattered studio of Vincent Van Ghoul.

Convincing Vincent to provide the posters was easy. Pongwiffy had hardly started outlining the idea before he was racing around excitedly, laying out brushes and jars of red paint and outlining his creative vision.

'I thought perhaps – um – you might use another

colour?' ventured Pongwiffy. 'Like, one that isn't red? Just for a change?'

'I am an artist,' said Vincent stiffly. 'I *think* you can leave the artistic decisions to me.'

He seemed a bit put out, so Pongwiffy didn't stay to argue. She had a busy day ahead. Next stop, royalty.

King Futtout was in his shed, admiring his lovely gardens through the small window. He had a kettle brewing on a small stove. The heady scent of cut grass wafted in. He'd been out mowing his velvet lawn all morning, and was sitting down for a well-earned rest.

The King liked it in his shed. He had got it kitted out very comfortably, with an old throne, a tin of custard creams, a bowl of home-grown tomatoes and a pile of old *What Coach?* magazines. He spent all his spare time there, mainly to get away from his wife and daughter who both nagged him a lot. Futtout was a small, weak, droopy sort of king, who wasn't very good at standing up for himself. Sometimes his loving family even followed him down to the shed and stood over him while he wrote out large cheques.

Not this morning, though. This morning they had gone shopping, and a peaceful time lay ahead. Or so he thought.

The door crashed open and, to his horror, a Witch came marching in, bringing with her a very familiar smell that instantly filled the shed, quite cancelling out the scent of grass. On her hat sat a small Hamster, casually polishing its nails.

'Oh,' mumbled King Futtout miserably. 'It's you, Pongwiffy.'

It should be mentioned here that King Futtout has had dealings with Pongwiffy in the past. There had been a nasty kidnapping incident involving her, the Hamster and Princess Honeydimple. Ankles had been bitten. Hair had been hacked. Harsh words had been exchanged. It had cost him money. He remembered it well.

'I want a word with you, Futtout,' announced Pongwiffy. 'They said I'd find you skulking down here.'

'Erm?' bleated King Futtout plaintively. 'Erm ... quite what ... ? What can I ... ? Erm ... do you have an appointment?'

'Nah,' said Pongwiffy breezily. 'Witches don't need appointments. Mind out the way, I need to sit down. Oooh. Tomatoes. I'll have one of them.'

She pushed past King Futtout, helped herself to a tomato and threw herself into the old throne. King

507

Futtout eyed her uneasily. He never got visits from Witches unless they wanted something.

'So,' said Pongwiffy cheerily, biting into the tomato. A squirt of juice shot out, narrowly missing his eye. 'How's the kinging going? Keeping you busy, are they?'

'Well, yes. I do have ... erm ... royal things to be getting on with,' said King Futtout nervously.

'Well, this won't take long. I've just come from Vincent Van Ghoul and I'm on my way to Scott Sinister, so I won't hang about. I just popped in to tell you that we're having a Sports Day called an O'Lumpicks and we need a big, flat space to hold it in.'

'*Stadium*,' said Hugo.

'That's right, stadium. And the only place is your garden, Futtout.'

King Futtout's jaw dropped. A *Sports Day*? In his *garden*?

'We'll need to shift a few things,' went on Pongwiffy. 'The rose bushes will have to go for a start, and the statues. Oh, and we'll need somewhere to store our costumes and flag for the Grand Opening Parade.' Her eyes flicked around the shed. 'This'll do, when it's cleared out.'

'Impossible!' The King's voice came out in a

high-pitched little squeak. 'I really cannot agree to this. This is taking things too far. The gardens are private property, you know.'

'And very nice they are too. Which is why you won't want an invasion of purple-toothed snails. Or big, mad space moles. Or Ninja locusts.'

Pongwiffy withdrew her Wand from her pocket and fingered it thoughtfully. The colour drained from King Futtout's face.

'You wouldn't,' he said.

'You know I would,' said Pongwiffy cheerfully, adding, 'But I won't need to, will I? You won't want it getting round that the King refuses to support a fun-filled sporting event that will benefit all the community. Besides, it's all arranged. The posters'll be up on the trees tomorrow. And *The Daily Miracle*'s doing a piece.'

'When?' croaked King Futtout, through numb lips. 'When is this – event – to be?'

'In three weeks' time. Everyone's got to get into training and there's all kinds of things to organise. You'll have plenty of time to get the shed cleared out. We'll send a party of Familiars to start chopping stuff down and marking up the lawn nearer the time.' Pongwiffy stood up. 'Well, that's it. I'm off. I've got a film star to visit. Nice tomato, by the way. I'll take a couple more for the journey. Oh, one last thing. You're the judge. So you'll need to come up with some medals.'

'Medals?'

'Yep. Gold, silver and bronze. We'll need loads, so I'd get cracking on that.'

And with that, she was off, leaving poor King Futtout stunned.

'I hope you noticed I didn't take any biscuits,' remarked Pongwiffy to Hugo, as they flew over the trees. 'That's because I'm starting to eat well. I think it's making a difference, you know. I'm already feeling a lot perkier than I was.'

They had been flying for quite some time. They were heading for Scott Sinister's holiday retreat – a rather smart castle that lay on the other side of Witchway Wood. It was surrounded by a high wall to keep out intruders. However, it had a big iron gate with bars, through which the curious could catch a glimpse of the blue, coffin-shaped swimming pool which took up most of the courtyard.

This is probably a good moment to tell you a few things about Scott Sinister. Scott is a rich, famous star of stage and screen. He has appeared in a great many horror films, including *The Rampaging Mummy*, in which he played the evil daddy, and *Return of the Avenging Killer Poodles*, which broke box office records. He has an on/off girlfriend called Lulu Lamarre, who Pongwiffy loathes. His career took a nasty dip at one point, but now he is back on top of his game, with a new film in the offing and a lucrative job on spellovision, advertising dental products. He is currently enjoying a short rest before filming starts. He is greatly adored by Pongwiffy, who cuts out pictures of him from magazines and drags him into any of her schemes that require a celebrity. He doesn't enjoy her attentions, but knows better than to turn her down. She is, after all, his number one fan – and number one fans should never be crossed, especially if they are Witches.

So there you have it. That's Scott. And his peace is about to be shattered.

He was lying in his purple silk hammock by the side of the pool. On a small table, set within easy reach, was a bottle of champagne, a single glass and a large bunch of grapes. His eyes were closed and he was just on the brink of a nice little snooze, when a dry voice said, 'So sorry to disturb you, sir. You have a visitor, I'm afraid.'

The voice belonged to the butler, a tall Skeleton in a tailcoat whose name, strangely, was Tubbs.

'Wha— ?' said Scott, struggling to open his eyes against the sun.

'He said you've got a visitor,' chirped a second voice. A shadow fell across his face, and he became aware of a horribly familiar smell. 'Surprise! Wakey-wakey, Scott, it's meeee!'

Scott fumbled for his sunglasses, set them on his nose and struggled upright, hoping it was a nightmare. It wasn't, though.

'Oh,' he said heavily. 'Pongwiffy.'

'Got it in one!'

There she was, beaming down at him. As always, her wretched Hamster sat on her hat.

'I knew you'd be pleased,' she went on. 'Thought I'd drop by. Just a social call. Have a little chat. Any chance of a cuppa?' She stared pointedly at Tubbs, who was hovering disapprovingly in the background, folding up towels and straightening grapes.

'I'm just about to go out,' lied Scott. 'I have an appointment with my director.'

'Good job I caught you, then. It's milk, five sugars.' Hugo gave a little cough. 'No, actually, skip the sugar. And the milk. And the tea. I'll have a large mug of

512

hot water, shaken not stirred. Got to think about the new me. Off you go, butler, Mr Sinister and I have things to discuss.'

'We do?' groaned Scott as Tubbs stalked off into the castle.

'We do. I've got a small favour to ask.'

'You have?'

'Yes. We're organising a big Sports Day, here in Witchway Wood. Everybody'll be joining in, it's very inclusive. We're calling it the O'Lumpick Games and we need you to do the commentating and give out the medals at the end. Oh, and you won't get paid because it's a Noble Cause.'

'It is?'

'Oh, yes. Everybody's going to be on their best behaviour, because it's Sport. There won't be any fighting. So, that's all sorted.'

'Look,' said Scott desperately. 'Look, I'm really busy, I'm not sure I can fit it in.'

'Oh, I think you *can*, you know,' said Pongwiffy mildly, helping herself to grapes.

'I don't think you quite understand ...'

'No.' Pongwiffy cut him off. '*You* don't understand. This is a great opportunity. This is *big*. There'll be crowds from far and wide. It's going to be spellovised.

513

The world will be watching. And there you'll be, in close-up, doing what you do best. Think of the exposure!'

Scott thought about this. Publicity was certainly a good thing. And filming wouldn't be starting for another few weeks.

'You're sure it won't end up with a fight?' he said.

'Certainly not. The very idea. Have some of Scott's grapes, Hugo, they're lovely.'

'It's just that things involving you usually do.'

'Ah, but this is Sport. It's different.'

She was right. It was.

Scott gave in.

CHAPTER ELEVEN
Plugugly Gets a Job

Plugugly stood gasping on the top doorstep of Stonking Towers. It was the biggest house he had ever seen. He glanced back at the distant gates, which seemed miles away. The rest of the Gaggle were back there, where he'd left them. He couldn't see them, but he knew they would be watching. It was up to him now.

Plugugly patted his bonnet and straightened his apron, staring up at the mighty front door. He felt nervous. Not only was everything really big, but there was a terrible roaring noise coming from somewhere within. It sounded like a wild animal. Maybe a lion, or one of those big grey wrinkled things with hosepipe noses. What were they called? Plugugly didn't know.

There was a huge brass knocker hanging above his head. He had to stand on tiptoe to reach it.

BOY-OY-OY-OY-OING!

The echoing crash made his ears ring. There was a short pause, then the sound of approaching footsteps. *Loud* footsteps. The huge door opened – and Plugugly found himself face to face with his first ever Giantess.

Actually, it was more face to knee. The Giantess's face loomed over him from a great height. She wore a grubby pink dressing gown and fluffy pink slippers. Her hair was in curlers and there were bags under her eyes. Her lipstick looked like it had been applied during an earthquake. By the looks of her, she hadn't been sleeping well.

'YES?' boomed the Giantess from on high. 'CAN I HELP YOU?'

It was all rather unsettling, but it has to be said that Plugugly rose to the occasion. A vision flashed into his head of him and the rest of the Gaggle sitting in the cave surrounded by sweet mountains. He had to keep his nerve and hold on to the dream.

'Good mornin',' he trilled in his nanny voice. He

bobbed a little curtsey. 'I is Nanny Susan an' I has come about de job.'

He wasn't prepared for the Giantess's reaction. Her eyes widened and she gave a gasp of excitement.

'BIGSY!' she bellowed over her shoulder. 'GET DOWN HERE RIGHT NOW! WE'VE GOT ONE!'

An answering distant bellow came from somewhere inside. Plugugly couldn't make out the words, though, because of that awful background roaring. Whatever could it be?

'You mean – I got de job?' asked Plugugly. He didn't think it would be *that* easy.

'OF COURSE'. The Giantess turned back to him. Her big face was wreathed in smiles. 'YOU DO LIKE BABIES, DON'T YOU?'

'Oh yes,' said Plugugly. 'Oh yes, I likes dem. Dat's cos I is a nanny. I has got de clothes an' de basket an' everyfin'.'

'SO I SEE.'

'Know what else I got?'

'WELL – NO. DO TELL ME.'

'Medicine,' said Plugugly proudly. He took the bottle from his apron pocket and gave it a vigorous shake. Liquid sloshed about inside.

The Goblins had made a real effort with the

pretend medicine. It consisted of nettle soup with crushed berries to give it a nice pink colour and a few handfuls of mud to thicken it up.

'MY WORD,' said the Giantess, clearly impressed. 'YOU ARE PREPARED. WELL, DO COME IN, NANNY SUSAN. COME AND MEET MY HUSBAND, HE'S UP SEEING TO THE BABY.'

'AH,' nodded Plugugly understandingly. 'Tryin' ter get it to sleep, eh? Must be difficult, wiv dat 'orrible noise goin' on. Wot *is* dat noise, by de way?'

'AH,' said the Giantess. Her smile wobbled and she bit her lip. 'AH. NOW, I THOUGHT YOU MIGHT MENTION THAT ...'

Time now to meet Baby Philpot. We've heard him quite a bit, but haven't yet seen him in the flesh. Prepare yourself.

The Stonkings had thrown money at Philpot's nursery. It was right at the top of the house. It was painted blue, with a border of charging elephants that matched the curtains. Big, clanking mobiles hung from the ceiling, mostly rhinos, hippos and other large, galumphing animals. Arranged on shelves was a huge collection of soft toys – again, following the big animal theme.

Philpot's crib was in the middle of the room. It was large and lovely, all draped in blue. It had ribbons and frills and was set on wooden rockers specially designed to gently lull the baby to sleep. It was the most expensive crib in the Giant Baby Catalogue – probably the whole world. It was a shame that it didn't come with a money back guarantee, because it certainly wasn't having any effect on Philpot.

Right now, it was shuddering violently and crashing to and fro on its rockers like a ship in a storm at sea. Its inmate was beside himself.

Baby Philpot was purple in the face. Drenched with sweat. Arms flailing, back arched. Eyes screwed up, hands clenched into fists. Mouth a gummy red O, and enough noise issuing from it to unplug drains.

Lying in the corner was a gigantic baby bottle, leaking milk on to the floor. Philpot had just hurled it at his father in a fit of pique. All around the cot lay the evidence of his unsettled state of mind – a torn blanket, a gnawed pillow and a cuddly gorilla with a chunk out of its leg.

Now, you know about Giant babies. You know that they are appalling for the first three weeks, when they do nothing but roar, vomit, thrash their arms and go purple. You know that they never ever sleep, as sleep would be a waste of good thrashing and roaring time. What you don't know is why. This is why.

They hate milk!

Yes. That is why Giant babies are so miserable. Milk disagrees with them. They don't like the taste and it gives them tummyache. So they sick it up, which means that they are always ravenously hungry. If only people would stop feeding them milk, they'd be just fine. But grown-up Giants can be a bit slow and haven't worked that out. By the time the babies have developed enough basic speech to explain the problem, they've forgotten they ever had it, so the traditional way of feeding babies – with milk – carries on to the next generation.

It would be funny if it wasn't so sad.

So there was Philpot, bellowing his hatred of milk to the world. Bigsy was cowering by the door, fingering a lump on his head and flinching at the barrage of sound.

The nursery door opened, and in came Largette, followed by Plugugly.

'THERE HE IS,' said Largette, pointing. 'THAT'S PHILPOT. OUR SON. THIS IS NANNY SUSAN, BIGSY. SHE'S COME ABOUT THE JOB.'

'Oh my,' said Plugugly. 'Dat is one unhappy baby. Someone should pick him up.'

'THEY SHOULD,' agreed Largette, not moving.

'DON'T LOOK AT ME,' said Bigsy. 'LITTLE SO-AND-SO JUST CHUCKED 'IS BOTTLE AT ME.'

Neither of them seemed keen. Both of them were casting hopeful sideways glances at the new nanny. This was the moment, then. The moment that Plugugly needed to demonstrate his credentials.

He picked up his skirts and marched to the crib. He stood on tiptoe, and peered over.

'RRRRRRRRRAAAAAARRRRRRrrrr . . . ?'

The roar trailed off as Baby Philpot suddenly registered a new face in baby world. A face he had never seen before. It wasn't a beautiful face, but it had a big, bulbous nose and was topped with a funny hat with pretty flowers. This was different. Who was this stranger staring down at him? Philpot said, 'GA?'

'Aaaah,' said Plugugly. 'Wot a fine big feller. I do believe he has your eyes. Dere, dere, never fear, Nanny's here.'

'I'M AFRAID HE CAN BE A BIT OF A HANDFUL,' admitted Largette. 'LIKE I SAY, HE ROARS ALL THE TIME. WE DON'T KNOW WHY, THOUGH, DO WE, BIGSY?'

'NOT A CLUE,' admitted Bigsy. 'PERHAPS NANNY SUSAN CAN TELL US?'

Plugugly didn't have a clue either. But it wouldn't do to say so. He was supposed to be an expert. Why did babies cry? He cast around for inspiration. His eyes alighted on the gigantic baby bottle.

'What is you feedin' him?' asked Plugugly.

'MILK,' said Largette firmly. 'NOTHING BUT MILK FOR THE FIRST THREE WEEKS. UNTIL HE CUTS HIS FIRST TOOTH.'

'SO WHAT D'YOU THINK, NANNY SUSAN?' rumbled Bigsy. 'WHY'S HE CRYIN'?'

'I is finkin' he has got de tummyache,' announced Plugugly. It was the only thing that came into his head.

'REALLY?' Bigsy turned to Largette. 'HEAR THAT, PETAL? NANNY SUSAN THINKS PHILPOT'S GOT TUMMYACHE.'

'I does,' agreed Plugugly. 'But dat's all right, 'cos I has got dis baby medicine.'

With a flourish, he produced the bottle. He gave it a proper businesslike shake. The contents sloshed about, making a very satisfactory noise. Then Plugugly began unscrewing the cap. The Stonkings watched in fascination. So did Philpot. For a moment. Then

522

he lost interest and opened his mouth to roar again.

'HAVE YOU GOT A MEASURING SPOON?' enquired Largette.

'No,' admitted Plugugly. *Darn!* A spoon. He hadn't thought of that. Was he about to be rumbled?

'SO HOW DO YOU KNOW HOW MUCH TO GIVE HIM?'

'He's a big baby,' said Plugugly. 'So he is needin' a big dose.'

And with no more ado, he crossed his fingers for luck and upended the bottle into Philpot's gaping mouth.

The roar that had just been about to burst forth turned into a choke as the mixture of crushed berries, boiled stinging nettles, rust and mud swilled into Philpot's mouth and spilled over, running down the sides and soaking the mattress. There was such a lot of it, he was forced to swallow.

And then – a miracle happened. To everyone's amazement, Philpot licked his lips. A big, goofy smile spread across his moon-like face. His fists unclenched and slowly, his purple cheeks faded to pale pink.

'GA,' said Philpot approvingly.

'OH MY,' gasped Largette. 'SEE THAT, BIGSY? HE'S SMILING! THE MEDICINE'S MADE HIM BETTER!'

He was – and it had! Nobody was more surprised

than Plugugly. From now on, he must trust his nanny instincts. They were *good*.

'WELL, LOOK AT THAT!' marvelled Bigsy. 'SHE PUT 'ER FINGER RIGHT ON THE PROBLEM.'

'Yes,' said Plugugly. 'I did. Now, I fink you should go away and leave him to me. We needs to bond.'

'OH,' said Largette. 'ALL RIGHT. SHOULD WE VISIT?'

'Not too often,' said Plugugly firmly. 'Just leave 'im to me. It's best. I'm de nanny now.'

CHAPTER TWELVE

Interesting News

Well, strike me sideways with great big green balls of fire!' spluttered Dave the Druid, dropping his fork with a clatter. Half a sausage rolled across the table and landed in the lap of Gerald the Just, who looked annoyed.

'Is that a *request*, or something you've seen in the paper?' enquired Frank the Foreteller, helping himself to a dollop of mustard.

'I don't believe it! They've come up with some batty ideas, but this one takes the cake!'

'Who have?' asked a disembodied voice from an

empty chair. This was Alf the Invisible, who preferred to take his reversing pills after eating.

'The Witches. Shush, I'm reading.'

The Wizards were in the dining room of the Clubhouse, eating breakfast. Breakfast mostly consisted of greasy sausages, and plenty of them. There was bacon and eggs and black pudding as well, but greasy sausages were the most popular, followed by endless rounds of toast and jam, all washed down with copious amounts of sugary tea.

There were seven Wizards, and six had beards. (You'll have to take my word about Alf the Invisible's beard. I know you can't see it right now, but I assure you he has one.) The only Wizard without the traditional chin shrubbery was Sharkadder's nephew, Ronald the Magnificent. He was trying very hard to grow one, but never quite managed it. Being the youngest and least important, he sat at the far end of the table near the door, in the draught.

'I don't see why you should have the paper,' said Fred the Flameraiser irritably. 'It's always you who reads it first.'

'That's because I'm the one who goes all the way down to the front door and picks it up off the mat,' explained Dave the Druid. 'I *bend down* to get it, don't I?'

'That seems reasonable to me,' said Gerald the Just. 'Dave makes the effort, so it's only fair he should read it first.'

'Well, at leasht read ush out a bit,' piped up the Venerable Harold the Hoodwinker, dunking a sausage into his tea. He was the oldest Wizard and liked his food soggy, because his teeth were missing. 'What doesh it shay about Witchesh?'

'They're organising some sort of *sporting* contest.'

'Sport?' exclaimed Frank the Foreteller. 'You mean – *running around*?'

'That sort of thing,' nodded Dave the Druid. 'The O'Lumpick Games, they're calling it. Open to everybody. They're to be held in the palace grounds. They're inviting teams to apply. All welcome, it says.'

'Good grief!' scoffed Frank the Foreteller, spooning jam on to his toast. 'What a thoroughly unpleasant idea.'

'Just imagine,' said Fred the Flameraiser, who had shredded up his napkin, made a little pile on his plate and was now in the process of setting fire to it with a candle. 'Running around Futtout's garden with a load of common riff-raff.'

'Quite sho,' nodded the Venerable Harold, dunking a fried egg. 'Why would one want to *do* that, I wonder?'

'It says here to get fit,' said Dave the Druid. 'And to intermingle.'

A chorus of braying chortles greeted this. Fitness wasn't high on the Wizards' agenda. The only exercise they got was shuffling between the table and the armchair. Apart from Dave the Druid, who had a daily bend down to pick up *The Daily Miracle*, and Ronald the Magnificent, who always did the weekly sweet run down to *Sugary Candy's*. As for intermingling – well! That was beyond the pale.

'It says that there are medals to be won,' added Dave. 'And it's going to be spellovised.'

'Good,' said Alf the Invisible. 'We can sit and watch in our armchairs and sneer. It's ridiculous, and we're certainly not getting involved.'

And then a lone voice piped up from the far end of the table.

'Oh, I don't know,' said Ronald. 'It might be ... fun?'

There fell a heavy silence. It was the pause before the storm.

'*Fun?*' Frank the Foreteller thundered. 'What has

fun to do with Wizardry? Are you *mad*? What d'you think, everyone? Is he *mad*? *I* think he's mad . . .'

Poor Ronald. He gets severely picked on at this point, and it's quite painful. It only stops when Dave the Druid starts reading out an advertisement for a new type of sweet called *Wizard Wobblers*. And then only because they want him to go and get some.

All over Witchway Wood, the various factions were opening *The Daily Miracle* and reading about the proposed O'Lumpick Games.

It should be explained here that the Wood is home to a wide variety of clans. Witches, Skeletons, Trolls, Zombies, Banshees, Gnomes, Fiends, Bogeymen, Vampires, Ghosts, Ghouls – they all live there, keeping themselves to themselves, doing their own thing and only mixing under duress. As well as the main clans, a number of odd individuals live there too. The Thing in the Moonmad T-shirt; a bad-tempered Tree Demon; a couple of bandaged Mummies called Xotindis and Xstufitu; the Werewolf from the sweet shop queue – it's amazing how heavily populated the Wood is. Of course, being a magical sort of place, it manages to accommodate everybody who chooses to live there whilst still remaining essentially wood-like. Quite how this works is a mystery. But it does.

Of all the reactions to the news, none was quite so volatile as that displayed at King Futtout's breakfast table. Queen Beryl was the first to read the headlines, because she insisted on having the paper first.

'Futtout!' she snapped, causing her husband to choke on his Kingios.

'Yes, dearest?' bleated King Futtout, as soon as he recovered his breath.

'What is *this* I am reading on the front page?'

'Urm – I really don't know, dearest. Something interesting, is it?'

'Have you consented to something called the *O'Lumpick Games* to be held in the palace grounds? Without consulting *me*?'

'Ah,' quavered King Futtout. 'Ah. I was going to mention that.'

'I want more ithe-cream,' announced Princess Honeydimple suddenly. She spoke with an annoying put-on lisp. She sat between her parents on a little golden chair with a pink cushion. She had long, curly yellow hair and big blue eyes. She wore a white frilly frock and white satin slippers. She was horribly spoiled and allowed to eat ice-cream for breakfast, which, as everybody knows, is not a good thing.

'In a moment, darling,' said Queen Beryl. 'I'm talking to your father. Explain yourself, Futtout.'

'It happened while you were out,' twittered poor Futtout. 'I wasn't expecting her, she just barged into the shed, you see, and ...'

'*Who* barged into the shed?'

'Erm. Her. You know. The Witch. Pongwiffy.'

'Oh, *poo!*' snarled Princess Honeydimple. '*Her! Thee* cut my *hair* off!'

Honeydimple was telling the truth. Pongwiffy had indeed cut off a hank of her hair. She had needed princess hair as a vital ingredient for a spell. It had happened some time ago, but Honeydimple was the type to bear grudges.

'What,' thundered Queen Beryl, 'were you *thinking* of, Futtout? Entertaining that appalling creature in your shed? After what she and that *dreadful* Hamster did to Honeydimple?'

'Yeth,' chipped in Honeydimple. 'How *could* you, Daddy?'

'I wasn't entertaining her, she just came in making demands and *threatening* me ...'

'Threatening you? How did she threaten you, pray?'

531

'She was talking about – about purple space snails and – erm – ginger locusts. She took her Wand out, you see, I had no choice in the matter . . .'

'You are the King!' roared Queen Beryl. 'Kings always have a choice. I will not *have* it, Futtout. I will not *have* that mad woman commandeering the palace gardens for some dreadful *sporting* event. Even if she is a Witch!'

'That'th right,' chipped in Honeydimple. 'You tell him, Mummy.'

'I'm afraid I don't see how we can stop her, dearest. She was very insistent . . .'

'*Nonsense!* You will write immediately and tell her you've changed your mind. The very idea!'

'But –'

'You heard me.'

'But –'

'Straight after breakfast, Futtout. You will get pen and paper and write her a very stiff letter which I will dictate. And that will be the end of the matter.'

So King Futtout wrote a stiff letter to Pongwiffy, which Queen Beryl dictated. He put it in an envelope, stamped it with the royal seal and affixed to it a first-class stamp.

He didn't post it, though.

CHAPTER THIRTEEN
Minding the Baby

'Dere, dere,' crooned Plugugly, bending over the crib. 'Oo's a good little baby, den? Oo's Nanny's treasure-poo?'

Philpot waggled his chunky arms and kicked his fat, dimpled legs. He was beaming. Plugugly reached in and tickled his fat, pink tummy. Philpot thrashed about in delight, giggling.

'*Oo's* a little sugar plum? *Oo's* Nanny's lovely boy? Baby Philpot, dat's who! Dat's *you*, dat is.'

'TEE HEE!' laughed Philpot, clearly loving it. 'TEE HEE!' And he threw out his arms to be picked up,

533

whacking Plugugly eye-wateringly hard on the nose.

'Aaaah,' drooled Plugugly, not minding at all. 'Duz 'oo want a cuddle? Duz 'oo? Den 'oo shall 'ave one. Up 'oo comes. Oooh!' He staggered back, legs buckling as he took Philpot's considerable weight. 'Whoopsie daisy! You *is* gettin' a heavy boy!'

'GA!' said Philpot, playfully biting Plugugly's ear with rock-hard gums. Plugugly didn't mind that either. He jiggled Philpot up and down.

'Is 'oo hungry? Is de bottle empty? Den let's go for our walkies. Is 'oo ready for walkies? *Is* 'oo? *Is* 'oo?'

Philpot kicked him joyfully in the tummy, and he didn't even flinch.

Let's catch up a bit on what has been going on.

It is Plugugly's third day as Nanny Susan, and you will be surprised to hear that things are going brilliantly. Plugugly has found his calling.

The Stonkings have given him his own room, next door to the nursery. It has a proper bed in it! Sleeping in a bed is a revelation. Plugugly lives in a cave with six other Goblins. The sleeping arrangements consist of slumping on top of each other in a pile, like hamsters. Plugugly is usually at the bottom, getting punctured by sharp stones and even sharper Goblin elbows, so having his own bed

534

is luxury indeed.

He gets proper meals too! They arrive three times a day on a tray outside his door. He can even choose what he wants. There are always three courses. Plugugly has decided that he likes pudding best. He has jam pudding for starters, treacle pudding for the main course, and chocolate pudding for pudding. Presumably, the Stonkings employ a cook, although Plugugly never sees her (or him). He never visits the kitchens. He spends all his time up in the nursery with Baby Philpot. He feeds him, winds him, sings to him and plays peek-a-boo with him. He even copes with the nappy side of things, although we won't go into that because this is not a horror story.

Philpot has stopped roaring. He is a very happy baby now. He does nothing but beam at Plugugly, who he loves dearly. Yes, that's right. You heard. Philpot loves Plugugly. Or, rather, he loves Nanny Susan. In particular, Philpot loves the thing that Nanny Susan provides: the *medicine*. He refuses all offers of milk now. Milk is a thing of the past. Philpot currently lives entirely on nettle soup, which he drinks full-time from his huge baby bottle. He can't get enough of it. What's more, he is thriving on it. Instead of roaring, he gurgles. He smiles. He sleeps like an angel. He is a changed character.

You may be wondering how Plugugly is keeping up with the supply and demand. Well, every day, he wraps Philpot up warm, heaves him downstairs (with difficulty, for he is a very *big* baby) and puts him in his pram. Then together, they set off down the long flight of steps to collect the day's supply of nettle soup. This is provided by the rest of the Gaggle, who wait by the gates with a bucket. Plugugly simply refills the giant baby bottle and gives it to Philpot, who grabs it, sucks madly and is once again content.

The Stonkings, of course, are over the moon. They can't do enough for Nanny Susan. They both agree that she is a treasure.

'THERE SHE GOES,' said Bigsy, gazing over the balcony railings. 'NANNY SUSAN. TAKING PHILPOT FOR A WALK.'

'I DON'T KNOW WHAT WE'D DO WITHOUT HER, BIGSY,' said Largette, coming up and slipping an arm around his waist. 'SHE'S A TREASURE. BABY PHILPOT LOVES HER. WHAT IS HER SECRET?'

'I DUNNO, PETAL. ALL I KNOW IS, HE AIN'T ROARIN'. AT LEAST WE gets SOME SLEEP NOW.'

'I KNOW,' said Largette, snuggling up to Bigsy. 'I

DIDN'T THINK I'D EVER SLEEP AGAIN.'

'HAPPY, PETAL?'

'OH YES, BIGSY. I'M HAPPY THAT BABY PHILPOT'S HAPPY. AND EVEN HAPPIER THAT SOMEONE ELSE IS DEALING WITH HIM. JUST WHILE HE'S GOING THROUGH THE MILK STAGE, OF COURSE.'

'OH YES,' agreed Bigsy. 'WHEN 'E STARTS WALKIN' AN' TALKIN', THAT'S DIFFERENT. WE'LL LIKE 'IM THEN.'

'I KNOW WE WILL. BUT RIGHT NOW, HE'S BETTER OFF WITH A PROFESSIONAL. I WAS THINKING, BIGSY. NOW WE'VE GOT ALL THIS SPARE TIME, WE COULD GO OUT ONE NIGHT, COULDN'T WE? TAKE THE BIKE FOR A SPIN. STOP OFF FOR A BITE TO EAT. PLAY THE JUKEBOX AND DANCE AROUND OUR HELMETS. LIKE WE USED TO DO.'

'YOU MEAN — LEAVE THE BABY?'

'WELL, YES. WE DON'T WANT TO DISTURB HIS ROUTINE. HE'LL BE ALL RIGHT WITH NANNY SUSAN. I DESERVE A BIT OF ME TIME, BIGSY. OH, SAY WE CAN!'

'WHATEVER YOU WANT, PETAL,' said Bigsy fondly. 'WHATEVER YOU WANT.'

Plugugly was down at the gates, where the Gaggle

538

were waiting on the other side of the bars with the bucket.

'You're late,' said Lardo.

'Yes, well, I had to get Baby Philpot ready, didn't I?' said Plugugly.

'Where's the bag o' gold?' demanded Eyesore.

'I hasn't *got* it yet,' said Plugugly. 'I keep *tellin'* you. I gets paid at the end o' the job.'

Hog stood on tiptoe and peered through the bars into the pram, where Philpot lay fretfully waving his empty bottle around.

'Gettin' bigger, innit?' said Hog.

'Is you referrin' to Baby Philpot?' asked Plugugly coldly. 'Because he isn't an it.'

'Yeah, whatever. I'm just sayin' it's grown. Don't you fink, Stinkwart?'

'I dunno,' said Stinkwart with a surly shrug. 'Dunno 'ow big it's s'posed to be. Don't care, neither.'

'Did Stinkwart speak?' Plugugly enquired of the other Goblins. 'Did I 'ear 'im say sumfink? I must say I'm surprised he's here. I'm surprised he isn't out *stick-collectin'*.' He leant into the pram and fussed about with Philpot's blanket. 'Take no notice o' dat bad Goblin, Baby Philpot. He don't know nuffin'.'

Stinkwart scowled and wandered off to kick

a bush.

'Hold out his bottle, then,' said Lardo, picking up the rusty bucket. 'I'll fill it up.'

Plugugly removed the teat and stuck the bottle through the bars. Lardo tipped up the bucket and attempted to pour in the contents. They came out in a rush. Most ended up coating Plugugly's hand. The rest formed a puddle on the ground.

'Look at dat!' said Plugugly crossly, wiping his gunky hand on his apron. 'You is one careless Goblin, Lardo.'

'You shoulda kept the bottle still,' said Lardo. ''Ow am I s'posed to pour if you keep wavin' it around?'

'But dere's hardly any in dere! What's Baby Philpot gonna do?'

'Ah, stop fussin'. We'll scrape it up off the ground.'

'But den it's all dirty!'

'So? He's eating nettles, crushed berries, mud an' rust. What's dirt gonna do?'

This was true.

'Well, hurry up,' said Plugugly. 'If he don't get fed, he gets sad.'

In the pram, Philpot was indeed getting restless. His brow was creased and his clenched fists waved around. His bulging eyes were fixed on the bottle. If he didn't get it soon, there was going to be trouble.

The Gaggle – well, all except Stinkwart, who was still away bush-kicking – set about the task of scooping up the spilled nettle soup with dirty cupped hands and transferring it into the bottle. A lot of it had soaked into the ground. Despite their best efforts, the bottle was only half full. And that included quite a lot of grass, leaves and twigs. It was a lot thicker than usual.

'GA!' bellowed Philpot from the pram, making everyone jump. 'GA! GAGAGAGAG . . .'

Hastily, Plugugly thrust the half-full bottle into Philpot's hands. He stuck it into his mouth and commenced sucking noisily.

'You see?' said Lardo. 'He likes it with extra dirt.'

He was right. Philpot did.

CHAPTER FOURTEEN
preparations

In Witchway Wood, all talk was about the forth-coming O'Lumpick Games. You couldn't avoid the subject. For a start, every other tree sported one of Vincent's posters. Black background with dribbly blood red writing.

THE O'LUMPICKS ARE COMING! they screamed. *OPEN TO ALL!*

The Daily Miracle was full of it and the spellovision news talked of nothing else. Not that anybody read the paper or watched spellovision much. They were all too busy doing knee bends and eating cauliflower.

Besides, you could have enough of Sourmuddle, who was never off the screen, claiming that the O'Lumpick Games were all her idea.

There was a new spirit in the Wood. Suddenly, everyone took to wearing shorts. There was talk of *getting fit* and *eating healthily*. If you took a stroll before breakfast, most likely you would come across the Skeleton team jogging, or the Troll team doing press-ups. Sometimes you might see the Mummies, Xotindis and Xstufitu, sharing a delicious banana before resuming their speed walk. If you were really lucky you might see the faddy Werewolf from the sweet shop queue sprint past, slip on the skin and fall over.

Everyone was taking the preparations seriously. The Banshees hired Witchway Hall every Monday night for a step aerobics class. On Tuesdays, the Zombies took it over for weightlifting practice. There were earnest discussions about what to wear for the Opening Parade, and what should go on the flag. The Witchway Rhythm Boys began practising marching music.

Nobody was keener than the Witches. Pongwiffy's rousing speech had pricked their consciences and made them take a long, hard look at themselves. All of them had gone back to their caves and cottages, rifled through their cupboards and thrown out all the bad stuff. Then they all went on a strict exercise regime. Sludgegooey took up jogging. Bendyshanks went in for Yoga. Gaga found an old bicycle and could be seen screeching around at all hours of the day and night. Ratsnappy, Scrofula and Greymatter met up twice a day to do stretching exercises. Macabre practised tossing large tree trunks around. (Everyone kept a wide berth.) The twins started skipping. Even Bonidle could be seen late at night, sleep running. Sharkadder started up a Keep Fit class on Wednesday nights, which was proving popular. And Pongwiffy herself ran around like a mad thing, organising.

Much to the Yetis' dismay, business at *Sugary Candy's* was beginning to drop off. The daily queues dwindled. Nobody wanted sweets any more. Sweets were out, sprouts were in. The Yetis finally put a sign on the door. It said: CLOSED UNTIL FURTHER NOTICE. Then they turned off the lights, fastened the magic padlock and went off to have emergency business meetings behind locked doors.

The Sports Committee were holding one of their regular meetings at Sharkadder's. They were gathered around her table, on which was set a healthy bowl of pickled cucumbers and a pile of entry forms.

'It's proving even more popular than I thought,' said Pongwiffy. 'Just look at all those forms. Everyone wants to take part. How many teams are entering?'

'Twelve,' said Greymatter, looking at her notepad. 'There's us, the Familiars, the Skeletons, the Trolls, the Zombies, the Banshees, the Mummies, the Vampires, the Ghosts, the Ghouls and the Gnomes. And that dithering Werewolf. He's in a team on his own. He's entering for the Relay, I'm not sure how.'

'My word,' marvelled Pongwiffy. 'Twelve teams! And they'll all have supporters. I bet crowds will come from far and wide.'

'Ah don't know how crowds from far an' wide'll fit in Futtout's garden,' said Macabre. 'It's big, but it's no that big.'

'It'll be a squeeze,' admitted Pongwiffy, 'but there has to be an audience, doesn't there, Hugo? To cheer and clap and stuff. Right, moving on. Have you thought about the Parade costumes, Sharky?'

'I have,' said Sharkadder coyly. 'But they're a secret. I don't want anyone to see them yet. They're rather marvellous, though. I'm thinking dazzling, vibrant colours.'

'Hmm,' said Pongwiffy, mentally resolving that whatever Sharkadder came up with, she would hide it under her old cardigan. 'What's next on the list, Greymatter?'

'Prepare the stadium,' read out Greymatter. 'Chop trees, pull up roses, remove statues, mark out running track with whitewash. Build podium. Bring over the chairs from Witchway Hall. And put up the bunting.'

'Where is the bunting?' Pongwiffy wanted to know. The bunting consisted of lots of rather faded little coloured flags strung out on a length of heavily knotted string. It always got dragged out on festive occasions.

'Under the hall platform, I think.'

'Well, somebody find it. I can't waste time hunting for bunting. I'll get cracking on the stadium straight away. I'll take a team of Familiars along first thing tomorrow.'

Hugo, Rory, Dudley and Speks rolled their eyes at each other and sighed.

'And you can stop all that!' scolded Pongwiffy. 'Just because you're in a team doesn't mean you get let off work. Any further business, Greymatter?'

'I think that's it, for now. Oh, almost forgot. There's

a special Coven Meeting tonight. Sourmuddle's asking for a report on how it's all going. And we've got to decide how we're going to organise the Witch team.'

'Do the Familiars have to come?' enquired Rory.

'No,' said Greymatter. 'You're our rivals now. We don't want you listening in. Spying and stealing our ideas.'

'As if,' said Hugo.

'Don't flatter yerselves,' scoffed Rory.

'I don't *think* so,' growled Dudley.

'We've got our own ideas,' sniffed Speks. 'We don't need to copy yours.'

'Well, that remains to be seen, doesn't it?' said Greymatter. 'Anyway, it's a Witches only meeting and you're not allowed to come.'

'Right,' said Pongwiffy. 'I think we've covered everything. My, I'm stiff with all that sitting. Time for a spot of exercise. You Familiars are dismissed. Everybody else on your feet. Deep breaths, follow me. Running on the spot, then three times around the table. Hup, two, three, four, hup, two, three, four ...'

The rest of the Familiars were gathered together in an old barn on the edge of the Wood, waiting for Hugo, Dudley, Speks and Rory to arrive. Just so that you are clear who they all are, let's run through them. The Familiars are:

Vernon, Ratsnappy's Rat. Currently eating a cheese sandwich on an upturned bucket.

Filth, Sludgegooey's Fiend, perched on a barrel, air drumming with his eyes closed. He has just finished rehearsal.

IdentiKit and CopiCat, Agglebag and Bagaggle's Siamese Cats, elegantly arranged on a bale of straw and looking bored.

Gaga's Bats, hanging upside down from a rafter.

Slithering Steve, Bendyshanks' Grass Snake, curled up on top of a flowerpot.

Bonidle's nameless Sloth, snoozing in a pile of hay.

Scrofula's Vulture, Barry, hunched in a corner, not feeling too well.

Snoop, Sourmuddle's Demon, is not present. Like his mistress, he has expressed disinterest in Sport. He considers himself too grand for it, particularly if it involves wearing shorts. (Tail difficulties.) He is currently back home doing the crossword in *The Demon Times*, watching his mistress being interviewed on spellovision.

Sourmuddle, whilst not prepared to actively participate in the O'Lumpicks, is certainly not averse to talking about them. She can be seen pretty well every night, appearing on spellovision talk shows, taking all the credit. She regularly announces that she has every confidence that the Witch team will win every event and take home all the gold medals. This is fighting talk, guaranteed to annoy everyone and make every team determined to prove her wrong, particularly the Familiars.

The Familiars don't often get together. They only meet up at the monthly Coven Meeting. Their Witches keep them very busy, and besides, they don't get on amongst themselves. There is a lot of inter-species rivalry and petty bickering. But they are entering the O'Lumpicks as a team, so for now it is important to set aside their differences. There's the flag to think about for a start. Everybody has strong views on this.

'It's got to be big,' said Vernon. 'It's got to be seen in the back row. I see a big white banner with THE FABULOUS FAMILIARS written on it in huge black letters.'

'Oh *purleeeze!*' drawled IdentiKit. 'Black on white, that's what *everyone* will do.'

'Far too obvious,' agreed CopiCat. 'Typical of a Rat to come up with something common like that.'

549

'Trust you two to be negative,' snapped Vernon. 'Suggest something else, then.'

'I always think green is a very nice colour,' piped up Slithering Steve shyly.

'Yes, well, you're green so you would say that,' said Vernon. 'We should keep it simple and use a white sheet.'

'Aw, man,' said Filth. 'What's with the sheet thing, dude? Where's the bling in that, bro?'

'I'm just saying,' snapped Vernon crossly. 'I'm just saying that using a white sheet is the obvious way to go. We can't spend hours making a flag. Not when we're supposed to be getting into training, not to mention all the other things we have to do . . .'

Just then, the barn door crashed open and in came Rory, Hugo, Speks and Dudley, hotfoot from the meeting of the Sports Committee. The barn was situated quite a long way from Sharkadder's and they had run all the way, for exercise.

'Phew!' panted Rory. 'Ah'm puffed oot! Ah think ma hooves are on fire.' He blew on his feet, which were indeed smoking.

'How did the meeting go?' enquired Barry. 'Did you learn anything new?'

'Zey vant us to start preparing stadium,' Hugo told

him. 'All Familiars got to meet in ze palace garden tomorrow. Start choppink ze trees down.'

'Not me,' said Filth. 'Band rehearsal, man.'

'You see?' cried Vernon. 'There's no time to fiddle around with complicated colour schemes. Keep it simple, I say.'

'Keep what simple?' growled Dudley.

'We're talking about our flag,' explained Steve. 'Vernon wants it to be white with black letters.'

'Which is like, dull, man!' cried Filth. 'Ain't no one gonna respect a banner like that.'

'I must say I agree with Filth,' said Speks. 'The Witches are wearing vibrant costumes. We don't want them outshining us. We're a team to be reckoned with. We want everyone to sit up and take notice when we enter the arena. Perhaps there should be some kind of logo.'

'*Oi* knows what'd make 'em take notice,' growled Dudley. 'A skull an' crossbones, that'd show 'em we mean business.'

'Is Sports Day, not pirate convention,' sneered Hugo. 'Zat rubbish idea.'

'You gotta better one, furball?'

'You talkink to me?'

'Yeah. Wanna make somethin' of it?'

551

'Yeah!'

'Yeah?'

'Oh yeah!'

We will leave them here. A fight breaks out, and it's not pretty. But you will be relieved to hear that they suddenly remember that it's all about Sport and teamwork and eventually get back to discussing the flag.

CHAPTER FIFTEEN
Solids

Plugugly sat in the nursery with Philpot on his lap. On the floor next to him was a large, empty pudding basin with a spoon in it.

'De wheels on de boat go in an' up, off an' down, on an' out,' sang Plugugly. He didn't know many nursery songs and usually got the words wrong, but Philpot didn't seem to care. 'De wheels on de boat go in an' up, dum-dee-long.'

'GA!' gurgled Philpot sleepily. 'GA!'

'You want it again? Den you shall. De wheels on de boat go ...'

There came a timid little knock on the door. Hastily, Plugugly kicked the pudding basin under the crib.

'Yes?' trilled Plugugly. 'Who dat?'

'ONLY ME, NANNY SUSAN,' came Largette's voice. 'CAN I COME IN?'

'Yes,' called Plugugly. 'But you has got to be quiet. I is gettin' Baby Philpot off to sleep.'

The door opened and Largette peeped in. She was wearing a pink leather jacket and matching leather trousers. Under her arm was a pink helmet.

'AHHH,' she breathed. 'MY BABY! HIS EYES ARE NEARLY CLOSED.'

'Yes,' said Plugugly. 'Dat's 'cos he is nearly asleep.'

'I DON'T KNOW HOW YOU DO IT, NANNY SUSAN. YOU HAVE SUCH A WAY WITH HIM.'

Plugugly glowed. It was true. He did have a way with Philpot.

'DID HE DRINK UP ALL HIS MILK TODAY?' enquired Largette, the concerned mother.

'Um – yes,' lied Plugugly.

'THAT'S WONDERFUL. NOT LONG BEFORE WE SEE A LITTLE TOOTH POKING THROUGH. THEN HE CAN GO ON TO SOLIDS.'

'Yes.'

'HE'LL REALLY BEGIN SHOOTING UP THEN.

554

ALTHOUGH HE'S GROWING QUITE FAST NOW, ISN'T HE?'

'Mmm,' said Plugugly.

'IS IT NORMAL, DO YOU THINK? HOW FAST HE'S GROWING?'

'Oh yes,' said Plugugly.

'IT'S JUST THAT HE SEEMS A LOT BIGGER THAN OTHER BABIES HIS AGE. CAN HE STILL FIT IN HIS PRAM?'

'Yes,' said Plugugly. 'Just about.'

'IT'S JUST THAT THE OTHER DAY I NOTICED YOU — WELL, JAMMING HIM IN. SORT OF RAMMING HIM DOWN. HIS FEET STICK OUT AT THE END, DON'T THEY?'

'Mmm.'

'WELL, HE CERTAINLY SEEMS HAPPY,' said Largette. 'YOU'RE DOING A WONDERFUL JOB.'

'Yes.'

'I JUST POPPED IN TO SAY BIGSY AND ME ARE POPPING OUT FOR A LITTLE SPIN ON THE BIKE. IF THAT'S ALL RIGHT WITH YOU.'

'Dat's all right.'

'I'LL LEAVE YOU TO IT, THEN.' Respectfully, Largette tiptoed out.

Philpot was properly asleep now. Plugugly stood

555

up, staggered across and heaved him into his crib, which sagged under the weight. It really was getting much too small. Philpot spilled over the sides. Even with his head rammed hard against the top end, his feet stuck out a mile.

This is all wrong, of course. Philpot should be growing a bit, but not this much. He is only one week old. By rights, there are another two weeks to go before he cuts his first tooth and starts shooting up. But Philpot is different. Instead of milk, he has been living on nettle soup, which has had the effect of vastly accelerating his growth rate.

Actually, soup is no longer the right word. Soup implies something liquid, something sloshy. But over the last few days, the Goblins have been experimenting with the pretend medicine formula. They have been adding all kinds of stuff to the bucket. Grass, twigs, gravel, leaves, quicksand, toadstools, anything they can find. The resultant mess is now so thick that it is more like cake than medicine. Plugugly has abandoned the bottle and feeds it to Philpot out of a bowl, with a spoon.

So. Philpot is now on solids. And boy, does he love them.

If you put a finger in Philpot's mouth and felt his gums – inadvisable, by the way – you wouldn't find just one tooth. You would find loads! All his teeth are coming through at the same time, much too early. Amazingly, this isn't hurting him at all. Philpot loves the fact that his teeth are coming through because he can use them to masticate his medicine.

Love is blind. Plugugly is vaguely aware that Philpot is getting very big, but he pushes any anxious thoughts to one side. After all, Philpot is happy now and Plugugly likes to see him happy. What harm can it do, spoiling him a bit?

Philpot lay crammed into his crib, sucking his thumb, deep in the world of nod.

'Rock-a-bye Philpot, in de tea pot,' crooned Plugugly tunelessly. The rockers creaked alarmingly under Philpot's weight. 'When you wakes up, I'll give you yer pretend medicine; when yer pretend medicine's gone we'll la lala la ...'

'MEDSIN!' muttered Philpot happily.

It was his first proper word.

The rest of the Gaggle were restless. The days were going by, and there was still no sign of any gold. They were getting bored of traipsing to and fro with buckets of baby food too. Instead of the whole Gaggle going, they were now taking it in turns.

Today, it was Eyesore's turn. He came marching back into the cave and threw the empty bucket into a corner.

'Still no bag o' gold, then,' said Hog.

'No,' said Eyesore shortly. ''E just filled the bowl an' went. I asked 'im, but 'e said 'e'd gimme a black eye if I mentioned it again.'

'I'm sure it's bin a week,' said Lardo. ''Ow many days in a week?'

Nobody knew. Sproggit suggested ten, but he was only guessing.

'Well, all I know is, it's been a long time,' went on Hog. ''Ow much longer we gotta wait? I wants to go shoppin' fer sweeties *now*.'

The Goblins had been talking a lot about shopping for sweets. They had long, argumentative discussions about *Sugary Candy's* and what it would be like. Plugugly's description of its glories had whetted their appetites and given their brains something to chew on. They desperately wanted to go and see it for themselves, but didn't dare because there was a lot of activity in Witchway Wood at the moment. The Witches in particular seemed to be doing a lot of running around, and as we know, Witches and Goblins don't get on. So the Gaggle had to restrict themselves to imagining. Goblins have limited imaginations, so the conversations tended to be samey.

'Sweeties,' said Sproggit dreamily. 'Rows an' rows o' great big jars, Plug said. Imagine.'

'I hope there's red ones,' said Lardo, drooling. 'I loves red ones.'

'An' green ones,' said Slopbucket. 'An' yeller ones. An' blue ones. An' orange ones. An' pink ones an' purple ones an' brown ones an' grey ones an' ...'

'That's enough colours,' said Stinkwart, adding, 'An' you don't get grey sweets.'

'How do you know? You gets all kinda colours.' Slopbucket went off into his drone again. 'Grey ones an' green ones an' yeller ones an' blue ones an' orange ones an' pink ones an' purple ones an' brown ones an' pink ones an ...'

'You said pink twice,' pointed out Hog.

'Ah, but that's 'cos there's two jars of 'em.'

'You don't know that,' argued Stinkwart.

'Niver do you, so shut up,' said Slopbucket.

There was a little pause.

'Someone should go an' fill the medicine bucket for tomorrer,' said Eyesore.

'Yeah,' said Hog. 'Someone should.'

Nobody stirred.

CHAPTER SIXTEEN
Getting Closer

Nobody was late to the full Coven Meeting. All thirteen chairs were occupied. There were no sweets to be seen either. Instead, everyone had brought along neat little plastic containers packed with celery, carrot sticks and apples. Even better, no one was complaining of aches and pains. Sallow faces and tooth problems belonged in the past. Everyone looked fitter and sat straighter. Clearly, the new regime was beginning to work.

'Right!' shouted Sourmuddle, rapping her Wand on the table. 'Attention, everyone. First, I want an update from the Sports Committee. Make it quick, though, I'm on the *Ali Pali Show* in half an hour. Speak up, Pongwiffy. Is everything on track?'

'Absolutely!' cried Pongwiffy. 'All the entry forms are in and I'm taking a team of Familiars along to sort out the stadium.'

'What's happening about our flag?' chipped in Bendyshanks.

'Ah'm workin' on it,' said Macabre. 'Ah'm thinking big banner. Moon, stars, an' thirteen Witches flying across on Broomsticks. *The Winning Witches* written on it in big letters.'

'Sounds good, we'll leave it to you,' said Pongwiffy. 'So now it's all down to talking athletics. We have to decide who does what.'

There was a hum of excitement. This was the moment they had all been waiting for.

'Pass me the list,' ordered Sourmuddle. 'I'm Grandwitch, I decide. Right. Who wants to do the Three-Legged Race?'

'Me and Ag!' shouted Bagaggle, before anyone could open their mouths. 'We've been practising, haven't we?'

'We have, Bag,' agreed Agglebag.

Indeed they had. They had taken to doing

everything with their ankles roped together. They even slept like it. Difficult in the mornings, when they forgot and got up on opposite sides of the bed.

'Fair enough,' said Sourmuddle. 'Moving on. Egg and Spoon.'

'*Me!*' came a number of voices. Pongwiffy was loudest of all. She fancied her chances at the Egg and Spoon.

'Sludgegooey,' said Sourmuddle decisively. 'You're covered in egg stains anyway, so it won't matter if you fall over when you're practising. You'd better not drop it on the day, though.'

'I won't,' said Sludgegooey smugly. 'I'll win for the Witches, you'll see.'

'You'd better. Right. Weightlifting.'

'Um –' began Pongwiffy, too late again.

'*Me!*' shouted Ratsnappy. 'It's got to be me, Sourmuddle. I've been doing press-ups with Vernon. I'm getting these huge muscles in my arms, see? Look how they're stretching my cardigan.'

'All right. Ratsnappy's our weightlifter. Next, High Jump.'

'Er –' said Pongwiffy, but was overshadowed. Gaga had leapt from her chair and was bouncing around, wild with excitement.

'Yes, all right, Gaga, you can do it, calm down,' said Sourmuddle, and Gaga leapt twice over the table before collapsing in a corner, overcome with happiness.

'Who wants to do the Sack Race?' went on Sourmuddle.

'I do,' attempted Pongwiffy, but was silenced by Sharkadder's sharp elbow in her ribs.

'*I* rather fancy that,' said Sharkadder.

'Fine. Tossing the Caber next. I take it that'll be you, Macabre?'

'It will,' said Macabre, adding threateningly, 'or Ah'll want tay know the reason why.'

'Hey, listen –' cut in Pongwiffy again, but no one was listening.

'That leaves four for the Relay,' said Sourmuddle. 'Greymatter, Bonidle, Bendyshanks and Scrofula. That's it, all decided.'

'Wait a minute!' shouted Pongwiffy. 'What am *I* doing? You've missed me out.'

'Have I? Oh well. Tough.'

'But that's not *fair*! The O'Lumpicks were my idea and I'm doing most of the organising and now you're saying I can't compete?'

'So? *I'm* not competing, am I?'

563

'But you don't *want* to!' cried Pongwiffy crossly. 'All you want to do is go on spello and take all the credit.'

'Yes? So?'

'So I want to be in them! I should be in them, shouldn't I?'

Pongwiffy appealed to the assembled company, who shrugged and looked away. What did they care if Pongwiffy wasn't in them? They were.

'Sharky?' she said piteously. 'Don't *you* have anything to say?' Surely her best friend would be on her side?

'Yes,' said Sharkadder. 'Get over it. I'm sorry, Pong, but you said yourself that Sourmuddle's decision is final. Now, I've brought my tape measure with me and I need to take everyone's measurements for the costumes. So if you'd all line up . . .'

'Stay right where you are!' bellowed Pongwiffy. 'I've been doing all the healthy eating and exercising and stuff. If I don't get to be in them, I'm going on strike and there won't *be* an O'Lumpicks, so there. Unless someone else wants to do all the donkey work. Any volunteers?'

Nobody put a hand up. Sourmuddle went into a huddle with Snoop.

'You see?' said Pongwiffy. 'I didn't think so.'

'All right,' said Sourmuddle suddenly. 'You can be in them.'

'I can? Doing what?'

'You can lead the Grand Opening Parade. You can have the honour of holding the flag. That's an important job, isn't it?'

Pongwiffy thought about this. Actually, it was. Participating in the Games would have been good, of course – but to be there up front, the first one in, holding the flag and leading the Parade – well, that was special. She could imagine the cheers.

'Really?' she said.

'Really. You're the official Flag Holder.'

'You won't change your mind at the last moment?'

'You have my word.'

'All right,' said Pongwiffy. 'In that case – all right.'

'Good old Pong,' sang Sharkadder. 'My Flag Holding Friend. I'll make sure your costume is the most vibrant of all.'

'Mmm,' said Pongwiffy. She cheered up, though, and even allowed herself to be measured.

'The paper hasn't arrived again, Futtout,' said Queen Beryl. 'I haven't seen it for days. I haven't a clue what's going on in the Wood.'

'Really, dearest? Deary me.'

It was the following morning, and once again the royal family were gathered at the breakfast table. King Futtout was having a soft boiled egg, Queen Beryl had strong coffee and dry toast and Honeydimple had jam doughnuts with hot fudge sauce and pink sprinkles.

'Write and complain, Futtout. Insist that they sack the paper boy.'

'I will,' promised King Futtout. He wouldn't, of course. He had cancelled the paper. He didn't want Queen Beryl to read the headlines, oh dear me no.

'Futtout!' rapped Queen Beryl suddenly. She had gone very stiff and her eyes were trained on the garden. 'What is *this* I see through the window?'

King Futtout's watery gaze followed her pointing finger. He gave a little start.

'Oh,' he said. 'Erm – oh.'

Slap bang in the middle of the lawn, under a spreading chestnut tree, was an unmistakable figure. Pongwiffy with a clipboard, surrounded by her working party of Familiars, all armed to the teeth with a number of businesslike tools.

'What is *she* doing here?' demanded Queen Beryl. 'And why has she brought that raggle-taggle band of – *creatures*? That great hairy *thing* with the horns! And all those evil-looking cats? And that hideous bald vulture!'

'Erm – pets, possibly?'

'Thum petth,' said Honeydimple, through a mouthful of doughnut. 'Don't be thilly, Daddy.'

'They've got axes, Futtout! Axes and buckets of whitewash! And spades, and ladders! And a great long piece of string with tacky little *flags* on! *Why*, Futtout?'

'I really have no idea, dearest,' squeaked King Futtout, bashing weakly at his egg.

'Surely they can't be going ahead with that appalling O'Lumpick idea! It's an outrage! After sending that letter.'

'Mmm.' Bash, bash, bash.

'You did *send* the letter, Futtout?'

'Erm. Yes.' King Futtout gave a little cough. 'Yes, most definitely.'

'No you didn't, Daddy,' said Honeydimple. 'You hid it under the cushion, I *thaw* you.'

'Futtout!' thundered Queen Beryl. 'Go out there now and tell her to go away. And take those dreadful creatures with her. There's a *snake*. Uggh!'

'But I still haven't –'

'*Now*.'

567

'But my egg –'

'*Do it!*'

Trembling, King Futtout abandoned breakfast and went off to do it.

Over on the lawn, Pongwiffy was issuing instructions. All the Familiars were present and correct apart from Snoop (back home keeping the Broom company), Filth (band rehearsal) and Bonidle's Sloth (excused on account of sleep. When it came to practical activities, it was more trouble than it was worth).

'Right,' said Pongwiffy. 'Steve, you're in charge of marking out the running tracks. Just dive in the bucket of whitewash and crawl along. *Straight*, mind. Try not to wriggle too much.'

'How many lines?' asked Steve.

'I don't know, do I? Lots. Keep going until you run out of lawn. You Bats, you can start hanging up the bunting. Barry can help with that.'

'I'd rather not,' said Barry. 'Bit of a headache, overdid the exercise. I'd sooner not fly.'

'Then make a start digging up those rose bushes, they're in the way. You Cats can help. Don't look like that, CopiCat and IdentiKit, we're all pulling our weight. Rory and Vernon, you can start dismantling the gazebo – oh. Here's Futtout, come to help. Dudley, give him an axe.'

Poor King Futtout came trailing up, looking terrified.

'Erm – my wife,' he mumbled. Dudley tried to hand him an axe, and he backed away.

'What about her?'

'My wife is not too – erm – pleased. Not too – you know – keen.'

'About what?'

'About the whole idea, really. This – erm – O'Lumpicks business.'

'Well, she should be keen. Very keen indeed. Everybody else is. Haven't you been watching spellovision?'

'No,' confessed King Futtout. They didn't have a spellovision set in the palace. The King would have liked one, but was overruled by Queen Beryl on the grounds that people might enjoy it.

'Well, it's wall-to-wall O'Lumpick coverage. The whole Wood's O'Lumpick crazy. The whole *world's* O'Lumpick crazy! Do you want it going out on the news that you've refused permission to use your grounds? At this late stage? There'll be riots.'

King Futtout bit his lip. Which was he more

scared of? Millions of rioting sports enthusiasts or Queen Beryl?

'*What* is going on here?' The sharp voice rang out from behind them. Queen Beryl came marching across the lawn, almost tripping over Steve, who had obediently coated himself in whitewash and was carefully wriggling out his first line. 'I demand an explanation!'

'Ask him,' said Pongwiffy cheerfully, pointing at King Futtout. '*He* knows. Oi! You Bats! Mind out with that bunting, you're getting it all tangled! Not in *that* tree, you idiots, *that* tree's coming down! I dunno, Bats, Vultures, who'd work with 'em, eh?'

'Futtout! Are you just going to stand there, or are you going to *do* something?' demanded Queen Beryl.

'She's right, you know,' agreed Pongwiffy. 'No room for slackers. Go and get your shed cleared out, Futtout. My friend needs it to store the costumes. Get Beryl here to help, she looks like she could do with the exercise. I can't stay chatting. Got things to do, places to go, people to see. Hugo, stay here and take over. I'm off to visit Scott. I'm calling for Sharky, she's coming with me. She says she needs a break from the sewing machine. By Scott I am referring to Scott Sinister, the

570

famous film star, you know, a personal friend of mine. A *proper* celebrity.' She gave Queen Beryl a withering glare. '*He* does what he's told.'

And off she went, leaving the royal couple to row amongst themselves. Well, Queen Beryl rowed. King Futtout just stood there and hung his head. I suppose we should feel sorry for him, but he is so very wet.

On the other side of Witchway Wood, Scott Sinister sat in his study, tongue out, madly scribbling on a piece of paper with a quill pen.

Once again he had been bullied into cooperating with Witches, which in the past had been disastrous. But maybe, this time, everything might turn out all right. After all, the O'Lumpicks were different. It was Sport. Everyone was supposed to play fair and be good losers if they didn't win. It wasn't all bad.

And of course, Pongwiffy was right. Think of the publicity! Scott was a professional. His many fans would be watching, both in the flesh and on spellovision, desperate for a glimpse of their hero. They would be hanging on his every word.

Scott was determined to do a good job. In fact, in a flash of inspiration, he had come up with a rather novel idea. Introducing the various competing teams *in poetry*, no less. Nobody had told him which teams were actually competing, but he thought he'd have a bash anyway and see how he got on.

'Wizards,' muttered Scott. 'Bizzards, cizzards, dizzards, fizzards, gizzards. Lizards. Blizzards. Hmm.'

'What are you doing, Scott?' said a voice in his ear. Scott jumped a mile, knocking over the ink-pot. A black tide spread across the desk and dripped into his lap.

Standing behind him were two Witches, Broomsticks in hand. Pongwiffy and Sharkadder, both smiling at him, a bit out of breath from the flight. Pongwiffy was her usual dishevelled self. Sharkadder was a vision in purple, with matching lipstick.

'Don't *do* that,' he snapped, dabbing himself with a hanky. 'Who let you in? Look what you've made me do!'

'We let ourselves in,' explained Pongwiffy. 'Flew straight in through the downstairs window. Can't be bothered with butlers. You remember my friend, Witch Sharkadder?'

'Yes,' said Scott shortly. 'I do.' His tone was rather bitter. There had been a certain incident in the past involving Sharkadder, himself and a beauty

572

demonstration that went horribly wrong. Well, let's put it like this. He lost a lot of face.

'Hello, Mr Sinister,' trilled Sharkadder. 'Lovely to see you again. I expect you're all excited? With it being the Big Day next Saturday?'

'Leave it to me to do the talking, Sharky, if you please,' said Pongwiffy firmly. 'He's my friend.'

'Did you say *next Saturday*?'

'Time flies, doesn't it, Scott?' agreed Pongwiffy. 'I hope you're prepared. It's a very important job, commentating. Nobody'll know what's happening unless someone's explaining it.'

'*I* don't know what's happening.' Scott pointed out rather crossly. 'I'd appreciate a little direction. I don't even know what the games are, or who's in them or *anything*.'

'Yes, well, it's all a bit complicated, organising a whole O'Lumpicks,' said Pongwiffy. 'We're still working things out. But it'll all come together in the end. If it's any help, the first thing you have to do is introduce the teams in the Grand Opening Parade.'

'Well, yes. I've been thinking about that,' said Scott. 'In fact, I've had a rather good idea. I'm thinking of welcoming each team with a short rhyming couplet. I have a couple here, if you'd like to ... ?'

'Go ahead,' said Pongwiffy. 'Although I don't know what poetry's got to do with Sport.'

'*Clap your hands and shout and scream,*

Here comes the amazingly fit and wonderful Skeleton team.'

'Not bad,' said Pongwiffy. 'Although I'd shorten it a bit. Cut out *amazingly fit and wonderful* and I think you're there.'

'I've got another one,' said Scott.

'You have?'

'*They come from the mountain, where there's blizzards.*

Welcome to the gallant, athletic Wizards.'

'They're not athletic,' scoffed Pongwiffy. '*Pathetic*, more like. Anyway, they haven't sent in an entry form, so you've wasted your time there. Have you done one for us Witches?'

'Not yet.'

'Well, make sure it's good. Make it longer than the others. We're far and away the best team, so we want the rhymiest introduction. Use words like *astonishingly fit and toned*.'

'And *vibrantly costumed*,' added Sharkadder.

'Yes,' said Pongwiffy. 'If you must. Although I don't think it'll be easy finding a rhyme.'

'But he'll try,' said Sharkadder. 'Won't you, Scott?'

'And he'll pop in a line about the Flag Holder, I expect?' added Pongwiffy.

Both of them beamed at him.

'Yes' said Scott wearily. 'I'll try.'

CHAPTER SEVENTEEN
A Meeting with Ronald

You may remember that the Wizards had refused to enter for the O'Lumpicks. Well, all but one. Ronald the Magnificent, Sharkadder's nephew, who we last saw being roundly jeered at for showing interest in them. It didn't put him off, though.

Ronald was really excited at the whole idea of the forthcoming Games. Of course, he didn't say so. But he couldn't stop thinking about them.

Every day, he waited impatiently until everyone had finished with *The Daily Miracle* and hurled it disdainfully into the bin. He would sneakily fish it out with trembling fingers and run upstairs to his room to pore over the latest thrilling O'Lumpick news.

The pages were full of pictures of the various competing teams, grinning at the camera with their thumbs up. Everyone wore shorts and clutched little bottles of water. There were interviews with Skeletons, Trolls, Ghouls, Banshees and Zombies, each claiming to have developed a unique, foolproof training programme. Instead of advertisements for *Sugary Candy's*, there were full page spreads dedicated to healthy eating. Sharkadder's Lemon Sprouts were proving particularly popular. Getting fit was the order of the day. There were a lot of gossip columns debating what costumes the athletes might wear in the Grand Opening Parade. Everyone was being very secretive, particularly about the design of their flag.

Sometimes, when the rest of the Wizards were snoozing in the lounge, Ronald tried turning on the spellovision, hoping to catch a glimpse of what was going on. He kept the volume low, but even so, someone always woke up and ordered him to turn it off, just to be mean. But the glimpses only whetted his appetite.

Just imagine it! A whole day devoted to Sport! Out in the fresh air! Wearing shorts!

Ronald had a pair of shorts. They were baggy and yellow. He had only worn them once, on a trip to the seaside. He kept them in his bottom drawer.

He pictured himself wearing them again. Strolling around casually chatting to his fellow competitors. Everyone saying, 'Who is that young Wizard in the yellow shorts? He looks like a strong contender.'

What a change that would make from eating sausages and sitting around in the overheated lounge talking vaguely about Magic but hardly ever doing any. Ronald got bored sometimes. The only time he went out was to do the weekly sweet run. Being the youngest Wizard, he either got ignored or picked on, with nothing in between. It didn't help that his aunt was a Witch either. He got a lot of stick for that.

Imagine if he competed in the O'Lumpicks, though! Competed, and won a gold medal! Things would be different then. The Wizards would have to clap him on the back and sing *For He's A Jolly Good Wizard*. Maybe carry him back to the Clubhouse shoulder-high. Frame the medal and hang it in the foyer. Show him a bit of respect, for once.

Ronald sent off for an entry form. When it arrived, he scuttled down at the crack of dawn, snatched it from the doorstep, then hurried up to his room to study it in secret.

He skipped over the first bit, which looked boring, and went straight to the list of games, looking for ones he thought he would be good at.

The Three-Legged Race was out because there was only one of him. The Sack Race was out because it needed practice with a sack. He could try begging one from the kitchens, but didn't hold out much hope because the cook didn't like him. Tossing the Caber was out. He didn't know what a caber was, or why it needed tossing. The elastic on his shorts was a bit feeble, so the High Jump presented major risks. Weightlifting sounded like hard work, and he would be up against Trolls and Zombies and probably Pongwiffy's Hamster, who was a lot stronger than he looked. The Relay was a non-starter, as there was no one to pass the baton to. That left one race. The Egg and Spoon. The Wizards specialised in breakfast, so getting hold of the props to practise with was easy.

Ronald filled in the entry form. Where it said TEAM name, he wrote *Ronald the Magnificent* in his best handwriting. He wrote it again in the space opposite Egg and Spoon. Then he sent it off, with a second-class stamp because he'd run out of first-class and didn't dare ask to borrow one in case he got quizzed about why he wanted it.

Every morning, when his fellow Wizards staggered from the dining room to the lounge, Ronald secreted away a boiled egg and silver spoon and slipped out the back way. He hurried down the mountain track, casting anxious glances over his shoulder in case anyone spotted him. As soon as he reached the sheltering branches of Witchway Wood, he made for a quiet glade that only he knew about. There, he removed his Hat of Mystery, his Robe of Knowledge and his Cloak of Darkness. Then, clad only in shorts, sandals and socks, he took the egg from his pocket, carefully placed it in the spoon and tried running.

It wasn't as easy as he had hoped. He had had visions of streaking along like a gazelle, arm triumph-antly extended before him, egg snugly lodged in the spoon, miles ahead of everybody else and reaching the finish line to thunderous applause. That was until he tried doing it.

The trouble was the egg. Well, the egg and the spoon. Well, the egg, the spoon and the trembling hand. And the feet. And the shorts. The fact was that he couldn't keep the egg steady and see what his feet were doing at the same time. Plus his shorts kept drifting downwards, on account of the limp elastic, so he had to use his other hand to keep them up.

He had been practising for days, but still couldn't get the hang of it. If he took his eye off the egg even for one second, it fell out of the spoon and rolled away under a bush. But if he didn't watch where he put his feet, he invariably fell flat on his face. Speed was out of the question. The best he could manage was a few shuffling paces at a slow crawl before the inevitable happened. It was all very disheartening.

He was on his hands and knees, crawling under a bush looking for the egg for the hundredth time, when Pongwiffy and Sharkadder found him. They had been flying overhead, on their way back from Scott Sinister's holiday retreat when Pongwiffy spotted a flash of yellow below. She pointed it out to Sharkadder, who recognised her nephew in an instant and insisted on flying down to say hello, although Pongwiffy didn't want to.

They alighted in the glade, propped the Brooms against a tree, folded their arms and surveyed Ronald's rear end.

'Well, well,' said Sharkadder. 'It's you, Ronald. Why are you crawling around under a bush? In those hideous shorts?'

'Looking for his brain,' sneered Pongwiffy, who didn't like Ronald.

Ronald crawled out of the bush, egg in hand, and scrambled to his feet, rather red-faced. There they stood, Aunt Sharky and her horrible friend, staring hard and making him feel self-conscious with his skinny legs and everything.

'Hello, Aunty,' said Ronald unhappily. 'Lovely to see you.'

'Is it?' said Sharkadder. '*Is* it indeed? Well, I'm glad you said that, because I was beginning to think you'd forgotten all about me.'

'I've been a bit busy,' said Ronald, squirming a bit.

'I don't recall getting a thank you letter for the money I sent you for your birthday.'

'I didn't have a stamp.'

'I see. Too busy to walk to the post office.'

'Well . . . yes, actually. I'm in training, you see. For the O'Lumpicks.'

'You've having a joke,' said Pongwiffy. 'You? Entering the O'Lumpicks? *You?*'

'I don't see why not,' said Ronald sulkily. 'It's open to all.'

'I don't remember seeing an entry form for the Wizards,' said Pongwiffy, adding, 'Not that

I was looking hard. Wizards and Sport. It's ridiculous, isn't it? I mean, they'd actually have to *move*. If it was a Sitting-In-An-Armchair-Looking-Beardy-And-Eating-Sausages Contest, that'd be different.'

'Now then, Pong,' scolded Sharkadder. 'That's not in the O'Lumpick spirit. You're not allowed to be mean to Ronald. *I* am, but I'm his aunty.'

'Actually,' admitted Ronald, 'actually, it's just me.'

'What – *Team Ronald*?' Pongwiffy guffawed rudely. 'I take it you're going in for the Egg and Spoon? Or is that your lunch?'

'As a matter of fact, I am.'

'Well, you can forget it because the form hasn't arrived. You're not allowed to be in the O'Lumpicks unless you've filled in the form, isn't that right, Sharky?'

Sharkadder hesitated. Rules were rules, but Ronald was family when all was said and done.

'It's in the post,' said Ronald anxiously.

'So you found a stamp for *that*, then?'

'It was my last one.'

'Too late,' said Pongwiffy ruthlessly. 'I've told Scott there aren't any Wizards, so he won't have a rhyme for you when he's doing the commentary. And anyway, we don't want thirteen teams, it's unlucky.'

Ronald looked stricken. He looked down at his egg.

'But I've been practising. Aunty, tell her.'

'Try that again. Not forgetting that simple little word.'

'Tell her, *please*. And thank you very much for the money. I'm saving it to buy you a big box of chocolates.'

'No chocolates,' said Sharkadder. 'You don't win sack races on chocolate.'

'Flowers, then.'

Sharkadder relented.

'Oh, I suppose so. We might as well let him, Pong. We're supposed to be intermingling, aren't we?'

'There are limits, though,' said Pongwiffy.

In the end, she agreed that Ronald could enter if his form arrived. It wouldn't do to appear to be a bad sport.

It had been a busy day, and Pongwiffy had had enough. She accepted Sharkadder's invitation to come back to her cottage for a healthy snack and a cup of water. After all that organising, she felt she deserved to put her feet up.

She sat on a comfy chair and idly switched on the spellovision while Sharkadder bustled around the kitchen preparing a bowl of prune and beetroot puree with a small jug of vinegar on the side.

The screen flickered into life. A short plump Genie stood before the palace gates, holding a microphone.

' . . . and behind these gates, even as I speak, the O'Lumpick stadium is being prepared by a hard-working team of Familiars. We had hoped to bring you footage, but it's rather dangerous in there at the moment, with all the tree felling. Unfortunately, King Futtout is unavailable for comment, but I have with me Hugo the Hamster. Hugo, how's it all going?'

The camera zoomed dizzyingly down and homed in on Hugo, holding a clipboard and looking business-like with a tiny hard hat on his head.

'Ah,' said Pongwiffy. 'Look at him. Sharky, come and look at my Hugo on the spello!'

'What about Dudley?' cried Sharkadder. 'Is he there too?'

'Well, no. He's inside the grounds, digging up rose bushes. Or he will be if he knows what's good for him.'

'In that case,' said Sharkadder, 'I won't bother.'

'Suit yourself.' Pongwiffy reached forward and turned up the volume. Sadly, she missed what Hugo had to say. He was scuttling off through the gates and the camera was wobbling up again.

'So there you have it,' said the Genie, beaming. 'The O'Lumpicks are on track for next Saturday. You have it direct from the Hamster's mouth. This is Ali Pali, returning you to the studio, where the Thing In The Moonmad T-Shirt Hour is about to begin, with special guest Grandwitch Sourmuddle, who once again will be explaining how she came up with such an unusual idea...'

Pongwiffy switched it off.

CHAPTER EIGHTEEN
Bigger

Plugugly was struggling down the stairs with Philpot. It was as much as he could do to manage it. Big? My, was that baby big! Plugugly could no longer get his arms around Philpot's ever-expanding middle. The only way was to hoist him up on to his back like a sack of potatoes, then bend forward into a low crouch. Even then, Philpot's huge pink feet flopped down, thumping on each stair.

'Hold on tight, Baby Philpot!' gasped Plugugly. 'Soon be down de stairs, don't choke me, dere's a good boy!'

587

'TEE-HEE,' giggled Philpot. *Thump, thump, thump* went his feet. 'MEDSIN.'

Walking down to the gates to collect Philpot's food remained a daily ritual. Cramming him into his pram was easier now he could sit up. There was more space for his bottom half with the rest of him sticking up in the air. His weight was still a problem, though, and the wheels were buckling badly. The pram wouldn't last much longer.

Philpot shouldn't be sitting up, of course. But as we know, his development is accelerating wildly. He is growing by the hour, not just by the day. He has other talents too. He can now say words (MEDSIN! MORE! 'GAIN! and NO!), has all his teeth and can take notice of things instead of just lying around gnawing his own feet. He is far too advanced for a two-week-old baby.

You will notice that Philpot's baby vocabulary does not include the words MAMA or DADA. This is because Philpot sees very little of his mother and father. Taking full advantage of Nanny Susan, Bigsy and Largette have been going out on long, carefree bike rides, coming home late and sleeping in every day, safe in the knowledge that their offspring is being well cared for by a professional.

Plugugly and Philpot had reached the landing where the Stonkings had their bedroom.

'NANNY SUSAN?' called Largette. 'IS THAT YOU? COULD YOU STEP IN HERE ONE MOMENT? BIGSY AND I WOULD LIKE A WORD.'

Plugugly's ears pricked up. Perhaps they were about to give him his wages. That would be good. Plugugly loved looking after Philpot, but he loved sweeties more. He couldn't wait to stride triumphantly into the cave, waving a big bag of gold! That would be the end of the nannying job, which would be sad, but not *that* sad. He was fond of Philpot, but a ton or two of sweets would certainly help him get over it.

'NANNY SUSAN? ARE YOU COMING?'

Plugugly hesitated. He had a dilemma. He couldn't spell it, and didn't know what it meant, but a dilemma was what he had. On the one hand, he wanted his wages. On the other, he didn't want the Stonkings to see Baby Philpot. They hadn't been up to the nursery for days, and Plugugly didn't want them to see him now. Plugugly could no longer be in denial. Even he could see that there was a real problem. And he had a bad feeling that it was all his fault. It was all down to the wrong diet. Plugugly suspected that he might be in trouble if the Stonkings caught a glimpse of their vastly oversized, frighteningly advanced offspring and the truth came out.

Of course, the truth *would* come out eventually. Plugugly couldn't keep Philpot under wraps for ever. But hopefully, by then he would have his bag of gold and would be a safe distance away.

He heaved Philpot off his back and set him on the floor by the stairs, which led steeply down to the hall. There was no rail or baby gate. It was a silly place to leave a baby, but Plugugly's Nanny Susan side wasn't working so well. His true Goblin nature had kicked in. He was thinking about gold and sweets.

He reached into his apron pocket, took out a gigantic dummy and plugged it into Philpot's mouth.

'Wait dere, Baby Philpot,' instructed Plugugly. 'Nanny'll be right back. Will you be good?'

Philpot regarded him solemnly, removed the dummy and said very clearly, ''ES.'

Talk about advanced development! He had only been up an hour, but already he could say another word.

'Ahhh,' said Plugugly fondly. 'Dere's Nanny's clever boy.'

Philpot casually replaced his own dummy and sucked contentedly.

Plugugly straightened his bonnet, adjusted his skirts, opened the bedroom door and went in.

Bigsy and Largette's gigantic bed was strewn with clothing. They were busily folding garments and stuffing them into a large motorbike pannier. Both of them were wearing leather jackets, boots and helmets. Largette was wearing a lot of red lipstick. Bigsy had all his gold chains on and was sporting goggles. The floor was awash with Largette's shoes. Hopefully, Plugugly looked around for the bag of gold.

'AH,' said Largette. 'I'M GLAD WE CAUGHT YOU, NANNY SUSAN. WE'RE GOING AWAY FOR A FEW DAYS. JUST A LITTLE BREAK. BIGSY'S TAKING ME BACK TO GIANT TOWN TO VISIT MUM.'

'Oh,' said Plugugly politely. 'Right. What about Baby Philpot? Is you thinkin' of takin' him?'

'NAH,' said Bigsy. 'NOT ON THE BIKE. GOTTA BE RESPONSIBLE.'

'WE THOUGHT HE'D BE BETTER OFF HERE WITH YOU,' explained Largette. 'IT'D SPOIL HIS ROUTINE IF WE TOOK HIM. HE MIGHT START ROARING AGAIN. THEN WHAT WOULD WE DO?'

This may seem odd to us, the Stonkings proposing to whoosh off for the weekend leaving their baby behind. But they are Giants. Giants aren't bothered

591

about babies until they become toddlers. It's tough, but that's the way it is.

'SO WILL THAT BE ALL RIGHT WITH YOU?' asked Largette.

'Oh yes. Dat's all right.'

'YOU'RE A TREASURE. SAY 'BYE TO BABY PHILPOT. LOTS OF KISSES FROM MUMMY AND DADDY. NOW THEN. DID I PACK MY PINK HEELS?'

And that was it. Plugugly left the room. It was only when he got outside that he remembered about the gold. He was about to go back and mention it, when he suddenly realised something.

Philpot was gone! He had been propped up against the wall, sucking his dummy, and now he wasn't there!

Plugugly's jaw dropped. Oh *no*!

Could he have toppled over and fallen down the stairs? Surely that would have made a big crash? Not necessarily. Not if he rolled down. But he might have bumped his precious huge head on the banisters . . .

Heart in his mouth, Plugugly approached the top of the stairs and looked down.

Philpot was indeed downstairs. He hadn't fallen, though. He had crawled.

Right now, he was halfway across the tiled hallway, be-nappied big bottom in the air, heading for the front door. Considering he was on his hands and knees, he had a fair turn of speed.

Greatly relieved, Plugugly picked up his skirts and hurried down to rescue him.

So. Baby Philpot has reached the next important stage. He is mobile. This will be even more difficult.

CHAPTER NINETEEN
One Day To Go

It was the day before the O'Lumpicks. All over Witchway Wood, the teams of dedicated athletes were getting in those final, critical hours of practice. Even before the sun rose, the place was awash with grim-faced joggers. Every glade was commandeered by determined-looking weightlifters. Everywhere you looked, there were sack racers and egg-and-spooners and high jumpers and relay teams clutching batons.

Every so often, from somewhere in the Wood, there would come a resounding, faraway crash. That was Macabre, practising Tossing the Caber. Even the

Trolls had declined to enter for that event, because whatever a Caber was, tossing it sounded dangerous. Macabre was the sole competitor, so she was certain of winning a gold medal. The trouble was, tossing a large, sharpened tree trunk was proving surprisingly tricky. It still landed on her own foot more often than she would like. But Macabre had her pride. She didn't want to make a complete fool of herself. Anyway, the exercise was doing her good.

Three whole weeks of healthy eating and vigorous activity had transformed the residents of the Wood. Mind you, they had paid the price. There were strained muscles, scabby knees and sprained ankles in evidence. There was quite a bit of under-the-breath moaning. Yes, all the teams were highly excited about the O'Lumpicks and determined to do their very best and win all the medals whilst remaining suitably humble and unfailingly polite to fellow competitors, which was in the rules. But getting fit had been *hard*. The noble athletes were getting a bit fed up with it now. They were looking forward to when it was all over and they could go back to normal. Slob around on the sofa with a big *Bog Bar* and a bag of *Hoppy Jumpers*, boasting loudly about their sporting achievements. Of course, nobody admitted this. It didn't go with the O'Lumpick spirit.

Everyone was practising intermingling too, because the rules stated that it was compulsory. This was proving a strain. Instead of ignoring each other, there were tight-lipped smiles and polite little waves and the odd courtly bow. The Ghoulish relay team politely gave way for a clutch of jogging Skeletons. A sprinting Vampire offered the twins a sip of his water. Instead of laughing in his face, they said thank you and waited until he had run off before spitting it out behind a bush.

Egg and Spoon athletes stood aside for Sack athletes, even though their instinct was to trip them up. A weightlifting Zombie put down his rock and gallantly came to Sharkadder's aid. (She insisted on wearing high heels when practising for the Sack Race and kept skewering herself into the ground.) Bendyshanks gave a passing Banshee one of her apples. It looked a bit wormy, but it was still quite nice of her. There was even the occasional insincere cry of 'Good luck!' or 'May the best team win!'

As well as all the sporting activity, there were lots of other things going on. Finishing touches were being added to flags. Parade costumes were being tried on. Shorts were being washed and ironed. The spellovision crew noisily staked out King Futtout's gardens, deciding where they should set up their equipment and accidentally setting fire to his shed, which caused a bit of drama.

In the Wizards' Clubhouse, Ronald was in his room in the process of sneakily glueing an egg into a spoon. Despite all that practice, he was still hopeless. Cheating was the only way to win. This was shocking, of course. He should have read the rules on the entry form. Although even if he had, I'm sorry to say he still would have done it.

King Futtout was in his treasury, also up to his armpits in glue. He was attempting to stick some of Honeydimple's red hair ribbons on to a number of gold, silver and copper coins that he hoped would do for the medals he'd been ordered to provide. Earlier in the day, Queen Beryl and Princess Honeydimple had taken the royal coach and departed in a furious cloud of dust, leaving him on his own. Honeydimple would make a fuss about the ribbons when she got back, but right now he was past caring.

Scott Sinister stood before a full-length mirror, practising his commentary.

'So! Here they come, the Witches' team
With vibrant costumes all a-gleam.
The fittest Witches in the land.
Stand up and give them a big hand.
I have to say they look so fine
I'm giving them an extra line
And a half.
And now, behold the Troll brigade
Who round the ground do now parade ...'

Yes. It was all go in Witchway Wood – and nobody was busier than Pongwiffy. There were so many last-minute things to do.

She began by inspecting the stadium.

King Futtout's lovely gardens had been ... well, transformed isn't quite the word. Ruined, more like. There was a newly built podium at one end, where the gazebo used to be. Miles of tangled bunting was suspended between the few trees that hadn't been chopped down. Rows of chairs were set around the edges, where the crowds from far and wide would sit. The lawn was a riot of wiggly, wobbly white lines. In one corner, two rickety poles had been set up next to a sign declaring High Jump. An area had been set aside for the Weightlifting. Several rocks of varying size and weight lay in a dangerous pile, ready to be hefted. Bushes had been uprooted and left in a careless pile behind the King's slightly charred shed, which was being used to store the Witches' Parade costumes.

After three weeks of ferocious sewing machine activity, Sharkadder had finally unveiled her handiwork. The costumes consisted of thirteen flowing cloaks in a wide variety of clashing colours. Each cloak had a sparkling hem, because she had gone seriously mad with glitter. Each had a matching pointy hat with a tassel and a matching pair of shorts. Sharkadder was thrilled with her efforts. Nobody else was quite so sure, but they didn't like to say so.

She spotted Pongwiffy running around setting out more chairs and made her come in and try on her costume. To Pongwiffy's horror, it was all white. The hat stood tall, white and pointy, not at all like the battered, floppy, comfortable one she always wore. The shorts looked ridiculous.

'White?' said Pongwiffy, staring down. '*WHITE*?'

'Don't you like it?' asked Sharkadder, sounding hurt. 'I made yours especially nice, as you're leading the Parade. I wanted you to look your best. I thought you'd like it.'

'But *white*. It's just not me. Don't you have anything in dirt?'

'There's no such colour as dirt.'

'What d'you call my cardigan, then?'

'I'd call it disgusting. But if you *really* want to spoil the Parade and let everyone down after I've spent all this time . . .'

'No, no. Keep your hair on. I suppose I'll get used to it. Anyway, I can't stop, I've got a million things to do. I don't suppose you want to help arrange the chairs? Or set out the programmes? Or anything?'

'I can't. I've got to hang up the costumes, then put in a few more hours' practice with the sack. You want me to win, don't you?'

'Nggh,' said Pongwiffy, which could have meant anything.

And off she went, leaving Sharkadder to pick up the offending cloak, hat and matching shorts from the floor.

And so the day wore on, until the sun dropped below the horizon and the stars came out. At that point, everyone went home to eat a last healthy supper, do a few last exercises, then fall exhaustedly into bed for a last, sensible early night. Tomorrow was the Witchway Wood O'Lumpick Games. They had put in the effort, and tomorrow they would find out whether it had been worth it. But now, they could do no more.

600

'Phew!' sighed Pongwiffy. She was in Number One, Dump Edge, lying flat on her sofa with a cold flannel on her head and her feet up. 'What a day. I can't be bothered to do exercises.'

'Got to exercise,' scolded Hugo. He was over in the corner with a tiny set of dumb-bells. As far as he was concerned, the Weightlifting medal was in the bag. 'Every night, every mornink. Like me. Last chance, tomorrow ze Big Day.'

'But I'm not competing. What's the point?'

'Duzzn't matter. You vant to stay fit, ya? So do exercises.'

'No. Leave me alone. I'll just have supper and turn in.'

'OK,' sighed Hugo with a little shrug. 'You ze boss. I get you nice bowl of radishes.'

'What, the ones Sharkadder sent round? The ones in lime jelly with a dollop of mustard on the top?'

'Ya.'

'Is that all there is?'

'Pretty well.'

'Well, I don't want them. I'm fed up with vegetables, particularly Sharkadder's. What I want is a big, greasy bowl of skunk stew. There, I've said it. And don't bother to tell me off because I don't care.'

Pongwiffy pulled a cushion over her face and lapsed into silence.

'Mistress?' said Hugo.

'What?'

'Sumsink ze matter?'

'Yes,' growled Pongwiffy, her voice muffled because of the cushion. 'As a matter of fact, there is. I'm fed up with the O'Lumpicks. In fact, I wish I'd never suggested them. I thought they'd be fun. That's what *you* said. But I haven't had any fun at all so far. It's been all work, work, work. And horrible food.'

'But zat good for you. Hard work, healthy food.'

'Yes, well, you can have too much of a good thing.'

'But is vorking! Look how much you change. Better colour. Not so creaky. I look at you now, I don't see old Pongviffy. I see new.'

'Old or new, I still ended up running the whole thing by myself. I'm worn out. Too much to do and no one to help.'

'Vot about ze Sports Committee?'

'What Sports Committee? They're all too busy practising for their event. They've gone all competitive. All they care about is winning medals.'

'Vell, ya. Athletes got to take Sport seriously,' said Hugo, flexing his tiny, iron-hard muscles.

602

'So I gather. You Familiars haven't exactly pitched in lately, have you? Even Greymatter's given up pretending to help. She just handed me a million lists and went off to practise the stupid Relay. And Sharky just leaps away in her sack whenever she sees me, then sends round more horrible food to poison me. I'm the only one not *in* anything, so it's left to me to organise where the coaches will park and where the crowds from far and wide will sit and where Scott's going to stand. And find him a megaphone, and put a glass of water on his podium. And decide where the Rhythm Boys and the television crew will set up and explain to Futtout how to judge. It's all too much and I'm sick of it. You'd think someone would say thank you, but no one ever does.'

'*I* do,' said Hugo kindly. '*I* say sank you.'

'Yes, but you're my Familiar. You've got to.'

'Cheer up,' said Hugo. 'You get to lead ze Grand Opening Parade, remember? Get to hold ze flag. Big honour.'

'Well, yes, I know that. And I was quite keen to start with. Until I saw my costume.'

'Vot it like?'

'White. I think Sharky hates me.'

'No, she don't,' soothed Hugo. 'You vant to know secret?'

603

'Yes. What?'

'She got Scott to make up special poem. For you. He goink to say nice sings. He goink to sank you for 'elping to make ze day so vunderful. He goink to read it out at ze end. You take special bow. Everybody give you big clap. Big close-up on ze spellovision.'

'Really?' Pongwiffy removed the pillow from her face.

'Ya. I hear zis from Dudley. He say not to tell you. Is s'posed to be surprise.'

'A special poem, eh?' Pongwiffy cheered up a bit. 'Well, that's different. Perhaps I'll get presented with an organiser medal. I wonder if anyone's organised that? If I'd known earlier, I'd have done it myself.' She gave a huge yawn. 'Oh well, too late now. I'm going to bed. Have to be up at the crack of dawn tomorrow. It's starting at ten, but the coaches will begin arriving long before that. I have to be there to greet Scott and put Futtout in place and make sure everything's ready.'

'You vant I get up, give you breakfast?'

'Would that be radishes in jelly, by any chance?'

'Funny you should say zat.'

Pongwiffy gave a heavy sigh. What she really fancied was a big, greasy fry-up, followed by one of Hugo's home-made cakes. But those days were long gone.

CHAPTER TWENTY

Philpot Walks!

Time now to catch up on developments at Stonking Towers.

Several days have passed since Philpot's loving parents roared off into the blue. For Giant babies, particularly an advanced one who has been prematurely weaned on unsuitable solids, even one day is a long time. The phrase 'My! How he's grown!' in no way does him justice.

Philpot hasn't just grown. He has expanded, like the universe. He has shot up, spread, widened, heightened, broadened and thoroughly enlarged. The crib cannot hold him. The pram cannot hold him.

Philpot is HUGE. He now towers over Plugugly, who has long given up trying to carry him. So it's just as well that he can now walk. Well, lurch. It's not so much walking as unsteady lurching, interspersed with intervals of mad, staggery running.

He can talk too. Not just DIN DIN, and NO and 'GAIN and 'ES. He can say WANT GO WALKIES. He can say MORE MEDSIN PEES TANK OO. He refers to him- self as 'POT, which is cute. He can say 'POT LOVE NANA SU-SU, which makes Plugugly almost weep with pleasure.

Mind you, it's no picnic. Keeping Philpot happy is a full-time job. Because his crib is too small, he now sleeps in Plugugly's bed with Plugugly, which is horrible. Plugugly spends all night hanging over the edge while Philpot blissfully slumbers on. During the day, Philpot is wildly energetic. His diet needs a lot of working off. He is constantly on the go, falling downstairs and bumping his head, crying a bit and needing to be soothed. Then off again to run full tilt at the front door and get poked in the eye by the door knob.

Somehow, though, Plugugly is coping. He plays peek-a-boo, which makes Philpot laugh. He feeds him and baths him. He can be strict too. If Philpot *really* misbehaves, he has to sit on the naughty step.

Plugugly has taken to going for long walks in the Wood with Philpot toddling happily along beside him, reined in by a piece of string attached to his nappy with a safety pin. Plugugly doesn't really enjoy these walks, because he's so exhausted he can hardly keep his eyes open. But walking is the only way to wear Philpot out. Philpot always goes to sleep on the way back, and has to be dragged up the steps and through the front door by his feet. Plugugly tiptoes away, leaving him snoozing on the doormat in the hall. It's the only time he can catch forty winks for himself.

Despite it all, they are getting on all right. After horrifying bath times, when Philpot thrashes around flooding the bathroom, giggling merrily whilst bashing Plugugly over the head with a giant plastic duck, he suddenly becomes all loving. He cuddles up in his big white towel, pats Plugugly's cheek and says, ''POT LOVE NANA SU-SU.' That always makes Plugugly's heart melt, although he is half drowned. Then comes the uncomfortable night, morning time, nappy changing, breakfast, then another walk. That is the routine.

The two of them are on one of these long walks right now.

'No, Baby Philpot,' said Plugugly. Philpot was straining sideways at the leash. He had seen a quicksand he always liked to fall in. He had done it two days running and each time Plugugly had had to fish him out. 'We's not stoppin' dere, you'll get all mucky again.'

Philpot stuck out his bottom lip. The swamp called to him. He *wanted* to fall in. Tears welled in his eyes.

'If you is a good boy Nanny'll give you extra medicine when we goes home,' promised Plugugly. 'Now, stay on de parf, dere's a dear.'

Philpot brightened up. He didn't stay cross for long, especially if medicine was promised. Anyway, despite his size he had the attention span of a gnat.

'MEDSIN PEES TANK OO,' he agreed.

Something caught his eye ahead, and he waved a massive dimpled arm and went charging off, yanking Plugugly behind him by his string.

'Slow down, Baby Philpot!' begged Plugugly. 'Nanny Susan can't keep up!'

The thing that had caught Philpot's attention was a flag. A small, red, triangular flag, hanging limply over the branch of a tree. (In fact, this had blown off the bunting that right now was adorning the O'Lumpick stadium, although neither Philpot nor Plugugly knew this.)

Philpot liked the look of the flag. He toddled up, reached out, plucked it from the tree and flapped it about.

'PITTY!' he roared. 'PITTY!'

'Dat's right,' gasped Plugugly, screeching to a halt. 'It *is* pretty, Baby Philpot. You play wiv de pretty flag while Nanny sits down for a minute.'

Scarlet in the face, he sank on to a nearby tree trunk and mopped his sweating brow.

'FLAG!' bellowed Philpot, his vocabulary swelling by the second. 'PITTY FLAG, TEE HEE!'

'Dat's it, you wave it, dat's de way.'

Philpot experimentally put the flag in his mouth. No. It didn't taste nice. He flapped it about a bit more, then put it on his head. He had a feeling it was a funny thing to do. Sometimes, Nanny Susan put things on her head, to make him laugh. He especially liked it when she did it with his plastic bath duck.

'LOOKA!' he demanded. 'LOOKA, NANA SU-SU.'

But his request wasn't met. Plugugly had toppled off the tree trunk and was lying flat out on the leafy ground, fast asleep.

'NANA SU-SU?' enquired Philpot. He toddled up to Plugugly and gave him an experimental pat on the cheek. No response. Philpot looked down at Plugugly's hand. The hand that held the end of his restraining string. Philpot reached down and one by one, bent back Plugugly's unresisting fingers. The string slithered out. Plugugly didn't stir.

'PEEK-A-BOO?' said Philpot. Still no response.

'MEDSIN PEES TANK OO?' tried Philpot hopefully. But no medicine was forthcoming.

Philpot stared around. This was getting boring. Nanny Susan clearly didn't want to play. What should he do?

'WALKIES,' announced Philpot to himself.

And he set off into the trees, trailing his leash behind him.

Some time later, the Goblins were lying around the cave doing nothing in particular when the front boulder rolled open with a crash. There stood Plugugly, bonnet askew, eyes bulging, wringing his hands, beside himself with anxiety.

'He's gone!' wailed Plugugly. 'I's lost him, he's gone. Oh, oh, whatever shall I do?'

'Wha— ? Who's gone?' enquired Lardo, opening one eye. He had been having a little snooze and didn't like being so rudely awakened.

'Baby Philpot! I was takin' him for his walk an' I musta dropped off an' now he's gone!'

'Ah, but 'ave you got the gold, though?' asked Stinkwart uncaringly.

'No! I hasn't got paid yet! Dey've gone away but dey're comin' back soon an' dey'll want to know where he is an' I don't *know*!' howled Plugugly, hopping from one foot to the other in a frenzy of panic.

'So you still ain't got the gold? After waitin' all this time for you to come back wiv it so we can go an' buy sweeties, now you're tellin' us ...'

'Stop goin' on about *gold*!' roared Plugugly. 'Baby Philpot's lost in de woods an' all you can fink about is *gold*!'

'Ain't my fault he's lost,' argued Stinkwart. 'You're the nanny, aintcha?'

'Stinkwart's right,' agreed Hog. 'We spends all that time gettin' you kitted out an' sits around waitin' for you to come back wiv the gold an' then you goes and loses 'im. So don't go blamin' us.'

'I cannot believe dis!' gasped Plugugly. 'Dis is a *baby* we is talkin' about. Suppose he falls in a bog? Or gets eaten by bears? Anyfin' could happen. What am I s'posed to tell his mummy an' daddy when dey gets back?'

'Tell 'em they owes you a bag o' gold,' suggested Sproggit.

'Is you *mad*?' cried Plugugly. 'Does you really fink dey'll pay up when dey finds out I've *lost de baby*?'

A little silence fell while the Goblins considered this.

'No,' said Slopbucket at length. 'I s'pose they won't.'

'Dere you are, den! Anyway, it's not about de money, it's about findin' Baby Philpot before somefin' bad happens to him.'

'Off you go, then,' said Sproggit. 'Let us know how you get on.'

'*Me*? I can't do it on my own, can I? We has got to form a search party. Come on, come on, don't just sit dere!'

Grumbling, the Goblins climbed to their feet, set their hats straight and left the cave to go baby hunting.

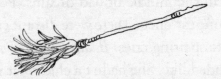

CHAPTER TWENTY-ONE
A Craaash!

It was the morning of the O'Lumpicks, and Pongwiffy rose at dawn. Despite an early night, she hadn't slept well. There had been a lot of nightmares, all based on the forthcoming day and the things that might go wrong. She had dreamed that Scott Sinister had backed out at the last minute, that King Futtout had sailed off to sea with the medals, that the Witches had come last in every single event and, worst of all, that she had tripped over and dropped the flag, making herself a laughing stock, and been thrown out of the Coven by Sourmuddle, who for

613

some reason was wearing a gorilla suit and carrying a tennis racquet. Sadly, there was no special poem or organiser medal in her dreams.

There had been strange noises out in the Wood too. Even when in the middle of bad dreams, Pongwiffy always had one ear open. There were distant crashings and weird, despairing cries. *Baaaby Fiiilll Pot!* That's what it sounded like. She hadn't a clue what that was all about, but it certainly hadn't made for a good night's sleep.

When the first light filtered through the hovel window, she climbed out of bed, thought about touching her toes, didn't, and reached for her boots. Pongwiffy always slept in her clothes because it saved time, but since the new fitness regime she had taken to removing her boots in order to give her socks room to breathe.

Boots on, she glanced across at Hugo, who was snoring heavily in the tea cosy he used for a bed. His little set of dumb-bells was placed within reach. Should she wake him? No. It was going to be a big day for him. He needed all the sleep he could get. Ratsnappy was the Witches' Weightlifter, and of course, Pongwiffy was hoping that she would do well, but secretly she wanted Hugo to win the gold after all the effort he had put into training.

Anyway, quite frankly, she wasn't in the mood for breakfast. The thought of the day ahead was making her tummy churn in a very unpleasant way. Of course, there was the specially commissioned poem to look forward to, but there was a lot to get through before she could enjoy her moment of glory. Best to take a brisk stroll along to the palace and make sure that everything was in place before anyone else arrived.

She found a scrap of paper and a pencil, wrote *gon to staddium gud luk* and left it on the kitchen table. Then she tiptoed out.

It was still quite dark as she walked through the Wood. It was deathly silent too, which is why she gave such a start when she heard the noise.

CRAAAAASH!

It was the sound of breaking glass. An almighty smash, followed by a hail of tinkling. It caused her to nearly jump out of her boots. Startled birds took off from the treetops. What on *earth* could it be? Pongwiffy hadn't been there for ages, but she felt sure it came from the direction of *Sugary Candy's*.

Heart pounding, she moved through the trees. She felt slightly nervous, but curiosity had got the better of her. Had the Yetis finally come to tear the shop down? Nobody had seen them for ages. Perhaps they had decided to collect all their unwanted stock, which she had heard was still on display behind the unbreakable window.

When she reached the glade, she could hardly believe her eyes. The crash had come from *Sugary Candy's* all right. But there was no sign of the Yetis.

Where the unbreakable window had been, there was a great, gaping hole. Millions of glass shards lay before it on the ground. And inside ... inside, in the shadowy darkness, something ... no, *somebody* ... was moving around. An enormous shape.

'Hello?' called Pongwiffy. 'Who's there?'

Silence.

She wished she had her Wand. All magical aids were banned from the O'Lumpicks, so she had dutifully left it under her pillow. But something interesting was going on, and she was burning to know what.

Cautiously, she left the shelter of the bushes and crept towards the shattered window, broken glass grinding under her boots. Heart in her mouth, she peered inside. What she saw made her go weak at the knees.

Standing in the middle of the shop, in a sea of glass shards and spilled sweets, was – *a Giant baby!* A Giant baby, wearing nothing but a big, droopy nappy and a huge, face-splitting grin. The soles of its enormous, bare pink feet must have been as tough as leather, because the glass didn't seem to bother it in the slightest. A long piece of string was attached to its nappy with a safety pin.

'DIN-DIN,' said the Giant baby, catching sight of Pongwiffy. It gave a delighted little giggle, and waved a huge, fat arm. 'TEE HEE! DIN-DIN!'

'What?' said Pongwiffy.

'DIN-DIN,' explained Philpot patiently.

He stooped down, scooped up a handful of red sweets shaped like little lips, crammed them into his mouth, slurped and added, 'MMMM.'

Pongwiffy didn't know what to do. It wasn't a situation she had come across before. She just stood hovering before the collapsed window, trying to make sense of it. A gigantic baby had broken the unbreakable window of *Sugary Candy's*, and was happily helping himself to free sweets. Who was he? She hadn't a clue. Where had he come from? Likewise. Where were his parents? Not around, hopefully. What should she do about it? Well, considering his size, probably nothing.

The Giant baby crunched and slurped. Sticky red goo ran from his mouth. Very suddenly, he sat down with a loud bump and began casting about for more sweets. He shovelled up two more fistfuls – a deliciously sticky, multicoloured mixture of *Minty Stingeroos*, *Beezi Kneezies* and *Wizard Wobblers* – and rammed them in his cavernous mouth.

'YUM,' said Philpot appreciatively. He crunched, swallowed and waved his huge arms around, pointing excitedly to the surrounding feast. 'GA?'

'What?' said Pongwiffy again. She wasn't used to babies.

'GA!' shouted Philpot. 'GA!'

'I don't quite get you,' said Pongwiffy. 'Could you be a little more explicit?'

'GA! DIN-DIN!'

'Well, yes,' agreed Pongwiffy. 'Yes, I suppose it is.'

Philpot's excited eye caught sight of a toppled mountain of broken chocolate bars. He rolled over on to his knees and took off in a jet-propelled crawl. Crushed sweets and broken glass did nothing to slow him down. He was possessed.

Pongwiffy watched him eat. The expression on his brown smeared face was blissful. Never was there a happier baby. Huge though he was, he certainly seemed friendly enough. He spotted Pongwiffy staring and gave her a rather sweet little wave.

'DIN-DIN?' he said again.

It was almost as though he was inviting her to join him.

Pongwiffy gazed around. Her shock at coming face to face with a Giant baby was ebbing away, particularly as he seemed so amenable. Her brain was slowly starting to work again. Thoughts began to form. Not particularly good thoughts, I'm afraid, but we're dealing with Pongwiffy here. Here are her thoughts, for the record.

Sugary Candy's window had finally met its match. Magic hadn't touched it, battering rams hadn't cracked it, hurled rocks hadn't dented the surface. But a Giant baby had arrived from nowhere and done what no one else had managed to do. How? Who knows. Probably just kicked it in, with bare feet. And now the place was awash with mouth-watering free sweets. *Free sweets!* After three weeks of munching on raw carrots. And not everything was on the floor. Some of the jars, the ones on the back shelves, remained intact. There was nobody around, apart from the baby. The O'Lumpicks wouldn't be starting for ages. She had plenty of time. It was oh so tempting. Perhaps just one, eh? One little sweet wouldn't hurt anybody. She deserved it, didn't she? A little reward for working so hard.

Briskly, she stepped through the window. She edged around the Giant baby, who was experimenting with how many lollies he could fit in his mouth at one time. (Thirteen.) She stepped over a mountain of spilled *Minty Stingeroos*, waded through a small desert of sherbet, marched around the counter, reached up to the top shelf, took down a jar of *Hoppy Jumpers* and unscrewed the cap.

'Here,' she said. 'Hold your hands out. Try some of these. They're lovely.'

'TANK OO!' said Philpot, just as Nanny Susan had taught him to say.

'You're welcome,' said Pongwiffy. And popped one in her mouth.

CHAPTER TWENTY-TWO
The O'Lumpicks

The sun shone brightly and a warm breeze blew across the stadium which was rapidly filling up. The long queue at the palace gates was getting shorter as excited spectators took their places and the various teams of noble athletes scurried around looking for places where they could change into their outfits for the Grand Opening Parade. The place was a hive of activity.

King Futtout drooped miserably in his best throne, which had been carted out of the palace and set at the end of the lawn, right by the finishing line. In one limp hand was a list of all the Games, with spaces to write the names of the winners. In the other limp hand was a pencil. Placed on a small table next to him was a box containing his home-made medals. Despite his best efforts, they hadn't turned out too well.

His tragic eyes surveyed the wreckage of his once lovely garden. Absent trees. Missing rose bushes. Wiggly white lines all over the lawn. A large podium where his gazebo used to be. A pile of boulders for the Weightlifting. A mound of sacks, a bucket of eggs, a collection of spoons and bundles of ropes. His washing line commandeered for the High Jump. Miles of tacky bunting. Rows of mismatched chairs, some from Witchway Hall and others pinched from his own palace. Chairs which seated the crowds from far and wide, some of whom had arrived a good hour or so earlier in ramshackle coaches which were even now cluttering up the palace coach yard.

They were a mixed bunch, the crowds from far and wide, consisting mainly of the various teams' families and friends. A lot of them sported cameras and picnic baskets. Flags on sticks and silly hats emblazoned with the teams' names were much in evidence. Sadly, there wasn't much mingling going on. The different factions tended to sit with their own kind. However, they weren't fighting either. Everyone knew about the good sportsmanship rule. No one wanted to let the side down.

You will be pleased to know that the Witches had supporters. Two, to be precise. Pierre de Gingerbeard, the famous Dwarf chef who happens to be Sharkadder's cousin, was there. He was sitting next to his brother, Wildman Willy Racoon, Sharkadder's other cousin, who is a famous wild man from the mountains. Both sported *Go Witches!* badges. That was all, but Witches don't have many friends. They were lucky to get two.

The spellovision crew had arrived and were getting their camera and microphones organised. On the bandstand, the Rhythm Boys were tuning up. Filth revved up with a particularly violent drum thrash, causing King Futtout to wince and clutch his head.

'No sleeping on the job, Futtout,' said a voice in his ear. Grandwitch Sourmuddle was standing next to him, wearing a bright orange cloak with matching hat. She had declined to wear shorts, declaring that they weren't a Grandwitch sort of thing. Snoop stood at her side, holding a large watch.

'I wasn't,' said King Futtout miserably. 'I'm ... erm ... just wondering what my wife is going to say.'

'Oh, she'll get over it. I hope you're going to sit up straighter than that when we get started. Which we will, as soon as Scott Sinister arrives. Which he's supposed to, any minute. And Pongwiffy, of course.'

'I think he's here,' said Snoop, pointing at the palace gates, where a long, low coach was drawing up, pulled by a team of coal black horses. The number plate read SS1. Scott liked to arrive in style. The coachman jumped down and opened the door with a flourish. Cameras flashed as the great man stepped out, swishing his gold and scarlet cloak and flashing his trademark sunglasses. He was holding a monogrammed briefcase, which contained his poetic commentary. A surge of fans rushed up clamouring for autographs and a teenage girl Troll fainted.

'Where is he supposed to stand?' wondered Sourmuddle. 'What do we do with him? Pongwiffy's supposed to be dealing with this. Oh, where *is* she? She promised to be here to greet him.'

'She's late,' tutted Snoop. 'Very, *very* late.'

'You don't need to tell me that, Snoop. The whole Coven was relying on her to get here early. If it wasn't the O'Lumpicks, I'd give her ten millionple black marks. Sadly I can't, because I've got to be a good sport. Where's Hugo?'

'With the Familiars, behind the bandstand. They're arguing about their flag.'

'Well, have you asked him where she is?'

Snoop shrugged. 'He hasn't a clue. She left early this morning and he hasn't seen her since.'

'Well, she'd better turn up soon. We can't start without her. Go and round up all the teams. We need to kick off the second she arrives.'

Snoop went off to do as he was told.

Macabre came marching up. She was dressed from head to foot in tartan, liberally sprinkled with glitter. It was an odd combination, particularly the shorts. Sharkadder had got the measurements a bit wrong and they ended at her ankles, in effect making them not so much shorts as longs. In her hand was a furled flag.

'What's happening?' demanded Macabre. 'We're supposed tay be starting the Parade as soon as that film star gets his act together.'

'Well, we can't, can we?' snapped Sourmuddle. 'Pongwiffy's not here. We'll have to get Scott to stall. I said she could lead us in, remember? A promise is a promise.'

'Since when?'

'Since now,' said Sourmuddle firmly. 'The

O'Lumpicks are all about being honourable and fair. I've been on spello explaining about it for weeks. Stop looking so grouchy, it's only for today.'

'Mmm. Well, all I know is she'd better not see me tomorrow.'

'Me neither,' agreed Sourmuddle darkly.

'Erm ... excuse me?' bleated King Futtout. 'I think the um ... film star needs some attention. He's looking a little put out.'

He pointed limply to where Scott Sinister was waving away Sharkadder, radiant in vibrant turquoise, who was attempting to manhandle him on to the podium. Scott was objecting because nobody had thought to provide him with a glass of fizzy water. Sourmuddle and Macabre hurried off to help, leaving King Futtout alone and ignored on his throne.

Behind the bandstand, Snoop was getting the teams lined up. It would take too long to describe them all in detail, but here's a quick summary of how they look. It's worth it, because they all had a very different take on what constitutes the perfect Grand Opening Parade outfit.

The Skeletons are in crisp white shorts and black bow ties. The Trolls have gone in for furry loincloths. The Zombies are in tight-fitting suits with half mast trousers. The Mummies (only two in their team) are in their usual bandages, with the unusual addition of top hats. The Ghosts are in traditional white sheets. The Ghouls are mainly in rags, but they've washed and ironed them. The Gnomes (including GNorman, who is entering for the Sack Race) are in little red pointy hats and green trousers. The Vampires are in black cloaks lined with scarlet, and smell strongly of toothpaste. The Banshees are in their best nighties, and weeping already at the thought that they might not win. The Familiars are all different shapes, sizes and species, so they haven't bothered to dress up in anything special. That's why they've put so much thought into their flag, which even at this late stage is causing dissent. They've finally gone with Vernon's black letters on a white sheet idea, but none of the Cats are happy.

There are two teams with only one member. These are the time-wasting Werewolf, wearing his best trousers and brandishing a relay baton, and Ronald in his yellow shorts, trying not to look guilty about what is in his pocket. (An egg glued to a spoon. Tut tut.)

Lining up first are the Witches in their technicolour cloaks, hats and matching shorts. In terms of vibrancy, they have certainly won the day, although it hurts your eyes to look at them.

The Familiars came next. Snoop scuttled up to give them their last minute instructions.

'Have you all got your flags ready?' he enquired. Nervous nods all round. 'Well, keep them furled until it's your turn to march in.'

'How do we know when that is?' asked Barry the Vulture.

'Just listen out for your poem. Mr Sinister's written some special verses in honour of the occasion. The minute you hear your name, you're on. He'll say a few words first, though. We're playing for time because Pongwiffy still hasn't arrived.'

Everyone turned and looked enquiringly at Hugo, who shrugged and mumbled, 'Don't ask me.'

Encouraged by Sourmuddle, twittered at by Sharkadder and prodded firmly by Macabre, Scott finally consented to mount the podium. Spectators hurried back to their seats, consulting their programmes, adjusting their binoculars, taking up their flags and finishing off their sandwiches. Filth began a little drum roll, then stopped when he saw Sourmuddle glaring and shaking her head. Apparently, they weren't quite ready.

Aware that all eyes were upon him, Scott slipped into professional superstar mode. He clicked open his briefcase and removed a sheaf of papers. Sharkadder came rushing up with his glass of water, then scuttled away to join the Witch team.

Scott waited until all the coughs died down. The spellovision crew moved in for a close-up. Taking his time, he arranged his papers, then took up the megaphone that Pongwiffy had thoughtfully supplied. He took a deep breath, then his sonorous voice rolled around the stadium.

'Friends,' said Scott. 'My very good friends. You all know me. Scott Sinister, the famous star of stage and screen, who has condescended to come here today and be your commentator. What's more, I'm doing it for free.'

He paused for applause, which dutifully came. He flashed his sunglasses, smiled for the camera and added, 'By the way, I've got a new film coming out, so fans, take note. But enough about me. I've got a job to do.' His voice became solemn. 'We are gathered here together on this glorious morn for an historic occasion. A momentous occasion. An occasion which, in a long line of occasions, stands out as the occasion which . . .'

'Get on with it!' shouted a cheeky Gnome in the front row. He wasn't a fan.

'As I was saying,' continued Scott, glaring at the heckler. 'An occasion which is probably the best occasion Witchway Wood has ever had. *The O'Lumpicks!*'

He threw up his arms, and the place exploded with thunderous clapping and ringing cheers.

'Yes!' cried Scott emotionally. 'Yes! Raise your voices! Let's hear it for the very first Witchway Wood O'Lumpick Games!'

'Hooray!' screamed the crowds, leaping on seats and waving flags.

'Fitness!' cried Scott. 'Health, fitness and dedication. That's what the O'Lumpicks are all about.'

'And shorts!' someone shouted.

'Yes! And shorts. And noble participation. And a lot of other stuff, but enough of that. We want to move on, don't we? The Games must commence! For your delight and amazement, we begin with a Grand Opening Parade . . .'

'Not yet,' hissed Sourmuddle from the sidelines.

'What?'

'Keep talking. We're not ready to start.'

'Eh? Why not?'

'Pongwiffy hasn't arrived. She leads us in.'

Scott frowned. He hadn't prepared for this. He

630

liked to stick to a script. Improvisation wasn't his strong point. But the audience was getting restless. The spellovision camera was trained on him and he had to say something.

'Ahem. Before we start the Parade, just a bit more about me. Not everyone knows this, but as well as an actor I'm a bit of a poet in my spare time. You'll be amazed to hear I've written my commentary in poetic verse. Now, I don't know if any of you have ever tried this, but it's not easy. Finding the right rhyme takes a lot of effort. For instance, nothing rhymes with *orange*. There are many other words which prove difficult. *Juggernaut*, for example. *Palaeanthropological. Zigzag*, that's a hard one. Um ... *rhubarb* ...'

Back at *Sugary Candy's*, it was a very different scene. Philpot lay in a sticky heap on the floor. His face was covered in chocolate and streaked with multicoloured trails of encrusted dribble. He was a total mess – and blissfully happy. Together, he and his new friend had eaten their way through enough sweets and chocolate to sink a barge.

Philpot felt great, but his new friend wasn't looking so good. She was stretched out on the counter, eyes tightly shut, groaning and looking green. Philpot heaved himself into a sitting position. It took some effort because he was lying on a heap of melted toffee and his back was stuck to the floor.

'WALKIES?' said Philpot brightly, reaching up and patting her on the cheek with a revoltingly sticky hand.

'What?' moaned Pongwiffy. With an effort, she sat up. 'Oooh. Where am I? What's happening? What time is it?'

Groggily, she looked around. Bright sunlight poured through the broken window. It made her head ache.

Wait a minute. Sunlight? When she had first entered the shop, the sun hadn't even risen properly. Could she have dropped off for a minute or two? In between finishing off the jar of *Gloopy Guzzlers* and getting stuck in to the *Minty Stingeroos*? It was all a bit of a blur. Something niggled at the back of her mind, though. She was supposed to *be* somewhere. There was something very important that –

Oh. Oh dear. Oh deary deary dear. In fact – *arrrrrrrgh!*

CHAPTER TWENTY-THREE
Late Again

'. . . and then there's *garlic*,' Scott told the puzzled crowd. 'That's a tricky one. And *spontaneous*. I'd defy anyone to find a rhyme for that. Anyone know a word that rhymes with *spontaneous*?' Deafening silence greeted this. 'No? I thought not.'

He took out a large white hanky and mopped his brow. He was feeling faint and his mouth was horribly dry, unlike the rest of him, which was bathed in perspiration.

'Keep going,' hissed Sourmuddle.

633

'I'm not sure I can,' croaked Scott. 'I'm losing my voice.'

'You're losing their interest too,' said Sourmuddle. 'Say something different before they start throwing things.'

She was right. The crowds were clearly getting bored with being lectured about poetry. They wanted the Grand Opening Parade. Someone started a slow hand clap, which was taken up with enthusiasm by athletes and supporters alike.

Scott reached out a trembling hand and took another swig from his water glass. He didn't think he could go on. His mind was blank. Not only could he not think of any more words that didn't rhyme with any other words, he couldn't think of any words *at all*. He had done what all actors dread. He had dried up.

And then he was saved. All heads turned as the palace gates opened with a loud clang, and a familiar, dishevelled figure stood framed in the gap. She had lost her hat and was panting heavily.

The slow clapping died away. A breeze blew. Somebody coughed.

Grandwitch Sourmuddle said nothing. She simply beckoned with a single curling finger.

Poor Pongwiffy. It was a horrible moment.

She set off on the long walk. The spellovision camera swivelled, capturing her every move. After what seemed like a week, she arrived at the podium.

'*Late*,' said Sourmuddle. 'Embarrassingly, ludicrously, unbelievably *late*.'

'Mmm … yes,' agreed Pongwiffy, adding rather feebly, 'Sorry.'

'*Why?*'

'Fell out of bed, banged my head, unconscious for hours,' explained Pongwiffy, and immediately came out in the pesky green spots. So everyone knew she was fibbing.

'Oooh,' muttered the crowd disapprovingly. 'Fibber.'

'*Spots*,' snapped Sourmuddle. 'Try again.'

'Lost my memory?'

'No, you didn't. Tell me another one.'

'Kidnapped by pirates?'

'*More* spots. Getting really bad now,' said Sourmuddle. 'Let's see how long before they all join up and you become one big green boil. I'm rather enjoying this. *Do* keep going.'

The entire watching arena nodded. Sport could wait. The Grand Opening Parade could wait. Watching Pongwiffy try to wriggle her way out of this one would provide a whole new world of entertainment. It certainly made a change from poetry.

Pongwiffy took a deep breath. There was nothing else for it. She would have to tell the truth. After all, this was the O'Lumpicks. They were supposed to be noble and truthful and fair. You shouldn't really tell fibs on a day like this.

'Well,' she said. 'Here's the truth. There's a wild Giant baby loose in the Wood. I saw him. He's broken the window of *Sugary Candy's*. He's in there scoffing free sweets. I've been trying to drive him off, and that's why I'm late. If you don't believe me, go and look for yourselves.'

It wasn't entirely a lie, although Pongwiffy can't resist an embellishment and it still veered slightly from the absolute truth. The spots subsided a little.

From all around came a muttering. The muttering grew to a grumbling. Little conversations were breaking out. What was this? The unbreakable, magically fortified, impregnable window of *Sugary Candy's* had finally given way?

There were free sweets?

Sweets. Ooh, that word! It leapt out from the sentence, overshadowing anything that had gone before, including even interesting words such as

wild, Giant, baby and loose in the Wood. *Sweets.*
That was the important word, the one that everyone
heard, the one they fixated on. And it brought back
such memories. Memories of what it was like going
to *Sugary Candy's* before the O'Lumpicks took over.
The fun. The anticipation in the queue. Drooling
over the labels, wondering what to buy. Placing
the order. Parting with your life savings. Coming
away with a thousand crackling packages of gooey
stickiness. Hurrying home, switching on the spello
and diving in!

Everyone forgot the bad things, of course. How you
always felt sick in the end. The tooth troubles. The
spots, the flabby tummies, the lack of get-up-and-go,
the sheer expense. All they remembered was the
wonderful, glorious, utterly all-consuming *taste.*

There was a collective intake of breath. A sort of
vast, communal, gasping sigh.

And then ...

STAMPEEEEEEEEDE!!!

The audience rocketed from their seats and, as one,
charged for the gates. And not only the audience.
The podium rocked threateningly as hordes of
well-honed, treat-starved teams of athletes surged
past, all thoughts of health, fitness, intermingling,

sportsmanship, games, medals and even shorts abandoned. Replaced by a single, primal thought.

Sweets!

Within a matter of moments, Pongwiffy was alone in an empty garden. Well, alone apart from King Futtout, who was unsuccessfully trying to untangle himself from his throne, which had been unceremoniously overturned by the mob. And Scott Sinister.

'Well,' said Scott after a long silence. He gathered up his carefully composed verses and placed them in his briefcase, which he closed with a sharp little click. 'I take it my services are no longer required.'

'Looks like it,' said Pongwiffy sadly.

'Yet again, all ends in chaos.'

'Yep.'

'I won't say *I told you so*,' said Scott bitterly. 'I won't say *I knew it*. I won't say your wretched O'Lumpicks are clearly an unmitigated disaster and it's *all your fault*.'

'No,' agreed Pongwiffy. 'Probably not a good idea to say those things right now.'

'I'll be off, then,' said Scott. Very deliberately, he dropped his megaphone on to the podium and stamped on it. It splintered into a thousand small pieces.

638

Then he stepped down from the podium and paused. 'One last thing. Don't ask me for any more favours. *Ever* again.'

Pongwiffy watched him stalk off, picking his way between broken flags, torn banners, forgotten picnic baskets, hats, vibrant cloaks, odd shoes, a cabbage, trampled carrots and other abandoned items.

'Hey!' shouted Pongwiffy as he strode through the gates. She had just thought of something. 'What about my special poem? I know you've written one, Hugo told me!'

What Scott said was short, sharp and luckily unintelligible. You could tell it was rude, though.

There came the sound of a coach moving off at high speed – and he was gone.

That was that, then.

Slowly, Pongwiffy sat down on the edge of the podium. She felt – crushed. After all that effort, everything she had worked for had come to nothing. There would be no flag bearing. No Grand Opening Parade. No Games. No one would ever intermingle. No medals would be won. The dream was over.

And to crown it all, she had given in and pigged out on sweets, after all the effort she'd put into getting fit.

Of course, she wasn't alone. By now, she had no

doubts that everyone was swarming over *Sugary Candy's* like ants on a sugar mountain, fighting over the best stuff, filling their hats and pockets and cramming their mouths like there was no tomorrow.

But she of all people should have been stronger. Or at least kept her mouth shut and said nothing. At the next Coven Meeting there would be Big Trouble. Sourmuddle would order an inquiry. She would get blamed for everything, as usual. Nothing had changed. She was still the same old Pongwiffy.

'But fitter,' said a voice at her elbow. Hugo was sitting next to her, little legs swinging.

'Oh, it's you,' muttered Pongwiffy. 'What did you say?' She hadn't realised she had spoken out loud.

'Still same but fitter.'

Pongwiffy shrugged. Somehow, without the spur of the O'Lumpicks, the whole fitness thing had lost its charm. She didn't care any more.

'You OK?' said Hugo. Pongwiffy didn't go in for silence often. It wasn't her style.

'I've been better,' she said.

'Lost your hat?'

'Yes. During my mad dash to get here. Not that it mattered.'

'Is true about wild Giant baby?'

'Yes. I said, didn't I?'

'You try to drive wild Giant baby out of sweet shop? All by yourself?'

'Yes. *Yes*, all right?' The spots returned, but Hugo didn't mention it.

'I help you find hat later.'

'Thanks.'

There was a little silence. Together, they watched King Futtout finally disentangle himself from his throne and wander off towards the palace, clutching his box of unwanted medals and moaning a bit. A footman came running out and led him away.

'He voulda been rubbish judge anyway,' said Hugo.

'He would,' agreed Pongwiffy. 'Too scared to say who's won. No powers of decision.'

'Big royal scaredy cat.'

'Don't know why we chose him.'

'Zoze medals!' Hugo gave a sneer. 'You see zem? Ze pits. Nobody vant vun, I sink. Not me, not you, not no vun.'

Pongwiffy fumbled in her pocket and brought out a handful of fluff-covered *Hoppy Jumpers*. They were all stuck together. They didn't look appetising.

'Want one?' she said.

'Sure,' said Hugo. He selected the least fluffy and

popped it in his mouth. Pongwiffy stared down at the rest, shrugged, then crammed them in her mouth.

'By the way,' she said indistinctly. 'I never did ask. Who was doing what in your team?'

'Me on ze Veights. Dudley on ze Sack Race, Barry and Speks on ze Three-Legged, Rory on ze High Jump, Vernon on ze Egg and Spoon, nobody Tossink ze Caber, Steve and IdentiKit and CopiCat and ze fastest Bat on ze Relay.'

'I'd like to have seen Rory doing the High Jump,' said Pongwiffy.

'Me too.'

'I wonder how Steve would have coped with the baton? In the Relay? Swallowed it or something?'

'Wound himself round it and rolled,' said Hugo. 'I see him practise. He voz gettink quite good. I sink maybe ve vin zat.'

'Maybe. It doesn't matter now though, does it?'

Together, they sat quietly chewing, staring around the deserted stadium. It was quite nice really. Peaceful. Companionable. The calm after the storm.

And then Philpot arrived.

CHAPTER TWENTY-FOUR
Philpot's Journey

You may be wondering what happened to Philpot after Pongwiffy shot out of his life without so much as a goodbye. Well, it's quite simple. He followed her.

For once in his short life, Philpot had eaten enough. Being weaned on a diet of pretend medicine, he had a cast-iron stomach. He had tried everything that *Sugary Candy's* had to offer. Together, more or less silently, he and his new friend had raided every jar – crunching, slurping, chewing and generally sampling everything except for the blinking eyeballs.

All that gorging meant that Philpot was full to bursting. The spilled mountains and open jars held no more secrets. He was all done with eating, bursting with energy and more than than ready for something new.

Finding himself suddenly alone and abandoned, he decided to see where his new friend had gone. Perhaps she was around the corner, hiding behind a tree, waiting to play peek-a-boo with him, like Nana Su-Su. Or even better, Hide and Seek. His eyes sparkled at the thought. He missed Nana Su-Su. He wished she was here now. But she wasn't, so his new, smelly friend with the pointy head would have to do.

Trailing his leash, he waded across the sticky, glass-strewn floor and stepped out into the sunshine.

There was no sign of his new friend. She must be hiding. Ooh, what fun, he would find her.

Giggling hopefully, he set off along the trail.

We won't bother to go into detail here. Philpot's journey is not that interesting. It goes in fits and starts and it takes a while. He fell down and cried once or twice. A bush scratched him. He saw a stone he liked but got bored with carrying it. At one point, he found a stick and waved it around a bit. Then he remembered his new friend and toddled on.

You may be wondering how he knew which way to go. It was the smell. Simple as that. Pongwiffy is nothing if not easy to trace.

At one point, Philpot found her hat. He picked it up and tried it on, but it was too small so he dropped it in the mud and stepped on it before moving on.

And so it went on.

The main event in Philpot's journey was probably the mob. He was quite surprised when he came face to face with that. He wasn't expecting a rampaging *mob* to come charging at him at all. He stood his ground, though. He stood swaying on his tree trunk legs, frowning a bit, waiting to see what the mob would do. He might be only a baby, but he was a big one.

The mob consisted of a motley assortment of Witches, Skeletons, Trolls – oh, you know who they were. It may interest you to hear that the faddy Werewolf was in the lead, closely challenged by Gaga, although Sourmuddle had a surprisingly fair turn of speed, as did Rory. Overhead was a collection of flying things, some of whose names we know.

The mob didn't even attempt to mow Philpot down. They just neatly parted and ran straight past him, like water round a boulder. So what if there was a Giant baby loose in the Wood? They'd think about that later. There were free sweets!

The howls died away, the dust settled and Philpot moved on.

In time, the trees thinned out. Ahead of him was something new. A high wall. Beyond the wall, he could see pretty flags fluttering in the breeze. There were gates in the wall and they stood wide open. In fact, one of them hung off its hinges.

Philpot's eyes widened. What adventures lay beyond?

He knew one thing. That was where his new friend had gone.

'Well, would you look at that,' said Pongwiffy to Hugo. 'If it's not the Giant baby. That's all we need.'

Hugo stared. There was certainly a Giant baby. He could see that. Philpot was hard to miss.

'Vill it attack?' he whispered cautiously.

'No. I'm afraid it rather likes me. Don't move, perhaps it won't notice us.'

The pair of them watched to see what Philpot would do. He stared around, thumb in mouth, observing the overturned chairs, the smashed spellovision camera, the thousand and one scattered items left behind in the mass exodus. None of it made any sense to him.

Then he caught sight of Pongwiffy. He broke into a delighted grin.

At last! His new friend! Found her!

'GA!' he bellowed triumphantly. 'GA! GA!'

And he came lumbering unsteadily across the lawn, arms outstretched in happy greeting.

'Oh bother, it's spotted me,' said Pongwiffy tiredly. 'I suppose this'll be something *else* I have to worry about.'

But just then, something unexpected happened. There came a shout from the gates.

'Baby Philpot! *Dere* you is!'

Philpot froze in mid-toddle. He knew that voice. He turned around. An even bigger grin split his fat pink face in two.

'NANA SU-SU!'

The two of them ran towards each other. You can add slow motion here if you like, but it's not necessary. At any rate, their reunion was emotional. There was a lot of smiling through tears.

'Hugo,' said Pongwiffy slowly. 'Am I dreaming, or is that Plugugly in a *dress*? Wearing a – *flowery bonnet*?'

'Ya,' said Hugo. 'It is. And look! More of zem!' He pointed to the gates, where the rest of the Gaggle were skulking nervously, clearly too frightened to enter.

'*Goblins?*' Pongwiffy was outraged. 'The whole Gaggle? Here? In *broad daylight*? Are they *mad*? If this doesn't call for a zapping, I don't know what does.'

'Ze brazen cheek of it!' cried Hugo. 'You vant I bite zeir ankles, get rid of zem? Just say ze vord!'

'No, hang on. I want to know what's happening. Why is Plugugly dressed like that? And why is he hugging the baby's leg in that ridiculous way?'

In the very centre of the arena, Plugugly was indeed hugging Philpot's leg. It was one of the few remaining bits of Philpot he could get his arms around. Philpot had expanded even more since the last time they were together. The leg felt unpleasantly sticky, as though he'd been rolling in something. But Plugugly was brimful of joy to see him. It was such a relief to find him safe and sound.

Philpot was delighted to be reunited with Nanny Susan too. He was chuckling with glee and trying to crawl into Plugugly's arms, which in effect meant knocking him over. Plugugly didn't mind one bit.

It would be nice to linger on this tender scene. But then ...

VROOOOOOOOMMMMMM!

There was a great, thunderous, roaring noise.

Through the palace gates came a massive, shiny red motorbike!

The Stonkings had returned from Giant Town!

The visit had been a partial success. Largette had gone shopping and bought some lovely shoes. Bigsy had had a tattoo done. It was across his stomach and said BABY PHILPO (the tattooist had run out of ink). The two of them had eaten well, gone dancing and caught up with old friends. The family barbecue hadn't gone too brilliantly, however. It had ended in a squabble, which is a shame.

On the whole, though, it had been a nice break. They were back now, and eager to be reunited with Baby Philpot. Had they missed him? Not a lot. But they were very keen to see if he had grown much. Besides, Largette had bought him a big blue bib, in preparation for that exciting day when he went on to solids.

How did they know that Philpot was to be found in the palace grounds, you may wonder. Had their way home taken them past *Sugary Candy's*? Had they overheard one of the ransacking mob talking about a Giant baby, in between hoovering up sweets? Or had they just driven past and spotted him by accident? Nobody knows. All that matters is that they are here.

The giant bike raced past the Gaggle, who scattered.

650

It roared through the gates and across the lawn, which was already badly churned up. It came to a screeching halt right in the middle, where Plugugly and Philpot were still hugging each other.

Bigsy turned off the engine. Largette planted a red high heel on the lawn and dismounted.

Over on the podium, Pongwiffy and Hugo watched the proceedings with drop-jawed disbelief. For once, they were speechless. They were used to strange things happening in Witchway Wood, it was that kind of place. But this was seriously weird. A Giant baby was one thing, but a couple of full-sized Giants arriving from nowhere on a blooming great giant motorbike was a step too far.

For a moment, nothing happened. Plugugly stared at the Stonkings and the Stonkings stared at Plugugly. Then they stared at their baby.

Their baby was a baby no more. He was a proper toddler. He was unbelievably filthy. He was clearly massively sticky. He was HUGE. My oh my, had he grown. Was this the same child they had left behind?

Philpot broke the spell. He stared shyly up at the two strangers, held up his chubby arms and said really sweetly, 'MAMA? DADA?'

Largette burst into tears and Bigsy fell to his knees and scooped Philpot into his arms.

651

He was absolutely perfect. They loved him!

Over on the podium, Pongwiffy and Hugo continued to watch the bewildering scene that was unravelling before their eyes.

What was this? Plugugly talking to Giants? Laughter, even? A lot of hugging and kissing and baby throwing? A large bag of gold being taken from a saddlebag and deposited in Plugugly's eager arms? More talk and happy laughter? Fond farewells? The Giants roaring off on the bike with the baby perched dangerously on the female's shoulders, screeching his delight to the wind?

And Plugugly's reaction when they had gone. That was worth observing. The short, noisy weep into the apron, followed by the instant cheering up when he suddenly remembered what he was holding.

They watched him pick up his skirts and race towards the rest of the Gaggle, who had regrouped at the gates, looking impatient. There was a brief exchange of words, and then they were gone.

That was it. Drama over. Once again it was back to a deserted stadium. Pongwiffy and Hugo were alone again.

'Well,' said Pongwiffy after a bit, 'I wonder what all that was about?'

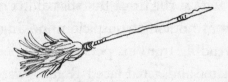

CHAPTER TWENTY-FIVE
What you may want to know

For those of you who like to have everything neatly tied up, here is a short summary.

RONALD

For Ronald, just like everyone else, the prospect of free sweets had proved irresistible. He had raced off with the mob, intent on getting there first and helping himself to the best ones. Sadly, he got knocked over and trampled on by a Zombie en route. Then his shorts elastic gave way and he had to slow down and walk, which meant that he was the last to arrive.

Sharkadder spotted him as he came shuffling into *Sugary Candy's*. She had her long arm stuck into a jar of *Bat Splatz* at the time. But that didn't stop her eagle eye from noticing a suspicious-looking spoon handle protruding from his pocket. A single barked command later and a red-faced Ronald was forced to disclose his shocking secret to the world. He was revealed as a sneaky cheat in front of everybody. Although it has to be said that nobody cared that much, because the O'Lumpicks were now over – well, they would never *begin*, put it like that – and the rules regarding sportsmanship no longer applied. It was back to the old ways, with every man for himself. Besides, they were all too busy scoffing sweets.

Ronald got punished, though. He got a strong lecture from Sharkadder. She wouldn't let him take any sweets either. He was sent back to the Clubhouse in disgrace, expecting another telling-off when he got home.

Luckily for him, his fellow Wizards never even knew that he had applied. They had forgotten that the O'Lumpicks were on and were watching something really boring on the other channel. So it could have been worse.

KING FUTTOUT

It took him several days to recover and many long weeks to set his garden back in order. He got it in the neck from Queen Beryl and Princess Honeydimple too, when they finally returned laden with dresses, handbags and shoes. Queen Beryl made him write a letter of complaint to Grandwitch Sourmuddle, and sent a footman to post it this time.

He didn't even get a reply.

SCOTT

Like the trouper he is, Scott put the experience behind him and moved on. He made a small bonfire of his poems, then went off to start rehearsing for his next film, which is currently doing good business at the box office. It has yet to be seen by Pongwiffy, although Hugo says it's good. It's called *Dark Night of the Mad Mutant Horror Hamsters*, so he would say that.

THE YETIS

They weren't too happy about things, particularly when they saw the state of their lovely shop, even though they hadn't exactly been paying it much attention since putting the notice on the door. They decided to abandon the whole project and go back to what they did best – kebab stalls, pizza parlours and greasy spoon joints. Although Spag is wondering whether an ice-cream parlour in Witchway Wood might catch on. They are currently away in the Antarctic, looking for a source of cheap ice.

THE GOBLINS

You will be interested to know that the Goblins finally made it to *Sugary Candy's*, armed with their bag of gold. Sadly, the mob had got there before them. When they finally showed up, there wasn't a single thing left. The place had been swept clean, apart from the untouched jar of blinking eyeballs.

But Goblins will eat anything. They fell upon the jar, wrenched off the top and got stuck in. While they were thus occupied, someone stole the bag of gold, which was a shame. They never did find out who.

Plugugly kept the dress. He still tries it on from time to time, in memory of Baby Philpot. Even though the others jeer at him.

THE STONKINGS

They moved back to Giant Town, taking Philpot with them. He is the apple of their eye and both his grand-mas adore him. He is the centre of attention at family barbecues, is growing bigger every day and can say whole sentences now. He has forgotten Nanny Susan.

So there you have it. You know what happened to everyone. Except Pongwiffy. Perhaps we'll pop into Number One, Dump Edge, one last time, to see how she's doing.

A week has gone by since we last saw her. Right now, she is sitting at the table, banging a fork and waiting for supper. Outside, night is falling and the stars are out.

'You know what I'm sorry about, Hugo?' said Pongwiffy.

'No. Vot?'

'I'm sorry I never got to hear Scott's poem. The one about me.'

'Mmm,' said Hugo.

'I wonder how it went? Sharkadder's pretending she's forgotten. I don't suppose Dudley said, did he?'

'No,' said Hugo quickly. 'Not a vord.'

He was being kind here. In fact, Dudley had repeated it to him, word for word. It went like this.

A word of thanks I'm forced to say
To she who organised this day.
She worked quite hard to sort it out
Of that I do not have a doubt.
We should have given her a prize
But we forgot, surprise, surprise.
I end now with a final plea.
Pongwiffy, stay away from me!
Do not visit, write or call.
I do not like you, not at all.

'Oh well,' said Pongwiffy. 'Perhaps it's just as well. I don't want to get big-headed.'

'Mmm.'

'And at least the O'Lumpicks weren't a *complete* waste of time. Everyone enjoyed the race to the sweet shop. And they all keep coming up and telling me how much fitter they feel these days and how they're going to keep eating healthy stuff and carry on working out. So am I actually. In fact, I'm quite looking forward to the Coven Meeting tonight. We're flying to Crag Hill, did you know? For the exercise.

Get *down*, Broom, not yet. Come on, Hugo, I'm hungry. What's for supper?'

'Skunk stew,' said Hugo. 'Your favourite. I make special.'

'Really? Well, that's very nice of you. I won't have too much, mustn't be greedy.'

In the event, though, she was very greedy indeed and had three platefuls.

But – and this is important – with a healthy dish of peas on the side.

Have you read all
of the other
Pongwiffy
stories?

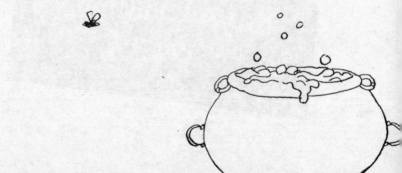

A spellbinding
children's classic

the Pongwiffy stories

Kaye Umansky

ILLUSTRATED BY KATY RIDDELL

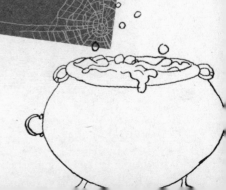

A spellbinding
children's classic

more
Pongwiffy
stories

Kaye Umansky

ILLUSTRATED BY KATY RIDDELL

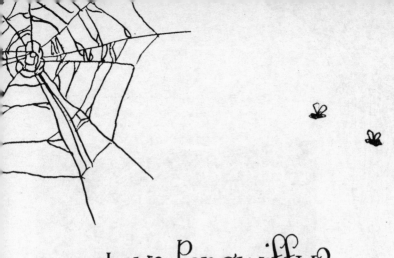

Love Pongwiffy?
Then get ready to
meet Elsie Pickles and
Magenta Sharp...

KAYE
UMANSKY

Witch
for a
Week

'Certain to delight any
witch in the making'
M.G. LEONARD

Illustrated by
ASHLEY KING

'BEWITCHING' M.G. LEONARD ON WITCH FOR A WEEK

KAYE
UMANSKY

Wish
for a
Witch

Illustrated by
ASHLEY KING

Look out for Book
Three coming
Spring 2019